Beyond the Softness of His Fur

by TammyJo Eckart

Circlet Press, Inc.
Cambridge, MA

Beyond the Softness of His Fur
by TammyJo Eckhart

Copyright © 2015 TammyJo Eckhart
Cover © 2014 Denis Tevekov | Dreamstime

Printed in the United States.
ISBN: 978-1-61390-114-4

Print-on-demand omnibus edition.

For catalog, information about our imprints, review copies, and other information, please write to:

Published by:
Circlet Press, Inc.
39 Hurlbut Street
Cambridge, MA 02138

Or visit us online at: http://www.circlet.com

Contents

Part II
Social Corruption

Part III
Private Revolutions?

Inspired by Fox

Part I

Wonders of Modern Science

Chapter One
Test Tube Pleasures

How long is this going to take? I uncross and recross my legs in the opposite direction as I try to sit patiently in the waiting room. Boredom room is more like it. This is taking a lot longer than I had anticipated, I realize as I check my watch again.

Didn't their ads promise fast, efficient, and satisfying service? Well, I should know better than to believe ads; I do design them for a living.

So why didn't Jim, Bailey, or Margaret tell me how long this would take? They all recommended this place—indeed, they insisted that I call immediately upon notice of my promotion. "You have to have a morph now, Emily," I can hear Bailey saying to me as he walked into my office without so much as a 'how do you do.' "We all have them," Margaret then insisted when I told her I wasn't sure it was for me. As to why it was important she simply wouldn't say though I've heard the rumors that executives have secret parties for years now. Wouldn't be a secret if she told me, now would it?

I've been so involved in my career these past five years I haven't had much time for a lover or a pet, let alone for both. Though the idea has intrigued me for some time. How could it not? To actually own something for my sole sexual amusement; isn't that every perverted bitch goddess' dream? Not really; most of my kind still follow that "safe, sane, and consensual" line developed a good century back. Which is great for dealing with human beings; just not what we all fantasize about.

I took Margaret's advice and dressed very nicely in natural fabrics of cotton and silk, both of which take up precious farm space, even getting a few real paper business cards so the folks here at the Institute for Sensual Morphology would be impressed before checking my financial records. First impressions are the most important thing; those get you in the door, and until you are in, you can't go anywhere. That's what my mentor taught me. Professor Randolf would be surprised to see me here today.

ISM is one of the elite pet genetics services. There are dozens and dozens of others. As with most technology, once developed and then utilized for the wealthiest and most powerful, middle level and cheap companies appear, as do knock-off brands. Since this is tied to my promotion for some reason I decided to go top-of-the-line as per my new colleagues' advice. I just didn't know they were literal about me needing to take a day off to get the best pet possible.

I check my watch again. Two hours. Geesh, people, some of us have to work to make the money to buy these things; we don't get to just play with them all the time. I'm relieved when the woman I interviewed with enters my line of sight and smiles at me.

"Ms Potter, we have found a good assortment for you to look at," the representative says. I see now that she is followed by a man in a white lab coat and another man in business grays.

"So everything checked out fine then?" I counter. I like to make sure of all my facts before I jump in. My company was so insistent that I get a morph that I didn't spend as much time researching this as I'm normally comfortable with.

The representative blinks, then stops directly in front of me. "Oh, of course, of course, I'm so sorry if you thought there was a problem. I've been spending most of my time looking for what you described," she explains.

I have been celibate for a number of years, living off of vids, books, and auds as I worked my way up quickly in the business world. I just earned vice president of administrative services, so now I think I can take a few risks. Getting a morph was not one of the risks, just a confirmation that "normal" wasn't normal in the company, confirming in my mind that I'd chosen a good place to work. Every executive has a morph of some sort, generally of the erotic specialty.

The man in business grays leans toward her and whispers in her ear.

"Of course, we'll discount our price for this inconvenience," she adds after a frown passes over her face.

"Good, I wouldn't want to have to go through this all at another company, but I will," I retort. The customer is always right; many businesses make the mistake of forgetting that, and when their customers leave, no amount of advertising will win them back from the consumer rights groups that monitor the net and airways like rabid hounds. Ironic choice of words here, I realize.

The woman blinks again, then motions to her companions. "This is Mr. Chase, our Vice President of Customer Relations and Doctor Batswinow, Head of Exotics," she introduced the men. Guess my records checked out very well to receive such personal attention.

"Yes, your interests are fairly unique, a good thing," the businessman assures me quickly. "We thought we might be of assistance to Ms Gaines in helping you chose the best ISM pet for yourself. The choice will, of course, be yours, but we hope we can answer any questions you might have."

"How very thoughtful of you?" I reply, though I'm wondering how much of a fool they take me for. I get it now: I have the money, so let's try and take her for all we can. It will work, just not if the customer is wise to it; they should have paid more attention to how I make my money, not just how much of it I have.

We walk further into the Institute, where I begin what I soon realize is a type of education process. It almost seems that they really do want contented customers. Of course, as the businessman points out, they never sell used morphs, and returns are fully refunded. Best to cut back on that possibility right from the start.

There are, it turns out, a few problems with my request. First is the requirement that it be male. Actually, fifty percent of all their morphs are male, so that isn't so much of a problem by itself as a complication to my other interests. Second, something unique or at least different; an exotic, they called it. Third, a pet which will be able to enjoy the rougher pleasures without wanting to return roughness and without getting moody about such sexual demands. The representative informs me that mostly such requests come from het male clients, so most of their stock in that category are female. I restate that I want a male morph. Geesh, haven't women gotten equality in being sadists yet? Most of the sadists I know are certainly female, but then I'm talking about consensual sadists, so maybe the wackos buy their victims.

They have three options for me at the moment—that's what they call a "good assortment?" They could specially design one, but that takes a bit more than a year to create and do basic training. This promotion seems connected to my getting a morph, hints are that I could find myself downgraded or at least denied future advancement if I don't get with the corporate culture, so that time lag is serious. I decide to see what they have. There are at least four other companies on Earth that deal in morphs, so if I don't find what I want I can look elsewhere.

We enter a fairly long white room with glass cages along each side. I'm informed that they aren't glass but one-way mirrors, so I can look in without the morph knowing that he is being watched. This way I'll see them as is and not performing as trained.

The first mirror cage houses a truly exotic morph-tiger. The size of the tiger has been curtailed, so the creature inside is equivalent to an average-sized man. It sits much as a cat would, tail twitching around, licking its paws in low strokes. It looks very bored and very self-absorbed. No, no cat morphs for me, thank you very much. If I want self-absorbed, I'll start dating again.

The next is a bear morph about the size of those furry warriors in the old space opera—what was it called, Star Battle or something like that? Chocolate brown fur, black eyes, and chubby. This one is pacing around the cage, first counterclockwise then clockwise; it makes a good three rounds each direction. Then with almost a shrug it lies down and curls into a ball. "It seems to tire easily," I say as I walk away. I could never get one of those. It would remind me too much of Mister Wentworth, my old teddy bear, and there are just some things that one should not do with a teddy bear.

The last one makes me stop before I reach the cage. A fox morph, and I can tell it is white—likely an albino, with those nasty little pink or red eyes. Now there would be something to have nightmares about. "I really don't like albinos," I begin to say when the scientist holds up his hand.

"Of course—who would?—and we would never sell such a defect. No; look more closely, and you'll see it was genetically engineered to be this color," the scientist instructs me.

"Very rare combination of white fur and blue eyes," the businessman adds.

This morph is also walking around the cage, though slowly, and pressing his paws against the one way mirrors. I stop just a foot from where he is heading and place my own hand on the glass. The fur is more light gray than white, really, but I recall something to that effect about all animals, or at least horses. I note the blue eyes as they move past me.

Then the fox morph does something that makes us all gasp. He stops, backs up, and places his hands almost opposite my own. "I thought you said these were one way?" I state.

"They are; he shouldn't be able to tell anyone is looking at him," the businessman scowls.

"I want him to see me," I say, surprising myself. "Can that be done?"

The businessman looks at the scientist, who merely shrugs his shoulders.

"Of course; we'll lower this front mirror," the businessman replies.

The businesswoman nods and presses a few buttons on the side of the cage. Slowly the mirror sinks down, and soon I see the morph jump back a bit as it reveals the four of us looking at him. The morph tilts his head, then moves back to place his hand opposite my own again. He's shorter than me by a good foot or so, probably weighing about seventy pounds, so a bit too thin.

I place my other hand on the glass, and he matches it with his own. Moving my hands slowly, I test him, and he matches my moves. After a few moments of this I glance back at the Institute trio with a grin. "He's very clever."

"Yes, fox morphs tend to be quite clever," the businessman says as though the thought annoys him.

When I look back the morph has approached and is licking the glass right over my palms. His jaw moves as though he's speaking every now and again between licks.

"They can talk?" I ask without looking behind me.

"Very limited; he's probably saying he likes you," the woman chimes in before the men can reply. "Fox morphs are very sensual creatures; very loyal too," she adds.

I take my hands down, and the fox morph presses himself against the glass. As the mirror is lifted again, he rises to his tiptoes and attempts to watch me for as long as his height allows.

"I want to see some information on him first, then meet him face to face, where I can get a better feel for him," I say as I turn to the trio.

"Of course," the woman replies as she takes me gently by my arm and steers me to the exit. "I think you'll be quite pleased," she adds with a glance back toward the men.

"Yes, he is a very interesting specimen," the scientist confirms.

As we walk down the hall, I catch bits of the conversations between the men. They seem concerned about something, and I'm not sure what or why.

i yawn and stretch a bit, my fur tingling as though from a long nap. Nap? Did i fall asleep? Oh, no! Customer, human, can't have fallen asleep, stupid stupid morph. i jerk up and find only white walls in front of me. Not the same ones as before, because these don't shine oddly; the room smells different too.

"Please," i beg softly as i launch myself at the walls. "Please, no big sleep, no, this one will do better, please better, be better," i plead as i press my body against the smooth surface. Figured out a while ago that white coats watch me when i'm in rooms like this, punish or reward based on what i do or don't do. If i'm here then i didn't get sold. "No big sleep, please," i beg as my claws try to crack the surface.

"So you can talk after all," a human voice says behind me, making me freeze, silent. i'm not alone. i should try to remain calm but instead turn around, my back pressed to the wall, my tail flat down in shock and fear.

She—i'm assuming female from the cues the videos the white coats have supplied—is sitting not more than a few feet from me. Dressed in colors, an oddity around here, and even rather bright hair falling along one side of Her face. The woman who was looking at me earlier. A buyer!

i drop to all fours and move toward Her cautiously. She must want to see me, otherwise why would She be in here? Be docile and submissive when approaching a human, the trainers say, so i inch forward then stop, head bowed and wait.

She leans forward, placing Her forelimbs—arms, i believe—at an odd angle, and rests Her head on Her hands. "It's all right. Don't be afraid of me. I've just come to meet you," She says. Her voice is slightly different from most of my trainers and the white coats, with something foreign but gentle in it. "I'm Emily, Emily Potter," she adds, placing one hand on her chest.

i crawl forward, pausing again once i'm within a foot of Her. She asks me to repeat her name. Don't blow this. "Em.. a.. lee," i venture, earning a shrug and nod in response. i jump a bit when She sits back and takes something sitting next to Her on the table in the room. There's Her, me, the table, and a chair. A quick but stealthy glance around reveals nothing else but a door opposite me.

"Here we go," She says, putting the container on the floor. She opens it, and the aroma of something meaty hits my nose. "They said feeding you might help with introductions," She adds.

"Food," i say, then dive in, pausing a second later, then continuing when there's no kick or slap heading my way. She must not have heard me—stupid morph, lucky morph. i attempt to eat as delicately as possible, but it tastes so good, and i've been hungry for so long, it seems. Once a day in the kennel, then when training

started maybe twice, depending on my behavior. Usually twice—
i can be clever when the goal is food, when the goal is no beating.
"My, you are hungry, aren't you?" She says.

i stop and wipe my jaw on one paw before glancing up at her.
i nod and blink my eyelashes as taught, making mewing sounds
in my throat. A whispered "thank you" emerges before i can stop
myself, but She smiles at that, so i venture again. "Tastes good,
thank you."

"You are welcome," She replies with a wide grin that i've been
told is a good thing. "You finish it, though, whatever it is," She
commands, so i turn my attention back to the container. i can feel
Her gaze on me, so i try to be as attractive as possible while eating.
Humans like to watch our tails, so i make sure to have mine move
a bit more than normal. Also i make eye contact several times,
showing that i am a good morph, focused on my superior, ready
at a second's notice.

After i finish, i push the bowl away and lick my paws and jaw
as well as i can. She's leaning down, one hand out stretched, so i
move closer. "Pet?" i ask as i dip my head under Her hand.

So rare this touch, a gift for the best behavior, a taste of favor
in a white coat, a reward from humans. She caresses my head with
Her hand, first just stroking it back then pushing it forward as
well. i arch my neck offering more of myself to Her hand, a soft
growl which i pray does not offend drifting up from my throat.
The fur at the top of my head is longer and different than the rest;
we suspect it is to mimic the fur on the tops of humans' heads,
though the white coats have never told us. They tell us very little,
but the songs sung in the dark since the time i can remember tell
us much.

"I'm trying to decide if I should buy you," Her voice reaches
down through the caressing, my ears going up automatically to
catch every sound.

"Fox morphs make good pets," i say as i rub a bit against her
leg. Her scent surrounds me; Her clothes are so strange and soft
beneath me; everything feels overwhelming, so i fight to stay
completely aware of Her movements and words.

"So I've read and been told," She replies. "But you are not inexpensive. Three months salary, you know?"

i look up at Her, rubbing my jaw against Her leg. "Buy 4753. 4753 will make best pet ever," i promise.

"4753?" Her voice goes up at the end, signaling a question.

i whine as i back up far enough to bat at the ear tag with my number. "Number. Will make best pet ever," i repeat. i can feel my body racing in ways i've never felt before. Is this what the songs call bliss? Is this what being owned feels like? Do i heed the warnings repeated in the choruses or give in? i sit back and watch as She examines my ear tag.

"Well, I am intrigued, but it is a huge amount of money. Do you know what money is?"

"Will make best pet ever," i say before laying down at Her feet, my head resting on Her shoes, my eyes looking up in what i hope is good form. "Buy," i whisper.

i jump back, my hands trembling as She stands up. Oh no, what have i done? Stupid, stupid, stupid morph! i'm surprised when she bends down and caresses my head again.

"Well, then, it's been a lovely visit, 4753," She says before heading out the door.

"Buy." The word i want to say is choked in my throat, so i just voice it internally, "me." i watch, then as soon as the door closes i rush to it and press my body against it. "Please," i whisper over and over.

i don't hear anything until they've entered the room; a grave mistake on my part, one i should know better than to make. i turn then relax a bit at seeing my regular handler, Frank, then tense at the sight of his new companion, a smaller man unfamiliar to me.

"So this it?" the new man says as he moves toward me.

"Now be careful, it don't know you," Frank tells him, putting out a hand to stop him. Frank has always been fair with me, never hurting me more than necessary, i think. Sometimes the white coats laugh when they hurt us, sometimes the dark coats laugh when they watch, sometimes the handlers laugh loudest; Ronald did when he corrected me. i'm glad Ronald isn't here anymore, even if it took several med visits to achieve. We are not really stupid; we know how to survive; the songs tell us how.

Frank looks at me with a grin and holds out a leash. "Here now, 4753, time to go." His voice is very different from the woman who visited, the one who will buy me, must buy me, rougher; the sounds are more what i'm used to, and his new companion sounds similar.

"Yeah, get a move on, morph," the new one says.

"Don't raise your voice, ain't no need," Frank says, lifting a hand to pet me briefly as i submit to the leash clicking onto my collar.

"No big sleep?" i ask. Frank is amused by my speech, so i've used that fact to glean pieces of information from him. Information is valuable—guard it, sing it, share it in the night.

"Big sleep?" the new one says. "Oh, you mean you think you're getting snuffed, put down, killed?"

i whimper and pull back on the leash, earning a frown from Frank.

"Hey, don't scare it! What are you, stupid?"

"Nah, it can't understand us, can it?"

"Of course, it can understand us, Joe," Frank replies. i drop to all fours quickly to keep up as we head out of the room. This door was hidden and must be how i got in. Little sleep, that's how they move us around. Could just tell me, i can go where i'm told. "Jesus, how many times I got to tell you. This here ain't just an animal, it's got some sense in it too."

"Looks like a big freaky fox to me," Joe replies, adding a harsh fondle of my head, which makes me tremble again. Not another Ronald, please.

"Damn it, Joe! Why I let my kid sister talk me into getting you hired here? You are so stupid!"

Soon this breaks down into yelling, and i'm pushed against the elevator wall at one point, unnoticed. We're going down, i realize suddenly. Down is big sleep. "No!" i scream and feel Frank grip the back of my neck.

"Calm down, there," he says. "See what your yelling is doing? Doc said to bring him in nice like. He's going to a nice lady who don't want him roughed up none."

i go limp in Frank's hand, and soon i'm released. "Woman buy 4753?" i ask, looking up at Frank.

"Yeah, kid, you been bought," he replies with a grin. So grateful, i yip and begin fluffing the fur on my face; must look my best for Her.

"See, told you it can understand us," Frank says.

They lead me into the med room, where i've been before; i'm not happy, but if i've been bought i can handle anything they have to do to me. i get up on the table when told by one of the white coats.

"We'll use a local for the punisher, then moderated for the sheath work," one of the white coats says. i'm concerned when my sheath is mentioned, but my arms and legs have already been strapped down to the table.

"Why not a full anesthesia?" the other asks.

"Too much of a risk that it won't wake up. One of those things the geneticists didn't think enough about." i realize now that the one speaking with authority is an older male, while the other is a younger female. Humans seem to place a lot of value on those things, but then they are only human.

The male white coat looks at my handlers. "Have you told it its name?" Name? i have a name, not a number?

"No, sir, wanted to make sure we had all the facts straight first," Frank replies.

"We should begin using it immediately; it will help with this last phase of training," the male white coat replies. "Denise, why don't you tell it its name?"

"We keep saying 'it'. Why not 'he?'" is her reply.

The elder white coat frowns. "Until purchase it didn't really have a sexual identity yet; certainly no sexual use has occurred. Correct?" the male white coat directs his gaze to my handlers again.

"Of course not, sir," Frank replies. "Only videos, tapes, and computer training in that area."

"It will become a he after this operation and delivery to its owner. Now give it a shot and a name, please, Denise."

"Yes, doctor." The woman leans over me and smiles. "This will just hurt a little," she says as she presses the gun to my head right next to my tagged ear. i don't believe her for a second, but at least she seems sincere. The shot works quickly, and soon i start to lose feeling on that side of my head.

"You have a name now, 4753," she continues. "Do you want to know what it is?"

What a stupid question! i nod my head eagerly, adding a whimper for good measure. White coats don't like our speaking much at all; it is wisest to be dumb around them unless they urge you to speak.

"Your owner has given you a name. The name is wynn. Can you say your name?"

i blink at her. "wind?" i reply. Isn't that something outside?

"No, no. No 'd' sound," she corrects but doesn't seem angry. "Just wynn. Try it again."

No 'd' sound. OK, i can do this. Very slowly i repeat, "win? wynn?"

"That's it!" She taps my head. "Feel that?"

"No," i reply, which is actually a lie. The sooner this is done, the faster i'm out of here. Anyway, how bad can this be; i'm bought, and anything else must be easy. It only hurts for a bit, then everything is numb anyway. That horrid thing that shocks me has been removed, but my joy is short-lived, because they place another below my ear on my neck and some type of decorative thing to cover it; the female white coat tells me everything as they work on me.

"Now breathe deeply," the female white coat orders me as she places a cup over my mouth. As i breathe i feel myself getting sleepier. No, what are you doing to me, my mind cries out as the last thing i see is the elder white coat picking up something sharp.

Pain. i feel pain around my pleasure regions, that special region we sing songs about and are trained not to touch before ordered by an owner, at least not if humans can see; my eyes struggle to open, but they are so heavy. Pain. Sheath, my sheath, no, not that please. i see white light and the concerned female white coat's face looking down at me. Twist of my head and i can see my sheath being lifted

off of my body. No, that is important; how can i serve Emalee
without it; fox morphs are pleasure pets; no, don't destroy me.

All my twisting and crying out loud only results in another
cup being shoved over my face. The attempt not to breathe is futile,
of course, and i sink down into the pain and the fear and the
horror of what is happening to me.

Chapter Two
Preparations

"Why does it need all this special stuff?"

I look up at my brother—no, half-brother—as he leans over my shoulder staring down at the computer form I'm filling out. "Anthony, are you sure you don't want a morph?" I say, hoping the insult will get him away from me. You'd think we were lovers, the way he is reacting to my purchase.

"Oh, that is uncalled for, it is," he replies, pulling a chair closer and straddling it. "I mean, this is gonna affect my life too, right?"

"Not really. I'm buying him; you are not to touch him, or tease him, or harass him," I state firmly. Anthony has never been very good with being told "no" about anything. Mother, however, kicked him out of the house over a year ago, and we have no idea where his father is—probably, like Anthony, he's claiming to be an artist when he's just a musician without work.

"But he'll be taking up space."

"In my wing, thank you very much," I remind him. "This is my house; I do pay the mortgage, remember?"

Anthony shifts uncomfortably in his chair. Could Mister Free Love himself have a moral problem with this? He stands up suddenly and glares at me. "Just tell it to stay out of my room!"

I don't reply as he leaves. According to the documentation the company gave me, once I've had sex with my morph, he'll be imprinted to me and not want anyone else as much as he'll want me. I assume that means he'll not be interested in Anthony, his room or his even being here.

Let's see, do I have everything? Contractors will be here next week to fix a bathroom for him. I've ordered all the pieces and the supplies to go with it. The Institute seems a bit perplexed by my demand for cleanliness. Well, it is still an animal, right? I want to make sure I'm safe, and anyway, certain pleasures are better when cleaner. I'm having a shelf put in for anything he might have or want, in the old linen closet, which will be his room. I mean, dogs and cats collect things, right, so why not a foxboy? And a nice circular low bed, sort of like a large basket for him to sleep in. Apparently when not engaged with their owners, fox morphs spend a good deal of their time sleeping—like cats, I guess.

Then I lean back and look at a few other items I've purchased for my playroom. He's very small compared to my past partners, so I've had to order some new equipment. And unlike my usual tastes, I've decided on blue, almost the same color as his eyes. It's a bit more expensive, but this entire situation is expensive.

I wonder how he'll feel underneath my hands and my body. I bought a piece of fur from the Institute that they said is the same texture as wynn—yes, I should start thinking of him by name now, shouldn't I? It feels... different. I rather enjoyed it last night in my private pleasures after my unwanted housemate went out for the evening. My neck, my breasts, my thighs, everywhere, it felt so soft and warm. But then I was moving it. Will it be frightening when a living creature is beneath that fur?

Well, I'll know in about two weeks, according to the confirmation note I received this morning. Training is progressing in good fashion, they claim.

"There you go; you are getting good at it, wynn," Frank says to me as i turn under the water and allow it to rinse off my front side. i feel so naked, my pleasure region so exposed all the time. It has hurt to move much these first few days after the med visit, so when i realize it isn't hurting today, i let one of my hands wander down my body with the water.

A scream rips from my throat as the punisher shocks me. i glance back to see Joe—that is my new handler's name—frown at me, his hand clenching the remote. "No touching yourself unnecessarily, morph," he sneers.

He's like Ronald, i think, though he isn't allowed to be alone with me, because i've been bought.

"wynn was just making sure the soap was being rinsed off," Frank states, then looks at me. "Ain't that right?"

"Yes, sir," i whisper. "wynn want to be best for Emalee," i add, hoping that her name will offer me some protection.

"Good morph," Frank replies with a grin. He grabs the remote from Joe and sticks it into his front pocket. "Let's try to just explain this next one, alright?"

"Let's just do it to it," Joe says as he slides the shower door open, which seems to also turn off the water. "Get out here," he orders with a wave of his hand.

i reach for the expected towel, but instead a bottle is thrust into my paws. It is clear plastic with some type of clear liquid inside of it. i look at Joe, then Frank; something is tickling the back of my mind about this, something in some videos, a computer program, but nothing solid is forming in my mind.

"It's an enema, stupid," Joe states harshly.

i cringe at the insult as much as his tone. Yes, now i recognize it, and the instructions are starting to form in my mind. "Yuck," i say out loud before i realize it.

Joe is angry now, his arms crossed over his chest in what i now know to be his attempt to control his temper. Frank is laughing, though, so i turn my attention to him. "Ah, come on, Joe," he says, wiping his eyes after a few seconds. "If it were you, you'd be doing a lot more than saying 'yuck' and you know it."

Joe's eyes never stray from me, and my hackles rise under his constant glare. "It should just do as it is told," he says slowly and steadily.

Frank nods and waves me back into the shower. "Joe's right, boy-o. You remember how to do this, or you need my help?"

i pause. The "how" is fairly clear in my mind, but whenever i've done something a handler was always there, hands over mine, guiding and instructing me; now, though, it seems wrong to be touched while i do this. She could teach me, but She isn't here. Of course if i mess up, then Joe will jump at the chance to show me how. i look directly at Frank, then bow my head. "Please, sir, help wynn do good."

Frank sighs, then turns and gathers a few things. Both of them are in blue slick clothes when we are in the cleaning stall—shower is what it is called—and now Frank adds some yellow gloves that reach up to his elbows. He adds a pair of goggles over his eyes that make him look funny, and for a moment i smile. If i have to learn to do this, then i'm glad that Frank is the one to teach me. i just hope it is truly what Emalee wants; everything is for Her now, i remind myself as we both step into the shower.

What happens next isn't so much painful as uncomfortable. Frank is gentle; he even ill-advisedly strokes my cock once as he pumps the liquid from the bottle into my ass. Only once, even though i purr a bit and glance up at him. When i glance around i don't see Joe, so i hope neither of us gets into trouble. Sometimes i've dreamed about going home with Frank, being his morph, wondering if he is as gentle in real life as he can be with me. This would feel so much better if he made me come.

He tosses the bottle, now empty and crumpled, out of the shower but remains over me, one hand on my back of my neck, keeping me bent over. "We're gonna hold that for a while now, so try to relax, kiddo," he says firmly.

After a few moments my guts start to clench and i can't help but moan. No slap or smack, but instead Frank releases my neck. "Stand up a bit, but hold that inside ya until I tell you otherwise," he instructs as he backs away. i slowly rise to an upright position, my jaw tightening with the effort to keep my ass closed tightly. In the video one of the morphs fails to hold herself well and is beaten for several minutes afterwards. There is no way i'm allowing myself to be damaged before delivery to Emalee.

In a few minutes, Frank announces that it is time for me to go to the toilet. i've learned how to use this thing a few weeks before the viewing, but to use it gracefully now with my guts distended by the liquid seems impossible. As though reading my mind Frank tells me to just sit down and let it out. A groan is the only verbalization i allow myself as the liquid gushes out of me. i feel so—i don't have words to describe it even to my own mind.

Frank examines both me and the toilet, then frowns at me sadly. "Sorry, kiddo, looks like we have to do it again." i groan but make my way back to the shower.

"Well, what do you think?" I ask Margaret, who I've invited over for tea and for her opinion as a morph owner.

She looks at the shower, then nods. "I didn't invest this much, but if you want clean, this looks like it will do the job," she says, but I note a wrinkle of her nose when her eyes run over the stainless steel enema system attached to its own outlet. She turns to her own morph, a female squirrel, gray in fur, standing about as tall as my own will be. "I prefer to bathe Violet myself," Margaret says as she caresses her pet and gets the huge, fluffy tail wrapped around her legs in response.

I smile at them; they seem happy, though I haven't heard Violet make a sound since they entered my house. From the way real squirrels chatter outside all day long at times, I expected a running commentary from her. I lead them back to the refinished closet and receive compliments from Margaret on how nicely I've decorated. "Of course," she adds, "I hope he is well behaved enough to not have to spend much time in here by himself."

I'm uneasy at the level of familiarity that this situation has forced on me and my colleague. I mean, we are friends, but I don't often discuss my private life with people. It just isn't proper. Of course, I realize that Americans have an entirely different view of that concept, so I just smile and agree with her as I lead us back out to the dining room.

There, over another serving of tea and biscuits, I allow myself to watch Margaret and her pet. Violet sits at her feet and takes what Margaret offers into her paws. I'm expecting her cheeks to puff out in that way that squirrels' cheeks do, but instead she eats one bite first before accepting another. I do mean accepting, too, for a few times when Margaret offers, the morph merely shakes her head and looks shyly down. Must have taken some serious genetic tampering and training to overcome that hoarding instinct, I find myself thinking.

At one point Margaret says something that I'm not sure I've heard correctly. "Pardon me, but would you repeat that?" I say as politely as my racing heart can manage.

"I asked if you'd like to try Violet out," Margaret repeats, confirming what I thought I heard. "I know that yours isn't a squirrel, but I know my first time with a morph was rather, well, distracting, and they can sense that. It might be better for you to have a bit of experience."

I just sit there as Margaret whispers to her morph, and then the creature approaches me. I continue to sit dumbly as the squirrel-girl stops right by my chair and raises herself up to full height in a slow sensuous sort of dance. Her tail folds around her, lifting over her body, circling her breasts and the edge of her mound; both areas are very lightly furred. Her eyes, which are almost a solid purple color, look directly at me as she moves closer.

I literally jump out of the chair as her tail touches my leg. "This isn't necessary," I say quickly.

Violet whimpers and cringes, shrinking back to the floor by Margaret's feet. I can tell she is trembling when my friend places one hand on her head. "She'll do anything you wish, Emily. She is a very good pet," she informs us both with a slight edge to her voice.

"I really don't need an introduction now," I reply, trying to be diplomatic. How do you turn down the offer of what is essentially a sex slave in a polite manner without endangering the slave? This isn't a problem I've had to deal with often; usually these sorts of things get negotiated ahead of the offer in the human world. "They've supplied me with samples at the Institute," I lie.

Margaret nods and pats Violet on the head; the morph sighs

and relaxes visibly. "I shall have to go there, then, the next time I'm in the market."

The afternoon ends soon afterwards, and I sigh with relief myself when I shut the door behind them. "That was all very sick." Anthony's voice behind me sends my defenses up.

"I didn't ask you to eavesdrop," I snap at him as I stride past him into the dining room to gather the dishes and leftovers. He stays out of my way the rest of the day. That evening when I'm lying in my bed with that piece of fur again, images of my fox morph with a squirrel morph tease the edges of my fantasies, but I forcefully push these aside. No orgasm for me tonight. Only a few more days, anyway, I tell myself as I roll over to try and get some sleep.

"Now who is this?" Frank asks me after i'm bathed, fluffed, combed, and readied. Today is the big day; today i go to Her home, to my home. i look at the picture and sigh a bit. "Emalee Potter," i say carefully. She looks very much like She did here—only the color of Her clothes are different, and She has Her glasses on in this one.

"Correct. Who is she?" he asks me the second of what i know are three questions in a group; i'm not stupid; we've done this drill at least a hundred times. i know all three answers.

"Owner, owner of this one," i add, placing one paw on my chest and fluffing up a bit more. This earns a soft smack on the back of my head from the other handler. "Sorry," i say when he complains about my messing things up.

Frank throws a glare at Joe, then taps the picture again. "What are you to call her?"

i know this answer, i do, but it doesn't feel right to be using the term here with Joe in the room. In the beginning he tried to get me to call him this as well until Frank intervened. i swallow, then glance down, focusing all my attention on Her image. "Master," i whisper.

"Good morph!" Frank says (with true affection in his voice, i think). He has been very attentive to me these two weeks, pushing me, punishing me, but never scaring me. It is clear he wants me to do well, to be a good pet, to be the best pet. i will be.

They lead me down a corridor i've never been in before to a large metal door. Joe pushes a few buttons on a pad by the door, and it lifts up into the ceiling. i want to ask how it does that, but i know better, so i just look up as we walk under it. There are many strange and big boxes here. No not boxes, i think as my mind tries to recall those computer images. Trucks. Yes, these are trucks. "To Emalee house?" i ask Frank with a tug on my leash.

"Yup, to your Master's house, foxboy," he says with a grin and a ruffle of my head. They lead me to one of the trucks, and Joe tells me to face him and be still. i can't help but whimper when he takes the muzzle from his pocket. "Quiet, Wynn," Frank orders with a firm grip on my shoulders. i try to steady my breathing as the leather and metal slides around my jaw and is fastened around my head and neck. we hate this more than anything else; we can't sing, we can't talk, we can't even make much sound, and i feel so sad in the pit of my stomach.

Next Joe places cuffs on my wrists and ankles, and i have to start a mantra to remain calm. "wynn is Emalee pet. Emalee be good owner. Emalee be best Master. wynn will please Master." They open the back of the truck and have me crawl inside and lay with my back against one of the walls. my hands are stretched above my head and locked into rings there, and my feet are likewise locked to the floor. It isn't that it is uncomfortable; i can wiggle a good deal and see out the glass part of the door once it is closed. But the white coats, the dark suits, and the handlers often bind us so to punish us, and we should hate it and fear it. i do, but the feeling is secondary for me, and that thought makes my stomach ache even more.

Joe and Frank disappear from my line of sight for a few moments, then i hear and feel the truck move and see them looking back at me over the chairs at the front of the truck. "Now hold on if you need to," Frank tells me with a grin. The sound the truck makes causes me to whimper as much as possible, and the vibration through the floor and wall feels like it is rattling my whole body. Looking as best i can between their two chairs, i see a much bigger metal door lift up and the blue of the sky.

i'm outside, i realize as we pass under it and i can see more blue above with white clouds, the green grass and the concrete like the walls in some parts of the Institute. Big is the only word i can think of to describe the trip. my eyes keep racing back and forth between the space between their two chairs and the glass part of the door i'm next to.

The world is so big! No wonder humans control everything, i would be lost in minutes out here on my own. And yet, as i watch the other trucks and smaller ones called cars whiz by and see the people walking, i also feel a strange yearning in my gut to be out there too. We pause a few times, and at one point i see something that makes me strain against my bonds to peer out the glass. There, on a leash, his fur a bit dirty but with a happy bounce in his gait, is a morph. A nice big canine one whose owner is a trim man who is bouncing along next to him. They both have brown fur, the morph's so much darker than the human's, and both wave at our truck as they cross out of my sight. The man and the morph appear briefly between Frank's and Joe's chairs then again on the other side of our truck before disappearing. When we are moving again i see them along side then behind us off to one side.

Maybe Emalee will take me out bouncing too. If i'm a good pet, the best pet, She surely must. i focus my attention on the decreasing figures until i can see them no longer. There was a time, our songs say, when we lived in the world in the place called the woods. we ran free with no humans to leash us, but we lived poorly and died horribly, as one stanza reveals. Lucky morph to be both owned and outdoors.

i see a few more morphs on leashes out with their owners. Most are not bouncing, though one appears to be jumping away from and then back to her owner in a big green space with big trees around it. Most just walk on all fours, as humans prefer us to do, and they seem a bit sad. *Stupid morphs, would you prefer the big sleep?*, i want to say to them, but of course i can only manage a muffled grunt or two and earn a comment from Joe in the process. As i continue to look i note that the morphs i see appear more higher quality as we get closer to Emalee's house. i'm not sure what it means but some times the gray suits comment about cheap knockoffs when they come to check on us.

Frank inquires about my legs and arms, and i wiggle them as much as i can in response with what i hope is a smile through the muzzle. Maybe if they tell Emalee i was good She'll take me outside. No, my training reminds me not to wish for that. Tonight i will see owner's house, learn owner's rules from Her, and then be played with as a fox morph should be. my cock is pushing against my stomach as my thoughts drift onto those vids and auds of my training. Maybe She'll bathe me, give me that yucky treatment, pet me, caress me, move my paws over Her body, touch me in those places that respond so frustratingly to the training until i feel like i'm touching the sky. The songs say that fox morphs reach the sky when we play with our owners—if we are very good, that is.

wynn will be best pet ever, i promise myself as i bring my legs up around my cock as much as the chains allow. Sometimes if i move just right, i've made myself touch the edge of the sky with just my legs or the mattress i sleep on. Technically i'm not touching myself, i claim in my mind. i'll stick to that claim if asked by any human. i am not stupid even if Ronald and Joe have stated otherwise.

Chapter Three
New World

The truck makes a sharp turn, and i see a big house in front of us. We stop, and the truck stops humming both physically and audibly. "We're here, kiddo," Frank tells me as he glances back with a grin. They both get out, and Joe appears at the glass of the door i'm by and smiles at me too. Is he happy with me? How odd.

It seems to take forever to get that door open, my wrists and ankles unlocked, and me out of the truck. i touch the muzzle but get a "no" from them both. They leave the cuffs on me as well. i drop to all fours and follow them eagerly to the front door of what i suspect and pray is Emalee Potter's house.

After a second i see i am right, as She Herself opens the door. By working hard, i am able to control myself enough to be led into the house, have the door close behind us, and see Frank give Her something. She looks at this thing, touches it, then takes the remote punisher from Frank. "Would you like him unmuzzled?" Joe asks Her in what must be the nicest tone of voice i've ever heard from his mouth.

"Yes, that would be lovely," She says. Her voice still has the musical tone to it, so unlike the Institute people.

Joe takes a key and unlocks the muzzle at the back of my neck. i am as still as my excitement allows as he slides it off of me, then hands it and the keys to Emalee. He touches the top of my head and pushes me slightly forward. "Greet your Master, morph," he orders, that rough edge back in his voice.

i crawl forward the few paces between us. As instructed, i lower my body to the floor, nice thick carpet beneath me, and lick Her shoes, nice shiny black boots actually, which reach to mid-calf. Now i should just wait until otherwise instructed, but i have been so good, so excited, that before i can stop myself, i've wrapped my arms around Her legs, my face pressed against her thighs, Her scent, that scent i smelled when she first talked to me, is there. "Emalee," i purr into her pants.

"Oh, whoa there, foxboy," i hear Frank's voice, then feel three pairs of hands on me. Stupid stupid morph! i curse myself. No blows land on me, however; i'm only pulled back from my owner's legs and held down by one of Joe's feet.

"wynn sorry," i say, then scream as Frank shows Emalee how to work the remote. It isn't humans that send us to the big sleep, one of our songs says, it is our own foolishness, our own dumb mistakes. "wynn sorry," i scream again and again during the time i'm shocked. i stay where i am when Joe releases me.

"Fucking great; already having problems with it." Another voice, masculine but with a similar musical tone like Emalee's, meets my ears. i now see another human enter my line of sight as i glance up from where i'm lying on the floor—the carpet is so soft, the color of a kit who had a cage next to mine in the nursery, i realize. This is another man. He looks a bit like Emalee, and She calls him "Anthony" and tells him to not bother us. He replies that he doesn't want to have anything to do with me, and Emalee seems pleased by that.

She turns back to Frank and shakes Her head. "I'm not sure that was truly necessary," She says.

"Got to make sure you maintain a consistent level of discipline," Joe responds before Frank can.

"My colleague is right, Ma'am," Frank adds. "Just use it to reinforce your rules, especially for these first couple of weeks. This one," he says, motioning to me, so i lift my head up and flutter my eyelashes at Emalee, "is a fast learner. He's just a bit enthusiastic."

Emalee smiles and crouches down, holding out one hand. "That can be a good thing," She says. "If it is done properly."

i crawl forward and lick her offered hand. "wynn sorry, Master," i say, that tightness in my stomach a bit less now when it is said directly to Her.

"See, what did I tell you," Frank states. "He learns fast, and he is eager to please."

"If that is true, gentlemen," Emalee says as She stands up and i merely contain myself at Her feet, "then I should thank you and ask you to leave."

Joe chuckles, and i hear an "oh, my god" from the unseen "Anthony." i stay where i am as Emalee sees the handlers out. i watch Frank, waving back at him as he turns and tells me to be good.

"So what the hell are you?" The voice makes me jump, and i find this "Anthony" standing almost on top of me.

"He's my morph," Emalee replies as She stands opposite this person—his hair is lighter, and he is taller and bigger, but there is a strange resemblance. Not all humans look alike; that is a myth i detected on my third day of training. "You are not to bother him," Emalee orders in what sounds like an angry voice.

"Just tell it to leave me alone then," Anthony retorts. One grunt toward my direction and he walks past us further into the house and disappears from my sight and sense of smell.

Emalee kneels down next to me, and the awaited petting begins on the back of my neck. The loose leash hangs down from my collar and rubs my cock and thighs as She strokes my neck, head, and shoulders a bit. "So do you remember who I am?" She asks me in a few seconds.

"Emalee Potter," i say reflectively. No answer, and when i look at Her i note a frown on Her face. "Owner, Master," i add, and this earns a grin from Her. No glasses today, so i think i even see Her eyes smiling.

"Good foxboy," She says and scratches behind one of my ears, the one with the ring in it for Her amusement. Almost as though She can read my thoughts, She tugs on it and says it is pretty. Then She motions me to follow Her with a "let's show you the house" comment. i follow, but my mind is thinking of playing already. i hope that Anthony isn't playing too; he gives me the same creeps that the mean handlers did.

I give him a tour of my house. First the parlor nearest the front door, then the dining room and the kitchen. I have set up a fairly elaborate feeding system in the kitchen, as the Institute suggested. "Do you know how to work it, wynn?" I ask when he tilts his head at it.

"wynn not hungry, Emalee," he says, so I remind him to use the proper title. I know, it is all so very proper of me; I'm British. What do you expect? Plus, it would give me a thrill. "Sorry, Master. wynn use Master from now on," he promises.

He works the buttons, and some food and some water are released into their appropriate bowls. The Institute sent me a few weeks of supplies yesterday, saying that this will give me more time to bond with my morph. Exactly why I'm taking a few days off of work as well.

I show him the entertainment room with my big screen television. I can't change the DNA settings on it to let him watch it himself but I've all ready made an appointment for a technician to come out and update several features of the house. Until then he can just watch what I watch. I don't demonstrate the fireplace now but instead show him the rest of the house.

I take great pains to point out Anthony's suite and add a slight shock from his punisher to emphasis that it is off-limits to him. My foxboy only whimpers and promises to stay out. I show him my bedroom but not my playroom. That will come later. This one is so flighty that I'm afraid of moving too quickly.

"And this is your room," I say, opening up the renovated closet. We go inside, and he hops onto the little bed at the center. He takes delight in the shelves, the few blue ribbons I've placed there, a mirror on the wall, the pillow, and the basket itself. He's as giddy as any small child on Christmas morning. "That's not all," I say as he begins to thank me with words and rubs his head against my boots.

The bathroom doesn't elicit as much happiness from him. He examines everything, frowning a bit at the first-class enema system and shower. "They did teach you to shower and clean yourself thoroughly, yes?" I ask.

"Yes, Master," he replies with what might be a sigh. He looks at everything, opening the easy-top containers of shampoo, soap, and enema additives, wrinkling his nose at the last when I inform him of what it is. Well, he is an animal, sort of; he has to be clean before much else. He looks very clean right now, so when he starts to step into the shower I tell him to just follow me.

It is only mid-afternoon, so I decide to sample him a bit before dinner. The booklet that came ahead of him said that it is vital to bond with him as soon as possible. Fox morphs, being very randy creatures, need to experience sexual use of some type very soon. Once bonded this way, he'll prefer me to all others, morph or human or himself. Sounds like some promises I've heard in my time; wonder if it is true.

I had grabbed his brush from his shelf as we left his room, so the first thing I do is set him in front of me on the floor at my feet in the entertainment room. I turn on the training channel and see a man talking about how important it is for a morph to be constantly thinking about what an owner wants. Sounds like excellent advice to me, so I leave it on. "I'm just going to brush this pretty white fur," I tell him as I push his head gently forward onto his chest.

The brush goes easily through his longer fur up on his head and along the back of his neck, feeling very much like hair in my fingers. The brush catches a few times on that silver collar around his neck. It is so difficult to see surrounded by his fur, but after a couple of nicks, I'm missing it. The fur on his back, not that icky back hair I can't stand, is different, very much like that dog my mother owned when I was growing up.

Soon his body is humming, and a steady purr is my reward for my brushing. When I have him turn and kneel for his front, I can see his cock already jutting forth a bit. "So, you are enjoying this, foxboy?" I ask with an amused grin.

"Yes, Master. wynn like fur brushed." He pauses, then tilts his head down. His blue eyes glance up at me as he asks, "Does Master like fur brushed?"

"Me brushing yours?" I reply with another grin. "Yes, I do, you are very soft."

"No," he says, though he purrs too as I trail the brush against his chest and nipples which peek out through his light fur. "Does Master like have her fur brushed," he carefully explains.

"As a matter of fact, I do." I stop brushing as his hands lift up and he offers his palms to me. "Ah, you want to show me that you can do the same to me?" I venture, taking the fur from the brush first. I hand it to him, and he nods as he takes it. He looks at the brush, then at me. "You'll have to stand up, if you can, and brush mine; I'm not sitting on the floor," I inform him.

He stands slowly, his hind legs wobbling. There is something amusing and arousing in this tremor and the hobbling gait as he moves behind me. I lean back and feel his paws taking my hair into his hands. He touches the barrettes, and I sigh and take them out. Then I find myself relaxing into what must be one of the best hair brushings I've had in ages.

"Master have beautiful fur," he tells me, and I feel his warm breath on my neck, his cool nose on my skin for a second. There is only a slight tightening in my stomach as I lean back further and just let him work. It is so wonderful to be pampered again.

I relax in the odd but delightful feeling of his fur and paws on my head and neck for many minutes as he brushes my hair. A few more times he leans down and nuzzles my neck; once I even feel the flick of his tongue, and he comments on how beautiful I am again. I wonder if I taste good, and that thought is enough to kill the relaxation for me.

"wynn," I say with a snap of my fingers. It is always a good idea to get a pet's attention, the booklet told me. I hear a bit of a soft snort and soon he appears in front of me, kneeling as best his body can, my hair brush offered up to me on the palms of his paws. A glance down reveals that he was indeed enjoying brushing my hair, as his black shaft, a bit of a shock to my eyes, peeks through his silvery white fur.

It takes me a second or two to figure out what to say. I suppose with a dog or cat, if I wanted them I'd use food as bait or just grab them. He is much larger than most dogs or cats, and those brilliant blue eyes with a look of attentiveness clearly states that he is more than a mere animal. "Can you remember which room is yours?" I ask gently.

He nods, glancing down at the brush with a small whimper.

"I can't hear your head rattle, foxboy," I inform him lightly. "You'll have to talk if you can. Can you?"

"Yes, Master," he says, looking up at me, even batting his eyelashes in a most flirtatious way. "Morphs talk if owners want," he tells me, then tilts his head to one side and inches slightly closer to me. "Emalee want wynn to talk?" he asks, batting those eyelashes again.

"Indeed, it would make things much easier," I reply with a grin. Come to think of it, I don't recall Margaret's morph talking the entire time they visited. I don't recall hearing many morphs say much at all, and usually it is almost a pleading or begging that I've heard out in the stores and on the streets. Sometimes they seem so sad to me. He doesn't seem sad, though; he is flirting even more now as I discover he's wiggled his way up to brush his tail across my shoes. That tail, that calls for investigation, but first things first.

"Go take this brush back to the shelf in your room where we got it, and use the bathroom if you need to," I say as he glances away. "Then come back here." He looks up at me, his jaw slightly open, those eyelashes batting again. "I want to play a bit with my pet."

He's wrapped his tail around my legs with what sounds like a giggle, then sits back like a shot. "wynn sorry, Master," he says; his breath sounds ragged. Oh, yes, he was punished the last time he did that. Should I do that now? I merely tell him to move it and hurry back instead.

I stand up as he scampers out the room. I left the booklet over by the fireplace, so I retrieve it now to refresh my mind on what it says about first time "play" with a foxmorph.

It is important to touch a morph sexually, if that is the type of morph you've purchased, as soon as possible. While all Institute for Sensual Morphology pets can be used in the greatest fashion immediately upon delivery, it is recommended that an owner take it slowly at first, working up to penetration by the end of a few hours of touching and teasing. Likewise, the rougher delights may best be left for later use, since this first sexual experience will bond your morph to you. Of course, our designs will accommodate any activity; these are merely our suggestions. Your guiding principle should be to enjoy your morph.

The booklet is just giving guiding principles; the actual ownership manual was more explicit. The foxmorph's greatest erotic zones are its tail, especially near the base, its genitals of course, nipples, ass, tongue—indeed, I recall that there seemed little about the breed that wasn't a hot button. They are, I remember, rather centered on themselves at first, though, unlike many humans, more eager to please after initial orgasm or arousal. I'm not sure exactly what that means, but right now I just want to get to know this new possession.

"Master?" I turn at the soft, almost childlike voice of my new pet. He is kneeling again right behind me so that I practically fall over him when I turn. The tip of his tail is laid over one shoulder and is dipping up and down his ear, the one I had a ring placed in, as he looks up at me.

I arch one eyebrow and he sits back at that, further when I next speak. "Are you sure you've never been played with by a human?"

"No, Master," he says, leaning forward after a second. His eyes are wider now, his voice slightly arched. "Only vids, computer, only learning, this one promises," he adds, bowing his head as though he knows that one of his selling points was the fact that all morphs are supposed to be trained, yet virgins.

I have to bend down in order to pet him as he kneels. At full height he reaches my shoulder; at an upright kneel he'd easily reach my groin, but now he is sitting with his rump on his feet. I can feel him tremble and purr again as I stroke his head fur. It curves around his ears, which are laid back against his head. Working my fingers down, I discover that the fur on his face is very light but clearly fur nonetheless.

After a few minutes my back begins to ache, so I straighten up, and he rises up to follow me. In this position I should be able to pet him for quite some time, but my back complains again. "Let's move back to the chair, where you can stand before me and let me get a good look at you, foxboy," I say. I kind of like that term, a cross between pet and human, possession and dependent, all-encompassing in many ways.

No need for commands; he follows me closely, his fur rubbing my leg every now and then as we walk back to the chair where we'd been earlier. I sit down, then motion for him to rise to his full height. He seems wobbly and shaking, not rising up completely until I verbally order him to. I wonder if it hurts, since his joints are slightly different from my own. I wave for him to move closer until his knees are touching my own. "Lights up twenty-five percent," I say, and my morph looks around as the computer turns the brightness up a bit more. "Don't worry," I begin, more to myself than to him really, "it will only respond to either my or Anthony's voice. You can't mess things up even if you tried."

"wynn never try mess up, Master," he says in a way that sounds like part pout and part anger.

"Good, then it lessens the need for that punisher device," I tell him. He nods rather vigorously, one paw reaching to the spot where the implant is located.

"Give me your paws," I instruct, and after the briefest pause he holds out his two front ones. I touch his palms gently at first, then more firmly. I push at the leather skin and feel the bones beneath each digit, I count a total of five on each paw, once more making him more useful on the human model. His nails are very short, not sharp at all, and if the Institute made the changes as I requested, they won't grow either. I've heard that clipping the nails can be painful for animals, and I'd rather avoid all unpleasant pain if I can.

The backs of his paws are covered with light fur again. His fur will also only grow to a certain length, but the doctors said that he will shed when summer arrives, though he will never lose all his hair. I recall a big debate in the Senate several years ago on morph laws. So many seemed trivial to me then as I pushed my way up the president's list to graduate with top honors as soon as

I could. But now, in possession of one, I can see that it is very important to have it clear who is the morph and who the human. We have laws against certain things I know I can do to wynn that I could never do to another human being. For example, there'd be outrage and possible future lawsuits if I changed the color, amount or type of hair a human partner had on the genetic level. Also human partners don't the need collars and tags but they are required for morphs. Some others I'm sure I'm forgetting, but for now I'm more fascinated by the feel of his fur as I move my hands up his arms.

At his shoulders I dip down and venture into the thicker fur that lines his chest. His purring increases as I trail down to his belly button, then back up. Around his nipples, which I can see are starting to get erect, the fur lightens again. A brief glance up at the ring in his ear makes me wonder what matching ones on his nipples would look like. But does he even like having his nipples touched?

I begin gently, just lightly caressing the nubs. Then more firmly I press them into his chest, and he makes a mewing sound. I back off again and instead start a soft tapping motion. His breathing deepens, so I make the taps more flicks, first with the fleshy part of my fingers, then my nails. His hips rock forward as he glances down at my hands on his chest.

"Master like wynn?" he asks, licking his jaw with his tongue as he flutters his eyelashes again.

"So far," I reply cautiously. I don't want him putting on any airs. I prefer my companions to be more focused on me and less on themselves. I think this is what has the greatest appeal for me in this situation. I won't and can't compete with him in anything because we are legally, physically, and socially so very different.

"I like reactions, all reactions," I tell him as I turn my flicks into light pinches. He sounds a bit like he's growling, though not in any threatening way, as I pinch harder and harder. His nipples are quite attractive—black, like his cock, jutting out from his silvery fur. They aren't large, giving me ample opportunity to increase them over time if I wish. They respond quite nicely, never losing their erection as I pull them out and twist them from side to side. It is only when he makes a sound that seems like pain that I back off and return to mere flicks and taps, occasional caresses.

A glance down and I find his cock; narrowed oddly at the end, a slight bulge a bit down the tip, then a regular shaft; sticking up and out. I pat his nose, earning a flick from his tongue in reward, then turn my attentions southward. His fur is thinner here, too, gathered around his cock and balls, lightly covering them. Wonder if they could be shaved safely? I only trace a finger down his shaft. I'll save that part for last.

His thighs are strong, and they part with only a minimal tremble when I prod with one hand. I weigh his balls in one hand; these are smaller than most men's, but then he is smaller than most men I've known. Any problem that causes will have to be compensated for with his tongue and paws, I decide as I caress and gently squeeze his balls. Right behind them I tap again and earn a moan from him. Ah, good. For some men that is a wonderful spot; for others an immediate turn off. Of course, being fox breed, being created for pleasure, it only makes sense that any part that could would get a sexual charge. I'll have to remember this spot when I fuck him. Not now, though; I'll go slow these first few nights.

I stroke his thighs, both inner and outer, then work my way down his legs. His knees are a bit odd, at a strange angle, which I suspect is why his upright position is a bit wobbly. His calves are strong as well. In fact, I can't say there is much extra flesh on him at all. I make a mental note to encourage him to eat a bit more. My rough tastes need more of a playing field than this. I move down to his feet and just tickle the tops, hearing a giggle as response.

"Turn around now," I instruct. He turns and lowers his tail at the same time. He's flirting again, I realize, as he only raises it when my hands move up his legs. "Tease," I call him. He looks back, eyes wide, and inquires if I'm angry. "No, not now, as long as you know who is the owner and who is the morph here," I inform him and earn a whispered "yes, Master" and a few flirty bats of his eyelashes.

At his ass, where the fur is lighter in coverage again, I suspect so that marks might show more readily, I push a hand between his thighs again with equal ease. I like full, firm buttocks, and his are caved in a bit on the outer edges. Definitely needs more food. I find that spot below his balls and caress it again. He responds by leaning forward so that his ass is poised outward. "You like that?"

"Yes, Master. Oh," he groans as I trace one finger along the crack but do not enter. "Please," he whispers, a flick of his tongue again accompanying the plea.

Later, my pet, I think as I decide to investigate his fifth appendage. I take it lightly in my hands, and he moans but does not resist. I caress it firmly enough to tell that under the fur is indeed flesh. This is a lot like the fur on his head, not exactly the same, but softer and fuller than on his body. I stroke it up along the length of his back and whisper in his ear, "Keep it up."

The base of a tail is supposed to be one of the most erogenous zones on a morph's body. I stroke his buttocks around it first, then dive in to circle the base with gentle caresses. He arches his back and groans again. Almost without thinking, I place one arm around his hips, taking his cock in one fist. I pull him back a bit and rest him on my knees so he won't fall. "Now I'm going to stroke and pet you until you orgasm. Come," I add in case his vocabulary is more simple.

"Yes, Master," he says looking back at me, the blue of his eyes very bright.

"Make sure you are giving me all the reactions you feel," I tell him. No words this time, merely a flick of his tail and a nod of his head.

I stroke and caress him slowly—I figure perhaps one stroke for every two semi-circles around his tail's base at the rate of one per three or four seconds. If this is his first time, I want it to be memorable, gentle, surprising. He tries to increase the tempo himself at one point, thrusting into my hand and wiggling his tail. I pull him closer and clamp my legs around his hips, earning a mumbled apology which sounds more like begging.

"Getting close, are we, foxboy?" I whisper into his ear.

He nods, then shakes his head, "Master, wynn don't know, please," he hisses, leaning his head back and thrusting as much as he can.

I'll be nice now; rough stuff later, control stuff later.

I increase my tempo now, with one stroke of his cock for every semi-circle behind. Then I place one finger on that spot behind his balls and one at the base of his tail and concentrate on stroking his shaft. I feel that bulge in it grow and tighten at the same time. His paws reach back and grab my knees as he bucks into my fist with gasps and growls. A few minutes, and I feel his cock throb and the bulge pulse. His warm come shoots out into my line of sight and slides down my hand.

Normally I'd either stop or slow down, giving my partner a second to recover. However, I can't recall if a fox breed needs this downtime, so I just keep stroking. He stops ejaculating for a few seconds, then the bulge pulses and his shaft throbs in my grasp again. He comes with a howl from his throat. I stop, and he collapses into my arms.

"Master," he moans as he starts to lick my neck and face, his arms stroking mine and my legs. I take my hand covered with his jism and hold it to his face. He merely turns his attention there and blinks once, then licks it clean. "Master, more, Master, more," he mumbles as he tries to turn in my grasp.

"Oh, there's going to be more, my pet. Much more." I begin to stroke his face with my cleaned hand as his tail wraps around me.

We both jump when the phone rings. I don't move but do place my palm around his jaw to quiet him. He doesn't like it and whines. Two more rings, then my machine picks up. At the word "emergency" I push him away and stand up.

"Maybe not tonight, though," I tell him as I run to my phone.

Chapter Four
Terror

She had to leave. Said emergency means She has to go immediately. i pouted, tried not to, but did. i accompanied Her to the door, hugging Her legs before She left. How long have i been staring at this door, lying on the carpet at the edge of the living room, waiting for Her?

She has one of those space clocks - where you tell time by how many spaces there are between the symbols and how far the big and little pointers are apart - on a wall i can see by just turning my head a bit. One, two, three, four spaces different for the big pointer, almost the same for the little pointer.

Not touching myself as She touched me is getting more difficult with each tick of that clock. i want to be good, i want to wait for Her touch, but it felt so much better than what my grinding into my bed at the Institute did, and my body is trembling just recalling what She did to me.

Maybe food will take my mind from it. i go to the kitchen and push the appropriate buttons to release some food and water. Same kind as we got back at the Institute, but now i get to decide when and how much. It only takes a few bites and swallows to realize this isn't helping my desires decrease.

Glancing around i decide that the other human in the house—what was his name, Andy, Anthony, something like that—won't notice, so I stretch out along the hard floor of the kitchen. In my mind i remember how She touched me, using my own hands as best I can to mimic Her touches. What my hands won't reach i use my tail for. i've never touched my own tail's base before. Though a caress from a trainer or doctor made me warm and frightened, Her touch made me shake with desire. Reaching it is a bit hard; the direction isn't quite the same, but i stroke the base as well as i can.

my cock is hard, so i roll over and start grinding into the floor.

It's hard and cold, not at all like Her hand, nor like the straw in the cage back in the Institute. Using one free hand, i wrap it around my cock as She did and begin rubbing it up and down, pushing with my hips into my hand. my balls tighten and ache as i feel my cock spasm and the liquid warmth ooze out.

After a bit it stops, and i realize i'm both sweating and breathing hard. It felt good; not as good as it did with Her, however. Oh, no; i sit up as i realize that I've made a mess on the floor and myself. There is a cloth by the sink, so i bolt and get it. i'm not sure how to use the water at the sink, so i just return to my bowl and wet it there before carefully wiping up the floor and my fur.

She'll notice this, i realize. i lay the cloth on the sink and walk slowly down the hall toward what She called my room. Shower, as much as i hate it; it will take a shower to cover up what i've done. Last thing i need is Owner angry at me; likely return me and i get the big sleep.

My intentions were to go to the shower, but outside the door She told me not to open i stop. Music—not just voices, but something else too is coming from behind the door. i press my head against the door, listening. If i don't open it, i'm not breaking Her rules, am i?

It sounds different from our songs. First, there is more than voices; it sounds good, a bit like on some of the training vids and movies. The voice is also strange, because it is only one voice. In our cages we all sang together after learning a song; all of us, so that the younger kits could learn easily and know they were supposed to sing too. The words are hard to understand, so i push against the door, and it opens just slightly.

Something about honey, baby, love, cry, what does it mean? i wiggle a bit further inside the door to hear better. i see no one at all, only some furniture, the carpet, some clothing on the floor, and more furniture. Ah, the song is about someone leaving him and he being sad and remembering him if the pronouns mean what I think they mean. The words are a bit scary at times too, talking about pushing, forcing, making the other person do what the singer wants. Not much like our songs but i have missed singing so much that i tune out the bad parts and focus on the music and the nice words. i listen a bit longer, then start to hum along. When he gets to repeated words, i join in as is proper.

"What the hell?" i hear, and the music stops. Faster than i can believe that other human who lives here is towering over me, his face reminding me of a very angry trainer or white coat. "I clearly told you both that you stay out of my suite!" he yells at me.

i back up, blinking at him. He did; i remember that and Her telling me again. If he tells Her ... i swallow in fear and back away, mumbling how sorry i am.

"Stupid, fucking animal!" he screams as he kicks me across the hallway. i land against the wall, my heart pounding in my ears as i realize he doesn't want to hear my apology. Instead i whimper and hold up my hands, head lowered, indicating how sorry i am for what i've done. Why can't i listen to the music though; i don't understand; isn't music for sharing?

"You stupid fuck!" he yells again as he lifts me up by the scruff which runs down my neck and stomach. i don't fight back; he's bigger than Her and fairly easily carries me a few feet before tossing me against the other wall again.

He touches his belt buckle, and i tense. Is he going to beat me? How do i explain that to Her? He's speaking again, so i turn my ears toward him, hoping there is some way to fix this yet. He has a glazed look in his eyes as he pauses and directs his gaze up and down my body.

"Of course, since that is what you're here for, why don't I try you out, huh?" He kneels down and grabs my arms in one hand. The belt doesn't strike me but instead is wrapped around my wrists. "So are you a good fuck or what?" he asks me with a smile that i think is the most terrifying i've ever seen.

That term, fuck, i know that term. It is when your Owner puts something into your mouth or ass to please themselves by using you that way. Can't imagine that it feels good, and can't imagine anyone Owner didn't want to could do that to me. i watch as though frozen as he lifts my arms above my head and undoes the button and zipper on his pants. Soon his own cock, much bigger than mine and the same color as his skin, is out and pointing at me.

Now i struggle in his grasp. i kick with my legs first, but he pins these with his own, forcing my legs apart. i do something strange next; i try to bite him, instinct almost overriding what the trainers taught us.

"What the fuck?" he yells again and slaps me so hard i can't breathe for a second. He pulls me down further, spreading my legs wider and pulling my own cock toward him.

No! This is all wrong. Only Owner can fuck a morph or someone Owner tells to fuck you. Not with you looking at them, either, for what he has in mind. At this angle i'll have to watch him, and our songs say that humans become monsters when they fuck you, so it is best never to look. I close my eyes, howling and begging for him to stop.

Pain. i feel a lot of pain as my asshole is parted by that enormous cock of his. "Be quiet!" he yells at me as he forces my hips higher and pushes my hands against the wall over my head. i can't be quiet. It hurts so much as he forces my legs and ass to part to the point where i'm sure i'm bleeding or broken in half.

Between my cries i try to hum this song that is supposed to help us cope with the horror humans can do to us. Now a new movement causes the tune to catch in my throat with sharp stabs of pain. He's moving my hips back and forth, forcing his cock in deeper, then out a bit, with each push and pull. my tail tries to whip around get between me and him, not that it would do much good, but it is trapped against the wall. Again my teeth clench, but i don't try to bite again.

It lasts forever, to the point where my throat is so dry and raw that i can't even whimper. He's cried out a few times too; he sounds like the pleased humans on our training tapes, and that makes me shudder inside. The white coats and handlers said that

Emalee liked rougher stuff; oh, my ancestors, did She mean this? At least it will be an Owner then, i find myself thinking.

It takes me a few seconds to realize that my arms and legs are free and the pain in my ass a bit duller. i open my eyes slowly after a few kicks land on my leg. He is glaring down at me, that same kind of look that Ronald and Joe got after punishing me. i try to listen to what he is saying something about this being my fault, but my head feels heavy and light all at the same time. Why do i still burn and hurt if he's standing above me now?

"Next time you want to hear my music or come into my room, remember what it costs, fucking animal," he growls at me, kicking me hard in the thigh before stomping down the hall and back into the forbidden room.

my entire body starts to shake after a few moments. Right now the big sleep might be a blessing, and that thought makes me cry and curl up right where i am. i wrap my arms and tail around me for protection, any protection at all.

"Wynn?" I say it a little louder this time, adding a gentle shake of his body. I found him curled up here in the hallway; the floor has something I'm afraid may be blood on it around him. I look at him as best I can with him curled up so tightly. His beautiful white fur is stained reddish brown around his legs, tail and ass.

I don't want to believe what I'm thinking, so I try to awaken him again. "Wynn, it's Emily. Please wake up."

His eyes flicker open, their color dull; the attentive spark there seems frightened. He pulls back to the wall out of my hand and glances around. "Emalee?" he asks softly.

"Yes, it's me; I just got back." I reach out to stroke him, but he flinches, so I stop and just rest my hands on my knees as I crouch there. "What happened here?"

"wynn sorry, Master," he says softly. He begins to rock into the wall and a bit away as he repeats this over and over.

My stomach is tightening; I know in my gut what has happened, but I have to be sure. "What happened here?" I ask with more firmness.

He whimpers and keeps repeating his apology.

I clench my hands into fists, and his words stop. I find his eyes frozen on me, focused on my fists. I force my fingers to relax a bit as I ask the big question. "Did Anthony rape you?" This only gets blinks. He's like a child; he'll need a simpler question, my reason informs me as it fights through the anger I feel building inside me. "Did Anthony, the other human here, hurt you, Wynn?"

My foxboy nods slowly and begins his chant of "sorry" over.

I swallow hard. To ask the question is difficult enough. I know my half brother is a selfish bastard, but could he actually rape someone or harm an animal? My flashes back on rumors I heard about him in school and in our neighborhood where we grew up and a cold knot forms in my stomach. Knowing that the answer is "yes" is like being hit by a truck.

"Stay right where you are," I tell Wynn as I stand up.

I took self-defense in college and a few other courses that dealt with violence and rape. In a daze I find myself following the "rules" for what to do in such a case. First I get my phone and dial the police. They say they'll be here in a few minutes; don't move the victim or confront the attacker if he is still in the house. Okay, fine; I'll kill Anthony later, I tell myself. Second, I call the Institute and report that my fox morph has been injured and needs a doctor immediately. Luckily, they have several doctors on staff, and one should be here in an hour or so. They repeat what the police told me about not moving wynn until after the police have left and then how to care for him until the doctor arrives.

I go and unlock the front door so that when the police arrive they can get in. Then I return to the hallway. I'm tempted to go to Anthony's suite and knock his door in, but my common sense prevails, so I just sit down across the hall from Wynn. He is still rocking and nodding his head and apologizing more softly. After a few minutes I call to him, "Wynn," and he looks up silently.

"That's it, just be quiet and try to relax; don't move. I've called someone to help you."

His mouth falls open, then he begins to shake. "Master, please, wynn be good, no send wynn back, no big sleep, please," he says as he clasps his front paws in front of him and shifts his position.

"Don't move," I tell him again. He stops and just sits there, shaking and making soft sounds. Oh, God, I think he might be crying.

Damn it! Of all the nights for an emergency, why tonight? It wasn't anything I needed to be there for, but Margaret, the branch manager called me in and asked me, no, told me, to stay around and make sure the editing was done correctly. How do you possibly screw up a thirty-second commercial so badly that the client threatens to leave entirely?

Now this. I have never been raped or sexually assaulted, but I have had a few friends who were, and an aunt on my father's side. I do know what it is like to try to help that person, the victim or survivor, depending on your political bent. But those were humans, and women. What do I do with a foxboy? Is this the right way?

"Ms Emily Potter?" I hear a voice call me as I also hear the door open.

"Yes, Officer, come in and turn right, we're down the hallway!" I yell back. Wynn is staring at me, frozen and silent now. He doesn't move when two officers, both women, enter the hallway. I stand up and reintroduce myself. "I'm Emily Potter, officers. This is my morph, and I believe he's been raped by my half brother," I say and close my eyes. There, I've said it; the tightness in my stomach changes to a dull, ill feeling.

"A morph, what breed?" one officer asks as she takes out a pad and her light pen; the other crouches down and begins talking to wynn.

"Fox, special exotic design," I add. I have one eye on Wynn but am forced to concentrate on the words of the officer talking to me. She wants to know where I was, when I returned, what my pet has told me, and finally where Anthony is.

"His suite is the first door on the left," I say pointing back down the hallway.

The officer goes and knocks on Anthony's door. It takes several knocks before he answers, then he glances down the hallway, his face turning red. It had better be fear and embarrassment and not anger; he has no right to be angry.

I can now pay more attention to Wynn and the other officer. She has something in his mouth, and when he opens his jaw I see that she's taken some type of molding of his teeth. "Okay, now I'm going to have you move a bit so I can take pictures," she tells him. She sounds like she's dealt with morphs or children or rape victims before. In the background I can hear the other officer having to raise her voice a bit with Anthony.

I can see that it is painful for Wynn to move, but he does so under the instructions of the officer. As she takes pictures my stomach grows more angry, and I can feel my head starting to pound. There is blood along his ass and thighs and tail, all seeming to come from his anus; he moves as though he were bruised everywhere, though how we could tell that under his fur I'm not sure until the officer parts some of his hair and takes some more pictures. She then has him assume the position that Anthony held him in, and I see tears rolling down his face as he complies.

I hear the doctor's voice and the door open as the officers are finishing their questioning. The doctor is a young woman whom wynn seems to recognize; he reaches toward her a bit when the officer moves aside. "Oh, my goodness," she says as she kneels down. She turns her face to me with a frown. "A little too rough for the first time, don't you think?"

"Hold there, Doctor," the officer who examined and questioned wynn jumps in. "The owner didn't do this; it was that man," she states, pointing down the hallway where the other officer is now putting my half brother into cuffs.

Anthony is cursing at both me and Wynn as the officers lead him from the house. I turn away afraid, that I'll lose control and smack him. Last thing I need is to get all emotional.

"I'm sorry," the doctor says, then turns to Wynn. No one tells me to leave, so I sit down again to watch and listen. The doctor goes through the same set of questions as the police officer and then some more. She asks him if I'd played with him yet, made him orgasm or come. When he describes what we did, he sounds both happy and sad at the same time.

The doctor turns to me with a smile. "Well, we'll hope that that is enough then. They are conditioned to attach themselves to the first person to make them orgasm or to penetrate them. Hopefully this attack was violent enough that he won't feel anything other than fear toward the attacker," she tells me in a very matter-of-fact voice.

There are blood samples, anal samples, mouth samples, and fur samples taken. All of them get whimpers and moans from Wynn as he is probed and poked. Finally the doctor and I take him to his bathroom and help him wash up. She puts a dressing over his anus and ointment inside, showing me what to do. Once he's sleeping thanks to a shot from her, I escort her to the door.

"I hate to say this, Ms Potter," the doctor begins with a frown on her face, "but the Institute can't cover this, since it had nothing as far as I can tell to do with the product you bought. A light beating from your half brother, was it, could be blamed on the morph's lack of obedience, but this is an overreaction that we rarely see."

"I just want my foxboy to be better," I reply. I'm insulted that she assumes I'd want to return him or get a refund or something. Are people really this heartless? "When will he be better?"

"Depends on whether or not you allow the attacker to live here and how much you expect from him. This one is a bit more sensitive than most morphs; the breed is very sexual but also very gentle." She pauses and digs in her black bag for a second. "Ah, here," she says as she hands me a small pamphlet. "We rarely have to hand these out, but, sometimes they are needed."

The handout is about morphs and the aftermath of non-owner extreme use. Nice way to avoid the term "rape" and enforce the idea that he's just property. "So, I'll just see how he reacts then," I say as the doctor opens the door to leave.

"Yes, that is the best way to deal with things. Not all morphs are the same; just don't treat him special if you can avoid it. They can be spoiled easily," she adds with a grin.

Gee, we wouldn't possibly want to do that, now would we? Right now I'm feeling more vanilla than anyone else in the world. He is my property, but damn it, he is also smart; he is aware. I don't allow myself to cry until I'm in my room.

Chapter Five
Shaken Foundations

If i don't open my eyes, maybe it will have been just a bad dream. In the distance i hear my name, "wynn?" but i try to push it aside. my name again, and a soft touch on my head, smoothing the fur on my brow. "wynn, can you hear me?"

Emalee? Master? i open my eyelids a bit. She is sitting next to me on something that feels soft underneath me. "Master?" i whisper, then whimper when my attempt to move toward Her causes pain to shoot along my body from my groin and ass to my pounding head.

"Don't move much," She orders, her hand petting my head again.

Why? Why do i hurt? A memory forms, and as i jump back against the wall i can almost ignore the pain. Something bad has happened. It happened because i was bad. Is She here to punish me more? "wynn is sorry, Master," i croak out. my throat feels hard and swollen as i speak.

"Hey, hey," She says, taking me by my paws, and i'm ashamed and flinch back again. "All right, no touching right now," She says, and i'm frightened by Her tone of voice. "I brought you some food and water, okay?" She says, motioning to one side.

There on a tray by my bed are my bowls from the kitchen. Am i banned from there? i look at Her as She stands up. She can touch the ceiling lots easier than me. i want to clasp Her legs as She leaves, but both my mind and body are too frightened to respond. Why? Emalee is Owner; She bought me; She hasn't hurt me, has She?

"I'll check in on you before I head to the ..." She says, pausing, then sighs, "before I have to leave."

i manage a whimper, and She sighs again.

"I have to go out for a while," She says. "You'll be here alone, and I'll lock your door just to be extra safe, even though he shouldn't be here. Okay?"

i bow my head. i've only been isolated a few times, because i've strived hard to be good.

"wynn, did you hear me, understand me?"

i look up, my face warm. "Yes, Master," i whisper a reply. Be careful; don't anger Her; remember what happened?

No! Don't want to! my body starts to shake as She leaves, closing and locking the door behind Her. It takes me a while to get calmed down enough to approach the tray. i think i'm hungry, but right now i notice my fur even more.

It is matted down as though it had been wet when i fell asleep, something i would not do. Also, there are dark spots here and there along my thighs. When i touch one, a jolt of pain rushes up my body, making me gasp.

i've got to get rid of these! i stumble to the connected bathroom and into the shower. i have to make the water as hot as i can stand. Over and over i suds up and rinse off. When i reach between my legs and in front of my tail, i freeze. Something is there between my cheeks. Flashes of a white coat and Emalee carrying me, washing me, and putting something inside and on me flashes through my mind. A little picking with my short claws and i remove what looks like a piece of cloth; it doesn't pull any fur with it but my ass aches now as i turn my attention to it.

With each ache, with each memory flash, i suds up again and rinse off. i even take that icky inside cleaner and use it, though i'm weeping as it goes inside my ass and the water fills me. i don't know how long my shower lasts, but i keep repeating the process of cleansing until i see blood and fur around my feet.

So big, bigger than Emalee, voice rougher and harsher, that glint in his eyes as he stood over me, his hand undoing his belt. "Stupid fucking animal," i hear him say over and over. Inside i'm screaming "no," but even here, alone and in pain, the word can't escape my lips. i find myself sliding down the cold, hard shower walls farthest from the door. "Since that's what you're good for," i hear his voice again, and my fur tingles as i remember his hands and legs on me.

"No!" i hear my scream echo in the bathroom. Soon my crying

is echoing as well. i want to disappear into the drain just like the fur and blood that is spiraling down.

i've just finished my shower and returned automatically to my bedroom when a knock sounds on the door.

"wynn?"

"Master?" i say as i kneel down right where i am, my fur dripping onto the floor.

She opens the door and enters with an unreadable look on Her face. "I have to go out for a while," She pauses and tilts Her head to one side. "Did you take a shower?"

"Yes, Master, wynn want to be beautiful for You," i whisper, hoping She'll believe that.

"Did you remove the, ah, the bandage?" She asks, looking around the room at the same time.

i close my eyes as i admit that i did.

"We'll have to replace it then," She sighs. She takes a small box from one of the shelves in the room and kneels down by me. "You can either lie down on your back or your stomach; I'll help you do this," She adds with gentleness in Her voice.

Before last night, if She had asked me to face Her while She fucked me, i would have complied, regardless of what our songs say. i wish i could do that now, but instead, shaking and repeating the calming song in my head, i turn away to kneel so i am open to Her.

Her touch is soft, and She speaks to me as She works, telling me what She is doing, even why. It is so hard not to tense up when She puts some ointment inside me, then around the outside a bit. i almost feel comfort as another piece of fabric is placed over my ass again.

"There, that should help, the doctor says," She tells me as Her hands stroke up my tail. Why am i shaking at Her touch? i hear Her sigh again and feel Her stand up, so i turn around, my head bowed, even though i want to gaze up at Her. "Like I was saying, I have to go out for a while, but I'll be back as soon as I can." There is another pause. "wynn, try to eat something, please," she adds.

"Yes, Master," i reply as i bow lower with my entire body. This isn't how it was supposed to be. i should be romping around with Her, entertaining Her, feeling Her hands on my body, learning how to touch Her, seeing the big world with Her.

"Right, then I'm off for now." i hear Her move a bit closer, but i flinch away as Her hand touches my head. "I'll check on you when I get back," She says after another sigh.

i don't move as the door opens, She leaves, the door closes, and i hear the lock click. i kneel there for a while, cursing myself. Why do i flinch from Her? Master didn't hurt me; Emalee bought me 'cause She wants me; She told me i cost a lot of money, three months money. i look up at the closed and locked door. Even if She had hurt me, wouldn't i have deserved it? Didn't i disobey Her?

i rub my hands over my eyes. It hurts my head to think too much right now. She said to eat, so i make my way to the tray, slowly, because it hurts to move. Maybe the food will calm my mind and stop my heart from racing every minute.

i have to make myself eat; the food tastes like nothing, the water like nothing. Yet once i've eaten a few bites i find myself buried in the bowl, eating every crumb i can find. Soon both bowls are as empty as i feel.

With a groan, i rise to my feet and hobble toward the bathroom again. It hurts too much to stand on my back legs, so i use the dryer as i kneel on the floor. Soon my fur is fluffed up more, and i examine myself again. Under my fur i can still see dark marks; they still hurt when i touch them, too. No dark patches on top, though, so the cleaning did well. i glance into the shower and see the bottles of shampoo and soap, half empty now. Will Master be angry with me?

i find myself shaking and crying again. i feel so empty inside, but i don't know what i need, what i'm missing. Please Emalee, come back to me; i'll be a good pet, i promise inside my head a million times.

Suddenly i tense. Is the door really locked? Back at the Institute the handlers and white coats might lie to us about such things. Sometimes there would be traps set on the doors or the cage bars, sometimes not. It became very confusing, so that the only safe place was at the center of anywhere a morph was. i move as quickly as the pain allows and check the door.

It's locked, just as She said it would be. Perhaps She'll be better at doing what She says? From the door i now look over what She called "my room" again. The bed is comfy, i suspect, though i can't honestly say i remember sleeping in it. The bed itself is certainly bigger than any cage i ever slept in back at the Institute.

Cage. i hated it as much as i loved this room the moment She showed it to me. Cages had no privacy and little comfort of any type but scratchy straw and cold metal bars. Yet there no handler or white coat or gray suit had ever dared touch me as ... Anthony— yes, that is his name, Anthony—had. That's why the door is locked; to keep me away from him. If i'd only been a good pet, none of this would have happened.

i didn't mean to enter his room. i realize that my paws are balled into fists at my sides as i replay the events in my mind. i didn't do it on purpose, but he was singing, and singing is for all. At least for morphs; maybe not for humans. Stop thinking about this, fool. Nothing you can do but be better now, a good pet—no, the best pet. i have to be the best pet now. i have to stop flinching away from Emalee; i have to work hard to please Her and stay away from Anthony.

i now look at the rest of my room. Other than the box on the shelf that She used on me, there are some bottles that look like the ones in my bathroom, a leash, and something shiny. i hobble over and take it down. A mirror, a small mirror. i look at myself in it but soon have to set it down, the shiny side downward. i look as tired as i feel.

Soon i'm lying on the bed, my body curling into a ball, my arms wrapped around me, my tail tucked between my legs. i feel my heart pounding and my body shaking until i lose track of everything but darkness.

For a couple of days She keeps me locked in my room. i don't really understand why until a vicious pounding on my door one night and Anthony's angry voice wakes me up.

"Oh, locked in, huh? Lucky for you, you stupid fucking animal!"

"Get away from his door!" says another voice i recognize as Master's.

"His door? It's a fucking morph!"

"I'll call the police again," She says, and i think if i could see Her and hear that tone i'd be flat on the floor wishing to be elsewhere.

"Oh, for fucking sake —"

"Forty-eighty hours, three down," She interrupts harshly. I press against the door to try to hear every sound; my body, still sore, protests against moving off the soft bed. "The judge spelled it out very clearly," She says now.

"And where am I supposed to go?" Anthony demands, pounding on the door and making me shake so much i'm ashamed.

Master's voice is louder, and Her scent seeps under the door and wraps around me; She must be right in front of it, blocking it—protecting me? "I don't care. You're a tosser. A bloody wanker!"

He curses and pounds on the door. my hackles rise up as i press into the wood. How dare he yell at my Master! my hand reaches the doorknob, but i freeze with fear.

"Fine! Just remember, bitch, that when I'm rich and famous I'll ignore you!" he yells again. His footsteps pound away until i hear a door slam.

"I'm not holding my breath," Master says.

A moment passes, then a gentle knock sounds on my door. "wynn, it's just me, Emily," She says, a little louder than Her previous comment. "Are you all right in there?"

i nod, then manage to say "Yes, Master," slowly into the door. my paws caress it—so hard, not like Her, and i struggle to voice my need for Her to come inside, to touch me, somehow, someway, anyway.

"I'm here at home for the evening," She says.

Take me out of here! i'm screaming inside, but only murmurs come from my throat as i continue to press myself into the door.

"I'll be back with your dinner in about an hour, okay?"
i swallow, then make a croaked "Yes, Master" in reply.

i nap again until another knock awakens me. "Yes, Master," i
reply to Her statement that She is about to enter. i sit up, pulling
my legs close to me, my tail wrapped around me reflectively. my
breath quickens as She enters. She looks so beautiful; has She
gotten more beautiful since i was last allowed to see Her? She sets
down the tray She is carrying between us on the mattress, then
sits down Herself.

my stomach growls, causing me to blush when the scent of
Her meal reaches my nostrils. Her food is, of course, human food,
not morph food, but my mouth waters anyway. i think it just
smells so much better, so many different textures in the scent,
whereas mine is the same old same old. When she visited me in
the Institute, i remember she brought me something not quite
human and not quite morph, and that it was delicious, so much
so that i almost made a fool of myself by eating impolitely.

She looks at me as she picks up one of my bowls. "If I set it
here on the mattress, can you manage not to spill it?"

i flinch at the question, which implies simply by being asked
that i couldn't help but make a mess. i sigh, swallow my pride and
then hop down onto the floor by Her feet. "wynn eat here, please,
Master," i say softly.

"you do seem a bit shaky, eh?" She says, then sets both bowls
next to Her feet—one on either side, actually. She's wearing these
dark shoes, slightly shiny, and i'm tempted to touch them when She
lifts up one foot and folds it underneath Her. i wonder if that hurts?

"We'll work on you eating a bit more civilized later," She says,
drawing my attention from Her shoes to Her face.

"Yes, Master," i reply simply, unsure whether answering was
required. She confirms it was by petting my head. There's that
stirring at my groin again, and my heart quickens at this touch. At
the same time, however, i realize that my eyes are darting back and
forth and that i'm gauging the distance to the door. i make myself
stop and focus on what She said. "Cibilised?"

Her eyebrows lift, but there is a grin on Her face. "Close

enough for now," She says as She adds another caress to my head. "Eat now, my pet."

While i eat, my mind is racing between two thoughts: What will She do to me now that i've been damaged? Stop thinking like that, you stupid morph! Why is She being so gentle and nice to me? You know you don't deserve it!

Her voice interrupts the confusion. "I told you, right, that I'm working from home for the next few days?" She says. i note that She's finished Her food, so i swallow my own last bites down.

"wynn doesn't believe so, Master?" i say.

"Well, I am. I'll be here at home for a while, at least until Anthony moves out," She adds with a frown.

i keep my eyes focused on Her, afraid that asking will only prove i've heard incorrectly or perhaps make Her change Her mind about his moving.

She seems aware of my fear and gently takes my muzzle into the palm of one hand. "Yes, he's moving out of here, and he won't be back," She promises as She massages the underside of my jaw.

"Never?" i whisper, my hands almost reaching out to touch Her foot or legs, but i dig them into my own thighs instead.

"Never. Not to live, not even to visit. I don't want him anywhere around you ever again."

i can feel tears welling up in my eyes as i realize that She is angry. But i need to be sure that She isn't angry at me, so i venture a timid question. "Master not mad at wynn?"

She leans toward me a bit, releasing my muzzle, then blinks a few times. i'm surprised and terrified when She grabs my arms and lifts me to my feet. i'm in for a beating now, or at the very least a shaking, but i decide to be quiet and will my body to relax. The surprise continues, but my fear drops when She takes my muzzle again and forces me to look Her directly in the eyes; with me standing and Her sitting we are almost at an equal height.

"Mad? I'm not angry, oh no, not angry with you, wynn, my pet," She replies with a few tears in Her own eyes.

As i say the words i regret doing so. "But wynn do bad, listen to music, open the door, make Anthony mad."

She releases my muzzle and pulls back, folding Her hands in Her lap. If She wasn't angry before, She certainly is now. There is a few moments of silence, then She sighs. "That doesn't matter," She begins slowly. "The only right Anthony had was to tell you to go to your room, lock his own door, and tell me what happened when I got home. I would have corrected matters."

"How?" the word tumbles out before my mind can stop it. Master's eyebrows snap up, Her eyes wide, at the question.

"Frankly," She says, then simply sighs and stands up, sending me wobbling back a few steps. She looks at me and shakes Her head. "They told me that you were very obedient and submissive, so I haven't thought much about punishments."

She picks up the tray and orders me to add my bowls to it. As i'm kneeling at Her feet to comply, i can't look up at Her.

"I'll check on you in an hour or so," She tells me as She turns toward the door.

"Emalee?" i say softly as i crawl a few paces toward Her.

She doesn't even bother to glance at me as She opens the door, saying, "I'm disappointed, wynn. Just disappointed."

i'm frozen where i am, silent, for a moment after She leaves. Next thing i know, i'm standing in front of the mirror in the bathroom, looking at my reflection in the shiny surface. "Worst pet in the whole world!" i declare as i smash my fists into the image. Hands sore, mirror askew, i sink to my knees and sob.

Chapter Six
Starting Anew

I count out a full ten minutes after the police pull out of my driveway to follow Anthony to the MTB territorial line. At ten, I call the "home security expert" I have had reserved all day so he can finally come over and change all the locks. Now, instead of just a number, it will also require a voiceprint as well. You aren't getting into my home ever again, half-brother.

As the technician finishes, I go and collect Wynn from his room. He hasn't been out in days and crawls next to my feet until he sees the technician. With a whimper, he hides behind my feet.

"Don't be scared," I say gently, bending down a bit to pet his head, and earn a glance upwards. "We just need you to say a few words for us," I explain as simply as I can.

My morph sits back and blinks at me as though I've just told him that the world was a cube—he'll do it, but I can see in his eyes that it makes no sense to him.

"The morph's probably never heard that before," the technician says as he closes the main security box. "To be honest, lady, I hadn't either."

"It's important to me that he be able to get in sometimes, like if I send him to get the mail or the paper, or run an errand," I offer. This only gets more blinks and frowns from both of them. What is so difficult to understand here? "So, let's do this!" I say with a clap of my hands that makes the morph jump and the human chuckle.

The tech has us each say our names and some other phrase into the computer system. I start, to demonstrate to Wynn how it should be done. "Emily Potter. This is my house, so please let me in."

Wynn stands on his tiptoes at first, but the tech is kind and lowers the microphone to him. "wynn. Please let wynn in Master's house?"

The tech looks at the computer screen and pushes a few

buttons, then smiles as he unjacks himself from the system. "Amazing what science can do, huh?" he comments, glancing between me, the system and Wynn.

Next we tackle an upgrade on the television. The tech explains that this is both more simple and more complicated, a statement that makes Wynn press his head against my calf again and my own mind turn a few flips of logic. In reality, only a simple deletion of Anthony is required; since I have the Master password, I can do that in less than ten seconds. But there are only certain channels that morphs are allowed to access on their own—a morph training channel, a nature channel, and an alternative sexualities channel. I make a note to check each of these out myself. This requires a DNA sample from Wynn for both the remote and the set itself. I hold his paw out as the tech draws a bit of blood and takes a snip of fur. He sulks by the couch afterwards, wary eyes on myself and the technician as we talk.

"Isn't it strange that the TV and the house security system seems geared toward giving a pet so much freedom?" I point out. It's an odd disconnect I've been noticing since I bought Wynn. Morphs are somewhere between object and person—a hot fantasy, but somewhat creepy when played out in reality. So far the hotness overpowers the creepiness for me.

The tech just shrugs as he hands me the computer pad with the bill displayed for me to approve. "Guess more folks want their morphs learning how to be better off on their own instead of having them out wandering the streets," he counters.

I bite back my surprise at the comment as I walk the tech to the door. After a few moments I realize that he has just compared Wynn to an animal, like some neighborhood dog or cat who meanders around getting into others' trash or flower beds. My morph wouldn't do that; he isn't just an animal. He isn't an animal at all, I add when that reflexive clenching of my stomach happens.

I call my morph into the kitchen so he can eat his own dinner and watch me cook mine. It will take a bit of time to relearn how to cook for just one again. Glancing back at him, I ask if he could eat my food but only get a "not good enough, Master" response.

It's probably in the manual the Institute sent home with me. I'd read it, but I think just exploring might be fun as well. *Slowly, Emily,* I tell myself as I finish my pasta.

He quickly learns how to set up my tray for me in the family room and bring me my food as I sit on the couch watching him. Carefully he balances the drink in both hands as he pads across the floor. The Institute should work more on the walking thing. After the glass joins my plate safely on my tray he turns and bolts back to the kitchen. In a few minutes he returns, his water bowl in his hands. This he sets down on the floor between my tray and the television.

"What about your food?" I prompt when he sits on the floor, half facing me and half facing the screen, curling his tail around him.

"wynn done," he says with almost childlike innocence. Then he pauses and glances at the bowl then at me before bowing his head in my direction. "wynn okay drink here, Master?" he softly asks—I'd swear I hear a plea in his voice.

I reach down to pet him but stop when his body tenses visibly. "That would be lovely. We can check out some television shows as well, give the system a try."

We watch the news first. When one of the ads I've helped design comes on the air, I ask him his opinion.

"Humans have lots to buy," he says with a sigh.

"What do you mean?"

He counters my question with another question. "Why water? Water," he asks as he laps up one swallow from his bowl, "not water?"

My thoughts exactly. This isn't the Middle East or the Western US, where we've never had or wasted our fresh resources; we aren't using desalination plants that jack up the through-the-faucet costs. But bottled water has been a big seller for over two centuries, and a client is a client. Heck, I buy a bottle myself every now and then when I go to the gym or on a hike. Damn, I've never really given much thought to it before, since all the materials are recycled and made of the new plastics that biodegrade easily.

"Well, some people have different tastes," I began.

"Water tastes?" he quickly asks.

"Yes, it does. For instance, some has minerals and chemicals in it; others might be from a different source. Then you can add flavoring to water too. And some places don't have a lot of fresh water," I try to explain, but am sure I see a frown.

"Source?" he asks during a pause.

"Source is where the water comes from," I say.

"Bottle, sink, server," he says, nodding his head.

"No, more like well, stream, lake, cave, where it originally comes from."

He nods and turns back to the newscast.

The nature channel is next, and Wynn asks a lot of questions I just don't have answers for. He seems very excited and appalled when wild animals hunt and eat their dinners, which are, of course, other animals.

The morph training channel is discussing walks. The leash law, the proper respect a morph should show to a human being, and basic traffic safety. A lot of browbeating about how great it is to be owned by a human.

"Did they teach you all this at the Institute?" I inquire during a break.

Wynn looks at me and nods.

"So why have it on the channel over and over?" I ask as I look through the guide on-screen. Every other show seems to be educational.

"Practice, to remind morphs," he responds. Tilting his head to one side, he seems confused by the questions. "Morphs not smart like humans, need work all the time," he says, looking back to the television, then he seems to smile when he turns back to me. "Now wynn be good pet with practice again."

He still thinks he's failed. Perhaps my disappointed comment was too harsh, but damn bloody true nonetheless. I'm not terribly interested in this channel, but he seems so engaged, even moving his paws and muttering phrases, that I let him watch while I go get a book to read.

He doesn't notice until I've finished a good five pages, then I feel his head on my knee. Lifting up the book I find him looking up at me, those blue eyes a bit moist.

"wynn sorry Master bored," he pouts. I feel his paws against my pant legs.

I sigh. "Perhaps this channel is more for you to watch when I'm at work." He frowns at that, then turns back to the television. I pick up the remote, then bump him with my left foot. When he glances up I hold it out to him. "You change the channel."

He takes it into his paw, and the sensor takes a few seconds to register who he is. When he pushes the forward button it skips forward to the last of the allowed channels.

There, on the screen, is something that makes us both freeze, our mouths open. I hear the soft thud of the remote as it hits the carpet.

The morph on the screen seems to be some dog type—I think female, but that's not so clear. Two human men are using the creature's mouth and ass in an elegant bedroom complete with silk sheets and draped canopy. The music is soft, like a soap opera love scene, and yet the content is nothing like any daytime or prime-time show I've ever done commercials for or seen. I can't seem to move. Am I horrified? No, not exactly, but I'm not turned on either. More like shock, I decide, then glance down at Wynn.

He's pressed against the floor, and I can hear his breathing and jagged gulps. His tail is flat up against his back, but his body is folded close together. His ears are cocked back, but his eyes are glued to the screen.

The man behind gives the morph a slap and orders, "Over." Both men exit her body, for now that she's flipped her sex is clear. The morph lies there, moving side to side and looking from one man to next. Her fur is brown, matted down and wet in places; her muzzle is parted, and her tongue is lapping out as she starts to lift her paws up to her body. The collar around her neck matches Wynn's.

"Wait," one of the men says, and the morph moans. The other man chuckles, then laughs out loud. "Charles, let her; I think it could be enough," he suggests as he strokes his cock.

"Sal, touch yourself," the man in charge says as he too touches his cock.

The morph uses her paws to caress her breasts, stomach, and thighs, but avoids her mound.

"Put on a better show than that," the first man growls.

Immediately the morph begins moving more, lifting her hips, flicking her short tail between her legs, rubbing her breasts vigorously, and groaning loudly. Soon the men are moaning as well and jerking off.

I'm keeping one eye on Wynn. He is moving a bit on the floor, but his ears and eyes are still fixed on their target.

On screen now the men are shooting ejaculate that falls onto the morph, who squeals and rolls, rubbing it into her fur. After they finish, the guest sighs, zips up, and leaves, and the first man, who I guess is her owner, motions to her. The morph scrambles forward and uses her tongue to clean off his cock. Once clean, the man zips up and pats her head. "Good girl, Sal," he says. "Now get the room and yourself cleaned up."

"Yes Master," she whispers. As the man leaves the camera zooms in on her face. One tear rolls down from her eye.

I hear movement, so I turn my full attention to Wynn, who's looking up at me. "Questions?" I ask, hoping he has none. I don't even know what the hell we're watching until the credits roll. "Southern Comfort" is the title.

"Why morph cry?" he asks, his voice sounding deeper, breathy.

"Could be several reasons," I begin. This is pure guessing and is based on people, not on morphs. "Happy because she had fun, sad that her Master's leaving, sad she didn't get to orgasm..." I let my voice trail off.

Wynn looks up at the screen, where a commercial for condoms is airing, and back at me. "Sad cause Master leave, like wynn sad when Master leave," he says.

I can feel my heart melting. I pat the spot next to me on the couch, but he merely moves closer, putting his head on the spot and looking at me with his bright blue eyes. A little more time, perhaps. I look him over and note that his cock is erect. Yes, a few more episodes, and he'll be ready.

I lean against the doorway of his room and watch him nap. I've gotten home early today, so I'm not surprised that he is asleep—morphs seem to sleep a lot; perhaps it is the fox part of him?

One month. That's how long he's lived with me. That first week had been hell, and these next three have been a matter of doctor visits and slowly reintroducing myself to wynn in simple ways like watching television, feeding him, and a bit of friendly but non-sexual petting. I don't think the Institute fed him well—I mean, I'm not overfeeding him, but he has surely put on some weight, and his fur looks so soft and shiny now. It feels so great in my hands and on my calves when we curl up by the fire.

Of course, there is more I want to do, but I've been very careful since that first day I left him here. The bruises and welts, which were visible under that white coat of his, are gone now, and the damaged tissue is healed, the doctor said three days ago.

He still pulled away from me after that visit, though, so I've been just acting like he's my dog, I guess. But he isn't, and I am fully aware of that.

That damned new television show isn't helping much with my self-control. One of the "adult" channels has put on an erotic morph show about humans and their very randy morph pets—I've noticed a high ratio of fox-breeds there, but then that is why I bought him, yes?

The truth is that I started watching the show in hopes it would get Wynn more interested in the things I bought him for. I sigh as I remember a particular shower scene from the other night.

I blink when I find his ice-blue eyes looking back at me. He hasn't moved otherwise—he's just opened his eyes and perhaps smiled; that's still hard for me to determine. Of course, with this first month, what has he had to smile about?

"I got back early," I say as I shift my position a bit to ease the tension that remembering that television episode has created in my groin.

He yawns a bit and moves so he is lying on his back. With one paw he smoothes down his fur from his chin to his stomach, then pauses at the edge of his own groin. "Master want wynn?" he asks suddenly, as his paw brushes the tip of his cock.

I just shift my weight again and raise my eyebrows. Maybe that television show is helping after all. I want to be sure, though, before I move in.

His tongue darts out and licks what would be his lips were he human, allowing me to see a quick flash of his teeth—he doesn't sleep well in the dark, I've learned, so the light in here is always on.

Still, I force myself to stand there. Yes, right now I need to know he's okay, that he wants this, and it flits through my mind that that is a very odd thing for a pet owner—heck, a slave owner—to worry about.

He whimpers then, slowly, his eyes watching me, as he rolls onto his stomach. He moves his tail up his body, seductively lifting it away from that part my dick-headed half-brother abused. wynn even squirms a bit as he arches up and pets his shoulders with his tail.

Then he says the words I've been wanting to hear. "wynn want Master, please."

I smile, and I do.

Looking around his room I decide to take this matter to my own suite—this should be his space, a place of safety, and once more it tickles my mind that such thoughts aren't quite right in this situation.

I motion with my hand, and he sighs but follows me, crawling and rubbing against my leg as we move down the hall. He looks at my bedroom when we don't enter, then silently follows me to the adjoining room that I've kept locked since he arrived.

I pause and place my hand on the door. This is probably too fast, way too fast for him, so I just smile as he rubs against my leg.

"Horny, are you?" I tease as I stroke his head, that longer fur soft and inviting in my fingers.

His ice-blue eyes are a bit darker now as he looks up at me, flicking out his tongue and licking my wrist. "Want Master," he whispers with a low growl in his throat.

"Indeed?" I tease as I continue down the hall to the living room we are so used to. I turn on the fire, then when I turn back I find him arranging pillows nearby. He's using his front paws and balancing on his hind legs. There was a scene in one episode of that television show where a morph was beaten for carrying such things in her mouth, and I suspect that is why he is acting this way. Seeing him standing touches something deep inside me, making me want him even more as he mimics human behavior.

At first one might think that the pillows are for me, but that would be misunderstanding how fox morphs think—they are, the owner's manual and the television show suggests, primarily concerned with self first. Not that they can't or don't want to please their owners; that just tends to follow their own sexual drive. Unlike some human partners, getting attention makes them want to give attention even more.

When the pillows are all arranged, Wynn reclines tummy-down on the pile so that his ass is lifted up invitingly. With one paw he pushes back another pillow and says with a purr, "For Master."

I grin and sit down on the offered pillow. My foxboy responds by wiggling closer to me, lifting his tail again, and flicking out his tongue as he watches me. I know that it is very difficult for his kind to ask for what they want; genetics can control a good number of things, and I suspect his training intensified any submissive inbred traits. Yet, what I am, what I like, makes me watch him silently for a moment.

That continues for a good couple of minutes until I must have reached his limit of patience. Wynn tilts his head, purrs again, and uses his tail to tickle my hands, which are folded in my lap. If they weren't folded I'd be all over him by now; that isn't my desire at this moment.

His tail gets a bit more active as he leans toward me and trails it up my bare arms; he's flicking out his tongue, perhaps offering other skills to me. After a few trips up and down my arm, I'm biting my lip to keep from giggling.

"Master not want wynn?" my foxboy asks me with what sounds like a pout. I can see his front paws gripping the pillows tightly as though even asking that hurts him.

I reach out and capture that tail as it lies against one of my hands. A slight tug causes him to growl softly and glance away from me. When he looks back at the next tug, he is indeed pouting, but in a rather desperate way. "Master want wynn?" He sounds as though he is pleading.

I don't speak but instead shift myself so I can also use my other hand. I smooth his tail up along his back with one while the other caresses his thighs. It is a very odd feeling to have something other than fabric or hair between my touch and the skin, yet not unpleasant either.

My foxboy responds by lifting up his ass a bit higher, his thighs pressed together, offering an odd image of wanting and yet not wanting attention to his nether regions. He purrs, though, when I use both my hands to caress his cheeks and thighs.

"Do you remember that I told you that I like to be a bit rough?" I say as I take a few hairs into my fingers and tug at them.

He shakes beneath my hands, then looks back at me. "Yes, Master," he whispers.

I move my body so that my arm nearest his head can be laid across his shoulders, pinning his tail to his back while the other continues to pet him.

A few gentle whacks on his ass and he is purring again, his tail moving under my arm ever so slightly. I'm very glad that I've changed into a sleeveless shirt after getting home so I can feel all these reactions.

My strikes grow in strength until he jerks back his head and his tail almost pulls free. With confirmed desire, I plant my arm firmly over that squirming appendage and push him down into the pillows.

"Master?" he asks when I pause and lean toward his head.

"I'm not done, Wynn," I begin, "but I really didn't tell you exactly how rough I like it." His eyes narrow as he looks up at me. "Do you still want to offer yourself to me like this?"

I hear him swallow and feel his body tremble slightly. "wynn want Master. Master is Owner."

In his simple language and maybe his simple thoughts, that perhaps says all there is to say.

I sit back up and swing one leg over his own. I intend to keep him as still as possible, something else I don't think fox morphs are very good at.

My spanking now takes on a decidedly sadistic bent as I lay into his ass with two dozen rapid, hard smacks. He is panting now, and I can feel his ribs shake with each breath.

The next two dozen pull a mewling out of him. Another two dozen, and I have to shift my weight to keep him in place as he pants and growls, his head snapping back as he looks at me and tries to pull away. It is hard to tell, but I don't think I see anger, just confusion and fear. His hips, however, have been rising up to meet my hand and then grinding down into the pillows. With a human I'd be sure he was enjoying this.

At the end of the next dozen blows, he has ripped a hole in the pillow he is holding. A volley of another dozen, and he is gasping as he finally speaks again, "Master, please."

I stop and sit back, swinging my leg free and releasing him completely. No safeword, and yet it feels like he said one, and did not abuse it either. As I'd hoped, he lifts up like a bolt, giving me access to his front.

His cock is hard and hot in my grasp. When I have it firmly in hand he half growls and half purrs as he looks directly at me, the blue of his eyes nearing neon in hue. A few strokes is all it takes to rip a howl from his throat and a spurt from his groin.

When his hips stop jerking, I remove my hand and hold it out to him. "Clean it up, foxboy," I command as calmly as I can play it. Without a protest or a sigh he begins.

His tongue is rough, sort of like a cat's, as he licks his come from my hand. At first he seemed uncertain of what to do, but now his tongue flicks around my fingers and palm earnestly. Those lovely blue eyes watching from under his longer head fur as it tumbles down his head.

I bet he'd be so pretty in blue ribbons and a blue collar over that silver one, which is barely visible under his pale fur. Maybe that would be too much, too gaudy. No, I think I could use the reminder that he is more than a pet, more than an animal.

When he has cleaned away all the remnants of his pleasure from my hand, he inches forward and continues to lick my wrist, then ventures up my arm. His eyes never break away from mine as a human might out of fear or shame or just awareness of being watched. Those are things my foxboy does not seem to feel; Master is owner, after all.

It is very true from all I've experienced so far with him that fox morphs are very self-centered about that first round of pleasure. But after that, as he is now showing me, they tend to focus on their owner with an almost inexhaustible randiness toward the human who has given them positive attention.

When his tongue reaches my shoulder, I reach over and grasp his head fur. I tilt his head back roughly, and he grips his thighs with his paws and gasps.

"Does my pet want something else?" I ask with as neutral an expression as I can manage.

The shape of his face enables him to flick out his tongue and lick my arm as I hold him. I shake him gently to focus him to my question. He blinks and sighs, then answers, "More, Master, more, please."

With a human we'd be talking, organizing, negotiating what we could and couldn't do, defining the relationship over and over, and arguing. Not so with Wynn; he is my pet, my possession, my property, my slave, to do with as I see fit with. Luckily I also consider myself an honorable and financially careful person—I shan't be doing anything to damage this investment.

I will do as I want, though.

I release him and stand up. He immediately wraps himself around my legs, eyes looking up at me as he caresses my calves. I click my tongue as his paws venture upward. "Go take a shower," I say.

Wynn whimpers, not moving but nuzzling my legs with his muzzle.

I pull my legs free, and he jumps back as though I were going to kick him. Instead I just poke him with one foot. "Go take a shower," I repeat, my voice a little harsher.

"More," he whines and sits up on his haunches with a wiggle of his body. Randy may be an understatement.

"Go!" I order with a wave of my hand for effect.

His shoulders rise up as he looks down at the floor. "Yes, Master," he sighs. Slowly he crawls away, looking over his back a few times as he moves to his room.

"Go, go," I repeat as I pick up the pillows that now need to be laundered. I shake my head at the ripped one, then frown at him as he pauses. He quickly opens the door, enters and shuts it behind him. Now I allow myself a very turned-on sigh.

I toss the wet pillows into the wash, then dump the ripped one into the maid's basket to be mended. Next time he'll have to be prevented from doing that, and the idea increases my own desires again.

I head toward his shower. I need to make sure he is following my instructions and getting completely clean.

When I enter his room I can hear the toilet flushing from the other side of the wall where the bathroom is. I also hear a "yuck" from there, so I can assume he's making sure to clean himself out. The company told me that it is difficult to train morphs to clean themselves this way, so I had to pay extra money. I think I might have a tiny clean fetish, though, because it is very important to me.

I count to ten once I hear the shower start and the door slide shut before I enter his bathroom.

Immediately he turns to face me, soap in one paw and the water wetting his fur, making it seem darker in color. "Master?" he asks, stepping closer to the glass door. He's gotten much better at standing up when he isn't bending over, though he still crawls on all fours most often when I'm around. I suspect he might have been punished for walking upright, and that memory keeps him cautious with me. I'll have to do something about that; I think he's more attractive upright—easier to access, too.

"I thought I'd come and watch you shower—make sure you know what you're doing, maybe see a bit of a show," I say as I walk closer and lean against one of the walls next to the shower door.

Wynn moves his body against the door and looks up at me as his wet fur drips water down his face. "Show like television?" he asks.

I nod as I trail a finger along the glass, outlining his face beneath it. "You are to get clean first," I state firmly. "And I'm not so sure you can put on a good show like on the television," I add with a shrug.

My foxboy straightens up a bit and snorts. "wynn can too," he insists.

"How can you be so sure?" I tease.

"wynn practice," he says, then leans his head against the door as though he's just realized what he's said. Supposedly, fox breeds, while being horny, have also been conditioned to not pleasure themselves unless directed to by a human. I suspect once more that that conditioning had to be violent to fight their natural tendency to enjoy themselves.

"Oh, is that one of the things you do when I'm at work?" I reply, a grin on my face and I hope the sound of pleasure in my voice.

He doesn't look up, though, and instead presses his body against the door as he asks softly, "Master angry?" He licks at the glass as I place my palm against it, his eyes not meeting mine.

"I doubt it," I say, "let's see how much your practice has paid off, Wynn," I state simply. He looks at me and blinks. I lean against the glass and whisper, "Put on a good show, my pet."

"Yes Master," he replies.

He steps back directly under the water and begins to mimic the television show to some degree. He can't, of course, do it exactly as the female did; he doesn't have those same parts, and the television show is more willing to show the fems than the studs, even though the statistics for ownership are fifty-fifty. If I owned a business I wouldn't advertise there until they got less sexist.

He begins by using soap on his backside, cleaning up that area he recently "yucked" about. He turns as he suds up so that he can bend a bit and show me what he does. "Still red, still hot, Master," he adds, and when he parts his fur I can see the marks from my spanking. "Feel good, Master," he says as he works the soap up and down and a bit inside. Setting the soap down he turns his ass to the water and lets it rinse off.

"You liked the spanking? That's what the thing we did in the living room is called," I add when he just glances at the question.

"Hurt," he says with a sigh as he parts his ass cheeks and lets the water rinse better. "Like Master touch." He straightens up again and looks directly at me as he takes the soap back in paw. "Rough, gentle, always like Master touch."

You haven't been to my special room yet, I think silently as I smile at him.

He works his special soap over his entire body, slowly, seductively, lifting and smoothing down his fur in turn, moving so I can see exactly what he is doing. "Now like water," he whispers, before rinsing his face. I'm not sure what that means, so I just watch silently.

The bottoms of his hind paws are the most difficult. No grace here as he grips the bar and balances with a tremor so he can clean his leathery feet. I find myself switching between using human terms and animal terms for his body in my mind and not really using any words at all to refer to him, just giving orders. Am I worried I'll offend him?

He next takes the shampoo from his shelf and does the fur on top of his head. It's not really like fur, but not like hair either; that's what my research has discovered. I've been doing more reading on morphs since buying him than I did before, and I should know better than that, since I help persuade folks to buy first, think later. None of his fur seems to be getting any longer, but it's only been a month. He builds up a lather on his head, then looks at me as he proceeds to make an odd artistic design there with the shampoo suds as sculpturing glue.

I laugh out loud, and he replies with a similar laugh. "Master happy?" he asks as he rinses his paws.

"You are very amusing," I simply reply. I watch quietly as he rinses out his creation. Who knew that animals could be so inclined, but then he isn't really an animal, is he? He moves to turn off the water when I make an observation out loud, "I think you forgot a part."

"wynn no forget, Master," he says as he instead turns the hot water down a bit.

Now I lean back against the wall. The show I've been waiting for is about to begin. For his first time masturbating in front of someone else, especially in a shower, Wynn does a fairly good job. His legs aren't really ideal for standing when in the throes of passion, so finally he just tilts the showerhead down and kneels under the water. He glances up at me, pausing in his stroking. "Sorry, Master," he says softly. When I smile and nod my head he resumes his self attentions.

Animals, of course, don't have sex just to have it. There is always a reason—primarily reproductive, but also for safety or chemical impulse or to bond with other members of their group. I wonder as I watch him whether somewhere in his mind that instinctive part is rebelling at the lack of a partner.

Now why would I think that? Didn't he just come over my hand a while ago? It's my mind again struggling with the dilemma of him looking so very much and yet so little like a human, performing for me as a human sex slave might.

This didn't bother me on the television show, I think for a moment, watching him grow more and more excited. His hips start to buck the air, and he throws back his head with a growl, his eyes fixed on mine. "Master?" he asks, and I know what is wrong with this scene.

"Stop!" I command as I step right against the glass shower doors.

He whimpers and strokes a few more times until my harsher repeated order makes him shake and take his hands from his groin.

"Don't move, foxboy," I instruct. "Watch me, Wynn," I add as I start to undo the buttons on my sleeveless shirt. His eyes get darker as I remove my shirt and pants and stand there for a moment in just my underwear. I pirouette around once and smile at him before removing my bra and panties. "See? No fur on me," I say as I step into the shower.

wynn looks at the floor as I step inside. "Master have some fur," he ventures to say softly.

I step closer to him, caressing his head. "Are you sure? You need to take a closer look, foxboy," I suggest as I pet him.

He shudders and slowly lets his gaze sweep up my legs, resting for a moment on my pubic mound, then up my belly to my breasts before meeting my eyes. "Master smell nice," he says, his voice husky, his eyes neon again.

"I'll smell better after I've come a few times," I tease.

He looks at me and licks his jaw, nervously or eagerly perhaps.

"What is it?" I ask as he makes no move toward me.

"wynn not know how please Master," he says, then lets his head bow again as though deeply embarrassed by the admission.

"I thought you were trained to be a good pet, a good sex toy," I say, a bit harsher than I really intend to. I am disappointed at the news, though.

"See, hear, on computer," he says, that last word more slowly. "wynn never do. wynn want please Master," he adds as he leans forward and hugs my legs so that his head is resting against my thighs.

I pet his head, and he purrs into my flesh, sending shivers up my body. "Then I shall have to teach you. The shower isn't the best place for a first time. We'll go to my suite," I decide out loud.

He begins to crawl after me, so I turn toward him. "Please walk; it makes me feel more comfortable," I confess.

Wynn blinks a few times, then rises to his feet, one hand on the shower door to help him balance.

"Good boy. Dry yourself, then come to my bedroom," I command as I pick up my own clothes and head out of his bathroom.

Chapter Seven
Training with a Personal Touch

i look at myself in the mirror and make sure that the blower hasn't left me a big puff. Sometimes i wish i could use personal pronouns when I talk to Her, but i know from the Institute that humans really hate that. i guess they prefer to think of us as less intelligent, less capable than we are. That's what the songs say, anyway. i would never want to upset Master.

i'm learning a lot from the television. i watch very carefully when She uses it, and now when She's at work—i hate Her going to work; She should be here playing with me—i watch it too.

There, that looks good, i think as i turn around watching myself in the mirror. Examining the surface again i'm still puzzled. It doesn't have an outlet or anything, so how does it work? That television has something in it, too, that only lets me watch certain channels, so what i'm learning is fairly limited i guess. How does this mirror work?

i look back at my shower and walk to the glass door. How does that water know what temperature to be? Where does it come from? my ears turn back as music drifts into the room, so i turn my head in response as well. That's probably Her nice way of telling me to get in there. i don't even want to guess what a less nice way would be.

i start to lower myself to the floor, then remember Her words. Why does She want me to walk? Not really something to think about; She is my Owner, and it sounded like an order, so i walk to my sleeping chamber, out into the hall and over to the open door of Her bedroom. At the door i pause and glance inside. The lights are dimmer, but not like sometimes in the television show about us. As Paul, Karen, Andrea, and Sam have their pets do, so does Master expect of me now.

i'm getting this feeling that my training might not be enough.

If i don't do this well, She'll send me back; She'll kick me outside; i swallow as my thoughts continue—the big sleep for certain.

As i'm about to sink to the floor in fear, She moves into my line of sight and smiles at me. my Master likes me, and that gives me strength.

"Come on in, wynn," She says with a wave of Her hand.

"Yes, Master," i say as i walk slowly into Her room. Sometimes when i walk i think that i could do much better with practice. When i talk i wish i could figure out how to make all those words in my head come out—but then humans like us talking in small words, so why should i care? Why do i care?

She is wearing Her—what did She call it?—oh yeah, Her nightie, and standing by Her bed. Hers is much bigger than mine and very strange to sleep in the few times i've been allowed. Wonder if i'll get to tonight. i like being that close to Her.

i turn my face to Her as She touches my jaw. She trails Her hand down my throat, i lift up my jaw. Whenever a human has touched me like this it makes me feel so small, so helpless; i'm horny again.

"I'd like to start exploring those pleasures that I was told fox morphs are good for," She says with that glint in Her eyes that makes me feel so eager and frightened at the same time.

"wynn want please Master," i reply, tilting my head so i can rub her hand with my nose and face. "Please show wynn how please Master," i add after a few seconds of petting.

"We're going to go slowly," She says as She continues to pet my face and jaw. i'm wondering what exactly that means as She backs away and sits down on the edge of Her bed. She lifts and extends one foot toward me. Covering it is one of her slippers, which are a kind of indoor and getting ready for bed type of shoe, i've figured out. Something i see some of my kind fetching on the television, but i'm afraid of harming them.

Of course that reminds me of the pillow i just ripped up and i bow my head in shame.

"What's wrong, foxboy?" Master asks as She touches my nose with Her slippered foot.

"wynn sorry for pillow, Master," i say very slowly, forcing that tiny but important word out. i flinch back to lessen the impact of Her kick. Instead i jump when my face merely feels Her caress, and i'm forced to look at Her.

"Next time I'll be more careful," She says with a serious look that soon transforms into a smile. "But that would be too fast for right now. If you are to be well trained, we must go slowly in some things. It will take time and effort. Are you willing to put in that time and effort, morph?"

"Yes, Master. wynn is Master's," i offer myself in words and what i hope she can understand by moving my body closer and lower.

"Good. Then our first lesson is feet," She replies as She sits back and extends Her foot again. "What do you see?"

i blink at the question, then focus my eyes on Her foot and slipper. As i look at it my mind races with how to answer the question. Simple, a statement of what is physically before me? A statement of what i feel? A statement of what She is in relationship to me? Unsure, i just start talking. Best to be punished for a mistake than for not trying, the songs say.

"Master's foot inside slipper. Slipper black, soft, thing on toe," i begin.

"That's supposed to be a flower," She corrects me.

"Yes, Master, funny flower." My comment makes Her giggle, a sound that means pleasure in humans. "Skin light color, no fur. Power over wynn," i say, starting to move to another possible meaning of Her question. "Power walk good, better than wynn, Master better than wynn," and i hear Her sigh and catch a smile on her face at those words, which encourages me further. "wynn want please Master's foot, show Master wynn know foxboy place."

i fall silent now and swallow. These are thoughts one might feel but never ever say to another morph. Our songs say that we just pretend, but right now, from my place at Her feet, looking at how much bigger and stronger and better She is, i am not pretending. She has given me a name, a home, a life; how could i pretend to be anything other than her creature?

"Now take my slipper off my foot with your," She orders,

pausing there, then continues, "paws, and set it by my bed. Be careful, foxboy."

i already know what the slipper feels like and most of Her other stuff too. i've rummaged through Her bedroom and most of the house when She's been at work. Now, though, i make sure to refeel them so She doesn't guess what i've been doing. "Soft," i say as i pull it off, careful not to let my very short claws touch Her. At least it is a slipper and not one of those other shoes with the straps that go around and around. That would be so hard. i place it near Her bed within easy reach and look up at Her. There has to be more to this.

"Now feel my foot too. You can scratch, but only very lightly, wynn," She adds, and i note the warning in Her tone of voice.

Using both hands i touch gently, outlining Her foot a few times, then take it into both hands. She keeps saying "paws," but i think of them as hands. Not as good as human hands, but what they can do would surprise most humans. Right now i just want to please Her.

Unlike my own feet and hands, Hers are smooth and soft for the most part, only a light down of fur—no, it's called hair on them. Her claws—no, nails—are very trimmed and thin. i stop all movement as She giggles again.

"It's okay, wynn," She says. "I'm just a bit ticklish; most humans are on the bottoms of our feet."

"Yes, Master. wynn continue?" i raise the pitch of my voice a bit as i've noticed humans do when they ask a question.

"Yes, but now use your face, your mouth, your tongue, explore that foot." Her voice is deepening as She speaks, and Her eyes seem to darken as i look up at Her. "That is how you pleasure a foot. But I want you to explore and see if you can figure out the best ways by paying attention to my reactions," she directs.

To use my mouth on that part of Her body which supports Her weight and protects Her from the ground seems somehow humbling, as though i'm placing myself under Her feet. When that thought finishes in my mind, i become aware that my cock has gotten harder and longer. i am not pretending to like being hers, i realize as i rub my cheek against her foot.

The scent is Her and yet somehow different from Her hands and arms, which i've been this close to before. Different still from the scent around her lower fur—hair—and that overall scent she sends out around me. i love her scent; at night when i dream of Her it is Her scent that washes over me first. What do Her other parts smell like, i wonder, then force myself to focus on the task at hand.

my fur makes Her giggle more but also causes Her to caress my back with Her other foot. i lift Her foot higher as i bow my body down so i can run my nose down the arch, breathing in Her scent, wishing to become one with it so I might never fear being sent back to the Institute. At Her heel i flick out my tongue and retrace my journey back up. When i reach Her toes i pause upon seeing Her lying back onto Her bed. "Master?" i ask softly.

"Keep going," She simply replies.

i flick my tongue along the ridge separating her toes and the rest of Her foot, and She sighs and slides down further toward the edge of Her bed. At another command to continue i decide that Her actions must mean She likes it. i lick each part of the bottom of Her foot, twirling my tongue between Her toes, and She reacts good again.

After a few moments Her other foot taps me on the shoulder, and i work on the first with my tongue while my hands remove that slipper. This is going to get difficult, so i move so the first foot is balanced on one of my shoulders and i can lift the other to my mouth.

"Good foxboy. Very clever," She whispers, and my heart swells with pride.

If i still had my sheath, which i miss on occasion, it would be pulled back now, my cock straining out from my own desire. With mouth, tongue, face, and hands i repeat my attentions to Her second foot. Then i begin to alternate between them. She is rubbing my chest with either free foot, grabbing my nipples between Her amazingly mobile toes. The pain, the pleasure, makes me moan into Her foot.

Her breathing is loud now, and i can see Her hands clenching the bedcover. After a few minutes more She screams, and i bolt back in terror, my entire body shaking, my cock deflating, my eyes focused on Her as i fight to stay where i am kneeling.

She just lies there, Her breathing slowing. Then She reaches out with one foot, but i stay at a distance, not moving. "wynn?" She says as She sits up, Her hair loose and falling around Her shoulders.

i swallow, flicking out my tongue a few times, then reply softly, "Yes, Master."

"That was very good," She says and holds out Her arms to me. i rush to Her, burying myself in Her embrace, breathing in Her scent, now more enticing for some reason than before, and enjoying Her petting. i think i have pleased my Owner, and my feelings about that are new and wonderful.

I need a vacation, I decide as I look at my briefcase sitting on the kitchen counter where I've just dumped it. I repeat this to myself as I return to the entryway to hang my coat up. This winter is going to be cold, if this early fall is any indication; I thought we were through the mini ice age. When I get back to the kitchen I can't help but smile. There he is, my pet, my morph, kneeling next to the counter, his eyes flashing. In these few weeks he's learned not to come jumping into me when I return home, but his whole body is moving as I just smile at him, teasing him for a moment.

I bend down and put my hands onto my knees. "Come here, Wynn," I order with a pat of my thighs. He may look small in comparison to me, but the energy he has as he rushes to hug me once more knocks me back a step or two. "Goodness, it's not like I'm leaving you out in the wilds to fend for yourself all day," I tease as he wraps his entire body practically around my legs, his head resting against my stomach, his eyes watching my face.

"Master gone every day, wynn so lonely," he says, and any illusions of his "canine like devotion" fade into the reality of the situation.

"I'm not gone every day," I start to say, attempting to defend myself from that pout that I now can recognize on his face. He is actually quite versatile in body language, and I'm just figuring out what it all means. "I'm here on weekends," I remind him as I loosen his grip enough to crouch down and return his hug.

"Weekends short," he continues. He must note my frown, because he begins nuzzling my neck and shoulder as he promises, "wynn so happy now Master home. wynn do everything make Master happy, happy, happy too."

"Oh, are you going to cook?" I ask, making my mouth gape in mock surprise. He just stops nuzzling and looks at me with that strange look that I haven't been able to decipher yet. He blinks silently at me, then laughs and bounces out of my reach to lean against the counter where my briefcase is.

"Master funny again," he says, then looks away, licking his jaw as though nervous.

"I bet I could teach you," I say, this time a bit more seriously. Not right now; I had a long week, and I think I'm low on choices here in the kitchen, but maybe someday. Yes, why not? He's got hands, he carried food for me, he's getting better on his hind legs, and he seems fairly bright for a morph, I think.

He's shaking his head, that longer head fur moving softly across his shoulders, as he still looks away. "wynn not that smart," he mutters.

"I don't know about that. You learned pretty fast how to work your way up my body," I say, reminding us both of last night's big climax, which celebrated my teaching him how the female human body really works.

"Fox morphs make good pets, not cooks," he replies, glancing at me.

"Oh, I think I'll have to test you a few more times before I can agree to the first half of that statement."

It takes a few seconds for him to understand what I said, then he walks over to me with bowed head. "Not good last night, Master?"

"It was... good. It will get better; we just need to keep

practicing," I suggest. One thing I learned with human submissives is that if you let him think that he is great, he'll stop trying, and soon he'll be mediocre at best. I don't intend to over-praise Wynn at any time—why should I; where is he going?

"Now?" he asks, and that grin on his upturned face and the brief glance down at his upturned cock confirm once again that he is horny so often.

"Maybe after dinner. I'm going to go take a nice bath right now, and then we'll eat." He whines and drops to his knees, his head cocked to one side as he looks up at me. He wants sex so badly, so obviously, and that is so exciting to see, but I just ruffle his head and motion to the living room. "You watch some television and see if you can learn anything to help you later."

"Yes, Master," he says as I walk past him. I glance down the hall and reassure myself that he is doing as told when I hear the set turn on and the sounds from perhaps the morph channel issuing forth.

It takes my nice large tub a good twenty-some minutes to fill with hot water and soapy bubbles. It's been a trying week: the annual reviews, the stockholders meeting, a big problem in accounting. Nothing bad for me and my teams, but still stressful. That executive party in a few weeks will be welcome. Now I'll get to see if all those rumors I heard before being promoted are true or merely envy. I wonder if my teams will gossip so much about me. Likely more.

Once the bubbles are swirling around me in the warm jets of water, I can relax. The weekend is here, so now I won't have to see his pouting face at 6:45 p.m. for two days. I think Margaret wanted to come over some weekend soon, before the executive party, she said. I'll think about it; that squirrel-girl gave me the chills last time, and not in a nice way.

Wynn gave me the good kind last night. He'd learned quickly how I like my feet pampered and pleased, at least sexually. I wonder if those paws could handle a pedicure or manicure? He's learned how to give a good massage, which feels very strange with tiny scratches and soft fur all the time. Both different and pleasant, so I don't plan to give up my bimonthly spa trips yet. He's figured out where my neck likes to be touched and how; he's almost Mastered my breasts and seems far less interested in mashing and squeezing than my human partners have been, much to my happiness. Then last night, he was shaking so hard when I finally ordered him between my thighs that I thought he might collapse. No; he did well, very well in fact, after a few light taps on his head for using his teeth too much.

I stretch out and remember the soft fur of his face, the hard, cool pressure of his nose right above my mound, adding to the clit stimulation all the time, the rough texture of his tongue. That tongue is so cute, very catlike, cupped and small. At first I thought he couldn't manage half as well as a man with something so small, but it is very flexible, and the shape of his head added to the feeling as his breath and fur flooded my thighs.

I moan and hear a soft one behind me. Turning my head I see two blue eyes amid white fur watching me from the door. "Out!" I say, firmly but not harshly. He squeaks and bolts away. Maybe for the first time in my life I might actually have someone who's more randy than me. Wonderful; the possibilities can be endless, then. Slowly, though; he's not going anywhere, and I have all the time I want.

Chapter Eight
The Public View of Miss Potter

i can feel the wind rushing around me, pushing my ears down and back, and it's sending shivers down my back, along my tail, and i'm horny again. The first time in a car, not a van like the white coats brought me to Emalee in, Master has informed me of the difference. Well, ok, not first time really, but first allowed more than in back seat, scared to move because i know we are going to see the doctor again and it will hurt again. No, now we go shopping, which must be fun because She goes every week, usually after work, and brings home lots of bags and boxes which She spends more time on than me. She made it sound like a chore, though, last night when She said we might starve if we didn't get to the grocery store soon.

my hands gripping the window, i lean out further.

"Hey! Don't go falling out that window! I paid a lot for you," my Master's voice calls out behind me, reminding me of where i am. With a sigh i pull back inside and sit down, adjusting that strap thing She ordered me to use. It is too big and feels weird. i won't whine, even though that is my first reaction.

She's taking me outside into the big human world. i don't want to disappoint Her; i can't disappoint Her.

She looks at me with that shake of Her head and a grin on Her face, which I find confusing. Is She angry, confused, worried, amused? "Did you enjoy that, foxboy?"

"Yes, Master," i reply quickly. It was amazing; it felt like, i don't know; it felt incredible.

She's shaking Her head again. "Just like a dog. I thought you were a fox, not a dog," and this time i believe She is teasing me.

"Fox morph," i state emphatically. i remember watching that

nature show with Her the first night I could use the television; i am not a fox like that. Yuck!

"Oh, excuse me," She chuckles as She reaches out Her hand toward an area of tiny lights and buttons between us.

i jump in my seat as music suddenly fills the car.

"Just the radio, like at home," She explains. "Now roll up the window like I showed you; no need to share it with the rest of the world."

i do as ordered with a frown. It was so much fun. Maybe if i'm good She'll let me do it again later.

After a few minutes i'm feeling uncomfortable. I look down at these blue shorts She put on me. Feel funny, tight, strange. She says She doesn't want the rest of the world getting a free gander, whatever that means. On the television morphs don't wear clothes in public, only at home when the owner wants it for "special reasons." We also don't walk around other humans, and She's already told me that She wants me walking today. As we pull into a big area with lots of cars in front of a big building, i feel my stomach tighten.

She is my Owner; i will obey, but i am worried.

i don't think She's noticing the stares and whispers that i am. Leash attached to my collar, i'm led through the parking lot (that's what She told me the place with the cars is called) and into the grocery store. i think everyone we've passed has stopped to stare or to comment softly to a companion. We even passed another morph, some exotic cat form, and his owner and he both stared. i think i saw envy in the morph's eyes, especially after his owner kicked him for not following quickly enough.

Just that thought makes me stay close to Master.

Inside She takes this metal thing from out of a section of many of them and pulls me to the back of it where a red bar is attached. "Want to learn to push the cart?" She asks, a big smile on Her face.

i look at the cart, then at Her. "If it please Master," i say, using a rote phrase i was taught back at the Institute with a swallow. i'm trying hard to concentrate on Her and not on the large number of people and things around us. Off in the distance i see another morph crawling behind a lady. There must be a dozen shoppers here, and at least two of us morphs. This must be the rich human store.

"It's easy. I'll tie your leash around the handle, and you can rest your paws on it and just walk where I direct," she explains in a rush of words. "Not hard to push at all; heck, it might even steady your steps."

Before i can even respond, i'm tied to the cart, my hands placed on the red bar. She takes the other end of the cart in one of Her hands and says "Come on," and i'm being moved down the hall.

This place is huge, as big as the Institute maybe. We go up and down the aisles, Her word for the hallways, which are lined with cans, and food, and stuff i can't place. In the back is a section of food for pets, one part specifically for morphs. She picks up a few things and frowns at them. "Why can't you just eat my food?" She asks, and before i can answer a man standing nearby smiles and comes toward us. Unlike other people, he doesn't stare at me, just gives me the once-over with a frown, then turns his attention to Master.

"Because this is loaded with more of the particular compounds that morphs need to stay healthy. Obviously you are a woman who values her morph," he says with a tone that makes my stomach ache more. "Plus, I have this coupon," he adds, handing Master a piece of paper.

"Ah, for the most expensive brand, I see," She replies after a glance at the paper.

"Yes, but the coupon, doubled here in this store today, makes it very reasonable to try," the man counters; that grin sends flashing warning lights off in my mind, but i'm not sure how to tell Master.

She looks at the food in question, then at the paper, then turns to me. "What do you think, wynn? Want to give it a try?"

The man now stares at me, and his frown returns.

i nod, my head bowed from the queasiness in my stomach.

"I can't hear your brains rattle. Answer me, please," She orders, one hand stroking my head.

"If it pleases Master," i repeat softly. Out of the corner of my eye i see the man step back from us.

"Alright, then," She announces, turning back toward the man, whose fake smile returns. "We'll try it once."

"I'm sure you'll be pleased, Ma'am," the man responds with a final frown at me.

The rest of the shopping trip i keep my eyes focused on the cart and my head bowed. There are indeed two more morphs in the store, both crawling and naked, ignored by all but their owners. i'm shaking by the time we are back out to the car. i think we've just done something very wrong, and i'm terrified of telling Her.

After i return the cart, i drop down to my normal position and sprint back to Her at the car. She's frowning at me as i kneel where i am, waiting for the door to open so i can jump inside and hide.

"I think you should walk," She repeats Her earlier command.

i cringe and glance up at her. "Faster to run, Master," i offer weakly.

She makes a strange noise through Her nose. "You can run on your feet too," She declares, using for the first time human terms to refer to my body, then opens the door to what She called the passenger's side.

Before i can step inside, a car stops, and one of the shoppers speaks to us from his window; in the back seat i see his own morph looking out the window from his place on the floor. "Interesting pet," the man snorts derisively, then drives off.

"Bastard; what did he mean by that?" Master says softly, then motions me inside.

i crawl in and curl up on the floor. The space is barely big enough for me, and it feels somehow safer that way.

"wynn, you have to sit up right; get your seatbelt on," She orders with a sigh. "I'll let you lean out the window again," She offers when i refuse to move.

Well, that is different! i climb up into the seat and let her strap me in. i think i like that feeling. But even the wind blowing through my fur and pushing on my ears can't erase this unease i feel in the pit of my stomach.

When we get home, though, Master merely kisses my cheek and puts away the groceries. She isn't worried, and i'm praying that tonight will be different than last. Mentioning my concern will only lessen that chance, and i think i'll explode if tonight doesn't end better for me. Master is training me to withhold pleasure but i don't like it much. i want to come so badly.

Chapter Nine
Temptation

"Master please, please, wynn so tight, so hot, please, Master," he gasps as I slow down my stroking again. Yes, the possibilities are indeed interesting. For the past two days I've teased him, spanked him, caressed and stroked him, even had him attend to my own needs, but he hasn't gotten off once under my hands. The way he's reacting, I don't think he's touched himself either, which is what I commanded after my bubble bath plan had formed. It is Sunday, and I have work tomorrow, so we do this either my way or no way until next weekend or so. The follow-up to all that review and stockholder stress is almost as stressful as being calm and in control to his cute whining.

There is one thing I am most unhappy with about that entire half-brother episode. I am a woman who loves to penetrate. Being penetrated can be good, can be fun, but penetrating is far superior in my mind. Who needs a penis? I got fingers; I got hands; I got my dildos in all shapes and sizes. I can enter and exit endlessly and make a partner beg for mercy or release or both while I stay physically detached if I wish. I love that feeling of being in control without being out of control.

I stroke my hands along his thighs, and he moans and thrusts upward. His tail is twitching somewhere off to one side, a bit trapped by his body since he's lying on his back. "Now, just two nights ago you were pouting because I don't play with you enough. I could just stop right now and go watch television if you prefer."

His whole body shakes as he begins to cry, and I have to steel my heart against it. No, this is the moment I've been most patient for, and I am getting it tonight. "Please, Master. wynn do anything but please, please," he says as he squirms down to me, wrapping his legs around me and pressing his ass into one of my knees.

"That's the part I want," I say, touching him below his balls where he is rubbing into me. He freezes, and his eyes narrow as he looks at me. "I realize that your first experience was very, very scary and very, very painful. But I won't be like that, I promise," I say softly.

He swallows, and a low groan begins in his throat as he opens and closes his mouth several times. "wynn is Master's," he barely whispers as his body stops moving.

I think for a moment then decide to be romantic in this first approach. It may have been a long time since I fucked someone, but I haven't forgotten how careful one should be and how intense the experience is for both parties. I slide my hands up along the inside of his thighs, and he makes a soft moan. "Let's go to my room and do it there."

He closes his eyes and nods. I back up and allow him to roll over and crawl out of the living room, down the hall and into my bed suite. No comments about walking now; let him be comfortable for a while. He stops at the foot of my bed, leans against it and turns his face up toward me. "Master? Where?"

I look around my room, suddenly not as sure as I was just a few minutes ago. "Get up on my bed," I tell him. "I'm going to go change clothes and get some supplies, and I'll be back." I cup his muzzle and smile at him. "Be ready for me, foxboy."

"Yes, Master," he whispers. He doesn't hop up as he has before but climbs slowly, carefully onto the cover. I can feel him watching me as I go into my dressing room.

"So, what's your problem?" I ask my reflection as I brush my hair out. I've chosen something long, silky and white to wear, and that surprised me. Earlier when I'd thought about this it was in this black satin teddy, with matching black latex gloves. "He's healed, physically; he's consented, and he doesn't have to, remember?" I point out to my reflection. I set my brush down and look at the lube and short latex gloves next to it. "No, he doesn't have to consent to anything, ever, never has to again, not with me," I agree.

Which way should i be? First thought is to repeat what we were doing out in the other room. Lying on my back, i close my eyes and try to recall all Her teasing and touching. Two nights in a row She played with me, had me touch Her. It was OK, not as good as if She'd played me all the way first, but Master did say that i have to be less focused on myself now. It's so hard! But now i'm not aroused, not even slightly.

Come on, stupid morph, get it up! What will She say, what will She do if She walks out and finds me lying here, completely flat. She'll think i'm not grateful, that i'm trying to defy Her. Whitecoats and trainers will come knocking on the door and take me back. Damn! The vids made this all seem so easy.

i hear the water stop running in the other room. Soon She'll be coming through the door, and i have to be ready.

Wait. The correct way, the way the vids mostly showed, isn't this way. i scramble onto my stomach and bring my knees up and out slightly so my ass is open and raised. One re-arranging, and i'm hoping all that can be viewed is the back of my balls. If i moan a lot, toss my head, yeah, She won't notice that anything is not exactly as it should be. i'm reaching for a pillow to prop me up higher when She enters.

She's all in white, something i've seen in Her drawers but didn't know would look like this. She sets a little bottle and something else white on the tiny table next to Her bed then sits down next to me. i'm facing the wrong way.

my sigh isn't faked when She pets my head first. "So, are you sure you're ready for this?" She asks me.

i tilt my head more into Her caress, ignoring the question. i could lie, i should lie, but i don't want to right now if there isn't a need.

She pets me some more in silence then sighs loudly, causing me to jump back a bit. "Yes, as I thought. You aren't ready," She says softly.

i lift up my head as she stands up. One swallow, then i make myself say, "wynn want Master fuck pet. wynn ready." i think She is the most beautiful in these nightie things, Her hair loose around Her shoulders, so smooth to the touch, Her scent surrounding me from Her head to her toes. How could i not want Her to touch me?

"Get up, wynn," She says, motioning with one hand. i obey, too scared, too confused to pretend and beg for something She has seen the truth of. i am the worst pet in the whole world. On that television show, the morphs beg and mew and move anxiously for any human touch. i slide off the bed opposite Her so She isn't insulted by my lack of arousal. As i slide, however, i realize that my cock is harder again.

"Help me turn down the covers," She says to me, then looks up at the ceiling. "Computer, fall night temperature."

We turn her covers down on both sides, and i watch as Master slips out of part of Her nightie, leaving a much smaller part of it on Her. "You're going to sleep with me, wynn," she tells me.

i freeze, certain that i have not heard Her correctly. "wynn sleep with Master, in Master bed?" I ask, looking indirectly at Her. i can feel my body tensed even though my cock is straining a bit. When I've slept with Her in the past it has been on top of Her covers or with Her in more clothing.

"Sleep with me, get used to me; I think that may help," She says as She gets into the bed and lies on one side facing me. After a further motion of Her hand i crawl up as well. "No, no, facing away from me," She instructs with a gentle push when i lick Her nose and grin.

my stomach is tightening as i roll. It could be a trick, but why a trick? No need for one. Did the trainers or whitecoats ever need a reason? Emalee not like them, i remind myself. The lights turn off at Her command as She pulls the covers up to our chins.

She tucks the blanket and sheet around my neck then slides up right behind me. my muscles are clenching, though i'm breathing as slowly as i can. One arm nudges my shoulder then moves, so i turn my head slightly to see Her placing it under Her head and pillow. Her other arm snakes around my back, over one hip, and briefly touches my cock.

"Do you want to come?" She whispers into my ear. She strokes me a few times, and i push back against Her, my ears turning back to hear every sound. "Do you?"

i find one of my hands lowering and covering Hers on my cock. i gently use it to raise her hand to my lips, where i kiss it as best i can. "Please, Master, just hold wynn," i surprise myself with these words, then bite my lip.

She snuggles in closer and pulls me back so i can feel the curves of Her body against my back. "Just like a teddy bear, then," She tells me.

From Her tone i know She is okay with this for right now, so i say one final word before closing my eyes, "Fox." Her response is to pull me closer to Her, and the best sleep of my life up to that point begins.

Snow. Soft and warm snow. "What?" My conscious mind tells me that this is not possible as it struggles to wake me up fully. At first it sort of looked like snow laying out over the cover of one of my pillows, flowing over one of my breasts. No, this wasn't white; it was more silver, or opaque perhaps, each individual strand moving with his breath.

Sleeping with him while mostly naked had been pleasant. He had made no more demands, taken up less room, in fact, than when I was in pajamas and he cuddled next to me.

"Wynn?" I say softly, brushing back his fur from what I expect to be his face, but instead I find one pointed ear turning slowly toward me. "Wake up, Wynn."

"Master?" he whimpers as he turns his face upward from his position of lying on his side. His crystal blue eyes open suddenly, and he starts to burrow into my chest with little flicks of his tongue.

"Here now, calm down," I tell him between the giggles his licking is causing.

"More," he whispers and begins licking downward. Of course he's horny again.

"No," I say firmly, and he withdraws with a whine. "No," I repeat. "I have to get ready for work. You know that."

"Hate work," he whines as he buries his head under the covers, refusing to watch me rise.

"You may lay there for a few minutes more, but then I want you to take your own shower and get very clean," I instruct as I grab my robe. "Hear me?" I ask with a swat on his butt as it lies like a lump under the covers.

"Yes, Master," he replies with another whimper.

Chapter Ten
Education

"Wynn?" I call to him from the front door when I return home. The week has been hectic, the processing of all those reviews a chore—next week won't be much easier as I write up individual reviews and respond to everyone. Right now may not be relaxing either, but there is some wisdom in doing this. As expected my morph is quick to appear, probably because he's been waiting in the kitchen for me. I'm late, for reasons good or bad— that's yet to be determined.

He turns the corner and freezes in mid-step when he sees we have guests. Our eyes meet briefly before he drops to all fours and scampers to me. When he is hiding behind my legs, I introduce him.

"This is Wynn, and this is my co-worker and friend, Margaret, and her morph Violet."

He looks around me as Violet looks around Margaret's legs, mimicking his shyness because I know that squirrel-girl isn't shy.

"An exotic, too," Margaret coos as she pets her own morph's head. "Isn't it amazing what science can do these days?"

I nod and pet Wynn, whose eyes flit back and forth, looking at me then them, his pink tongue flicking out nervously. His manner and speech changed from the moment he saw them, and it's making me uncomfortable. "Well, why don't we all go into the living room and relax a bit?" I suggest with a sudden but soft clap of my hands.

"And get to know each other better," Margaret adds with that sexy tone only a native North American can manage. She and I hang our coats in the hall closet then lead the way to more comfortable surroundings.

Right before I sit I inquire whether either of them would like a drink or snack—normally we'd be preparing dinner now, but honestly I had hoped Margaret had forgotten her plans to visit, so I have nothing for four, or even two, I guess. "Wine would be lovely for me," Margaret says while Violet merely sits on the floor by her feet.

"That sounds good for me as well," I agree with a nod to Wynn.

Margaret tilts her head as my morph disappears and I sit in the chair opposite her. We chat politely about the upcoming executive party that will be my big introduction to all the company executives. I stop and turn as her eyes widen and she says, "That is an amazing trick."

Wynn comes in, balancing a tray with two goblets of white wine on it. It seems a bit difficult for him to manage; the balance isn't the same as when it's just a glass for me and a bowl for him. Actually he has nothing for himself on the tray at all. Part of me is a bit embarrassed by the fact that he still can't kneel to serve—his legs just don't seem to bend that way very gracefully yet. However, Margaret seems either pleased or shocked as she takes one of the goblets.

"Wonders. Simply a wonder what you've accomplished in a little over a month, Emily."

"Thank you," I say, first to her, then to Wynn as I take my own goblet. "I didn't really do much, merely encourage him; he's still a bit wobbly on his hind legs," I add so as not to sound as proud as her comment has made me feel.

Margaret chuckles. "That's a thought. But why?"

I pause in mid-sip at the question. "Why?"

"Yes, why have him do this at all? I mean, it is entertaining—a bit risqué too, I suppose—but why spend that time?"

"To serve me," I reply, then frown. Why do I suddenly feel like I'm on display here and that it isn't a good thing? "Don't you have Violet serve you?"

"In the ways she was designed for, of course," Margaret says matter-of-factly. "She could never grasp serving wine on a tray or—for god's sake, Emily, I just realized, he had to pour it too!"

She takes a deep sip and watches him as he puts the tray on an end table. "I heard that fox breeds were clever, but I had no idea. It must have taken a lot of work on your part."

I nod and sip my wine until Wynn has returned and is safely curled around my feet. Who feels safer? Him? Me? I can almost feel his discomfort as his body shakes from his fast breathing. I return us to the reason for this visit, hoping that whatever it is that Margaret insists I must do before the party, it can be done quickly. "You said you needed to see me before the party?"

"Yes, yes," she says and hands Violet her goblet. The squirrel-girl frowns at the glass as she holds it and herself upright. "Since this is your first, I'm concerned that you might be nervous about attending. I was a wreck, and I made a few mistakes that shook my confidence for weeks."

I find that difficult to believe. Margaret has been my mentor more than anyone else at the company, a mentor because she was the first female president for the financial side of things and was anxious to bring more women into the company as a way to reach a wider and more profitable clientele; you'd think we'd come farther in centuries, but still it can be a man's world at times. "Well, I'm assuming that it's like your average party or meeting," I suggest.

"No, more like a time to—bond, shall we say," she begins mysteriously.

"Bond? To the company, to other executives?"

"In a way. It is a time to celebrate our successes, discuss new directions, and to make sure we are all of the same mind, so to speak."

"Why bring the morphs?" I ask, stroking Wynn as I bring him into the discussion.

"That's part of what makes us of the same mind. Many of our clients own them or work for companies that have some connection to the erotic bioengineering field. Most of them have very special concerns about how they are perceived, so by having all of us own morphs, we hope we can understand them better." She takes her goblet again, so my eyes are drawn to the squirrel-girl, who doesn't meet Margaret's eyes but merely smiles at me and Wynn. "And it was discovered many years ago that it is also good for the company if we share certain beliefs and hobbies."

"Now you're starting to worry me. You're being so mysterious that it sounds like the morphs will be passed around among us, like Roman sex slaves," I say with as much of a giggle as I can muster. There are some fantasies that make me uncomfortable in real life even, if the idea can be a turn-on.

"Oh, no, no," she replies as she hands her now-empty glass to her morph. "Anything that might happen between humans and morphs, well, that won't happen at this party. But you like to watch that new television show, 'Southern Comfort?' I thought I heard you talking about it the other day?"

"Yes, we were approached to do a commercial, and I was advising my team to watch a few episodes. What does this have to do with the party?"

"Erotic morphs are just that, erotic. Sexually charged in ways that I still haven't fully grasped, and I've had Violet for four years now. At these parties they tend to relate to each other in sexual ways, ways which we encourage." She says this last word with a hint of force. "We watch them, and by doing so, we learn what each other likes. Is this making you uncomfortable, Emily?"

Damn straight, as my half-brother might say, but I'm too new to make a fuss over what is probably nothing like what she's saying. "No, I just haven't been so open with my sexuality in a group in a very long time. Co-workers, at that," I say and finish my wine in one large swallow.

Margaret looks at me silently for a moment then smiles and settles back into her chair. "I understand; I was uncomfortable my first time, too. Which is why I wanted to give you and your pet a chance to mingle before the party. Violet was very frightened her first time with as many morphs as humans in one room. Since he is so clever, though, I think yours will do quite well if he can just get comfortable with different breeds."

I don't know what to say. Without being blatant, I and mine have just been propositioned in my own house. I blink a few times and feel the hair on wynn start to rise as he presses himself closer to my legs. I set my goblet down before speaking. "Are you suggesting that Wynn and Violet have sex?"

Margaret chuckles again. "Of course not; we can't be encouraging such fraternization among morphs," she says.

I start to sigh in relief when her next words make me freeze.

"They'll perform for us, in front of us, do whatever we tell them, or if you prefer, we'll just tell them to amuse us and themselves."

"How is that not having sex?" I hear the question issue from my mouth.

"Technically I suppose it could be said that they have sex," she agrees, but her voice and the movement of her hands tell me that I've made her uncomfortable now. "But it is only for our amusement, when we tell them to. Morphs can never think they have a right to their own bodies or the bodies of others. That is one of the philosophies behind legalized erotic anthropomorphism."

Why is something that previously sounded so hot suddenly so—not? "Wynn doesn't know anything about squirrel-morphs," I say, then add, "nor do I."

"I can direct them, then, and you can learn as he does," she offers with a sincere smile.

I feel like I've been slapped. "I don't think this is appropriate," I state as I start to stand up. Margaret grabs my hand with more strength than I would have guessed she had.

"I like you, Emily. You are a gifted manager and a gifted artist. I'm the one who worked for your promotion, so if you value your job and mine, you'll let me help you and your morph," she says in a low and even tone.

I have always been amazed at how calm some people can be when threatening others. This isn't a tease between mates; she is quite serious, and for the first time I'm feeling uneasy about my company. I sit down mutely. After a few moments of her intensely meeting my gaze, I turn wynn's eyes up to me. "Wynn, do as Margaret tells you."

"Everything I tell him," she adds, causing my bile to rise into my chest.

"Everything she tells you," I amend. I can feel the questions burning from him as he looks at me with those abnormally blue eyes. "Go on, foxboy; put on a good show, now."

After a few seconds he crawls to the squirrel-girl, who has already moved a few feet from us and is waiting for him. She stands there like a whore, one tip of her tail at the corner of her mouth. I'd be angry if not for the concern I'm keeping at bay by gripping the arms of my chair. What kind of place do I work in?

By the time Violet and wynn have finished an hour later, I have a much better idea of the kind of people I work for and with. I don't think I like it too much.

Wynn just stays in the front room as I see our guests to the door. When I come back he's sitting waiting for me, looking up at me with his big blue eyes. "Are you all right?"

"Yes, Master, wynn fine," he says, nodding his head and watching me.

I sigh as I sit down and put a hand over my eyes for a second. "Are you sure? I mean, I didn't know," I start to say when he interrupts me.

"Violet have huge mouth!" His comment makes me glance up, and he's lying on his back just as he was during most of their performance; it was clear that the squirrel girl had experience in these sorts of things. "wynn think she swallow him all up!" he says, turning to lie on his side with a chuckle.

That makes me smile. It was a bit weird for a while when she had his cock and balls in her mouth at the same time. And those teeth ... "She didn't hurt you, did she?"

He shakes his head and crawls to place his head on my knees. "No, no, Violet Master train her good, no use teeth, though they funny."

I smile and run a hand through the longer hair on top of his head. He whimpers and nuzzles me with his cool nose. "Master pleased?"

"Of course," I lie, my first falsehood with him. "It was very entertaining to watch."

"wynn like Master best," he declares as he rubs his face against my legs.

I want to cry because I certainly don't like myself right now. He doesn't know better; he seems content. I'm making this a bigger deal than it needs to be, I decide.

"I'm going to order a pizza for myself, so fetch the phone for me," I order. As I watch him scamper off to do as ordered, I hug my knees up to my chest for a moment, reminding myself that this will all be worth it and that it can't possibly do him any damage. Can it?

Part II

Social Corruption

Chapter Eleven
Business Days

I can see Lake Superior in the distance from one of my office windows. This, as far as I'm concerned, is the true perk of my promotion. Overseeing our three teams is more stressful than overseeing just one, which I did as team leader, or watcher, as we call them internally. I suppose my teammates had less kind words for me when I suggested to our previous VP that we shake things up, but after two years and the resulting benefits, everyone apparently gave me a good review, or I wouldn't be sitting here today.

I look down at my desk, see the photo of Wynn, and smile at his furry face and bright eyes looking eagerly up at the camera and me. I can run the vid on the photoframe, but for now the stillness is reassuring to me, given that the R-H2O campaign is meeting in the conference room. Amber told me yesterday that there were some differences of opinion in the team, so they are presenting three instead of our normal two ideas. Rainwind Corp is one of our major clients, given their homeland status, and if the big dogs in Turkey aren't pleased, no one's allowed to be pleased. I draw my fingers across his face, and the image then moves, his head tilting to follow my finger before returning to the static pose. He pouts—foxmorphs are very needy, I'm learning—but I think about how at home, I don't worry about whether or not a client is going to keep investing in us. I do worry about this executive meeting coming up in Egirdir, Turkey, a concern that makes me frown until I hear my door sigh, signaling someone is coming inside.

I look up as Lindsey enters with a cup of steaming mochaid. He hands it directly to me, then moves behind me and starts rubbing my shoulders. "Tight much?" he comments as I make a pained sound. In a few minutes his gifted hands have me relaxed enough that I can enjoy my drink.

"That's better then, boss," he decides and moves to perch on the edge of my desk. "Nothing yet from the pit, but they did send out for more drinks, so they are still talking."

I nod my head. "That means they either narrowed it down, or they aren't arguing as loud as they were yesterday. Hopefully not at all."

"They aren't arguing because I made sure both Vartan and Maggie had an extra treat in their mochaids this morning," my executive assistant tells me with a grin.

I look at him over the edge of my glasses, and he waves one sparkling nailed hand dismissively. "Just enough to tone them down; got to put my chem degree to some use."

Oh, that's right—before he just gave up, Lindsey had been one of the top students in a highly-rated pharmaceutical program, India maybe, hard to say, since he also came with the promotion. A year in tech school and a few years here, and he's up to First Executive Assistant for the Vice President of Administration. Looking at him you'd think he was a boytoy, but I know he's smart enough to be more than this. I don't bother with another suggestion for him to check out our education program, because that only gets me cool mochaids and warm water for a few days. He's content where he is behind a desk, making drinks, ordering meals, and filtering anyone who wants to get through my double doors. He leaves the actual filing and data work to Connie, who likes to hide out behind her screen.

"Emily, they are going to be a while, and the other teams are active as ants," Lindsey says as he slides off the desk onto his knees. "Shall we see if your feet are bit tight as well?"

This, too, is part of his job, and until I got Wynn I didn't hesitate to use his full services, as he calls them. The world's a competitive place where those not on the top find themselves doing things that my grandmother tells me could get you thrown in prison when she was my age. As long as there is a legal contract and you are a signatory, why should anyone care? If you can't pay your way, you'll find yourself outside the cities, outside the agribusinesses, and life is damned horrid beyond those zones. Of course that makes me think of the R-H2O campaign, and my body tenses again, so I nod my head and turn my chair so he can get to my feet better.

"Excellent," he says as he grins up at me, flashing his brilliant teeth that offset his tan and blond hair to the fullest. "I was starting to worry that you weren't going to use the full facilities and thus be wasting Inandirmak's money," he comments, just loud enough for me to clearly hear as he slips off my shoes.

"That would be foolish, so when you finish down there, go lock the door," I tell him with a deep edge to my voice. My eyes lock onto his when he glances up, and his smile fades into his face, though his eyes light up more. "Yes, boss," he says as he starts to tend to my left arch.

After a few moments I try to relax more, but my mind keeps wandering back to how much better Lindsey is at this than Wynn. That's unfair on so many levels that my eyes glance over at the furry face in the photo frame. My pet didn't know how to do much of, well, anything when I got him—and then there was my wanker stepbrother—and he's smaller; his hands are shaped differently; there's the fur.

"I know I am good at this, Boss," intrudes Lindsey's voice, drawing my attention down to him on the floor. "But you have to do your part, too. Try and relax. Deal?"

I give him a tight smile and lay back my head, closing my eyes, trying to focus on his firm, smooth fingers working the muscles, caressing my skin, moving my toes back and forth, side to side. A gasp releases further tension in my body as one of my toes pops and Lindsey makes a sound of triumph.

Wynn would be asking questions right now instead of just watching my body, feeling it change under his care, listening for heart rate and breathing to give him clues. I open my eyes again and look at his furry face. He doesn't seem to know how to read humans at all. He's constantly messing up pronouns when we watch television. I wonder if there's something I can do to help him with that.

"Ahem." Lindsey's voice again interrupts the flow of my thoughts. "Seriously, Boss, the meeting will go fine. But if you can't relax this foot you are not gonna be ready for my executive skills anywhere else."

I frown. One of the reasons I went to college and got a degree was so I'd never have to spend time down on my knees to rise up through a company. My father and mother both did it the hard way, and I swore I'd never do that to myself or anyone else. Yet there he is, my first executive assistant, on his knees with a very concerned frown, holding one bare foot and looking at me like this is the biggest insult he's suffered in years.

"Lindsey, go lock the door and pull the curtains. I think I just need less potential distractions."

He arches an eyebrow but lays my foot gently back onto the floor and stands up gracefully, smoothing down his trousers before turning to the door. I take the few moments he's looking away to turn off and lower my photoframe back into the desk. When he looks back he sees me turning down the lights on my desk and putting my computer on sleep mode.

Lindsey walks around the office and closes the curtains, bending unnecessarily and moving more than needed, giving me a nice view of his firm, round ass and nicely sized groin, which always seems firm but never demanding. He stops behind my desk and touches my shoulders again. "Let's take your jacket off, too, Boss. Get your skin some air."

This is another subtle difference between my assistant and my morph. Wynn is demanding, but it is always about him, getting me to play with him, to have sex with him. I sigh in frustration, which makes Lindsey look back from where he's hung my coat up just a few feet away. "We getting on with this, or what?" I say, more roughly than I really should. Lindsey is contracted to the company, not to me; I should respect his position, even if it is on his knees or under me.

He just smirks and comes back, unbuttoning his shirt. "We are not yet ready for the advanced relaxation techniques, Boss. I will surely let you know when we are," he says, letting his shirt fall to the floor, where he just leaves it. "Let's face facts; I was assisting you well before you occupied that chair."

That's true. I always figured it was because he saw my star rising and wanted to make sure that if I got the corner office, he'd keep his position. Reynolds was a good VP, but he'd gotten comfortable in this chair, demanding evening work sessions that everyone in the office knew had little to do with reviewing the clients or campaigns. The fact that he took early retirement was an indication of how Corporate in Egirdir disliked his business attitude. The Turks are tricky about such things; they put a great deal at our disposal the higher up you go in the company, but there are also limits to what they consider appropriate. Or so Margaret told me the day before my promotion became official.

I let Lindsey set the parameters, figuring he was the reason that Reynolds left. How else would the big bosses on the other side of the world have learned about the overtime for a salaried employee unless his assistant revealed it? Business is a complex dance of power, authority, profits and debts. I learned to never take anything here for granted.

"I have always enjoyed being of assistance to you, Boss," Lindsey continues as he unbuttons his trousers and lets them shimmer down over his hips and ass, his cock swinging free, half hard already. The rings on his nipples glint in the dim lights, and those in his ears swing as he strikes a pose. "Now that I'm clear about helping you relax, let's get serious so all our transactions flow smoothly today."

A giggle escapes my lips. I realize I've missed this banter after weeks of attention to matters at home. I push my chair back and turn so he has lots of space when he gets back into position down on his knees. I lift my bare foot and put it on his chest, stroking his flesh, tweaking his nipples and getting a soft chuckle from him in return before he catches it and places a solid kiss on the top.

Lindsey trails his tongue lightly along the top and works his way up my ankle and calf with tiny strokes while his hands knead the muscles. His deep mocha eyes are on mine as he works to the edge of my skirt. Then he glances down, placing the bare foot on the floor before turning to the shod one and rendering it equally pliant with his skills.

His tongue and fingers artfully work up my other leg, then he pauses at my skirt again, reaching out with one hand to stroke the first leg, which has lain neglected. "You're feeling more relaxed now, Boss; time to add the right amount of good stress to fully ease your mind. Would you lower your chair a bit, please," he instructs before turning his attention to lifting my skirt and nuzzling my knees.

These chairs were especially designed for Inandirmak, and the first time I tried mine out I just thought this feature was for napping, as the company's public infosheet claims. It was a huge accomplishment when this firm bought my contract from Reman, Shire, and Niobi, where I'd been employed since earning my first master's. Inandirmak always receives high ratings from both internal and external evaluations for workplace environment and public stewardship. They offer unspeakable perks to their officers, of which Lindsey is merely one, but also demand a certain level of professional conduct that stretches outside the office walls.

Oddly, one of those was getting Wynn. I feel the chair go down too fast as I push that furry face from my mind again.

"Whoa there, cowgirl," Lindsey chuckles as he jerks back from the descending chair. "I'd suggest the floor if you really want me down to work, Boss, but I didn't vacuum this morning."

I frown, wondering if he forgot on purpose or because he's also worried about R-H2O. Three types of people are happy in the position of first executive assistant. The first likes to be in charge without the stress of answering to the higher officials and finds a way to manipulate their bosses, generally through scheduling as well as the sexual benefits. I suspect that Connie does most of my scheduling. The second type of assistant wants to be totally submissive, barely exercising any authority and constantly needing direction with rewards and punishments meted out. I just can't see that working in any of our branch offices, though perhaps at the main headquarters. So that makes my Lindsey, who is now looking at me after telling me he's failed in one of his assigned tasks, the third type of executive assistant. These love to be of service but realize that those of us who must exercise authority over big decisions sometimes want to lead and sometimes need to be led.

When my stress is overwhelming, Lindsey knows what I need to bring me relief, as any decent service assistant would.

"You didn't vacuum?" I narrow my eyes and pull one leg free from his hands as I sit up. "Well, now, Lindsey, that is just unacceptable." I push him back onto the floor with one shove from a bare foot. He looks down at the toes then slowly up my leg until his eyes meet mine. "However, focus on the task at hand, and perhaps I'll take that into consideration later. You have earned demerits, and I will pay them out." I finish the promise by beckoning him back to me as I lie back down, carefully lifting my skirt up to bunch around my hips.

He's grinning as he kneels up and parts my thighs with his hands. "Of course, Boss. I've really needed you to keep me on task lately." With that he bows his head and begins nibbling at my outer lips.

An hour later Lindsey walks a bit more slowly out of my office, and I watch with a grin tugging at one side of my mouth. While I tend to go a bit carefully with my pet back home, here Lindsey's spanking was the real deal, his demerits paid off in the form of a sore, turning-purple ass that has him leaning down over his desk, not sitting. Connie's eyes are wide when she catches me looking at her, and her blush is almost sweet until all our eyes spot the conference room doors swinging open.

I touch my hand to my hair, double checking to make sure it is in place as Glen escorts our clients through the door followed by Amber at his heels. Our liaison ignores me and the rest of the office to lead the trio from Rainwind to the elevators while Amber turns back to the conference room for a moment before heading toward me, folder in hand.

"Glen is taking them to the airport, and I'm planning a debrief with the rest of the team," she tells me as she hands me the contracts.

"I'll look it over, and we'll meet back in the conference room as soon as he returns." I glance at Lindsey, who has moved close, his pad in hand to confirm that the room will be open the rest of the day. "Guru and Click-back work it out?"

"Yeah, they were surprisingly calm this morning after a rough start," Amber says with a tight smile. She looks exhausted but keeps her eyes on me, her back straight, and her hands behind her back, probably clenching and unclenching her fists. That's what I would have done in her place.

"Lindsey, get them all something cool to drink," I order, and he just smiles, nods his head and goes to the water cooler. I turn back to Amber and say, "Take a quarter break, tell everyone to get outside while we have a break in the sun, and then come back to debrief. Trust me," I cut off her concerns just as her mouth opens slightly, "I've been there."

"Yes, Boss," she says with a more relaxed smile. Reassurance and acknowledgement that my team had just won a big client was rare when I was in her position. Offering more feedback and more support: that's another change I was determined to make when I got the better office. Besides, it will give Lindsey some time to figure out what to add to their drinks to help them relax but keep them sharp for analysis.

"Connie!" She stands when I address her. "Let Nanna and Kaya know I want reports on their projects by tomorrow at noon." With that I turn back to my office, leaving the door open but determined to look over the contracts and see which campaign R-H2O chose.

After Glen has a few minutes to settle back into the office I walk swiftly pass the team pits, groups of desks where the leaders for each marketing team sits, even though their specialized units are on different floors or wings of our building. My movement causes everyone to look up, but only Team 1 knows where I'm heading and why. Soon they have all filed into the conference room, taking seats facing me at the head. Lindsey is still standing behind me, pad in hand to record, while Connie checks it as it goes into her computer for storage and quarterly reports.

I slap two separate contracts down on the table as I settle my gaze on each team member in turn. Glen and Amber exchange looks; as client liaison and team leader, they have the most to lose if I've found something wrong. Roger just looks at me blankly, unconcerned since his real work won't begin until I've given my approval. The three whose differing visions are clear in these contracts and campaign proposals, Vartan, Thomas, and Maggie, all lick their lips nervously, though I see that Vartan still feels his idea is superior from the way he refuses to look at the table or the floor, keeping his eyes steady on mine.

It is Elsbeth Fluri, though, who speaks up. "Ms. Potter, I know it is very rare for clients nowadays to want to invest in more than one ad campaign at a time, given the current economic and habitation situation. However I believe strongly that this particular product requires a different approach, given the two very distinct demographics Rainwind wants to target."

Amber moves in her seat, so I make a small hand gesture toward her, and she sits back, her mouth closing with an audible gasp that makes everyone flinch just a bit. I recall Margaret's words during our lunch meeting after I received word of my promotion almost two years ago: "Approachable, helpful, respectful, all of that is wonderful, but if you are assigned to your home office as VP, never forget that a little fear is a wonderful thing."

With that in mind, I say, "I reviewed the contracts, the proposals, and of course the meeting tapes." I don't know why that still makes people cringe. We all grew up being watched almost 24/7 in all public places, by cities protecting their water and companies protecting their employees. "I could see that you two," I go on, aiming a look at both Maggie and Vartan, "were still in competition right in front of the client. That is not acceptable." Both sink back into their chairs at my words.

"Thomas, you and Glen did a good job of reassuring the clients. Amber, your attention to the meeting's needs was good, but next time do not allow anyone to leave the room as I saw. Once they leave those doors," I explain, motioning to the conference room's main doors, "there is always a chance they won't come back. That's why we have an in-suite restroom, folks."

I look at Roger, who is hardly looking at me until my gaze pulls his eyes to me. "I know you feel like your part is rather vague until a campaign is contracted, but I want more next time. I think we could have cut this meeting by a good half hour if the clients could have had reassurances of both campaigns' feasibility right from the start." He agrees with both a nod and a verbal reply.

"Elsbeth, let's get back to your strong feelings on these two approaches," I say, turning my full attention to our strategist, whose research into the target audiences and the markets should be the foundation for any proposed campaign. The entire table looks to her as she sits up straighter and nods her head, her lips tight.

I smile as I speak, my entire body lit up with pride. "Well worth your defense, and you've won us the first multi-campaign contract in four years."

The team members begin laughing or sighing, both chastising me and thanking me at the same time. Of course, that last multi-campaign was from my old team for Bio-Mandrema, who still uses our continental and gendered approach that many business leaders declared unnecessary two decades ago.

"Now don't get too cocky," I remind them all, "but take this evening out at Inandirmak's facilities, and come in late tomorrow morning. Amber, Glen, Elsbeth, I want reports on the T-R Farms and BFC campaigns by next week."

"Yes, Boss," they say as they all start gathering up their things to head out to a much desired mini-vacation. My history classes told me that at one time families and individuals made vacation choices and had time off from work, but the impotence of governments and the short-sightedness of people required that cor-porations step up to protect their workers. Instead of the much-feared mega-corporations, though, smaller firms were able to provide more consistency for their employees and their customers, resulting in the regional web system that links various suppliers with consumers and support staff. Inandirmak has offices in North America, of which we are one, and in most other Earth regions, as well as on the lunar base and the Mars station, and our Asian branch has made headway into the Titan Project in regards to product placement. Corporate still claims that we are a small firm, though, part private and part employee co-op.

I have my time off, so I turn to Lindsey and tell him to get Connie. We have reports from the other two teams to begin looking at before we can head home today.

After what I feel is enough time, and a quick glance at the clock on my desk confirms this, I dismiss both of my assistants with the customary inquiry into whether or not they want a lift home. Connie is on my way, and I can drop Lindsey off at a club he often likes to relax at after work. I find having good relations with my assistants goes beyond using their services in the office.

As always, Connie accepts and collects her things from her desk quickly to meet me at the elevator. Lindsey turns to me while she's gone and grins. "I can catch a bus from your place."

I look at him and blink slowly, unsure whether I'm hearing him correctly. "You know your services really end at the building's door," I say stupidly.

"Actually they don't, as buying plane tickets and getting meals attest to from time to time," he replies, crossing his arms over his chest. "But my ass is still sore, so I'm not looking for that."

I shush him and glance at Connie, who is locking her desk.

"I want to check out your pet, you know," he intimates, making his voice into a low whisper as he leans toward me, "the kind they make you get when you get a big promotion."

I sigh and do some quick calculations of the risks of taking him home versus not. "Just a quick visit. Wynn gets nervous around other people."

"Wind? You named it Wind?"

"Wynn, no D sound," I correct him and then smile at Connie as she looks at us patiently.

"Oh, sure thing, and yeah, a quick visit," Lindsey says with an even bigger grin. It takes him seconds to grab his stuff and lock his desk.

Having three of us in the car along with the company card allows us to drive in the private lane and get to the residential area quickly. The buses and the trains move through, and the delivery vehicles are chugging along the slowest, but everyone needs to be off the roads before the sun falls and the highway's electric supply decreases, and with it the right to travel on the streets.

Connie thanks me softly and scurries from my car into her building, a subsidized complex run by several companies, including Inandirmak. She lives there with her wife, their child, her mother, and I think her wife's younger sister, or is it disabled sister? I try to be aware of all their families, but she's so quiet that I rarely get more than a few words from her. Lindsey gets out and takes the front passenger seat with a smile.

With only two of us I have to switch to another lane, but we don't have far to go. My house is right outside the corporate city proper, another perk from the promotion that came in the day after I heard the news. I had a year to get Wynn, and I pushed it to almost that limit.

"You sure?" I ask as I nod ahead to the usual club. Lindsey just shakes his head and waves goodbye to the neon-lit building as we go past it.

I can feel my hands start to sweat on the control panel.

Chapter Twelve
Daily Solitude

i can see the backyard from my spot on the window seat. So nice to see the big world instead of the white and silver walls of the Institute all around me, all the time. Emalee's walls are nicer with color and photos and things She calls gadgets. i like looking outside, but we haven't been out there in what She calls the backyard yet. She says that we will when the weather clears up a bit. i don't really understand this weather thing, but the people on the TV sure spend a lot of time talking about it. It looks like outdoors to me, wet or not, gray or black sky or sometimes that off-blue. Sure, it smells different when She opens the windows or the door or when we go shopping, but that isn't being out in the backyard. i glance toward the back door then sigh, remembering Her orders not to leave the house without Her. i miss her so much every day.

i get up and move so i can look at the big family vid display by the entry to the kitchen and watch as the images of Emalee, Her parents, some friends, and some people She called exes go by, playing clips of them talking or laughing. i push the button She showed me when it gets to the one i love best. She's in this flowing black thing and has a flat hat on her head with a big drab color thing hanging off one side. She's smiling and holding up a big frame with something in it that has a big red symbol on the bottom. "I do think that we can make the world a better place through advertising, Dad," She says, then this male voice questions that, and she just shakes Her head. "How do you think people ever know about these things if not for advertising? Education? Their temple? Their families? That's so old-fashioned, Dad."

She seems so relaxed there, not at all like She is here at home. Sighing, i think hard about why that might be. Things got harder after that squirrel girl and her owner came to visit Her. i'm not smart enough to know why. i had fun, though, but i don't tell Her that, because She gets this angry frown when that lady calls now. Something called an execute meeting or something that is big and important.

i look up when the door bell rings.

i'm not allowed to open the door—can't 'cause humans are smart about that—but i go to it anyway to look. There is a man, i think—i don't see the shape of breasts, and his clothing is dull, so it might be a him—leaving a box in the holding pen Emalee has for such things. i'm so excited 'cause i remember what to do. Once the box is inside, i push this little button that blinks a light at the person, who waves some flat thing at it, then smiles and says, "Have a good day, Ms. Potter," before leaving. The voice confirms he was a he, and i smile, very pleased with myself for guessing correctly. Human gender was much easier to figure out back at the Institution, like everything else was easier, but more boring.

i called her Ms. Potter once, but just like Emalee, that didn't make Her happy, so i'm sticking with Master for right now. Not stupid, i know She is so much more than me, i call Her like She wants, but still, here, inside me, in my head, thinking of her as Emalee is more good feeling. i shake my head and try to focus on the next task to do when a delivery is made while She is out.

i push a series of buttons and wait, holding my breath for the green light to flash inside. It takes a while, 'cause Emalee says it has to be scanned for dangerous things. When the small door opens and the box comes rolling toward me i hunch down to grab it. This one is heavy, but not too much, so i push it over to one side next to Her house shoes. It has writing on the top and a picture of a human face with long head fur and her arms spread wide and her breasts bared, indicating female, a her. After sniffing at it for a good long time, i give up trying to figure it out; it smells like humans and machines, just like everything usually does.

i go back to the window seat and look outside again. Does it smell only like humans and machines?

i'm frowning at the TV as I watch the one channel i can access. The show claims to be about how we morphs think and feel, but it is very wrong about this thing i've decided i'm having right now, every day when Emalee is away. They called it "boredom." Humans get bored when they have nothing to do, and the show claims that most of the time a morph is happy to sleep and look outside. That's nice, but i am bored, i realize, as i keep watching until the man doing most of the talking—his voice and brightly-colored shirt declare his gender—turns and speaks with a group of morphs settled around his chair. He isn't wearing a white coat, but he sure talks like them, so that's how i label him because he hasn't given a name.

The TV must know we can watch this channel, because it keeps talking to other morphs on these shows. Always starts with the humans, and then these morphs appear, and the handler or a white coat—it changes—talks to them. i feel like this one is talking to me when he says, "You miss your master when he's away, yes?" and the morphs all nod their heads.

"Unlike you lucky things, we humans have to work to make that money that we use to buy your food, keep you in a nice house, buy you toys, all those things you like," the white coat on the show says. "Work isn't something we'd choose to do if we could just be like you and enjoy life every second. No, no, it is stressful. Do you know what your master looks like when she feels stressful?"

The morphs on TV nod their heads, and i nod mine, thinking back to all the times that Emalee has come home from Her work with a tired expression, Her voice less happy, and sometimes with a bag or box of human food that She calls take-away. "If you want your master to play more with you, then you have to help him de-stress. Want to learn how?" the white coat asks, and now i'm standing up and nodding my head rapidly along with the other morphs on the TV.

"I knew you were all good pets. Today we're going to talk about attitude and service, something you may not have learned much about back in your clinics." Clinics? i don't have time to think much further, because the white coat on TV starts talking about having the right pet attitude, and i want Emalee to pay attention to me lots more, so i move really close and listen hard.

my Master is super smart, but i knew that already; i didn't need this man on television to tell me that. This is a series, so i followed the instructions they gave on how to set the show to turn on every day or record it so i don't miss it. That's what the white coat said to do, anyway; he said owners would be angry if we didn't learn what he had to teach. Today he talked about speaking and making noise. How some owners want more noise than others, and how the way we are trained in the clinics may not be what is required when we get bought. i not from clinic, i from Institute, so maybe TV white coat not as smart as he thinks. Not want to risk it, not now, after my disobedience early on. The memories scratch at my mind, but i just push them aside.

Emalee tell me all this and teach more, but maybe this white coat on TV have some ideas. What else i do for the long times she is gone. Backyard only so interesting for so long, even with strange animals moving around. Must be sad to be so stupid, not knowing this is Emalee's house and stealing Her plants, digging in Her dirt. i growl and pounce on the window, sending the stupid animals scurrying away.

Poor stupid animals. i nestle down and look out at the backyard again. So many rules, too many for them to learn, about who is in charge, what you can do, what you shouldn't do, what you can't. Humans own everything, then morphs 'cause we are best of all pets, then the stupid animals, some that are food for the rest of us.

When the clock's lines are a certain way, i know i can go to the kitchen and use the dispenser to get my own food. i wonder which animal it is made from as i eat. Today i feel a bit naughty, so i sit back on my rump like Master does so i can look around better as i eat. One of the songs i learned from the other morphs tells about a place like this and an uppity catmorph who climbed into her owner's chair to eat when she thought he was not around. The old breeders would argue about the meaning of the story after they sang how she was found, beaten and turned out into the streets to die in the big human world.

i may sit up now, but i know better than to do more than lay my head on the soft chairs around the table. Not as nice as Emalee's lap, though this seat has Her scent on it. my cock stirs, and i reach down to stroke it a few times before nipping my tongue to help control the urge. i hope Emalee not have this stress thing tonight, 'cause i need Her to play with me. i glance up at this thing She put up last week She called a whiteboard with dates and marks She put on it. When i don't obey, when i fail to control my urges, i get these demerit things that can only be erased by punishment—the thought makes my stomach clench 'cause it is not fun at all—or from extra good behavior. At the Institute punishment was swift, and i never forgot what i did wrong. i frown as i look up and try to remember what i did wrong yesterday morning.

i force myself to finish eating and drinking then head back to the window seat to scare off some more stupid animals. Someday i go out there and scare them off for good. That would be extra good, maybe worth a couple demerits getting removed for me.

The afternoon goes so slow when Emalee is away. The television is boring; the stupid animals are boring; i nap, but i don't really need to, and it only makes me want to do the things i'm not supposed to do on my own. i look at her computer but know better than to touch it. i try to switch to some other channels on the TV, but i get a mild shock from the remote and give up after a while.

Then i hear the garage open, and i jump up from the window, the spot i keep returning to again and again. i run to my room and check myself in the mirror. Takes Emalee a good time to get in and do Her car stuff before She comes inside. i try to smooth down my fur but decide i look great; i always look great.

Emalee only uses the garage door when we go shopping, something i wish i liked since She seems to like to do it so much— the real shopping stuff, looking at things, and then buying things— but She does talk to me a lot, which makes it less boring. Others notice when She talks to me; others glare at me; others say things i don't think Master (remember to call Her that) hears, because they aren't nice things. i pat the box that was delivered earlier. This is the best shopping, i decide as i kneel down to watch the door.

Her scent floats through the door as it opens, and i lean forward eagerly until another scent mixes with Hers. She walks in, and Her face lights up when she sees me, "Good, boy, Wynn, waiting for me," She says, and i hear it, though my eyes turn to the human behind Her. This one has on more colors than She wears to work and is carrying a colorful bag, not the plain brown leather one She takes to work. It takes off its glasses—Master says these protect their eyes from the sun—and looks down at me after stepping in and closing the door. Its eyes are like the drink Master likes, mochaid, but mine are much prettier.

"Is this it, Boss?" the new human asks in a voice that is slightly deeper than Master's, suggesting the newcomer is male. But he isn't dressed like human males i've known before. His brighter clothes, colored fingernails, and general appearance make him appear more like some animals i see on TV who show off their gender by how they act and dress, the male being more colorful, loud, and active in some ways. Humans are so difficult to figure out because Master is active, colorful, and pretty, even for a human.

She touches my head, so i turn my attention to Her, one ear attuned to the newcomer, my nose trying to sort through the scents coming from it. "Wynn, this is my first executive assistant, Lindsey, he's just here for a little bit. He heard about you, so I said he could come meet you. Say hello to him."

"Hello," i repeat automatically, but i don't say it with any enthusiasm, since i don't see another morph behind him, now that i know for certain he is a male human. If he didn't come to see me play with his morph, why is he here? i think back to my first night here, then shove that thought away as quickly as i can.

"Whoa!" he says as he takes a step back and then chuckles before crouching down to be more on my level. "It can talk! I'd seen that in movies and on the TV, you know, but I figured it was special effects." He's talking, but not really to me, i decide quickly, so i just keep one ear on him and look up to Master.

"They can talk, though I think he was trained at the Institute not to talk very much. I've been encouraging him to talk more."

"Him? Oh." i can feel his eyes moving down my body, coming to rest on my primary pleasure zone. i turn my face to him and narrow my eyes, but his attention is elsewhere. "Oh, wow, it's black and kind of small."

i huff at him, and he looks up at me. "Didn't mean to insult you, Wynn." He says my name, and i scurry back to hide behind Master's legs.

"He's a bit shy with strangers, particularly men," Master explains as i hug her leg and look around it at this first something of Hers.

The man stands up and sighs. "Yeah, the deal with your brother...."

"Half-brother."

"Half-brother," he amends and then steps closer to Master. "You should have let me call those guys I know to teach him a lesson."

"You know a lot of guys who can do stuff, Lindsey," Master says with a chuckle, but i can hear there's a dark edge to it.

"There are many benefits to having me for your assistant, Boss," he says and reaches out and touches Master's hand.

Her scent. Her scent is one of those i'm picking up from this person, and not just Her scent but the scent She makes when we play. i bound around Her legs and get between them, growling and yipping up at him.

He steps back and puts his hands up, palms flat, "Hey, there, little fella, calm down."

"Wynn!" i was going to turn around at Her voice, but Master grabs my collar and jerks me back, sending me to the floor at Her feet. "You do not growl at my guests, do you understand me?"

i pout, but then he reaches out again for Her hand or arm, and the growl rises up and out of my mouth unbidden. i yip in pain as Master grabs my head fur harshly, more harshly than She's been with me ever.

"He doesn't like me touching you," the newcomer states, and i nod as best i can, my eyes trying to confirm his words since i'm afraid to speak right now.

Master is frowning at me now; Her eyes are narrowed as She shakes me a bit. "Go to your room," She orders and releases me with a little push in that direction.

With a sigh, i sink down to my paws and slowly move away until

She orders me to hurry up and to not crawl. She doesn't seem to know that those are difficult orders to obey together, but i stand up, knowing that is one of the new things she is insisting i learn now.

Sometimes i am a bad pet, but my reason is good—at least, that is what i tell myself when i stop in the hallway to listen, hoping i can't be seen by either of them. Her first is speaking again.

"Do you think he knows what we did this morning? Is that why he's acting so... possessive?"

"That's ridiculous," Master replies, but Her tone says She is thinking about it. "How could he possibly know?"

"He is an animal," the man starts, but She interrupts.

"He is not an animal; he's a morph, an erotic pet," She corrects, but i can hear a wobble in Her voice.

"Yes, fine, sure, but still, he has those huge ears, which I bet hear better, and that muzzle nose like an animal; I'll bet you he can smell a lot better than us, too. It's not like we showered afterwards."

"Hell," Master says softly, but there's stress in Her voice. A few silent moments follow before She speaks again. "That shouldn't matter. He's my pet, not my boyfriend."

The other human laughs. "Yeah, and he's a he. He's male; I think jealousy sort of goes with the hormones, Boss. Some of us just learn to control it and channel it."

Now Master's voice sounds lighter when She laughs in return. "You can't get jealous, Lindsey; I doubt you have a jealous cell in your body."

"You'd be surprised. That's one of the reasons I took this job and I don't date for the long run. No commitment to one person unless you move up and take me along for the ride; I wouldn't mind that."

There's something in his voice that makes me growl, but i grab my muzzle with both hands to keep it from escaping.

"Did you hear something?" Master says, so i turn and scurry down the hall to my room, closing the door softly behind me. i try to slow my breathing by lying down on my pet bed and closing my eyes. i keep hearing that man's voice saying "jealousy" over and over again. i don't know what that is, but it is clear that the thought of my having it really displeased Master.

How can a mere morph find out about that jealousy thing without making Master more angry? Who can i ask? i go back through all the vids and white coat training sessions, but i don't recall this jealousy thing being mentioned.

i try to go over everything i heard and match it to the training and the things i see on the television. It isn't really that hard, though for some reason i think it should be hard for me to do. Then i sit up when i realize the answer. i am Her pet; She is not mine. When i acted because of Her happy scent on him, i was acting like She was my pet. That made Her angry, and with good reason—i can recall the white coats, the vids and the TV telling me the same thing in different ways.

i roll over to look at my mirror and i look very hard at my face. i trace the tag on my ear, the collar around my neck. Sitting up, i look at the nubs of my nipples and remember that Master mentioned tags—no, rings, She called them—being placed in there in the future. She can do any of that, all of that, to me because i'm Her pet. i must make her happy so She keeps me.

i don't know how much time passes before Master opens the door and looks down at me, Her hands on Her hips, Her head tilted to one side, Her voice edged with the same tones She had after long, hard days at work. This is one of those times the human on the television said that a good pet has to think about their owner first, so i sit, then hurry to Her, rising on my knees to hug Her.

"Wynn is sorry, Master, very sorry. Tell Wynn how to make it better. Wynn want to be good pet please."

Her sigh goes through Her entire body, and i feel Her hands on my head and then my shoulders, pushing me back a bit. i follow; i don't struggle, but i keep my eyes on Her, afraid that if i look away it will make Her more angry. "Come out of the closet, Wynn; let's go talk where there's more room," She orders, so i follow Her out, standing up on my hind legs when She shakes Her head at my crawling.

She stops back at the entryway, but there's no first Lindsey there anymore. His scent is starting to fade, and i'm glad, but i hold that feeling inside and look up at Her. "I can tell from looking around the house, from this package being brought inside, from your dishes, that you've been a good pet all day. Why did you growl at Lindsey? That was an unusual thing for you to do."

"Wynn sorry, Wynn not do again, promise, Master." As i say it i want to kneel down, but She reaches out and grabs one of my arms so i stay standing.

"I don't want promises. I want to know why you did it at all. Do you even know?" She shakes me a bit to add weight to Her already harsher tone.

So much to lose right now. Truth or lie? The human on the TV said that lying was always bad, but omitting some information for a certain time to lessen your owner's stress might be fine. She looks angry—i can tell that emotion from years of seeing it on lots of human faces—but is She angry 'cause She doesn't know why i did it?

Any words are a risk, so i just say my thoughts as they come, knowing i can't stop Her from punishing me either way. "Lindsey smelled like You do after Master plays with Wynn. Wynn job to play with Master not other human. Master come home and play with Wynn and get happy and get scent on pet, not him."

Her grip on my arm tightens, making me whimper, then loosens until She's released me and is using that hand to rub Her forehead. That's a sure sign of stress, the TV human said, but i have to be careful and watch and listen before i can make any attempt to ease her head. "Actually, it is also Lindsey's job to take care of me, sometimes in the same way you do," She says in a softer voice.

i just stare at Her. Lindsey is Her pet, too? Humans have other humans as pets?

"It doesn't mean anything; it's just the benefits of the job. Expectations of the job, much like you, this house," She continues, looking up and waving one hand around as she talks, "certain vehicles and clothes. If I don't use them, I lose them. Oh, you don't understand, do you?"

i shake my head, then nod it, unsure how to answer because i do and i don't understand what She is telling me. i'm not a stupid animal; i know that humans need humans for things we morphs just can't do. But playing with Her is something i can do, i should do. "Wynn come to work then with Master, play with Her when She needs it," i say, offering a good solution, but She just chuckles and pats my head.

"That would definitely be against company policy. Look, I realize that you must feel trapped in here all the time while I'm away. I'll look into some sort of day care program or something, all right?"

i don't know why She asks me questions like this, so i just nod. Sometimes i think humans' questions aren't real questions, but i don't want to make Her angry by not answering, and i don't want to make Her angry by disagreeing, so i just nod all the time.

"Good, we're in agreement then. Let's see what's in the box," She states as She picks it up and carries it into the front room.

i like this, sitting by Her as she does something at home, Her hands petting me, Her voice telling me things i sometimes do and sometimes don't really understand. The fact that i can't have the goodies Her mother sent over from England doesn't even bother me as long as i can be near her.

i think She has forgiven me until She sends me off to bed that evening without play time. i know that is a punishment, so i just cry myself to sleep quietly and remember the feeling of being surrounded by Her scent and Her body.

Master got upset once when we were watching a show and a morph was beaten by her owner for misbehaving. She said that it wasn't right to do that to a pet. Later after She is asleep i get up and go into Her bedroom and watch Her sleep for a while. i wish She'd just hit me and get it over with, but i don't know how to tell Her that.

Luckily things return to long, boring days and then nights of play time soon, and i almost forget what happens, so i start working on reminding myself daily by looking into a mirror and repeating "you are Her pet, She is not your pet" over and over again.

Chapter Thirteen
Annual Upheavals

"To a well-earned bonus from Euro-Glas," I say as I lift my wine glass high into the air.

Team three all lift their glasses and agree, then Ekon—Details for this team—adds, "To Kaya and Xin for keeping us all cool when the numbers took a dive in the third quarter!"

"Hear, hear!" I agree before taking another sip of my drink. Looking around the club where the company always celebrated, I see the usual—the lithe dancers working the stage, the drinks flowing from relatively conservatively dressed servers of all sexes and genders, the company tables with groups of three to ten people pretending for a moment that this is a real break from work. Such celebrations, on the company credit, are one way to ensure loyalty, just as certainly as are the subsidized housing, medical care and childcare provided by any decent company I've ever known that wanted to last more than a decade or two. I imagine this is more than just a profit issue; profit as the main business concern died along with a whole lot of species that disappeared in the past century and a half. With declining populations but increased difficulties supplying basic and luxury needs, yet with a never-ending demand for both, companies will do anything to ensure you'll come back to work the next day.

Hasad and Lila get up to dance to the cheers of their teammates, but I can only smile and shake my head when both Gayla and Ekon ask me in turn. They aren't quite sure of where I fall on the continuum of sexuality, a state of uncertainly Margaret told me years ago was wise to maintain. My predecessor's forced retirement for various reasons only confirmed that her unsolicited advice was true. I blink and turn to look when someone touches my arm. It's Lindsey.

"I said, MTB to Boss, come in Boss." He's chuckling, but I can see the concern in his eyes. His coming to this celebration is stretching the company rules just a touch. The reasonable excuse is that's he's here to make sure I get home safely and to take any business calls that might interrupt me, though the only people who'd call would be the Turks at this time of night, since it is day to them and they thrive on keeping us off balance, it seems. Of course, if I ever earn another promotion, then he could come along to any event I wanted, becoming what we half-jokingly refer to as a company spouse though that is really an official title, one I doubt either of us has thought about yet.

Lindsey leans in, pouring me another drink from the bottles we had our servers leave, another excuse for him to be here. "So where is your head?"

"At home," I say simply as I pick up my glass. Wynn did not take it well when I called to say I was going to be late getting home. He'd been doing so well, too, thinking more about me and less about himself: pointing out programs he thought might please me on channels he can't access alone when I'm planning my recording schedule. Pleasing me, it turned out, was really code for things he wanted to learn more about, like dancing, yard care, and most oddly, household care. He can actually do a fair amount, so much that my once a week housekeeper commented that there was so little work for her to do that she was worried about me. Translation: I can clean someone else's house for extra cash if you don't need me so often. Result: I put her on a ten-day rotation instead of seven, and she didn't seem worried anymore.

"Wynn not take the night out well, then, huh?" Lindsey guesses. When I nod, he taps my hand, then motions to a table not far away with another company celebration—or maybe it's private, hard to say—where two morphs are with the group. "Maybe you should have brought him?"

I can feel my eyes widen at that thought and shake my head. "I doubt everyone would be happy with a 70-pound growling jealous ball of fur."

Lindsey waves one hand dismissively. "He hasn't growled at me now in weeks." That's true. Ever since that first encounter, I've had Lindsey back to the house four or five times to help with some last-minute work and honestly to test out Wynn's ability to accept another man in my life. Plus any extra excuse for work is one less entryway into my mind about the approaching meeting in Egirdir.

As much as Lindsey may say it, and as much as I said it to Wynn, I do think of Lindsey as "my man" in some ways. I like the comfort of knowing that if I call he'll get a bus over, run to the stores on his lunch break, or whatever I need at a moment's notice. After all, if he can play the "perks of the job" card to get me to use all the services he enjoys, I'm going to use all the services I'm allowed to show him I'm still the Boss.

"You want me to make an excuse, Boss?" Lindsey says with a glance toward the team, three more of whom are watching their teammates dance. When I nod, he winks and then stands up, his headset covered by one hand as though he's received a call.

"Boss?" I turn to find that Ann, this team's media guru, has moved closer to me. "I know that I should put this through proper channels, but before I take that time, do you think I could get some time off to go visit my family on the coast?"

"Connie will have records of your vacation time, and I can't recall right now that the team has any new clients or campaigns that need immediate attention," I say as I search my mind for personal information about her family. Ah, yes, she probably means her brothers who moved south to work in the aquaculture business. It may pay well and have benefits to rival the best city company, but I can't imagine wanting to live on the constant threat of the coastlines myself. Still, we need water and food, and those working in the outlands have more theoretical freedom than we in the metros, so I can understand why someone unskilled in other work would be drawn. Then I pause and frown. "Isn't it storm season still?"

"Isn't it always? Seems to be getting worse, not better," Ann says with a tight smile. "My brothers tell me that there is a break now for a few weeks. I only want to go maybe for a week or so. I haven't seen my nieces and nephews in about three years."

"Like I said, Ann, if you have the time, I don't see why not. File the forms with Connie tomorrow, and let your department know so they have someone to back up your team if something should happen."

Ann swallows, and her face pales a bit. "Losing a job is a risk, might be twenty others out there with her talents. She grew up in Metro Thunder Bay, and most of her family was here before that move. Inandirmak is the only ad agency in the Superior North region, a coup that the company worked hard for before I was born. "Thanks, Boss," she says but looks up, which gets me to as well.

"Boss," says Lindsey's voice even before I can see him clearly. "Had to move your conference call up earlier tomorrow. Sorry."

I sigh and then turn back to my team, most of whom noticed Lindsey returning and have thus returned to the table as well. "That makes it a night for me, people. You stay on and celebrate. You earned it," I add as I stand, and Lindsey helps me back into the blazer I ditched once we were at our table.

Lindsey refuses a ride but heads toward the bus stop once I retrieve my call. He's a good assistant, giving up his time in the club just to keep up my excuse the next day. For once I can go home and relax with Wynn, which I can't do every night.

I'm curled up on the sofa looking over some reports from my three team watchers, the folks from my old department, when something brushes against my bare foot. "Not now, Wynn, I have to finish reading these tonight."

After a few months you'd think I'd have learned that he doesn't take "no" very well. Oh, he's learned to say some nicely submissive things, but someone should have told me that morphs aren't as submissive as the publicity suggests. There are days I wonder if that tiger might have been less demanding in exchange for a mirror, or the bear too busy sleeping his days and nights away to be too demanding. Of course, that's not what I really feel, and I know that when I can feel his cold nose and his fur slipping along the arch of my foot.

I'm expecting his furry little face to pop up under my files any moment. He did that once when I was looking through some information about a new hire for the admin department. His sudden pointed muzzle and big blue eyes looking at me gave me the scare of my life. Sent the datapad flying out of my hands, across the room and into a wall. Thank goodness those things are built to withstand a good deal of abuse. I still sent him to his room and locked him in for a good day as punishment.

Now I'm expecting another such action, but instead I see a blur of white off to my left side. When I turn my head my glass is gone, as is Wynn. I hit "save" on the screen and am about to get him when he comes tottering back into the room holding my glass in both hands, looking very focused on it and the floor, where his feet are still uncertain. He glances up when he notices me and then comes over to the sidetable and kneels down to place the glass back where it was. It is full of cirtaid and a few shavings of ice, just like I like it in this hotter time of year.

"Master tell Wynn if She need anything, yes?" he says, pleading more than making a statement, so I nod and reach out to scratch behind one of his ears. He purrs, then shakes himself and ducks down slightly. "Wynn wait by window for Master need him," he says, then scurries to said window, climbing up to lie down, his face turned partly toward the glass and partly toward me.

Well, I'll be damned. He is learning something from those TV shows after all. I'll have to send Dr. Brownstone's TV show that he has recorded a thank-you note. Just a few weeks ago my pet's eyes would be burrowing into me from his position at my feet or, worse yet, half lying across my knees, trying to distract me from my work.

Without the distractions I'm able to get through all three finalists and leave Connie a note to send my recommendations to our President of Administration, whose office is in Brescia, the control city of Lake Garda, just as MTB controls Lake Superior. Of course, the area included in either extends quite far out, but I don't have to worry about such details unless I get a promotion that moves me there.

One thing at a time, though, as I close off the datapad so I can go to the window. I sigh very softly as I see that he's fallen asleep again. I crouch down and pet his head until his eyes open sleepily to look at me. "Master need Wynn?"

"Yes, I need you to come to bed with me."

"Play?" he asks but yawns part of the way through the word, causing me to chuckle.

"We'll play in the morning, perhaps," I assure us both. Who said that having an erotic pet would be as much sex as any one could handle? The pet and my will isn't the problem. My work schedule has been the real challenge recently.

Without protest Wynn crawls after me, and I'm too tired to urge him to walk. He helps me take off my clothes and slip into a basic sleep shirt. Then he hops up into the bed and snuggles with his back to me so I can drape my arm over him. I sleep better with his soft, warm mass next to me.

In the morning I feel myself smile awake as something touches my body in all the right places. Soft fluffy touches caress my inner thighs, and I part them, only half awake. When a warm yet coarse touch slips up my outer lips, my eyes open fully. A glance to my left reveals no Wynn, but the touches on my body and the lump under the bed just below my waist reveal where he is.

I blink a few times, wondering what he is doing, but all thought leaves when that wet, warm coarseness parts me to find my inner lips. He works his tongue up and down, tickling my clit, and I spread my legs wider. I briefly wonder exactly what those TV shows are demonstrating to him as he gives me the best oral I've had since Lindsey at the beginning of the quarter, before everything went crazy, taking up days and nights both.

I hear Wynn yip softly as I thrust upward and he has to adjust his position to continue. I feel all my muscles tightening, and my hands jerk out from underneath the bedclothes to grab the pillows.

Everything in my body, every sensation, every nerve, every thought whirls down to my clit, where he's licking in slow strokes. It is slightly maddening, given the rushed attentions I've allowed myself these past few weeks, both here and at the office. Then I sit up and gasp when the powerful first unclenching of my orgasm bursts from me. Wynn doesn't stop but continues in a quicker, harder fashion as I basically melt back down onto the bed and toss my head to and fro, saying something that probably sounds ridiculous.

After either a very brief time or an eternity of floating away from the decreasing waves of pleasure, I feel a softness move up my body. I blink, clearing my vision to find his furry face looking at me as he props himself up on one side. "Master wake up now?"

"That was a new way to wake me up, pet! Where'd you learn to do that?"

"Master like? Wynn do good?" His eyes are staring at me in all seriousness.

I turn to my side, running one hand up the length of his body, fluffing his fur and hair up against the natural flow and watching him shiver, his eyes flittering, his muzzle opening just slightly. "You did good, pet, but now I want to play with you a bit."

"Yes," he declares as he flops back with his arms and legs spread, body open and ready for anything I want to do to him. A glance at my clock tells me that I have a bit of time this morning, so I continue to fluff his fur in the wrong way, making him squirm and try hard to accept what might be a creepy feeling. No, he always says anything I do feels good, and I will test that later once we have a decent break.

I adjust my position so I'm sitting over him, and he looks up at me, bats his eyes, and rolls his hips under mine. I haven't ridden him yet, and this morning there's not enough time for that, but I do enjoy the feel of his length and heat against me. I wonder if I'd feel much, given how much smaller he actually is than a human male. But what's that old, old expression—it's the motion in the ocean, not the size of the boat?

I turn my thoughts away from that and take his black nipples into my fingertips. He arches up when I pull them into taut peaks. As I roll them, gently at first then with increasing pressure, he growls softly, which no longer frightens me at all, since I've learned his responses fairly well.

He's on the verge of begging me when the phone rings. I put one finger over my lips and release him, earning a moan and a wiggle. "Yes, this is the Potter residence, Emily speaking, and there better be a damned good reason why you are calling me, Lindsey." I use his name since the house puts his name up on the wall to identify the caller.

"Sorry, Boss, got a call from Connie's wife. She's been rushed to the hospital this morning."

Like a torrent of ice-cold water, any pleasure I felt this morning is doused. I get off Wynn and snap my fingers, pointing him toward the hallway. "Put out my briefcase by the front door, pet, I have to get going."

"Master?"

"Just do it!" I barely register his flinch as I bellow out the order then turn a much calmer tone to the phone as I pull off my gown and head to the shower. "Why the hospital? What's going on?"

"Something about chest pains and trouble breathing, Boss. You don't have to head in; I'm on my way."

"Don't be ridiculous, man. Call the office, then send a taxi for me. I'll be ready in fifteen minutes. Then get the benefits office on the line; I want to know this is being taken care of."

"She's at the company clinic, Boss." There is silence as I hop in the shower and quickly start bathing. "Taxi is on the way. Boss?"

"Yes!"

"I'll have breakfast for you here."

With that my entire day reverts to stress and juggling corporate benefits with Connie's wife and their kid. Before I hang up I order one more thing. "Lindsey, first look up her wife's employer; I want to know that before we talk to Benefits."

"And that is why you will be getting a promotion," Lindsey says softly before acknowledging the command and hanging up.

Wynn's just staring at me by the front door, where he's waiting with my briefcase. "Wynn sorry, Master," he mutters against my hand as I pet him.

His rejected tone makes me pause, even though I hear the taxi's horn outside. I crouch down and cup his muzzle in one palm. "I'll be back as soon as I can, and then we will continue this. Do you understand?"

His eyes light up as he nods. "Wynn make everything ready, Master. Wynn best pet ever," he adds with a nod as I release him.

I want to stay, but the taxi honks again. Bloody bastards with their traffic perks. I'd drive, but the mass transit and company vehicles can move quicker than I could on my day off, and putting those beneath you before your private life is one of the codes of Inandirmak that I swore to uphold with my promotion. I'm twirling that in my mind as I see Wynn's furry face pressed up against the glass, watching me pull away.

Chapter Fourteen
Haven

Emalee got home later, but not when it was dark or right before dark. Been trying to work out how to tell time, and i think She was home three first numbers sooner than normal workday. i tried to be clever and went to the clock, looking back at Her after she was in the house. She frowned for a second, then smiled slightly, adding, "Yes, I am home a bit earlier. It's only 15:27, isn't it?"

15:27. i put that in my mind and added that the three numbers later looks like two circles on each other. i don't ask what that number is because Her frown might mean i did something almost bad.

Don't want to be bad pet. Don't want be locked in room again away from Master.

i rub my head against Her hand as She pets me, letting contented noises rise up so She can hear them. Whitecoats didn't want speaking, but they and Handlers always liked positive noises. Master does, too, though i also add a few words i know will please Her. "Wynn so happy Master home."

"Technically vacation does not start until tomorrow, but since it is really too late to go back to MTB, I'm starting a few hours early." She leans down and catches my muzzle in Her hands, looking into my eyes. "That make you happier, pet?"

"Most happy ever!" i exclaim as i try to put a bunch of feelings into my eyes. She still seems unclear on my mouth's feelings, but my eyes She can read well if i try hard. i lift up and snuggle into Her legs and stomach as She releases my muzzle to hug me. Her scent and something i don't like but can't place washes over me, but soon i can tune into Her scent alone.

After too short a time She pushes me back and looks down at me. i can feel Her eyes traveling down to stop on my main pleasure region, that area She calls cock. "Wynn, have you been touching yourself while I was gone?"

Her voice has that edge to it that i don't like. That edge that says She is angry, and if Master angry then big hurt could follow. Emalee not mean and not hit me in punishment way so far. i swallow when She grasps my arms and looks at me. Her eyes narrow, and She repeats Her question.

i glance down and see my black firmness bounce when She shakes me just a bit. It's been like this ever since She left, but I don't know if She'll believe me. "No, Master, no touching, Wynn tell truth. Miss Master so bad all day after You play with pet."

Her eyes narrow more, then She releases me and goes to the computer in the next room, me at Her feet following anxiously but silent. "Maurice," She says—that's what She calls her computer, which is sort of like a very smart TV or a machine pet, i decided a while back—"Display erotic foxmorph arousal diagram, male."

Since She sits down, i can stand and look at the computer, but i kneel instead by Her feet. i'm not sure what all the words She said meant, but i know i am erotic foxmorph, so i worry something bad will be told to Her. Stupid computer! Master should ask me what arousal diagram is. i could figure it out, 'cause i smart pet.

After a few minutes She sits back and sighs, "Damn." After a few moments of silence i rub my head against Her leg and look up at Her silently, hoping She isn't more angry.

"Let's go take care of this," She says, suddenly standing up so i have to scramble back. i blink up at Her then hurry after out of the office into Her bedroom. "Up on the bed," She orders, and i hop up, kneeling to face Her, my paws on top of my thighs, thighs spread so She can see the state She left me in this morning.

i'm not sure, but given that sparkle in her eyes i think She's going to play with me more, hopefully lots more. But She ignores me to go to this fancy box She has in one corner of Her bedroom. i wiggle a bit and let out a yip that makes Her chuckle but not look back at me. i know what's in there. Toys! Lots of toys for me, for Master, lots of play fun that She rarely has time for.

i cross out all bad thoughts i've had about computer taking Master away from me now that it's told Her to play more with me.

i'm wondering what to give the computer to say thank you when She turns around with two objects in Her hands that look a bit strange. Then i yip again and let my tail swish about as i recognize the lube and the dildo.

She frowns slightly as She comes to the bed and sits on it. Now i see that She has gloves on Her hands up past Her wrists. "Now if this makes you feel bad, pet, if this reminds you of my half-brother, you tell me, understand?"

i sit back for a second at the mention of the human who hurt me in Her house that first day i was here. That was my fault for not obeying Her and his fault for taking me without permission. Looking at what She has, i'm confused for a few moments, then it makes sense. She thinks Her toys are like him because they'll go inside me.

As soon as i realize that, i feel my stomach tighten up, but i push that feeling aside by looking at Master's hair, breasts, hands, so strong but gentle. Letting my gaze go up again, i smile, hoping She recognizes it. Her head fur is much different from his; Her face is much nicer than His; everything about Her is much better, 'cause She Master, but also 'cause She Emalee. Emalee, who people call and She go to them. Emalee who big important at work so She get house, and car, and me; best is me.

"Wynn want Master inside," i say with a dip of my head before i flop back on the bed and spread my legs. i let my hands outline my body, but i do not touch it. i wiggle and lift up my hips, keeping my eyes on Hers.

"Good lord," She whispers, and i spy Her setting the lube and the dildo down as She watches me. That is not what i want.

"Wynn good pet all day, Master. Wynn so hard and aching," i pull some words from the TV shows where male morphs are begging for attention i really need now myself.

i should roll over onto my stomach or flip over and kneel on all fours. i should do that—that's what all the vids at Institution tell us—but i want to see Her eyes on me; i want to show Her how much i wanted Her touch all day long. i reach out with one paw and plead, "Please."

Master moves up, and soon one slick hand is on my shaft, stroking it, making me growl softly and thrust up into Her grip. i struggle to keep my eyes on Her as She takes one of my nipples into Her mouth and bites a bit, not hard, but enough to make me groan. Rougher attention has always made me lose control of my surroundings faster, that condition our songs say means both danger and approaching bliss. Spankings are fun, but sometimes i want more from Master, so i make sure i watch Her and plead with sounds and words for more.

All too soon, or maybe not soon enough, my head feels fuzzy, and Master releases my nipple and my cock to rub the lube on the outside of my bottom channel and then into it with a circling motion that enters me gently. Back at Institute we had training rods we mounted ourselves on or laid back to be mounted by, always with machine, never by human hand, Whitecoat or Handler. Bad human hurt me by no lube and sudden mounting, but i push that quickly from my mind when i feel a bit of pain.

Good pets do not feel pain unless Master wants. Good pets only feel desire, need, for Master at all times. i'm a good pet, "best pet ever" i repeat to myself, relaxing my muscles and watching the top of Emalee's head, whispering "more" when She glances up at me.

"One more finger, then; relax," She commands, and i sigh when She adds the next one and makes a motion that seems to stretch me then let me return to a smaller size. i think i'm getting bigger, though, and soon i want even more. She only shakes Her head when i beg for more and her fingers disappear.

Something that isn't moving except to push inward and which feels firmer next enters me. "That's it, pet, relax; let my little toy in, then we'll have different fun than ever before."

It is very smooth until one point, when i moan as i'm stretched a bit further, seeming to swallow the dildo. Master does something that shakes me a bit, but the dildo does not move. Now i know i was mistaken; not dildo but plug, and i wonder if She'll make me move around like the Handlers used to do. Plugs for training for bigger and bigger, for stretching and making us want more and more inside of us. Without further playing we are left wanting and wanting with no sky in our reach.

i won't be bad pet; i won't beg for real dildo or more play, really won't, but i'm wiggling and whimpering at Master anyway. i can feel it is right on the edge of that spot inside where shocks make us come and come, but i know the knot in the toy will keep me from pushing it further inside.

Maybe this is rougher stuff that Master likes? Make Wynn crazy for more, test Wynn's ability to be focused on Master before self. i can do that, i can do that, then She caresses my shaft again and i'm arching up into Her hand, saying "Master, Master," over and over as She strokes me slowly.

"Since you went all day, pet, I didn't want to rush things," She says with a smile that gets a nod from me as well as a needy groan.

She leans over me and lowers Her teeth to my nipples again. Her head fur flops down over one shoulder to sweep over my face, and i'm washed with Her scent. After several moments i'm wiggling hard, so She has to release my nipple and use Her weight to hold me down more. "Please, Master, please let Wynn reach the sky," i beg, and then i realize i've used a phrase that humans don't know about.

"Reach the sky, huh? That's so poetic; I'm surprised," She says with an odd tone to Her voice that makes me pause but does not make me afraid.

"Let's take a moment to thoroughly test things out before the rocket, then," She says, and i'm curious until something warm and wet surrounds my shaft. The sensation reminds me of what the squirrel girl did, but this is bigger; the tongue moving around me is larger and works in long strokes, not her quick jabs to get me ready for play.

my eyes snap open wide, and i freeze when i realize that Master's mouth has swallowed me. i can't see it; all i see is Her head moving up and down just slightly. my first instinct is "NO," but while i never saw vids of Masters going down on pets, that is what we were told to call it: going down or worshipping, never eating, though i don't know why anyone would use that term; i never thought Master would do this to pet.

i swallow again as a terrible song floods my mind. In that one the pet is so bad that his Master gets so angry that he eats him—takes his shaft first and then pulls apart his body. i feel afraid and start whimpering, saying "Please no, Master, please no," clenching my paws to keep from touching Her, though something inside is screaming at me to push Her away and run.

She looks up at me and frowns, then strokes my thighs and tummy gently. "You don't like receiving then? You like giving, so I thought... That's all right; I have something else that should send you to the sky," Master tells me.

The hand on my thigh moves down toward my ass, and then there's a whirring sound, and the plug in my ass begins to move. This isn't the pushing and pulling, or sometimes the pounding away, that the training machines do. This is just a small movement, fast, that bumps against that spot inside and makes my entire body stiffen.

One of my paws reaches up, and then i firmly plant it on my stomach next to Her hand; i put every feeling i can manage into my eyes and stare at Her as i feel my shaft start to pulse. She takes my paw in Her hand and then moves us both so i'm lying across Her lap as She gazes between my face and my shaft.

"You're all right, pet," She chuckles as I start to thrust against the nothingness of air and grip Her hand tighter. "I think I found something you aren't used to—two things, I think. That pleases me greatly," She confesses, and hearing that seems to push me up and into the sky with a howl.

Master says i have a short down time, and soon my shaft goes from slightly limp to full again, and i'm howling over and over until it starts to hurt below. i wiggle, licking my lips and looking up at Her, hoping She can't tell it now hurts and wanting to stop, or worse, go bigger and harder inside me. Little pain is nothing if it keeps bigger pain away.

"There we go; your cock says you are done, I think," She says and leans over me. Her breasts, even under Her shirt, are sending out that special scent that tells me She is ready for pleasure as they move across my muzzle and She reaches down. Immediately the fast movements inside stop and the pain recedes.

Master rolls onto Her back so i sit up and nuzzle a close thigh, looking up at Her. "Wynn please Master now?"

"You already did, pet. After today at the hospital, you already did. It's nice to have some positive control and not the tired bureaucracy to wade through. Who knew spouses with different companies could complicate things so much. They really need to be loyal to one, but I don't want to lose Connie."

i let Her talk and just touch Her body lightly with one paw and my muzzle as i listen. i have no idea what She is talking about, but it makes me dislike work again. Bad morph; humans work hard to give you good life. "Connie?" i ask, pretending i want to know more about the people who take Her away from me many days a week.

Master shifts, and I move back a bit so She can lean up and look at me from lying on Her side. "Connie is my secondary executive assistant—my secretary is a nicer sounding way to say it, I think. She does all the detailed stuff so Lindsey can focus on the personnel and scheduling matters for me. You remember Lindsey, right?"

i nod and reach out to caress Her thigh and hip lightly, trying to distract Her but not be demanding about it.

"She's going to be fine, the doctors said, now that the coverage is there. Genetic corrections should fix the problem, and luckily with the month of holidays she'll have time to go through them without missing work. We'll think about negotiating testing for their kid later, since she was the donating mother."

Master reaches out and touches my nose, making me chuckle and wiggle a bit more to show Her i like it. "Doesn't mean anything to you, though, does it?"

She sits up and pulls me into a hug, and i nuzzle Her breasts lightly. "That's what I love about coming home to you, pet. You just don't care about these sorts of things, so I should just let them go and enjoy a break. Right?"

"Right!" i agree, looking up at Her then nuzzling Her neck until She giggles and lets me pleasure Her until we both fall asleep.

The first day of this vacation thing is my favorite day so far with

Master. We get up late, and She checks Her messages and talks to Her mother and father both, who have sent colorful wrapped boxes that She opens while they watch on the phone. Then She watches them open some other boxes from Her while i crumble up the paper that She tossed on top of me with a chuckle.

All three humans laugh at me, so i crumble more and crawl around in it, getting them to react more. Laughter is usually good, and her parents mean a lot to Master, so i want them all happy. They say something about a visit after Her trip, and i feel Master's scent change as well as Her tone of voice. "I'm not sure how long I'll be in Egirdir, Mum. I'll try my best to stop by and see you both."

"We understand. Business before family, that's the way of things," Her father replies, but Her mother only nods her head silently.

"I'll have Wynn with me," She adds, with a pat on my head. With Her? I'm going with Her to meet parents and this Egiry person?

"Oh, your morph? Can you take those on flights, overseas?" Her mother asks. Flights? Overseas? What does that mean, i wonder.

"Yes, yes, I've been told that I can," Master says, and I look at Her and then lie down on Her lap, where She pets me and continues the conversation.

"It looks rather large, doesn't it? I mean, do you put it in the pet compartment of the plane? That seems like a waste of precious space and fuel, doesn't it?"

"Let it go, Aggy," Master's father says, and he's frowning and looking off somewhere that doesn't seem to be at Master's mother. These telephone things are so confusing to me, so i just bury my face in Emalee's lap and try to let their voices wash over me. Acting like i don't hear but picking up anything that might have to do with me is a trick our songs teach us.

"Do you not want Wynn in your house, Mum?"

"No, no, of course I want to meet your pet, but I do worry about the resources these things are taking up."

"He, Mum. Wynn is male, I assure you of that." i snuggle against Master's leg and She scratches behind one of my ears.

"That is not what I want to hear, young lady!" i stop snuggling at the angry sound of the mother's voice. She sounds a lot like Master, and that is scary.

Her father's voice is lower but still clear to my sharp ears as i turn them slightly toward the speakers. "Good god. Let it go, Aggy."

"I will not let it go, Will. Ignoring things is your specialty. Now, dear, Emily, your brother told me about the situation, and I worry...."

"You listened to him?"

Master's scent has changed, and i scurry off Her lap and to the side, my body low, my eyes and ears focused on Her.

"You listened to him? You believe him over me? Over the police?"

"I know you both differ on the details, but I'm sure you are both exaggerating...."

Her father snorts, but the women ignore him.

"There is the truth, and there is a lie. That you would believe anything that perverted, freeloading bastard has to say... I... I...." i sit up as Master suddenly turns off Her mother's face and voice. She never does that, never just turns off anyone, though She's complained about them calling and refuses calls from the one who hurt me.

There is a silence that is scary for several minutes, then a chuckle comes from the other screen. Master has two phone screens, but i've seen Her split them into more faces before. "Damn! I didn't have an opinion one way or the other about him, but now you better bring your pet with you, and you better come see your old dad, 'cause I have to check out what has made you into someone who can stand up against that bitch."

Master smiles, then frowns when another call appears on the control panel for the telephone. She hits a button, and a red light appears for a moment, just like the ones She made appear when She refused to talk to the one who hurt me. "She can be on blocked until she learns some manners and who is the truthful child in this family," Master announces, and that makes Her father chuckle more.

"Now that that's out of the way, would you let me look at your pet more closely? I've frankly only seen a tail tip and the top of his head." Her father emphasized the "his" part, and Master smiles again and motions me toward Her.

i hurry to Her lap and sit up in it, looking curiously at the man on the screen. He has head fur that is lighter than Hers; he also has fur on his face that looks like several colors. He has different color eyes, though, and his nose is bigger; i wonder how good he can smell things. i lean forward, and Master grabs me and tells me to not be so anxious.

"He seems smaller than you, a bit thin."

"I've been trying to bulk him up a bit, but I think his genetics might be restricting it or something."

"Well, it is all about that, isn't it? His name is Wynn?"

"You can talk directly to him, Dad. He can understand, and he can talk, too."

"Really? Make him say something."

Master looks at me and pats my back. "Wynn, would you say hello to my father?"

i raise a hand and wave with an opening and closing of my paws i've seen friendly morphs on TV do. "Hello Master Father."

"By Saint Maurice's Badge. It... he can talk!"

Master giggles, and i look at Her, relieved that She seems pleased with me. "Yes, not a lot though. I think he could talk more, but it seems to upset people if we're in public."

She notices that?

"Well, I'll want to hear more about it. I'll check on my end of things and make sure all the forms that need to be filled out are and update your passport. Has to be a benefit to being an officer, so I'm sure it will be fine."

"Thank you, Dad. Love you. I'll send his specifics, then, and work on amending my flight."

"When is that, by the way?"

Master's body temperature cools a bit, and Her scent changes again. This time the changes urge me to kneel back down and snuggle around Her, wrapping my tail around Her to help warm her up. She smiles down at me and places a still hand on my head resting on Her knee. "We're leaving in two days, a little less actually."

"You don't seem too excited, Em. Last year you didn't get to go to the big dance, right? You had to staff the office over the holiday. New girl thing, I suspect." Her father's voice has changed too, and when i look up he has his head tilted to one side, his eyes narrowed, but not in an angry way.

"Yeah, new girl takes care of things, though Ashton in Tahoe is staying on the continent this time."

"We've heard there's been some attacks there."

"I'm sure the city and the co-ops have it under control, Dad. Don't worry about it."

"My job to worry about things like that."

"For The Alps, Dad, for The Alps. I'll talk to you later." What are alps?

"See you soon, Em."

We sit there for a while. i'm content to stay here, though i know Master's legs and back get uncomfortable—that's the word She uses—after a time. Humans are made to be up and about, looking around, controlling everything. Morphs are meant to be below them, looking up, helping. Yes, that's right, no doubt about that. i sigh as She strokes my fur and rocks back and forth a bit.

Her scent and body temperature still aren't quite right, but without Her direction, i don't know what to do to help. Sometimes, rarely, i think i should tell Her that, but that can't be good pet behavior.

"All right, pet. Let's go pack, then. We have a flight at 0600 the day after tomorrow." She stands, so i stand up with Her at Her urging. She puts Her arm around me—She's never done that before—and leads me to Her bedroom, saying, "We'll get to see headquarters, a new region, a new culture, lots of other morphs, too. Won't that be fun?"

Her tone, body language, nothing is matching Her words, so i just nod and wait to see what will happen over this Egir and father trip.

Chapter Fifteen
Executive Lunch

I've been so focused on watching my manners, eating at the same pace, keeping up the falsely light conversation, and trying to ignore the fact that I feel like I haven't breathed since we entered the airport yesterday at 0400 sharp and stepped out here in Egirdir around 1900 last night, that I jump slightly when Wynn rubs his head against my leg. Margaret, who has stationed herself between the podium and me, glances at me with a tight smile. I can feel her squirrel girl's eyes looking up at me, too, so I reach down and pat Wynn a few times on the head to calm him.

Or maybe it's me who needs to be calmed.

Wynn was fine with the doctor from the Institute when she came to do a last minute check-up for customs. He was fine with being felt up by security three times in the airports. He was fine when they insisted I chain him into his special pet bed on the floor by my feet. I'm the one who kept asking if all that was really necessary.

Apparently my fuss was reported, because Margaret appeared at my room not more than half an hour after I arrived. We are staying at corporate headquarters, or the Reizis family compound if you prefer, but there is even less division between business and family here than back in North America. Her room is right next door in case I need anything. Faye from Winnipeg is on my other side, while Zandy from Detroit is kitty-corner across the hall. The guys are just in the next wing. All of North America is one big happy family, minus Ashton, living together, eating together—all this togetherness isn't reflective of how the business actually works.

So why does it feel like everyone's watching the new girl to make sure I don't screw things up for our continent?

Ashton's face on the computer at the head of the table, looking at us and rolling his eyes when anyone takes a bite of meat, is more like how we do business every day. Of course, I feel his eyes on me more often than not, and I wonder if he wishes he were here, though he told me in a private letter that he was happy to stay at home where conspicuous consumption wouldn't be expected.

"Your morph didn't cause any problems on the flight, did he, Emily?" Bailey asks in his blunt fashion, looking directly at me over his fourth course. In just this one luncheon I've had the equivalent of three days of meat, but I think it's the tension that is really making my stomach clench. Bailey's morph looked kind of mean when I saw him last night, but today he's not just under the table like the rest at our feet—human, morph, human, morph—but also muzzled, his eyes on the ground, head hanging low. Bailey has all the tact of a bomb, but he runs the Chicago branch well, overseeing all of the Accounts department's needs, though how he ever got to be VP of that is beyond me. People skills are not his strong suit— they aren't even his weak suit; they simply seem beyond him.

"Wynn was perfectly well behaved. If you've heard otherwise, I shall have to lodge a compliant against the stewards," I reply with what I hope is a light tone but a serious expression.

"Ignore Sir Grumps," Zandy tells me as she nudges me with an elbow lightly. We're sitting around the table with the women on one side and the men on the other, just like at the other eight tables. "He's jealous because you have the exotic he wishes his Chewy was."

"At least Chewy isn't a slut like Sammy," Bailey retorts, and my eyes widen at the bizarre comment until Jim jumps in to calm everyone down.

I briefly met everyone's morph this morning at breakfast, an affair of just the six of us and our pets on a balcony off the end of our hallways. One big balcony per two halls or wings, it seemed, from the light laughter I heard every now and then from other directions. Below us but off to one side was another balcony with six people and six morphs sitting at an identical table. If every continent is housed like this, not to mention the Presidents and the Reizis family proper, who created our company last century, this house must be a monster.

Sammy is a cat morph, also male, making three male and four female morphs in our group, if we include Ashton's pet ferret girl Renee, and of course Margaret's Violet. The other two female morphs are Faye's poodle morph named Lily, who seems detached from the events around her and somewhat slow, and Jim's Libby, a female cat morph who keeps looking at everything with wide childlike stares. It was difficult to see after some of the tables were already seated, but I didn't see any other fox morphs until I noticed that our CEO's pet is also a fox morph, reddish-brown in fur and definitely female.

I'll ask Margaret later if I stepped over some line by getting such an exotic pet.

My mentor now changes the subject as the servers come to take this course away and bring in dessert. I smile at Margaret as she leads us gently toward less hostile topics. She and Bailey really should change departments.

After dessert, rather subdued compared to the rest of or meal, the lights dim, and our CEO, Madame Eser Reizis, great-great-grand-daughter of our founder, stands to address us. "Hoş geldiniz!"

"Hoş bulduk!" we all reply. Our company still uses some basic Turkish for introductions and farewells, though beyond when I'm supposed to use them, I can't say I understand them. Really, beyond scholars and natives, who uses more than one language these days?

"I recognize many faces here today, and I welcome you back to my father's father's father's home, our home as the Inandirmak family whom you all are part of. But one of you is new to us this year, as in many years. Will Emily Grant Potter from the North American Office please stand?"

I've already placed my napkin and taken hold of Wynn's leash in preparation for this. "Stay at my heels, keep up, and don't look around," I remind him in a whisper as I stand.

"Ah, there you are. Please come up, so I may greet you properly."

when we say it looks like she made some excellent decisions by taking the time to think through and research them."

Madame Reizis glances down at Wynn, and suddenly I feel every eye in the room looking at him as well. After a second the crowd erupts into applause and odd exclamations of "he looks like he'll do the job," "exotics are worth the wait," and "my Rita calls dibs," which draws some whistles and hoots.

I feel like I've been hit over the head, but I'm still left confused.

I feel Wynn suddenly grab onto my legs and rest his head on my hip, moving it slightly. The crowd's volume goes up another notch. Alarms are going off in my head now, and the next announcement confirms my unconscious worries.

"We will establish this rotation system for teams in our European markets next and give it two years to test. If that works, then we will redesign our project teams around the globe, though I think for now Lunar and Titan can wait."

This brings much subdued applause and now comments. It isn't that all my peers and superiors don't think it is a great idea and a proven method, I realize, so much as this isn't about the company or me. It's about Wynn.

Chapter Sixteen
Business & Pleasure

Everyone at our table nods and smiles at me, even Bailey, though his eyes are narrowed a bit. With their gaze on me, I walk as confidently and smoothly as I can, Wynn crawling behind me. I just tell myself it is his exotic nature that is starting the muttering around us as we approach, because our CEO is still smiling as she steps around the podium and a man I assume is her son helps me up the few steps to the platform.

Madame Reizis smiles at me and then bends down just slightly to look at Wynn, who is kneeling at my feet with his head bowed. There's that twinge again in my stomach when she takes his muzzle in her hand and tilts his head up to look at him. She smiles and stands up straight to look at me. She's just a touch shorter than me, and her smile seems sincere. "Good choice," she whispers as she puts a hand on my shoulder and guides me to turn to face the audience.

"Emily was part of the Administration Department headquartered in Metro Thunder Bay on Superior. While there she had an idea to rotate certain team members out to keep the flow of creativity and stem the chances for personality conflicts. After this proved successful, we, by executive and stockholder vote, promoted her to the new branch manager at that office and new Vice President of Administration for all of North America, which as we all know is still one of the biggest and most competitive markets on Earth."

She looks directly at me now but raises her voice a bit further to compensate for turning from her audience and uses another formal phrase for our company. "Hayırlı olsun."

"Teşekkür ederim," I say loudly enough for the room to hear.

She nods and then faces those watching us again. "As you know, Emily took great care in managing her new perks of promotion, so she wasn't able to join us last year. I think I speak for everyone

"Master?" i'm reaching through the bars in the door as Emalee backs up.

"Be a good pet; do as you're told. I'll collect you in no time at all," She tells me before leaving with the squirrel girl's owner.

violet smirks at me then scampers off to the room where dozens of other morphs are waiting for something. The room is big, with a rough carpet, and strewn with dull colored pillows. violet rushes to join a group of morphs sitting on a collection of these pillows. There are several groups gathered around, hoarding the pillows, and i don't see a free one.

There are no white coats or handlers or owners, and soon i hear a rough voice behind me. "Oh, your mommy go and leave you, baby?" Chuckles follow, so i turn around.

The entire room of morphs is staring at me, some whispering behind paws to each other as this leopard morph confronts me. he is a bit larger than me; breeds like his tend to be. It's like being back in the nursery, struggling for attention from the bitches or the breeders.

"Emalee Master, not mommy," i say simply, then try to walk further into the room to see if i can figure out why we were all brought here tonight. i liked time with Emalee at meals, and i loved the time with other morphs in the pools set aside for us in the huge house, but i don't like how things smell in here, not one bit. Fear, anger, depression are rolling off the others.

"Where you think you're going, exotic? You think that makes you something special, huh?" the leopard morph adds as he pokes my chest with one of his fingers.

i look down at his finger, and i can feel the hackles rise up on my neck as i trail back up to his black leather collar and spotted face. "you exotic, too," i point out.

"That is his point," a feminine voice that sounds like a sister's voice interrupts us, and the leopard drops his hand, stepping back to let a red fox morph girl through. No, she's not a young morph; she's older, if her graying and thinning fur is an indication, and the others shut up the moment she speaks. Around her neck is a silver collar with shining green stones in it and matching bands on her limbs near her paws. her adornments and the fear and arousal i smell coming off of everyone as she speaks mark her as the pen leader, so i lower my gaze a bit.

"we are only as special as they tell us we are; at least in their minds, they only care about two things: The Show or The Sharing," she continues as she steps very close to me and lowers her voice to a growl. "you will not mess up either of these in any way, or you'll have me to answer to. Do you understand, todd?"

i ignore her use of a human term for me and look up at her, shaking my head slightly. "No. What's show or sharing?"

she smiles and narrows her cold-looking eyes as she puts a hand on my shoulder and starts to lead me further into the room as the others move aside to let us past. "If i told you, they wouldn't enjoy either as much. Just do as the humans tell us and don't make any of us look bad, even if you have to fake."

i feel a bigger presence move closer to my back and glance back to see the leopard spots. "Do you understand how you should act now?"

i nod and say, "wynn be good pet."

"As we all need to be," she adds before walking away, leaving me with a group of morphs who all move in and trail their hands over my fur and body. they aren't mean; they don't try to hurt me, but they all stay away from the pleasure regions of my body. i keep my eyes on the leader and her leopard beta, watching, listening, and smelling, trying to figure it out.

After some time a wall opens up and the group around me steps back. Following the example of all the morphs, i kneel down, looking up from beneath my bowed head as a man walks among us with two others, one a woman, the other another man, writing things down.

i turn my ears so i can hear what he's saying. It's a list of names, but only one i know, "violet," reaches my ears until the man stops in front of me. He reaches and tugs my muzzle up so i have to look at him. He's taller than Emalee, but the others with him are about her height. They all have darker skin, dark eyes, and darker head fur, though the man talking has little of that, but a lot above his lips.

The other man says something that i can hear now, but his voice is very quiet. "The new one, from the MTB branch. Wynn, exotic white fox breed, age four and some months, male."

"Stop announcing the sex, Armand; I see that for myself," the balding man says, and the other bows slightly. "What was the name of the one shouted out?"

"Rita," the woman says in a low voice as well. She shows him the screen, her touch pen poised.

"That will work; a good molly and todd pairing will be unique," he says and then moves on. my eyes follow, wondering what a todd or molly is.

After more time, the man stops, and the humans face us by the wall they came through. Now i can see there is a door there just the same color as the wall. The balding man speaks into the same device Emalee and the people who have been talking loud have been using since yesterday's lunch. He calls out the names, and the morphs start to move. i stay where i am, since i don't know who rita is.

i jump slightly when something brushes up against me. Turning, i see a cat girl about my size with very short fur sliding around me to stand in front of me, our bodies almost touching, but really it is just our fur. she rests one paw on a breast that is larger than the squirrel girl's and smiles with her elongated eyes fluttering open and closed. "rita," she purrs, twisting her body slightly from side to side.

i try to copy her movements, but i'm not as fluid. "wynn." she chuckles, so i grin back. "wynn think we need to find todd and molly."

rita blinks slowly at me then giggles. "No, that's just Master words describing us. They like a lot of different words for things."

i nod 'cause it is true. Almost everything Emalee eats has a specific name—She never just has "food" or "drink"—and clothes are all called different words, too.

After a moment of silence, rita's face turns worried. "You have no idea what we do for them? Something easy, please," she begs, but i can't figure out who from.

After watching a few of the morph groups, i know what we are doing for the humans. Looks like fun, 'cause all i see are pets giving each other pleasure without fear of being punished. Humans are watching, though i can't see Master from where i'm looking at the screens around our big room, where we wait until our names are called, along with some other words that usually correspond to the different types of pleasure i learned from training and from the TV back home.

When they state our names rita releases a breath, and she does it so loud that she must have been holding it a long time.

"Rita and Wynn. Oral."

rita grabs my paw and leads me out into a big circle with walls, the humans looking at us from above. i turn my head around until i find Master. i wave, and the crowd applauds with chuckles, but Emalee only stares back at me and leans forward to put Her hands on top of the railing, Her eyes locked on mine.

rita takes us up to the top of a round platform that has pillows and odd furniture of different angles and heights. i stay standing with her, copying her position as much as i can, but i really want to keep watching Master, who is nodding Her head while another human, the one who brought the squirrel girl over, is leaning with her and seems to be saying something in her ear.

The voice tells me to go down on rita first, and she lies down on an angled bench that has another smaller bench in front of it, set lower to the floor. i hear a buzzing noise and look up to see a machine move down and off to one side. i want to bat it away, but rita shakes her head vigorously.

rita then opens her legs and lifts her feet up one at a time to rest them on these sidebars. This bares her, and i can see the pinkish area that looks like a smaller version of Emalee, only more round and with the opposite amount of fur. i lean in and sniff, but she smells like fear, not arousal, and i lean back, blinking at her.

The floating machine turns and looks at me with what i now see is a camera lens like the one i had to pose for back at the Institute several times. They are watching and see rita's eyes widen as she whimpers. None of the morphs before us said anything, only made lots of noises, so i huff and then kneel down and lean in again.

i open my jaws enough to lift my nose above her fur and then use my tongue in long slow strokes waiting for her scent to change and moisture to grow like it does in Master. i'm working for a long time and nothing changes, so i speed up. rita pretends, she purrs and wiggles her hips, and the tip of her tail swishes around as best it can in this position. That's all it is though, pretend, and that makes me growl.

rita freezes, and a bit of moisture appears at her channel. i growl again, my jaw closed now and close to her, and more moisture appears. A few different things, and i think I figured it out. she likes vibration, not licking. Does that count as oral?

The camera bumps into me, and i turn to glare at it; the humans start chuckling again and clapping. Not sure what they liked, but i put my hands on both sides of rita's pink hole and tap with my fingers between hums and licks. Now her scent is changing, and she's wet, but the voice tells us to stop.

i can see her breasts heaving as she pushes me back with a foot and sits up again, looking up at the humans. i see her gaze directed at one man, who seems to be looking at something in his hands more than at us. rita is trembling slightly until the voice says she should go down on me.

she knows what she's doing, but her mouth is much smaller than Master's, and rougher. It really sort of hurts, and yet i can see my shaft firm up a bit, though nothing like it does for Emalee. Rita does something different then and pounces on top of me, nuzzling my face and then whispering in my ear, "please pretend, or they'll hurt us bad," before nuzzling her way down my body to my shaft again.

Glancing around i can see several humans frowning, so i close my eyes and think of being home, being with Master, being touched by Master, pretending that this cat girl is Master. Soon the roughness feels fine; it feels normal; it feels like what an Owner has the right to do to any pet.

i huff and stick my chest out with a twist of my body, making myself move more, pretending that Master is driving me crazy but wants me to be still, even though it is so hard. Rita can only get a bit of my shaft in her mouth, but she licks it all the way down and along my balls. Sometimes she gets the tip in her mouth and sucks, and it is one of these times i can feel myself tighten up, knowing i should have Master's permission before coming, when the voice tells us to separate again.

i groan as Rita moves away and cover my eyes with my paws in frustration. The crowd claps loudly and yells out a few things, more sexual positions, and calls that i'm a slut. Some Owners use words like that with the morphs on TV, but Emalee never calls me names other than pet or foxboy or my name. i don't mind if She does, but these voices make me shiver.

rita takes my hand and leads me off the platform but not back through the door we came in. The voice asks people to applaud Emalee and Douglas for the good show. i smile at rita 'cause now i know her Owner's name and i can thank him myself, 'cause i feel that rita helped me a lot tonight to please Master.

When we walk by Master's seat, though, i can see She's turned away and has one hand over Her mouth; the other lady has one hand on her back, but She's looking down at me with a broad smile and a nod.

i didn't pretend enough for Master, i decide as i think over it all during a quick shower they make us take before we are sent to another room to wait.

Later i get another chance to pretend better when i'm paired with another male named lockin, the leopard who questioned me earlier. he barely acknowledges me, grabbing a wrist and jerking me after him back to the platform. "Don't mess this up, todd, or this tom will hurt you bad," he growls in my ear as he starts feeling me all over with his paws as the voice commands.

i want to make sure he understands that my name is wynn, but he pushes me down on the bench so hard when the voice tells us to change positions that i can't breathe for a second.

he isn't as nice as rita, so i have to do a lot of pretending when he pushes me around to the positions the voice wants and drives his shaft into me over and over again. he isn't nearly as big as Emalee's brother nor Emalee's toys, but there is a scratchiness as he pulls out and pushes in. Since i don't have much to do, i make a lot of noise, and hold on tight to the top of the bench when i'm facing down or the sides when i'm facing up.

When we are done and the humans are all standing and clapping, lockin puts an arm around my shoulders and leads me out, his other arm raised to the humans, his face a mask of no emotions. "That was OK," the leopard boy tells me before slinking off to his shower stall.

"Not OK. Great!" i call after him, fluffing up my chest in anger for a few seconds until the voice tells me to shower again.

Master tells me that i'm randy—that's how She says horny—but as i look at the next male i have to pretend with, a dog boy with a face that looks mushed up and a slightly pudgy tummy, my shaft wilts. It isn't so much his face or his tummy, and it isn't the fact that he introduced himself as bryce after the Voice told us we were paired; it's his penis. Now i know i'm not the same breed as him, but i saw that something was missing below his exposed shaft when i gave him a quick once over in the room we waited in after the showers.

Then the Voice makes me freeze when it announces our position once we are on the platform. i have to fuck him? i'm terrified of him. Did he lose his balls because he not please master? Did he lose them because he not please humans watching? Or were they taken just on his Master's idea with no reason at all? Humans always doing that. Making rules then changing them, changing minds, changing world, changing us. Guess they own everything, so they can, but right now my heart is pounding in my chest.

bryce kneels down and takes my limp shaft into his mouth, looking up at me with sad brown eyes. i'm facing Emalee, so i look up. At least She's looking back, though She's sort of limp in her own way, sitting back, Her eyes watching, but no smile on Her face, while the others are chatting or watching and pointing to us.

i've lost my mind, because before i can control myself one of my arms is raised toward Her and i whimper.

She blinks and then sits forward, watching me more intently. She holds out Hers to me and then draws them toward Her chest where She wrapped one hand over a fist and makes a petting motion. She understood me; Master is so smart.

i reach down and start petting Bryce's head, and his eyes sparkle a bit. i can feel my shaft firming up as i look up to see Master nod Her head at me but still without a smile. Emalee will smile, will be happy with me, will see i'm best pet.

i take one of bryce's ears in a grip and nod to the bench lockin took me on. he rises slowly with a look down then up, and i understand he's now pretending, too. Watching the others after showers and between pairings, i can see there are stories being told. The shy bottom, the lovers, the rough top, the fighters, several games that we are playing to make the humans less aware of how little this is actually doing for us in terms of pleasure.

Our pleasure doesn't matter, not really; isn't that what they tried to teach me at the Institute? Isn't that what the TV shows try to tell me? i have been trying so hard to put Master's pleasure first, but She is so nice to me, helping me reach the sky many, many times. i've seen no sky yet tonight, but i won't take that out on bryce, like lockin did to me.

As i help bryce lie down on his stomach and run a paw over his body from head to foot then back up to his raised ass, the crowd lets out sounds that seem like happy ones. i even hear a "that's adorable" and "he's a sweetie" and finally one that makes my shaft get fully hard "good pet, Emalee." That's why i'm here, to make Master look good to those She works with, 'cause work is what lets Her keep me.

bryce lifts his rather short tail up and looks back at me. i kneel down and check him out, since i've never fucked another male before—haven't fucked a female yet either. What i see makes me pause. i know what i have—shaft, balls, asshole that is both yucky and yummy. i see those, but then something that looks like rita down there. Male and female? Wow! Humans change everything. i touch the female hole first, and bryce nods his head slightly. i touch the asshole next, and he shakes his head slightly.

"Wynn has discovered Bryce's secret, Ladies and Gentlemen!" the Voice announces, and the crowd chuckles. i try to tune that Voice out when it isn't telling us to move on to another position or to switch spots.

From what i've seen males simply push it into the females when it is two morphs. It hurt me when lockin did that to me, but maybe female holes are special and don't hurt so much. i line up and push inside, and Bryce's face relaxes, but his paws are gripping the sides of the bench. his mouth is opened a bit, and he's panting already. Yes, i think i did that, too, just sort of did it when it hurt.

Inside he's tight but also wetter than i thought just from looking. i work my way in and out, never leaving entirely as the close-ups on the screens in our rooms showed was the way to do this. It's feeling good; my balls are beginning to tighten up when the Voice says to fuck his other hole.

bryce moves a bit, adjusting legs and body, and then gives me a slight nod. i don't wipe myself off, and as i'm struggling to enter, i'm glad. This is tight and not wet at all. he's panting more intensely, his hands gripping the top of the bench, but I can see he is working on keeping his butt relaxed. i should have thought of that when it was me in his position.

After a few thrusts i get an idea that may be too clever, but fox morphs are supposed to be clever pets, so i hope the humans and Master like it. i reach down and slowly insert one finger into the female hole, and this makes bryce look back at me, his eyes wide and a smile forming on his face. he nods his head, and i use my finger in pace with my shaft to fuck him.

i use my other hand to steady his hips as he begins to push back. i look up at Master, but She's sitting back again, Her hands still on her chest, still making that petting motion. Bryce barks softly, and i yip back. The crowd starts saying something that builds up in voices. "Finish! Finish! Finish!" a chant i've heard only twice today, and it seemed like the morphs stopped pretending for a moment and reached the sky.

bryce understands them, and he releases the head of the bench with one hand and uses it to wrap around his shaft, stroking it in time to my pace. i'm so close, and yet i keep hearing the trainers tell me that i can only orgasm with Master's permission. i look up, and Emalee's friend is whispering in Her ears again. In a few minutes, bryce is whimpering and looking at me, begging me with his eyes to come so he can do so as well; apparently the bottom needs to wait in this room, though Emalee usually sends me to the sky first before Her.

i look at Her, begging with every part i can in this position and without words, 'cause She won't hear me from here or the other humans will hear, too. In a few moments She leans forward again and gives me a very clear nod of Her head. i'm howling my release, and bryce follows immediately.

The crowd is clapping and making noise as we are dismissed and head to another shower. i ache in ways i didn't know i could, and i pause before the next room's door, wondering who i'll be paired with next.

This is the room we started in, and there are morphs just lying around, eating and drinking. Our pen leader walks up to me, a bit of stiffness in her gait, and she holds out a small bowl to me. "Good job, todd."

"Thank you," i whisper before emptying the bowl of water.

"We're done for tonight; that's the end of The Showing," she says before turning and taking a few steps. Lockin steps up to her and she glances back at me. "Of course, since you were a... sweetie was the word they used, i believe. Yes, since you were a sweetie, they're going to really enjoy hurting you during The Sharing."

"And that's how you learn," the leopard boy announces as he takes her paw and leads her to some pillows to sit on while two waiting morphs begin feeding her pieces of something.

"Ignore them," bryce says as he puts a hand on my shoulder. "Come on, you can eat with rita, lessa, nick and me over here."

The food is fresh, not the canned and bagged stuff Master gets. It should taste good, but i keep looking over at the other group and thinking. Too much thinking; i should know better. Thinking is never a pleasing thing in a morph.

When Master comes to collect me, She says nothing, only clips my leash on my collar and leads me away. Her scent, Her body language, all suggest disappointment. i see a few morphs hit or hugged by their owners, but Master does nothing until we're in Her room.

She takes me to the bathroom and makes me get in the tub. She bathes me by hand, scrubbing very hard, but i can only cower down and keep quiet. Something is wrong, and the words i want to say are stuck in my head. Finally She stops commenting on how i smell right again, but i don't really know what She means, 'cause i don't think i've been cleaned so much in one day forever. Maybe Her sense of smell is stronger now, but i only smell soap and water until She dries me with the hair drier, making my fur fluff up until She brushes it down.

She takes me to bed, and i scramble up, eager to please Her and get Her scent all over me, since that is more important to Her than i realized before. i'm eager, telling myself i have a lot of randy for Master, but She just lies down and pulls me close to Her, my back against her front.

"I'm so sorry, Wynn, so, so sorry," She whispers and begins to cry.

i'm trapped in Her arms and by one of Her legs over mine. Her grip on my fur hurts if i move, so i just stay still and count out my breaths until She's only making sleeping sounds.

i lie in the darkness feeling cold until i don't know when and the alarm is making Emalee scramble out of bed.

i whine quietly, and at one point She stops to stare at me, Her eyes narrowing until She shakes Her head, grabs a coat and slips into Her shoes. "I'll bring you back something to eat. Don't want to share you this morning," She tells me before leaving me alone in Her room.

Something is very wrong, and part of me is telling me to run. However, i'm a good pet, so i just wait for Her to change me into what She wants.

Chapter Seventeen
Personal Property

I was the only one without a pet at breakfast, our morning meeting, lunch, the afternoon meetings, and now also at dinner. Up until then my colleagues have said nothing. Then Bailey has to change that with his blunt comment, "Where's your pet, Emily?"

"It was his first time for... Showing. He's tired, and I don't like to present the things I own unless they are at their best," I offer. I want to say I'm tired, too, but how foolish would that be. I wasn't the one being violated repeatedly for close to a hundred voyeurs.

Bailey looks down at his German shepherd morph, who sits up straight, watching his master closely. "Of course he's tired. I'd be tired too after all of that, but you can't coddle him too much—give him some extra care, sure," he says as he puts a treat into Chewy's mouth, then taps his nose after a moment. Chewy lowers his head and starts eating. "You can spoil them, and retraining is tiring."

"Sharing starts tomorrow; you'll have to bring him then." I turn and stare at Faye, who has said perhaps a few dozen sentences since this executive retreat began. She looks right back at me, but I see she's petting Lily, her poodle morph, while she talks. "That's with near strangers. Been easier for you both if you could have arranged a sharing among us first."

"Sorry to add to the pile, Em," Jim's voice draws my attention next, "but this isn't just about you, and what was his name?"

"Wynn," Zandy tells him but keeps her eyes locked on me. They are all looking at me, even Ashton on the monitor.

"Wynn. It isn't just about you two. This affects all North American branches. We can be asked to take early retirement and replaced. While that may not be a big deal for Bailey, Faye or me, I doubt the rest of you have enough merits yet to warrant a cozy retirement."

"You don't want to end up like that African Click-Back who

Madame called out the year I was first here," Zandy states. "He got so jealous and so possessive that he locked his in a closet, and when that didn't work he tried to poison her just enough to make her too sick to be shared."

"Almost died," Faye adds with a glance at me that sends shivers down my spine.

"I wouldn't do that," I start, and then I feel Margaret's hand on my leg, patting me as though I'm her morph.

"Emily is perfectly fine sharing. We've already shared, several months back, right after she got Wynn. Eager thing, but not terribly skilled yet, though we also did a show, and I think Violet taught him a few things. Isn't that right, Emily?" She says it looking directly at me with intensity in her eyes and a tone that makes me nod for a moment.

"Yes, yes, Margaret was kind enough to help prepare me for this." Then I have a thought and run with it. "Actually I'm fairly tired too. After all of that showing last night I wanted a bit for myself, and the time just flew by."

"That's one of the things I miss most," Ashton comments from the monitor. "So compliant after the show, so easy to use."

"Oh, yuck, trying to eat, here!" Zandy says with a chuckle.

That gets everyone laughing and talking about the fun they had after the Showing. Everyone but Bailey, who is looking at me like he can see my lies.

I'm standing on the shared balcony when he approaches me and just leans on the railing with a nightcap in hand. Bailey doesn't even look at me as he speaks. "You know what kills a career fastest in Inandirmak? Jealousy. Possessiveness."

"I'm not," I start to say, but he cuts me off.

"Not done," he states, turning to look directly at me, using his back as a brace against the railing. "You have your pet because of Inandirmak, just like you have your house, car, health care, food, everything. It's a team, and a team takes care of itself, or it can't win. We aren't the only company in town that helps educate and persuade folks to choose this product, service, and candidate over another. The only time we'd get to rest would be if Inandirmak was the only company that offered these services, and please tell me you do recall from classes what happened a hundred years ago, with the monopoly and cyber systems debacles."

"How can my behavior or choices, which have been to show Wynn's quite charming skills last night, be related to that?"

"Last night was last night. Now we're moving forward, just like on Titan or the lunar station. Moving forward is the only direction to go. As a team, we go as a team. Am I clear?"

I am silent for a moment, thinking about his words, the looks I've gotten all day, and the compliments last night as I made my way from the stands to the pens, comparing these with the facts I've learned from the past. Returning to the good old days was a big killer for us as a species, because we didn't learn from the past, only idealized it, as my father would say. We're still paying for that every day, and the only salvation has been the cooperation between companies for the good of their workers and their world. Companies are still competing, so we don't repeat the megacorps, groups helping each other instead of just trying to get ahead—a new paradigm, our teachers and trainers told us.

"Yeah, you're clear as glass," I reply. "Wynn will be ready and eager tomorrow after a full day off. Trust me," I say, leaning toward him a bit then downing my own drink.

"When have I ever misled us?" I add with a grin as I start to walk away.

"Not yet. Make sure you keep it up, Emily; keep moving forward for the team," he tosses at my back, but I just keep walking.

Wynn is waiting for me when I get back. He's kneeling on the bed, and I'm sure he hasn't been like this all day, even though when I checked in before lunch and dinner with some food for him he was also in this position. I frown at him and ask "You been kneeling all day like that?"

He flicks at one of his ears for a moment or two of silence that I've decided means that he's thinking about what to say. "No, Master. Wynn hear you outside so kneel up. Wynn rested all day like you say."

No comment this time about his being a good pet. He must say that to me two or more times a day, but not today. Not since last night.

"Damnit." I let myself verbalize my frustration softly, but he jerks back a bit anyway until I'm sitting on the bed. Then he rolls onto his back and rests his head next to my lap, his blue eyes looking up at me from beneath partly lowered lashes, giving him a vulnerable look, not the seductive ones I'm used to receiving from him.

I reach out and rub his exposed neck, and he arches back to offer me more, keeping his legs spread and his arms at his side. Inwardly I sigh. Now he's all submissive to me, not demanding, just when I'm feeling about as nonsexual as I've ever felt.

That's bad, because Sharing isn't just about them now; it's also about us. I have to share myself as well as him, and somehow I doubt just watching TV or petting someone else's morph is going to count as taking part in these team-building exercises.

"Wynn," I say his name, and his eyes open wide to look directly up at me. He's moving even less now; I can't even see the rise and fall of his chest. Last night has terrified him, and now I have to terrify him more by telling him that he has to go and be with others, but humans this time.

"Wynn, tomorrow is something we call The Sharing around here. We'll—you and me both—we'll spend time with other morphs and humans. Do you know what I'm saying?"

He pauses, flicking one ear again before quickly lowering his paw. "Like last night?"

I swallow and bite my lower lip. "No, not like last night. Just you with another human and me with another morph. Alone; I won't be watching you," I add slowly with a deep sigh.

He doesn't say anything, but just tilts his head and looks at me. My petting of his neck has gotten a bit firmer, but he doesn't move or complain. When I thread my fingers into his fur and lift up his body by his neck just barely off the bed, he moans, then sighs as I lay him back down.

He slips up to rest his head on my thigh and lowers his eyelids again before looking up at me. "Wynn like Master rough," he assures me as I grip his fur tightly in a fist. I can feel him swallow and breathe beneath my fingers.

The lights in the room seem to dim as he moans when I use my other hand to pinch one of his ears. "As much as you liked playing with the other morphs last night?" I can even hear the harshness in my voice.

His eyes open wider, and he looks at me, swallowing beneath my fist, and absently bats one ear, the one I'm pinching. Then he puts his hand over my fist and lets it sit there. "Wynn do for Master. All others do for masters. Wynn not pretend enough for Master?" he whispers.

"What? Pretend?" I'm so stupid. Bailey, Faye, all of them were right. I'm feeling jealous, looking at last night as though it was either one big rape or just morphs enjoying each other. I didn't think of how he, they, would look at it. Every TV show I've seen on the morph channel has been about the morph serving the human, submitting to the human. I was finding it boring to watch the same old thing over and over again, but he seems fascinated each show. Each week, though, Wynn became less and less focused on his own pleasure and more and more on me. I'm starting to think I understand when he speaks up again in a hurried voice.

"No, no pretend, Wynn say wrong thing. Stupid. Wynn like others, like Master watching, Wynn figure out the positions fast, 'cause Master watching, and he want to do it good, feel good." He's babbling and confusing me at the same time.

This isn't what I wanted. I don't want to share, not him, not me, especially with someone I have to pick from a group. Lindsey pops up in my mind, but I push that aside, because that's different.

"Just shut up!" I finally say, and Wynn's mouth closes with a snap. He places his hands behind his back and tilts up his face again, exposing more of his neck. I release the fur there and just smooth it down as I take a breath or two.

"Let me finish what I was saying. Tomorrow and for a few days we do this Sharing thing where you'll go visit with another human for a few hours, then come back to me."

"How many?" he says, then clamps both hands over his muzzle, tears welling up in his eyes.

What am I doing wrong here? It can't be me; I'm trying to be as rational and gentle as I can be, I quickly decide. "How many? Well, it is a three-day event, so at least three times? I don't know, honestly, Wynn. This is my first time here, too, with my new job."

He nods his head but keeps his hands around his muzzle. He looks too much like Bailey's pet, so I brush at his hands. "Put them down; I don't like you muzzled." When I say it he smiles at me and captures one of my hands in his, bringing it to his mouth and licking it a few times.

"I'm not completely certain, but I believe I'll meet with the other Administrative folks tomorrow, and I'll try to pick someone good for you. You are coming with, so if you don't like someone, let me know."

"How?"

Good question. I've not heard another morph speak this entire time. Few of them make much noise when we are in groups, and some of them barely move at all, though others do seem to be pressed right up tight for petting and food. "That's it." He looks up at me attentively now. "You stay close and keep your head touching my leg if we are in one place. If you don't like someone, you pull back, and if you do like them, just rub against my leg more."

He narrows his eyes briefly and looks worried but remains quiet while I continue. "That should be something I can't miss and which doesn't draw too much attention to you. You think you can do that?"

He swallows again, and I can see his throat rise and fall as his hand brushes an ear. "Yes, Master, Wynn remember and do good."

The best-laid plans never seem to work out for me. I've had more success in my life when I took a risk, spoke up with an idea, or simply tried something different alone.

That's why Wynn is looking back at me with a confused look on his face as he's standing with the other morphs, being moved around by the group of Administrators on this odd platform in the center of our circle of chairs.

Of course, since I'm the new girl I just followed the example of the others, even making sure I would be the fourth one in the room, not too late and not too early. Each of the three before me had their morphs in the center with a leash from their collar hooked through a ring in the center. The center was really a platform that was raised about a foot from the floor, and that turned slowly even before we began.

"Be good," I told Wynn gently as he looked around while he slowly rotated away from me.

One of the compound servants, or maybe they are really company employees—I'm not sure any more around this crazy place—gave us each a pad with a list of each of our morphs and boxes to fill out about what we liked to do with our own pets as well as a section for our reactions to each other's pets.

We had some time to fill out the top section while the pets slowly moved around, all of them kneeling as straight as they could, though Wynn looked around a lot at first. Strangely this questionnaire refused some of my answers until I gave it more honest ones. Yes, I was lying about some of my rougher interests, but how did the pad know that? I'm creeped out just thinking about it.

Then when the last of us put down the pad—I made sure I was not the last one to do so—the platform moved a bit faster, causing each morph except for one, the dog girl the senior executive owned, to struggle a bit to maintain their balance. The circle paused, and I had a honey-colored bear boy in front of me. Oh, my god, not Mister Wentworth....

I pick up the pad and start going through the checklist. When I see others are touching the morphs in front of them, in some very intimate ways that make me glare at Wynn, I have to shake myself mentally. The bear boy has moved and is right in front of my knees; I can feel his eyes watching mine even though his head is bowed. His hands are at his sides, and he's brushing his fur up and down just slightly as he waits.

I suck it up and think of the team, not my old teddy bear, and force myself to stroke the fur on his chest. I notice that his hands stop moving and a slight shudder passes through his body. His fur is softer than I expected, and shorter as well, just as on Wynn's body the fur varies in length, mimicking human anatomy without losing the appearance of the animal they were designed from.

My history classes always said we used to do this to ourselves—manipulate our bodies with genetics and machines. Then the Zombie Wars happened, and companies worldwide banned the use of such technology beyond that needed for specific jobs or to cure disease and disability. Instead we turned to manufacturing other beings that we could control without fear of hacking or artificial intelligence.

I see Wynn jerk a bit, and I have to make myself focus on the creature in front of me. I look at the form and find that his name is Benny... cute, Benny the Bear. From the Meersburg branch, owned by Erich Becker. He's had Benny for four years; he had him especially created to need less sleep than the normal bear morph. Does that mean that Benny will expect a long workout with me?

I write down my observations and then add a note where I can that says I would prefer not to have "Shared time," as the form calls it, with a bear morph for "personal reasons." I'm forced to continue to pay attention to the poor thing, though, until everyone has placed their pads back down and we can move on again to the next pet on the platform.

I note that four of the pets are all dog breeds, one bear, which I rejected, and then this strange creature that looks very different, so different that I'm sure the stats on pet ownership for the company must be wrong, because this has to be an exotic. "I'm sorry," I say, looking directly at the representative from Australia, Jonathan Walker. "What is a bandicoot?"

He laughs and pushes back his longish light brown hair as he talks. In another time or place I might find him attractive. "The animal ones are just these horribly overpopulated critters, maybe like rabbits, though those damned things bloody near did the continent in, my teachers told us."

I look at Nari—the form tells me her name—and she doesn't look much like a rabbit at all. Short ears, short nose or muzzle, and hairless tail that looks a bit ratlike. But she's looking at me with big dark eyes, even though her head is bowed and her hands are clasped in front of her.

"Nari there is a good example of how we saved animals by changing them. Back up around Nyirripi, ain't much animals left with all the extremes nowadays. Don't take me long to get to a damned desert," Jonathan continues. I'm trying to learn first names from those in my departmental group, just in case we ever need to confer on things.

"Doesn't take most of us long to get to damned desert," Bryan Madraa from Kampala on Lake Victoria points out. Everyone laughs, but when a Reizis younger son who is overlooking the first round of Sharing looks our way, we all return our attentions to the pets before us.

Nari is brown with black sections on her fur, mostly on her head, where it is longer, and she has beads worked into a few sections, giving her a further exotic look. She seems a little skittish when I touch her but looks up quietly, even attempting a smile and making a more passable one than Wynn can.

I wonder how he's doing as Wanda Deng from the Lake Qinghai Shaliuhe branch is looking carefully at him. I watch for a moment, but she is only having him moving his arms and legs around at the moment. I told myself not to watch, so I force my eyes back on Nari, who has turned her head to one side considering me.

As I have with the other females on the platform, I rank her higher than the males, hoping that I can use that as an excuse to do less to, with, them. Why am I resisting this? Haven't I jilled off to fantasies of slaves my entire life? Didn't I enjoy the roleplaying with my past partners?

"Not human," I say softly, but Nari steps back a tad, her ears flattened down. She comes to me, though, when I hold out my hand and make a shushing noise. "You aren't, but you are a cute little bandicoot," I tell her, though the three-toe thing is a bit weird.

I'm guessing it's a holdover from the actual animal stock but I know nothing about this type of creature.

Every pet is a mammal here. I recall a science show a few years back explaining that not only did people not want non-mammals, but they were much harder to alter appropriately. Altered she has been, to have a sort of hourglass figure with larger breasts sporting rings in each nipple. I make a mental note to look into that for Wynn when this entire affair is finished and we can go back home.

The Showing is very public, and I felt as much on display as Wynn, even though I know that is foolish. Margaret's leaning in to whisper in my ear that we are being watched didn't help with my fears one bit, but it has made me more conscious of trying to control my outward display of feelings. That's why I'm sitting in this alcove for The Sharing, running successful ad campaigns through my mind, trying to get lost in the jingles and slogans as I wait for my first shared pet to arrive.

I don't know which one it will be. I was pissed that they didn't tell me who Wynn was going to but simply told us to have the pets follow one of the company assistants, who are all very similar in form, enough so to make me think family, while we were each assigned an alcove to enjoy our colleagues' pets.

I get up and look through the supplies here again to kill some time. There is a big bed, though not as large as in my room, and it doesn't have sheets or blankets. Guess I know it isn't for sleeping, huh? There is a sink, countertop, and small mirror with a brush, obviously for the pet, given its size and shape. Under the sink is a fridge, very odd, and inside is a small selection of acceptable food and drink, listing general pet types with each on a laminated card attached by a small chain to the mirror.

Then there is the toy chest I'm looking through again when the door slides open with an airy sound. I turn around to see that a white Samoyed morph named Sonja is being pushed into the room.

Not pushed so much as she simply enters and kneels down in the center of the floor, a soft carpet that blends into her coloring.

The door closes, and the digital numbers above it come on. Two hours until the door unlocks, unless there is an emergency. I decided about five minutes after entering that we'll probably be watched if not live, then later if I can't do this right. I just wish I could figure out what this all has to do with team building and brainstorming about taking Inandirmak to the next level.

They can watch, and they can lock me in here, but I've decided they can't make me be someone I'm not. I sit down on the floor in front of Sonja and smile at her while I speak. "In this room, Sonja, I want you to look at me at all times."

She lifts her head, and I can see that grin on her face, serene and accepting.

"I also don't like silence, so if you feel like making noise or saying a word or two, I won't punish you. Do you understand? You should verbally answer me now," I urge her, since this was a huge shock to Wynn when I required him to speak more.

"Yes, Master, this one understands, will try to be good pet," she says, and her voice is a bit rough, like it hasn't been used in a while. She bats her eyelashes and smiles a bit more.

She's still smiling at me when they come to collect her, even though I've spanked her soundly, vibrated a few orgasms from her, and required her to kneel a long time, giving me a foot rub after all of that.

If they want more of a Show from me, they can tell me directly. I head back to my room to take a hot shower.

Chapter Eighteen
To Please Master

Miss Wanda didn't want too much from me. A massage—she was thrilled i knew how to do that—and then for me to lie very still. i still feel like my skin is on fire from all the needles she put in me. Very scary. Didn't move, not so much 'cause of her order as 'cause of worry she'd really hurt me, and that would make Master very angry.

Old, old technique, she said, from when China was a unified country, not a series of associated city-states like it is today. She talked a lot, too, like Emalee often does. Keeping quiet makes me a good pet but also lets me learn more. Not that i told her that. The few words i did use to confirm i understood her instructions earned me a slap so hard my head rang for some time.

Needles had to be big to be seen through my fur, she told me. Different colors for different regions or reactions she wanted to create. Looked pretty after the putting-in pain. Then she touched them, and i lost control of my body completely. One moment screaming in intense pain, the next moaning in pleasure or sighing with gentling of my muscles.

Just lying there made me so exhausted that i'm stumbling a bit as the handler takes me back to Master's room. At least i got a shower, just like the ones during the Showing. Miss Wanda didn't even take her pleasure from me, so i wonder if i'll smell like anything now.

i'm pushed into Master's room, and i can hear the shower running, along with some music that doesn't have words. Not sure what the point of that is, but Emalee often plays such music when She's stressed or trying to work. Not good. i kneel on the floor at the foot of Her bed, paws on my thighs, thighs spread, head down slightly as Master prefers, even though it is with great effort i remain upright.

She's in there a long time before the water stops. i wait, but then the sound of a hair dryer reaches my ears. Maybe that means She had a good time with Her morph? A growl escapes my mouth, and i slump a bit, because it is a useless feeling to have.

i should be happy if Emalee had a good time. Good time means happy Master. Happy Master means She play with me. i roll onto one shoulder and wince from the ache.

Whatever She wants of me tonight, i'll smile and beg for more. Anything has to be better than last night.

The air sound stops, and i straighten up, bowing my head again but looking up as well to see Her come in. In a few moments She comes in, dressed in a robe but nothing else i can see. my shaft moves a bit, and i'm grateful i'm not too used to respond to Her as i should.

"You're back," She says, but Her tone is difficult to read, rather flat. She steps around me and circles me before disappearing out of my view. "Back in one piece, I hope," She comments, but it doesn't sound exactly like a question, so i think for a moment, my hands moving, but i grip my leg fur tightly to maintain position.

"Wynn back for Master," i simply say. She's there petting my head for a few seconds before moving away again. Good, i answered right. i'm so smart sometimes.

Turning my head i see Her getting into pajamas, not the ones i like best that are open on the bottom, her "nighties", but just pants and a shirt; this one leaves Her arms bare but covers Her breasts and stomach going down to Her legs. It's Her "time to get comfy" clothes, She calls them. So probably no play tonight, but probably not angry at me either. Maybe She brush my fur and let me brush Hers?

She comes to me and crouches down so She's at my level, which always makes me a bit nervous. "Look at me."

i look up and bat my lashes for a second or two, trying to be very good.

"You bathed already?" At my nod She smiles. "Hungry?"

Yes, i want to scream, now that She mentions it, i feel like i'm starving. Don't know why; i only lay there mostly. She's looking at me expecting an answer, a word answer, so i nod my head again and whisper, "Wynn hungry if Master hungry."

She sighs and rolls Her eyes, something She does when She is annoyed, getting angry, and i flinch back just a bit. "I'm not hungry yet, but you very well may be, so let me call the kitchen."

i watch Her stand up, wanting so much to wrap my arms around Her, beg Her not to send me off with someone else tomorrow. Instead i listen to Her call and then watch as She lies on the bed on Her back, letting Her head hang down over it, her long fur, darker than mine, hanging down to pool on the carpet. i heard Her and Her assistant, that man Lindsey, once talk about whether or not She should get it cut, something about water, but balanced by the uniqueness and that She only washes it every other day or so. i was so glad, because i love Master's head fur second best of all Her fur. My shaft lengthens a bit at the thought, so i turn my head back away from Her, suddenly worried She might not like to see that right now.

i hear a big sigh behind me but keep my position. "Wynn? Are you injured? Did something bad happen to you?" She then mutters something i can't fully make out before speaking again. "Come here, pet."

That's what i want to hear, and i'm at her side leaning against the bed, leaning into her caresses, watching her upside down face as quickly as my sore muscles let me. i try so hard, but sometimes She touches a sore point and i whimper or flinch again.

"What did you have to do? Wynn?" She tilts my face toward Her and looks at me with Her big eyes that are a lighter color than Her head fur and often hidden behind glasses when She's working. That's different, too, something Lindsey has also mentioned makes Her stand out in a good way. One of the whitecoats back at the Institute wore them as well, and the others sometimes teased him about them, but he said something about his eyes not being bad enough for the treatment. Emalee's eyes beautiful, not bad at all.

"Wynn, answer me. I won't be angry. I promise, but I want, no, I need to know if you are injured."

"Not injured…" i start to say, then stop to think about what that word means. No, it isn't the right word, 'cause i could do anything Master wanted, just might be sore at times, only a little bit really. "Not injured. Sore," i offer with a turn of my head so i can lick Her hand.

"Oh, right," She releases me and looks up at the ceiling. "I don't want those details," She says softly. In a moment She smiles and looks back at me. "I suppose that is to be expected. Sonja might be a bit sore, too."

i growl at the mention of another pet's name. i remember that one, a white fluffy thing, sort of like me but a dog with a smile. She was very bouncy the entire Showing until the third round, when the humans had the leopard morph boy do something very icky to her that made me turn away. i growl again, and Emalee makes a shushing noise that grabs my attention.

"Nothing to be jealous of, pet. She didn't mean anything to me. Just a tool to connect with my colleagues, really that's all it was." Another sigh, and She rolls over, pushing Her hair back with one hand and failing at getting it to stay back very well. "That sounded mean, didn't it?"

i just look at Her. Sounded like the ways things are to me. i don't think Miss Wanda felt anything about me, Wynn, that she wouldn't have felt about another morph. Maybe for her own she feel more, like i hope Master feel more for me.

Emalee sits up and moves Her hair out of Her face. "Fetch me a brush and a band, will you?"

That i can do, so i jump up with a gasp when a muscle hurts but go quickly to the table where She keeps these things for Her head fur. She put some clips and things in my fur a few times, and it just felt weird. i jerked around a bit at first because they were odd, then when She smiled and laughed in a good way i did it more to make Her happy.

i carry the items back and stand looking at Her. "Wynn brush Master's hair?" i use the word she likes better.

She nods, when there is a buzz at the door. "You get the food in, and I'll just pull it back. We'll have all the time we want for hair brushing later," She tells me as i lay the items on the bed in front of Her.

i open the door then kneel down by it. One time i stayed standing like Master wants at home, and the woman there yelled at me in a language i don't know, but it sounded very angry, so i kneel now around anyone else unless they tell me to stand up. It's a man today, and he rolls in a cart with two levels covered with bowls and containers. "Miss Potter?" he asks.

"Just set it all on the table. We'll nibble throughout the night."

i watch as he sits the human food in nicer bowls and containers on the top of the table that folds down from one wall. Then he places other bowls on a lower shelf that i can eat right from and be within petting distance of Master. This is the one thing i like best about coming to this place, and i'm trying to figure out how to ask Emalee for a table like this at Her house. i like eating from Her hands but can't do that with water very well and often just have food on bowl on floor. This up a bit higher and feels easier to eat well.

Master's head fur is now up in what She calls a ponytail, though i not see ponies or pony morphs with such things on the TV. She nods at me as the man leaves, and i shut the door behind him by crawling and pushing the door gently.

When i turn back She nods at the table, and i move toward it. Part of me says to wait until She is hungry, but part can smell the food, both what i can and cannot eat, and my tummy growls. At Her "Go on then," i move to the table and lift the lids off of two bowls, one of water and one of these meaty gray things that have a little spice to them. Also must find way to ask Emalee for these back home.

No play today, but Master brush me, hold, have me brush Her, and we eat, drink off and on. She never asks for details, and i don't offer or ask.

The rest of the week is much the same. Two days i go with Master and sit by Her side after the moving table lets other humans look at me, touch me, move me around and note things on a pad, they call them, just like Master has at home. i don't like it, but it doesn't hurt much, most of time not at all.

Then all us pets are ignored and just sit on the floor under the table, moving quickly out of the way of feet and legs while humans discuss and do things on a big table for most of two days. It is all very big words and sometimes yelling that Master's voice stops. She seems in charge of whatever they are doing, because She is so very smart and everyone likes Her lots.

After a meal on the big table, the humans leave, but Master always looks down at me by crouching and looking under the table. "Be good, Wynn; do as you're told. I'll see you in a while."

A bit after that i'm led to a room, and the Sharing starts over again with someone new.

Three times i'm taken to a room that looks like the last one i was in, but the human is different. i sort of remember them from Her big table and the moving table meetings, but those groups change after the Sharing night, and i never see these same people. Except for one—one is from the first group, what Emalee called her home team group. i never go to one of them, but i don't know why, 'cause no one tells me anything before i enter the room.

The second human to claim me in these little rooms sounds a bit like Emalee but more intense and loud, and not just because he's a man. He says he's Master Jason but tells me nothing else. He spends a lot of time measuring me, every part of me, even handling me until my shaft is hard and aching and measuring that, too.

When he takes out a black rope, i understand this will be another occasion for me to be very still. Emalee doesn't have ropes; i've looked in all Her shelves, boxes, and drawers while She's gone. She has these cuffs, but they are too big for me, and She hasn't used them yet. She could; what could i do about it? Don't want to do anything about it if Master is touching me, but my muscles tighten up a bit as Master Jason begins a simple tie-down. He grabs my muzzle and looks at me with a frown. "You need to relax, mate, or do you like it rough?"

i shake my head, lying, but then i decided after Anthony hurt me that i only want Emalee to be rough. Concentrating, i will my shoulders to ease downward, flex my fingers and toes, swallow a few times to try and calm myself. Soon i'll be helpless against him, even more than i already am, but i can try to control my insides right now before i feel overwhelmed again.

First he crisscrosses my arms behind my back and lays the rope over my chest and back to hold them in place. This is easy to do, because while we may be designed to crawl and resemble our stupid animal cousins, the whitecoats made us so that our limbs are flexible and can be moved in many ways by an owner.

Once he is done he moves me a bit and then puts a blindfold on me, chuckling when i huff and toss my head a few times, testing it, testing him. i hear a click and feel a flash of heat, then he's untying the rope but leaving the blindfold on.

He pushes me to the ground, pulls my legs out at an angle, and then uses only a few passes over my arms and chest to secure my torso. Then he wraps rope around my neck, and i freeze, my eyes darting to and fro in the darkness, until the rope is wrapped around my ankles then comes back up to my neck. He does this several times, and I'm bent over, barely able to move. i'm left alone, and there is another click and flash of heat before he unties me again.

He always ties my chest and arms in some fashion, but the lower half changes. Next he spreads my thighs but ties my ankles to them, lifting up my balls so they aren't crushed beneath my weight, fondling them just long enough for my shaft to stretch up before more clicking and heat.

i'm bent almost over backwards, with something that feels wooden and smooth between my legs and hands and a lot of the smooth rope, including one that seems to be holding me up by my chest, making it difficult to breathe. i am lucky he never leaves me long in any position and seems content to click and heat at me until the end.

The last position is like the one with my thighs spread and the one with just my arms behind my back. However, he adds more ropes, and i feel them pull on my legs and chest, then i feel the floor beneath me pull away until i'm floating. i tense, biting back my pleas because he never gave me permission to speak or make any noise. i fear spinning most of all. Handlers and whitecoats did something similar then spun me in circles until i vomited, then punished me for being dirty. Emalee does not play games like that, never makes me be bad then hurts me for it. Master Jason is not Emalee, so i'm glad some time has passed since i last ate.

There is a click and more heat, then the sound of a zipper. i feel myself lowered a bit, and then his hands are on my ass, caressing and kneading me. He pushes something inside of me covered with something wet and a bit chilly. Unlike the leopard boy, this human opens me up first, getting me wet, but never talking to me. When his flesh parts my cheeks, he feels as big as the one who hurt me, but it doesn't hurt, not down there, not at first.

my teeth are aching as i clench them against the force of his thrusting and the swinging of my body in the ropes. i gasp when something firm but flexible grasps my shaft, and then i realize he's stroking me. Emalee said to be good, so i hold it until he tells me to come when he rams into my body and stays still for a few moments.

i feel achy and a bit confused after he releases me and the handlers take me to the showers to clean up. i use the yucky soap inside to clean myself out in hopes Master will not be angry and smell the other human on me. She says to be good, but Her scent and body told me something else when i was taken from her tonight.

Emalee is out of the shower and has food waiting for me when i am taken back to Her room. She doesn't ask me what happened and only holds me in Her arms to sleep again.

Lady Lisa is how the next human introduces herself to me for the next Sharing two nights later. Her skin is darker than Emalee's, her eyes very brown, and her face wider, but she's very strong, something she demonstrates by picking me up by the scruff of my neck and plopping me face down on the bed. In a few moments she has my arms tied down in front and my legs tied together on the other side. i wait for a blindfold and more clicking and heat, but she only comes around to look at my face.

She states, "You may make all the noise you like," before getting out the equipment that i know is going to hurt me. At first i pray it is only a mind game—humans like to play those with us because they are so clever, but our songs tell us how to lock up part of ourselves in our heads, too, while we react to their games. She begins with her hands, just caressing, pushing my fur up the wrong way, then back down.

Then she begins to tap on me, every part of me, a relentless tapping of her fingers. Sometimes one at a time, sometimes a few, and sometimes all ten of her fingers making rhythms on my body. The tapping turns to thuds that build to enough force to earn some gasps and moans from me.

"There we go, a bit of music from you as well. Let's turn up the volume," she says as she moves away. i feel something dragging over my body next, then feel something falling lightly on it. Twisting my head i can see a rod with strands of leather in her hand, and i swallow because i know what comes next.

Emalee has such tools in Her house, but She hasn't used them on me yet. The rougher stuff is coming, She's told me this, and for a moment i feel very betrayed that my first time will be at another human's hands. Why isn't Master here doing this instead of Lady Lisa?

The flogging begins to build up, and once i'm gasping and groaning, she stops and changes to another tool. This is a hard flogger with only two strands, and it stings, but i think i have figured out the game. She'll move on when i react to it. i hold on, biting my tongue, thinking of Master, thinking of Her backyard, anything to keep my mouth closed and my mind distant. We have only a certain amount of time in these rooms for the Sharing, so if i can hold out long enough—

A particularly strong strike forces a scream from me. i whimper as she goes back to the tool case and selects another device, this one a long flexible rod. She begins slowly, but i can feel the welts under my fur, rising up on my flesh, making me feel puffy and hot at the same time.

i can't hold out when she strikes my feet and i beg her to stop.

That was an error i won't repeat, because she lays into me viciously with the rod until i've screamed and cried myself hoarse.

The handlers have to carry me and wash me up, then let me crawl back to Master's room. Emalee asks them some questions as i lie at Her feet, then she dismisses them and picks me up to help me walk to Her bed. She leaves and comes back soon with a bucket and washcloth. She lays very cold water on the bottom of my feet, confirming that the handlers gave me a shot for the swelling.

Master cuddles with me, careful of my sore body, whispering She's sorry in my ear. i turn my head and smile at Her before licking Her nose with my tongue once. That always makes Her chuckle, but now She just looks at me sadly. "Wynn want to please Master by be good pet for others. Master, Wynn try so hard to be good pet," i say to Her.

Her voice shakes, and She pulls me close. i swallow down the pain this causes and just melt into Her body. "You are being a very good pet. I'm being a very bad master," She says softly as She strokes my head fur with one hand.

The last man i'm Shared with just looks down at me for some time after i'm delivered to his room. He is darker skinned yet with some fur around his mouth and more on his arms and legs. i wonder if he has morph ancestors, then decide that is stupid, and i'm not a stupid animal, so i make myself stop thinking like that. Humans are humans, and morphs are morphs; we cannot breed, so there can be no morph blood in humans.

Finally after what seems like a very long time he crouches down like Master does and smiles at me with big brilliant teeth. "You are allowed only four words in here, little furry friend. Please, more, and Sir Samuel. Do you understand?"

i nod my head and swallow. i won't make another error like i did in the last room.

He's strong too, and he has to move me around a lot as the time passes. Foxmorphs are horny—i heard whitecoats, handlers, even Master say this—but we have our limits.

His cock is big, almost too big for my mouth, but our jaws, like our limbs, are designed to be used by humans as they wish, so i just adjust and keep my feelings damped down as much as i can.

He takes me from the front, back and even side, with some bending over and even being hung up, but not as comfortably as Master Jason did. He never hits me, never flogs me or strikes me, never makes clicks or heats me up beyond the motion of his body into and against mine. His cock feels so big, and yet after a few positions it also feels so good, so much that i feel embarrassed that i'm reacting to him like i should react to Master. i haven't reacted to the other humans in ways i had to pretend with the morphs, and i feel ashamed. my own shaft starts to wilt. He never touches my shaft, and i don't dare, so i'm glad my mixed feelings are keeping my horniness under control.

He takes a few pills at one point—the only time i get a break—and offers me one but takes it away when i shake my head. He comes only twice in all this sex, and i wonder where he gets the ability to keep going and going. Our songs say that human males have short drives that rebuild during the day, so while they may use us often it is not for long, unlike human females, who can spend hours but only a few days a week. Emalee seems to want me often when Her job is not with Her and the time isn't short, though not long enough for me.

i'm thinking about Master as Sir Samuel pulls out of me, flips me over and onto my knees on the floor. i'm blinking and wondering what is happening when he comes over my face. He snarls at me and spits down at me before stalking into the bathroom. i'm still kneeling there frozen when the handlers come and take me to the showers.

i scrub and scrub, and clean out my ass many times until the handler tells me i have to stop. i feel so dirty, so worried, so confused when they walk me back to Emalee's room. i'm only walking a bit stiffly, so i can hide it from Master by kneeling and crawling to Her.

She doesn't ask again but only motions me onto the bed where

She begins to brush my fur and hum to me some song She plays at Her house. When i start to hum along She laughs, then pulls me into a hug. "We're almost done. No more Sharing," She tells me.

At least i got time between the last Sharing and now, but i had to spend it with the other morphs, either under the big table or silently watching from an area not far away. i felt my tummy clench and a growl rise up in my throat when the other humans at the big tables came and took their morphs away for a while. Emalee never took me away, only came over to pet me or called me to Her for food. Our songs say that we should hold ourselves back, keep a divide up between us and humans, or our hearts will break. Why is this so hard to do with Master?

She's left now to see Her boss. She's not happy. She's not angry at me, i think. Yet She left me here with the luggage waiting to be back on the plane. i wonder if i'll stay with them or be allowed at Her feet again.

Chapter Nineteen
Financial Servitude

Madame Reizis bids me sit down when I visit her office. We have to catch a flight in four hours, and I desperately want to be out of here as soon as possible, but I keep my face relaxed and smile at her, thanking her for her hospitality. She smiles and then tells her assistant to leave. Her assistants must be her children or grandchildren; they all look so much alike.

"Emily Potter," she says my name with a very regal tone, and I feel myself shudder just a bit. I've read about royalty in history classes and seen the dramas and comedies featuring them, but this is the closest I've ever come to a modern queen.

"Your work has been refreshing. Far too often once we achieve some level of success we allow ourselves to become closed off to the words and wisdom of those under our authority. I've watched the tapes of your team exercises here at headquarters and, of course, from MTB. Your leadership skills are perfect for our type of service."

"Thank you, Ma'am," I begin to say, but she shakes her head, so I fall silent.

She pushes a few buttons, and a double-sided screen rises up from her desk to face both of us. I feel the blood drain from my face as I see a close-up of myself watching Wynn's first time in the arena for the Showing. My face is white, perhaps paler than it must be now, and my eyes wide, with tears at the corners, my lips trembling, until Margaret leans in and whispers into my ear.

"You don't look like you enjoyed yourself," Madame Reizis says and pushes another button. This time I'm on the screen in my room, crying into the sink in the bathroom after the second Sharing when I took a break from comforting Wynn.

I stand up on shaky legs. "You had no right to tape there," I start to protest, but Madame Reizis freezes me with her cold glare.

"Don't I? Don't we? Aren't we all part of the Inandirmak family? Should we have secrets from each other?"

She pushes another button, and I see Lindsey and me going at it like bunnies in my corner office. I sit down slowly as she hums and nods. "This is wonderful. Just what first executive assistants should be used for by all of us. I can tell by your faces that this isn't just a job perk for either of you. He might make a good executive spouse."

I just stare, hardly believing what I'm seeing. Do they have cameras in the house? I always think of it as my house, but it isn't really mine; it's part of the promotion, so they could have cameras anywhere.

"I know you did enjoy yourself a bit with the Sharing," Madame Reizis tells me as she shows a succession of clips of me with each of the four morphs I used. "A bit repetitive, though, given your past history."

My mouth falls open as the screens now show a clip of me in one of the clubs near campus where I used to go with different boyfriends and girlfriends because our dorms could hardly hold the bondage equipment or block the sounds they loved to make under my hands.

"When you interviewed, we started watching you. Standard procedure for all companies, I assure you," she tells me.

I do not feel assured.

"Every organization has its skeletons, its corporate culture, its family peculiarities. Our recruiter could see that you would fit in nicely with us. Yet you were very uncomfortable here. Why is that, Emily?"

How dare she use that tone of voice? That's the same cadence that my mother would use as she tried to comfort me and help me think of the best choices without telling me what to do in a direct fashion. I hated it from my mother, so I certainly hate it from this woman who confirms my weekly credits. I damp my anger down and think before speaking.

"I'm possessive, Madame Reizis. I don't like sharing."

She smiles and shakes her head. "But that's so childish, isn't it? I mean, you aren't a child, are you, Emily? We can't have children working for us, that's against global statutes."

I feel my heart start to pound in my chest. She just threatened my job. Without a job one has nothing, is nothing. I react out of immediate fear. "No, no, I'm not a child. I understand we're all part of one team, one family," I add, trying to soothe her.

She smiles, but her eyes remain cold. "Excellent. I'm glad we understand each other, Emily. I would hate to lose our future President of Administration to such an outdated concept as jealousy."

"Future?" I repeat that one word in shock. Did she just go from threatening me to promising me something?

"Of course," she says as her eyes take on a twinkle and she leans back. "You aren't the first to react this way. I myself had moments of jealousy when I was young. We get over it if we have the potential to sit at the big table and help take Inandirmak into the twenty-third century and beyond. We don't achieve our full potential by keeping things solely in the blood, shall we say."

My head is spinning, and my heart can't decide if it should speed up or calm down. This woman is good at keeping me off-balance, something I hate, and yet her offer is intriguing. No one, no one in the entire history of my family, has ever risen above my level in any corporation or metro, even when those were focused almost exclusively on their employment.

"Sitting at the big table," she continues, "means more responsibilities, but also more perks, like a better house, more morphs, a spouse, even more travel, and I know your parents are back in Europe, yes?"

"Yes," I repeat in a daze.

"I believe you need to go catch your plane, then, so you can see your Father, is it?"

When I nod she stands up, as do I. She holds out a chipdrive to me, and I take it. "This is a copy of the Showing and the Sharing with your pet. Remember, family protects itself; we all have a stake in this," she adds as she rests her other hand on mine before letting the chipdrive and me go.

Wynn is waiting for me with the luggage, but I make him sit on the floor, his head in my lap, on the drive to the airport. I hold him during the jaunt to Lausanne, where my father is waiting in full uniform to pick us up.

"What's wrong?" my father asks me, and Wynn looks up at me from his place at my feet. Neither of us had said anything that wasn't required since leaving headquarters.

"Is your house safe?" I ask my father. When he frowns at me, arching one eyebrow, and I just stare at him and repeat my question, I can see the light of understanding go on in his eyes.

"It is indeed," he simply says, then launches into a list of various sightseeing activities he wants us to check out around Lac Léman when he must report to patrol duty.

Wynn looks up at me from where I've had him lay his head on my lap. My father hasn't spoken to or even really looked at my pet yet. My mother would have disdained to notice him, insulting him in some fashion by now I'm sure, but I expected my father... I don't know what I expected. I sigh as I pet Wynn's head.

"You must be tired," my father says. "We'll get you settled, and you and your pet can relax after your business holiday. Doesn't look like it was really much of a holiday, from the stress in your face," he adds, reaching over and patting Wynn, then looking at me sharply before laughing. "Your lap's full, so I'll just have to be all emotional about it and say I'm glad you're home."

My father should have been a doctor or a therapist instead of in the military. He picks up on little things and knows exactly how to get me to smile, which I do as I reply, "I'm glad to be home, Dad."

My father's house is at the end of a block of condos in the Guard off-base area of Lausanne nearest the lake. He gave me a tour of the base once, where the major equipment, maintenance buildings, clinic, and supplies are kept, but most of the Guard stay in these condo camp stations at ten points around the lake to protect it from water bandits and pollution, as well as misuse by those allowed on the banks. Father told me that they used to allow both boats and swimmers, but now it's too risky to allow any potential pollutants in. Even fishing is restricted and controlled, though you can picnic on the beaches and visit all the farms and areas around it.

Compared to my house, my father's is a bit smaller, and built vertically. The building looks old, like it's simply been maintained over the decades. I stop when Wynn does and smile as he stares at the line of doors. "I think Wynn believes the entire building is your house, Dad. Looks so much bigger than my place."

My father chuckles, then puts down one suitcase and looks directly at Wynn, who kneels down and holds my legs, turning his face away. "That true? You think I'm some city manager to own all of this?"

"You can talk to my Dad, Wynn. He won't hurt you," I say, patting his head.

"Wynn don't know, sir," my pet replies, then ducks his head back down.

"Aye, that you don't," my father says as he stands up. "So let's go see my fine mansion."

"Dad," I say as we follow him inside his door.

"I'll add your signature to the locks there, so you can come and go when I'm on duty. I picked up a packet about morph pet laws for the area for you, so you can figure it all out," he adds, motioning to a pamphlet on the table not far from the front door. He takes us up two flights of stairs to the top floor, which has a bathroom, a bedroom with a small balcony, and a storage area.

After setting our luggage down he gives us the brief tour. The second floor is his bedroom, bathroom, and his home office. The ground floor is the living space and dining room all in one, with a kitchen and a back deck that leads to the communal garden. The basement has his years of military souvenirs as well as two bikes and an inflatable raft, "just in case," he always says.

Wynn looks at everything but touches nothing, watching my father but saying nothing further. He's been increasingly shy—no, let me be honest with myself at least—afraid. He's been increasingly afraid since the Sharing began. Just thinking about it makes my head throb.

Of course, my father notices, and he suggests we sit on the couch while he makes a late lunch or early dinner, whatever we want to call it, before he has to get to the watch tower to start his rounds.

"You have to go in today, even?"

"Yup, unfortunately we had an incident this past weekend, so we've increased patrols. I can understand poor families, but what would the world be like if we all took water whenever we felt like it? All of us would be thirsty, dying even; that's what it would be like," he begins his normal lecture on how rules are an important aspect of any civilization.

I feel like that's just been ground into me repeatedly in Egirdir, so I change the subject, asking him about other morphs he may have seen around the area. He tells me that there aren't many in this part of the city. He could get one given his last promotion but is waiting to see what exactly they do and what they need, because he's gone a good part of the day and sometimes evenings.

"They can be demanding of attention," I comment and then turn my eyes in surprise as Wynn make a huffing noise and turns his head away from me while lying on my lap. I look back at my father and roll my eyes to emphasize my point.

"Yeah, and it never worked for your mother, so I doubt it would work well for a pet."

"Actually Wynn is very clever," I say, which gets him to look back at me again, "and I suspect many other breeds are as well. He's been learning to help out with some household chores for me. I imagine you could teach a morph to help out a bit."

"Hadn't thought of that," my father admits as he flips something in the frying pan. "Just something light here for us. You can make whatever you fancy if you have a mind to," he tells me, and I know a not-too-subtle hint to help out around the house when I hear it.

"I'll take a survey, then, while you're out, then check out the nearby shops. Is the Isler shop still here?"

"Yes, and she was asking about you the other day, so she was thrilled when I told her you were coming for a visit. The Wirths were also asking about you."

"I'll be sure to visit with everyone, then." My father has been stationed in Lausanne for many years, and the city made a decision decades ago to limit company size, so that many small shops and family corps are still around. Not many folks take vacations, but those that do want to see a bit of old world charm when they travel—forget about the modern conveniences hidden underneath it all—pretending to live in an idyllic past that probably never existed.

I've never understood that desire, because I'd rather live with the truth than the lie any day. Except maybe today or this week. I make a decision as I lean over and kiss the top of Wynn's head, making him yip up at me and wag his tail. I'm going to go back and pretend I haven't learned so much so I can relax.

It's so nice to just get away for a while. No phone calls, no pressing deadlines, no cameras watching my every move that I know about. I'm getting our third picnic basket from Ms. Isler when I see someone approach Wynn, whom I've had to leave outside, leashed to the bicycle rack. Why have the laws if you don't have the facilities, but I don't want to get my father or us into trouble, so he's had to stay outdoors when I'm shopping.

There is a young woman talking to Wynn, bending down, since it looks like he's back as far as his leash allows toward the shop. His ears are down, his tail flat, and I tune out what the shopkeeper is saying and start toward the door when the woman outside takes his hand and places something in it. Then she simply leaves, and Wynn looks down at his hand before going back to curl up on the sidewalk near the bike rack.

"Do you have security cameras?" I ask Ms. Isler, who blinks at me. "I'm so sorry. I saw this person outside talking to Wynn and... that just isn't done where we're from."

Ms. Isler blinks again, then calls over her assistant to watch the front counter. I follow her back to her office, throwing one look out at Wynn before entering the windowless room. After a few minutes she pulls up the front camera, and we watch this young woman approach Wynn. At first he ignores her, then when she reaches out to him he scrambles to his feet and hops backwards as quickly as he can before hunching down and staring at her.

"Oh, I've seen her around here before. Seems like a nice girl, the Kaelin girl, I can't remember her name," Ms. Isler tells me when she pauses the camera. "Mostly a good girl, though she moved out to that commune a few years ago. Not that they do anything, but still, very odd when we've kept this part of Lausanne so nice."

We watch her say something else, and whatever it is seems to make Wynn relax and hold out his hand. She places something in it, tells him something else with a laugh, and then leaves. "What could she have possibly given him?"

"Probably a flier," Ms. Isler replies, though my question wasn't expecting an answer.

"A flier?"

"Ja, they always having events out there, art things, performances. Some folks go, but I say we have enough here, and if we don't support the city then soon the companies will move in. Not that I'm saying all are bad, mind you," she adds quickly, likely worried I'll take my business elsewhere since I work for a company, one far worse than she might imagine. "We need a balance of power, or, well, we still paying, yes?"

"Yes," I say out of habit. Criticisms of the past are rarely discussed in public; we merely accept that things are better and that we've fixed the conflicts of the past. Out of necessity or not, we pretend it is because we are wiser than our ancestors.

"Thank you, Ms. Isler," I say as we both stand up and head back into the main shop. A quick glance confirms Wynn is still there waiting for me. I pay for our picnic and arrange for a cake to be delivered tomorrow evening for a little party with my father before we leave.

Wynn doesn't show me the flier until we have eaten some of our picnic and are watching the birds come pick up the crumbs we've tossed out. "Master?" he says to me in a soft voice that draws my attention. "Woman give Wynn something for you. This pet sorry he mess it up," he adds, unfolding it and laying it on the blanket.

He has messed it up; it's dirty and torn in a few places, but I can still read it. In five languages it says that they have a morph retreat for loving owners and their pets called Monroe Village, a very un-Swiss name. It would only be a good thirty-minute ride from here—I see that it's a bit more than that when I call up my GPS and note that it is further into the mountains along a bike trail. Wynn is watching me, and I read the flier to him, but he just wrinkles up his nose and eyes with a little sniff.

I wait a few seconds before asking the question that's been threatening to burst out of my brain since I saw the scene through the window. "Why did you let that woman give you something?"

Wynn immediately bends down, his head low and his ears and tail down, and he whimpers.

"I'm not angry. I'm just curious. I want to know. This isn't a bad thing," I try to reassure him.

After a few more whimpers he looks directly at me and licks his tongue out cutely. "Woman say Wynn smart pet, Master must like smart pet, this is something special for such owners and pets that she would want to know about. Wynn do wrong?"

Smart pets? I was about to dismiss this as a tourist scam, but Wynn is quite clever, and the more I've interacted with the morphs, the more I think it isn't just a trait that ISM routinely breeds. At least one of the others I... shared... was from ISM, too, and he wasn't a quarter as clever as Wynn. I pet him to reassure him more and make up my mind. "Let's go check them out; the exercise will do me good."

It is a bit of an adventure, it turns out, to find this retreat; the roads are small and clearly not maintained by the city. When we do, it looks very much like a traditional Swiss village until I notice all the solar panels, as well as the windmills and generators attached to every building. The GPS guide says there is a fairly large body of fresh water in the immediate area, but I don't see it with my eyes. Of course, any community worth a drop of water would hide such a resource as well as guard it. Visitors need not see what the citizens are willing to protect.

The place is much bigger than I imagined; shops and

apartments line the streets. The signage is in German, Swiss, and English, so I can find our way around easily. I don't know what I'm expecting in terms of smart pets and their owners until I stop at one point as a woman and her female canine morph walk across the street, both of them upright and walking, the morph not cowering at all. I hear Wynn make a noise from his pet wagon, which I'm pulling behind me on the bike. He's shocked too, but what little we've seen so far and our reactions spur me to go to the welcome center listed on about every third sign I see.

The man there is very happy to see us, standing when we enter the main room of the tiny welcome center. "Welcome to Monroe Village; I'm Lukas," he says and offers Wynn his hand after I shake his. Wynn just shrinks back behind my legs and looks up at me with wide eyes. Lukas just smiles softly and motions for a morph that is sitting in the corner to come to him. The creature stands and walks over; it has white fur like Wynn's, nearly black eyes, and long ears and facial features that make me think "bunny." I think it is male, though there is no obvious penis to identify it. Maybe the receptionist didn't have the surgery I was told was necessary, and that makes me frown for just a moment until Lukas introduces us. "This is Addis, my pet." Addis is shorter than Wynn by a good half foot, but he stands tall and smiles at me with a dip of his head, his ears twitching a bit. "What brings you to Monroe Village?" Lukas asks, and I can sense a hint of more than mere curiosity behind the question.

I take the flyer out of my pocket and hand it to him. "A woman stopped and gave this to my pet, Wynn, when I was shopping."

As though on cue, the woman I saw with Wynn joins us, a soft brown catlike morph following at her heels, this one female from the gentle rise to her chest. "That would be me," the woman announces, holding out her hand. "I'm Catria, and I hope I didn't offend you by talking to him. He seemed so aware of his surroundings, so very smart, that I thought you might be interested in our little community. This is Etta, my pet," she says, introducing us, and I can feel Wynn tighten his grip on my legs and his head turn to look at the two humans and their morphs before us.

"Oh, no, no offense," I reply with a forced chuckle. "I'm always interested in checking out unique communities." That isn't completely a lie, but to be blunt, unless I've had to go there for business or family, I tend to stay in the city, where I know there is protection as well as water.

"It's a slow day, so why don't we give you a tour?" Lukas suggests, and I agree, because I had little else planned. I'm not a fool; I know how tours should go. We show our visitors—our potential customers—the best, sidestepping any negatives and steering them toward those areas we maintain for such display.

These people are insane. No one has taught them the basics of advertising their community, I soon realize as we literally walk the entire village, including a quick peek at their water supply, hidden back in the mountains and guarded in a fashion that would make my father proud. "The goal of Monroe Village is to allow the individual full freedom to become the best person she or he can be. Granted, we need certain guidelines to guard our water and to protect our persons and our property, but ultimately a community thrives when we feel like one big family," Lukas tells me as we pause at the fence that blocks the cavern.

We visit every shop, and Catria notices me as I check out the corners and ceilings of every building and room. "We have few cameras installed in the village. While that all-seeing eye may be necessary in the cities, and corporations want to guide their employees' every step, we prefer to rely on each other for support," she tells me. It all sounds like well-rehearsed lines that could be good for business if they were only better written.

Wynn walks, because the other pets are walking; in fact, so is every morph we see, except for one in a wheelchair pushed by an older woman. I don't even notice that Wynn is holding my hand and walking with me until Lukas chuckles, lifts his own pet's paw, and kisses the back of it. "You're both comfortable with his walking. See, I knew Catria had found fellow spirits. She always does."

I look at Wynn, who begins to kneel again until I shake my head. "I just find it more convenient," I offer, but both of our hosts only smile and continue their tour.

They tell us all their secrets: that their community allows morphs unprecedented freedoms and even a voice on the community council. The one thing I haven't heard, though, is any morphs speaking, not like Wynn can. Oh, there are a few "yes"es and "please"es, but no titles for humans, and certainly nothing like a sentence. I wonder how they have a voice in the council if they don't talk. Maybe they aren't as crazy as I fear and they all know to keep that subversion private. All in all, it's like some sort of fantasy novel or fairytale. "This is all quite lovely, very idyllic, but I'm surprised that Lausanne allows you all such freedoms."

"We're... privately supported, you might say," Lukas replies, watching his colleague carefully.

"I think you might be interested in meeting James," Catria says, and they take me to the biggest house in town, right at the edge nearest the water caves.

Individual landowners are almost unheard of except among the most wealthy, whom I've only seen on TV shows about their vast property and unparalleled freedom from laws—at the cost of having no voice in governing matters outside of their estates. The Reizis family may own Inandirmak, but they don't own land or water, and this place has its own water supply, power grid and everything. Mr. James Monroe is much younger than one would expect given those TV shows, perhaps in his late 40s. He shakes my hand and insists on shaking Wynn's but doesn't react negatively when my pet then hides behind my legs, on the floor by the chair I'm seated in. He tells us that his father's father acquired this land right before the Grand Consolidation, right after the Zombie Wars, when things were in chaos and Lausanne needed funds to rebuild.

"My grandfather was a forward thinker, Ms. Potter," he says with pride. "He owned a first-generation morph, and he felt that she had greater potential to be a true companion and not merely a pet or a toy. Let's face it—science and business, they tend to get so focused on advancement and profit that they don't fully think things through. Every generation of morphs is a bit smarter, a bit more human, and the majority of humans are not going to like that one bit. So we are here to protect what God gave us the intelligence to create. We are looking for like-minded people to help us further our love for all of this world's creatures." He continues on and on, sounding more and more like a cult leader to me, so I start tuning it all out until he asks us to stay for the night.

"I'm staying with my father, a Guardsman, rather high up," I drop that fact in the hopes that they won't do something aggressive. "We're spending most of the afternoon and evening with him before heading home."

"Metro Thunder Bay, correct?" Mr. Monroe says, and my blood freezes. I can't say anything, though my eyes are darting around, wondering whether I could overpower three people to escape, and if not, whether Wynn could run out, find my father, and let him know. My thoughts are interrupted when Wynn touches my hand with his cold, wet nose. "The storm, you haven't heard about it," Mr. Monroe tells me in a tone that suggests he has said it a few times.

"I don't know what you're talking about, but we need to leave now," I state as forcefully as I can manage.

I hear Wynn growl and find him between me and Lukas. "He's loyal; that must mean you treat him well," Mr. Monroe says.

"Of course I do. What kind of fool do you take me for?"

"Not a fool at all, Ms. Potter, not a fool at all. In fact, I hope you will contact me in the future, because I think you could be a valuable asset to our community, and I know we could offer you what you are looking for," Mr. Monroe says before telling his people to take us back to the bike and let us go home.

Catria insists I take a book with me about their commune, and I accept, tossing it into Wynn's wagon before biking back into the City as hard as I can.

Once we are safely at my father's condo I look at my messages and the news. A storm has developed over the North Atlantic, blocking all cross-ocean travel for at least 72 hours. Inandirmak says I am welcome to come to their Lausanne headquarters if I need to check in at all, but please just enjoy my extended vacation without penalty.

Penalty? I'm caught between a company that watches my every move and demands my obedience to their sick desires and a cult that offers us an escape from the restraints of society in exchange for all my worldly possessions, money, and loyalty—I just know it. This is some vacation.

My father isn't concerned about our staying; in fact, when I tell him about the storm that evening, he says he is coming up on a bit of a break himself, since he's picked up so many tours lately. He'll be able to spend time with me, and I'm so happy that I cry, or that's what I let him believe. Surely no one, neither Inandirmak nor some cult, would risk coming to harm us if a Guardsman is with us all the time.

Spending time with my father is wonderful. Unlike my mother, while he wasn't thrilled that I went the company route, he didn't nag me about it either. We go on more picnics, see a concert, wander through a museum that lets me bring Wynn inside, and cook together. I even catch my father and Wynn asleep together on the couch where they were watching the TV when I get a call from Lindsey, just checking in to make sure things are going all right and letting me know that the teams are functioning fine.

Sneaking back upstairs, I start packing for our afternoon flight the next day. The storm will last about ten hours longer, but they've gotten so good at predicting these things that it hardly seems frightening anymore. No, I'm more frightened about using the device my father gave me and discovering that my company is spying on me in my own home as well.

That's when I see the book from the commune again. The people and morphs all look so happy on the cover, and their motto, "One Community for Us All," seems so sincere that I open it up and begin to read.

Wynn finds me as I'm on the telephone with Mr. Monroe a few hours later. "I can bring him tomorrow. Are you sure that my visiting will be fine? I can't really leave him with my parents; it might harm their own positions." I smile at my pet, excited to tell him my decision. "I'm sure it won't be a problem. Tomorrow morning, then, before my flight."

Wynn is looking at the book on the bed where I left it. I sit down next to it and smile at him. "You liked that place, right?"

He backs up a step and shakes his head.

"What do you mean, I saw you looking at everything."

"They scare Master, Wynn no like that," he says in a halting voice and takes another step back.

"That's because I wasn't ready; I hadn't considered that there might be others like me, you know, who want more functioning pets. I can't stay, but you can, and I'd come visit."

He blinks at me and takes another step back. "Emalee leave Wynn?"

"I'd come visit; you'd be with others who aren't afraid to show how clever they are. I could just say you were a distraction, that I needed to keep you somewhere, or maybe, no...." I realize I haven't thought this through at all, and I must sound like a babbling idiot. I'm just so enamored by the idea of having a place I could get away from all the cameras and company eyes that I'm not noticing how upset Wynn is becoming.

"Maybe we can just visit with them; we can buy a little place there, come back and forth; I can visit my father, too; it won't be a lie. After the company meeting, we could certainly use it."

I vaguely hear him object again, and I nod my head. "You're right; it's too far away. You know," I say, grabbing the book again and flipping through it, "they mention that they are better than other similar communes, so I bet I could find one closer; then you could stay there and I could visit more often. I bet I could spin it so Inandirmak wouldn't think twice about it—"

I stop dead in my words and look at Wynn. He's right up next to me, looking up into my face. He swallows and shakes himself, then backs up, so I grab his arms. "What did you just say to me?"

He shakes his head, so I tighten my grip. "Wynn not want to leave Master," he offers, but that isn't what interrupted my babbling.

"No, no, you didn't say that; you said something else. Something I've never heard you say before, never heard any morph say before."

He's shaking his head and muttering, "Wynn sorry, be better pet, be best pet, please Master."

"Stop it!" We both freeze as my father's voice comes from outside the door.

"Everything is fine, Dad, just a small discipline problem," I call.

I wait until I hear his footsteps go all the way down to the ground floor, and then I lower my voice to a hiss. "Now you stop lying to me and you repeat what you said before, or so help me God, I will discipline you."

I don't think I've ever threatened him before—punished him for small infractions, yes, but I can feel my heart ready to pound out of my chest. I have to be sure he said what I think I heard him say. "Tell me," I order, bringing him close to my face, his blue eyes tearing up, his mouth trembling.

"I don't want to leave you," he whispers.

I let him go and just sit down on the floor. He crawls onto my lap and keeps repeating that phrase over and over as I stroke him. I've just found out that I've got a much bigger problem than I thought I had.

Morphs aren't supposed to read, talk, or even think like us. Clearly Wynn thinks a lot more like me than I realized. I tease him about being selfish about sex, especially at the beginning, but he's worked hard on that. I thought it was biological, something the genetic manipulation couldn't or didn't want to sort out. If it was biology, he couldn't overcome that.

On TV, in the book, and even at the commune, none of the morphs use personal pronouns. No one whispers "I" or "me" or "my." Everything is "pet" this or "girl" that or insert-name-here. Objectification: they objectify themselves, just as we do to them.

Except he doesn't, does he?

We get looks when we go shopping and I make him push the cart. We get stares when I tell folks he helps me out around the house. Margaret warned me several times in Egirdir to make sure I kept his odd habits under control, because not everyone would share my fetishes.

This isn't my fetish.

I look at him, lift his face up, and make him look at me. "I don't want to leave you," he says again.

This is him.

Chapter Twenty
Guarding The Hearth

i am so confused. Master was so angry when i said what i was thinking without more thinking to talk like the white coats want us to, like the humans want us to. After the weird, scary ideas She was talking really fast about at Her father's home, She told me to keep on talking like i always had, 'cause it wasn't safe to use words like "me," "I, " or "my"—i already knew that, but it seemed important to Her, so i promised i'd stop.

She took this little box thing out when we got home and went all over Her house many times. Then She sat down and did that frustrated stuff of rubbing Her hands over Her face and head. She told me it was fine if i wanted to talk like i do in my head here at home if no one else was around. So i tried to do that more—difficult when for most of my life i have to watch it so carefully.

She got angry though, when, i called Her Emalee once. New rule: i can use forbidden words to talk about myself, but not about Master. i need to work harder on never using Her name in my head. Such a pretty name, though; sounds like music when i hear it out loud.

Master starts asking me weird questions, holding out Her pad to me, pointing to things on the TV, asking if i can read them. i shake my head, and that seems to relieve Her, but She keeps asking. i think she thinks i'm lying. i don't lie to Master, not if i can help it. She is too powerful; She got me to talk this way, didn't She? She'd see my lies for sure, so i don't tell real lies, only sometimes don't say everything in my head or body.

Like now. She's put my hands over my head, attached them with cuffs to a place in the ceiling, and she's been using more of Her toys on me. She leans in, Her scent heightened by Her working on me with these toys, and asks, "Are you OK, Wynn? Can you take more?"

"Yes, Master, more, more," i say when i really just want Her to toss me on Her bed and fuck me hard. Before i would have whimpered and whined, rubbed my body against Hers, knowing it wasn't safe to say what i wanted. Now She says it is, but i'm not a stupid animal; i know She is owner, and owners must be pleased, or more bad things like at that company place will happen.

She steps back, and soon Her flogging is hitting my butt, thighs and upper back again. i can feel my shaft leaking from need, but i just moan and brace for each blow. She has a pattern i'm starting to understand from our playtime and watching in the mirror She always sets up in front of me. Starts slow, just Her hands, then softer toys, then harder, faster toys. She takes breaks between each one to ask me how i feel, what i can take. i can smell Her arousal, and i try to last until Her scent starts to overwhelm me.

If i can last that long, Master will take me hard, and for a long time, using other fun toys and telling me how to pleasure Her. She smells more real then; She seems most happy afterwards. She says She wants to know how i feel, what i think, but i can think, i can remember, humans like us best when we are pleasing them first. i won't be selfish anymore, and then She will not send me to another place and just visit. If i'm very good, maybe She won't take me back for more Showing and Sharing. Give Her what She wants as often as She lets me, and i can keep Her from talking about that trip.

Lindsey is no help at all. He is always talking to Her about the trip, about the company, about "moving up," as they call it. i don't know what that is, but i like it here where i can watch Her back yard, play with Her to distract Her, and do more things in the house to get more play time.

i lean back into Her arms as She stops the flogging and presses close to me. "You are so pretty," She whispers, forcing my head back with a hand when i turn away from the mirror.

my fur is matted down, the longer fur on my head is hanging in my face, my paws are clenching the chains the cuffs are attached to, and i'm poised carefully on my legs. i don't see it, but i nod and moan as She strokes a hand down my chest to grasp my shaft. Her smell is right, so i lick my lips and plead, "Master, i'm so hard for you, so horny."

She smiles and holds me against Her with one arm as She releases the cuffs with the other but leaves them on my wrists. She likes to put things on me now, around my wrists, my ankles, my throat, but no more clothes. Those always felt so weird to wear, but these feel good.

i've put on some weight since we got back home, something She says that She likes, but i miss Her carrying me or lifting me as easily. i refused to eat once, and She got angry and shook me until i told Her why, then just held me, saying that She'd just need to work out more. She works too much. Right now She guides me to Her bed, which i sometimes think of as our bed, though i'm not brave enough to say that out loud yet. She only seems to get angry at me when i don't say what i'm thinking or feeling and She's asked. Never asked about what i call bed in my head, so i say nothing.

She lays me on my front, on the edge, my feet and legs hanging down, so i raise my ass up a bit, knowing what is coming. Sometimes i'm on my front and She swallows me whole, but my shaft is clearly ready tonight, and i prefer Her inside instead of around me. Every now and again She says She'll ride me sometime, but i'm not sure what that means, and all the TV shows with morphs and humans only use that word when the morph is on top doing more of the work for a tired master. i could do that, though not right now, since i'm still floating.

Master is kind and always prepares me with one, then two fingers, slicking me up, though i recall white coats saying several times it wasn't necessary like with a human. i growl and lift up more, pushing back. "Horny indeed," Master says and adds a soft smack to my already hot ass.

She continues to play with me this way, making me moan when She withdraws the second finger. i know what She wants to hear, but i keep holding back, my head racing with a lot of songs, rules, and images until She takes that finger away and steps back.

She is so mean at times.

i look back and whimper, wiggling my butt, "Please," i beg. She just smiles, and i swallow before the words spill out in a rush, "i want you to fuck me, Master." It feels so bad and so good to say the words out loud.

Mostly good, 'cause in a moment She parts Her robe and shows the leather clothing underneath that She'll put the toy into. i turn my head and watch, licking my lips as She takes it from the drawer and fastens it on low, right in front of the area She loves me to stroke Her best. She turns it to a new angle, and i moan. A few times She has said that human men aren't as easily pleased this way; they have a spot that needs to be touched. i think whitecoats made many spots in me, because She always feels good inside of me.

When She does not add more slick i smile and bend my head down, bracing. She enters suddenly, grabbing my hips when i buck up at the burning and filling, my shaft twitching and bursting, then quickly hardening again. That we can go and go is one of the best things about fox morphs, i recall Frank explaining to the new handler as they did tests before i was brought to Emalee, Master. Hardest to remember to not use Her name when She's making me feel so good.

Soon i'm lost until Master makes a lot of noise Herself before finding Her own great pleasure. Afterwards She cleans us both up, and we go to bed. i snuggle close when Her scent changes, telling me that She's thinking work things again. It calms Her, and soon She is asleep, while i stay awake to watch and drive bad dreams away with more snuggling. So many bad dreams since we got home. i can sleep in today while She goes to work, so i've decided to guard Her like our pen mothers tried to guard us.

I'm getting a headache as Lindsey tells me that Vice President Steirwalt is coming to MTB for a visit with our Strategy people. I've been able to avoid any more Sharing since getting back, but I have this horrible feeling that when VPs visit, we are supposed to entertain ourselves with our pets. My first executive assistant says nothing about that, only that he wonders if he should coordinate with her people and get her a room at the office or a hotel. "Lindsey," I say his name, and I can feel Wynn's eyes turn in my direction from the window seat he adores that looks out on the back yard. "I trust you to do what is best for the company and for Zandy—Vice President Steirwalt," I quickly amend.

Lindsey chuckles and mentions that that is what all good corporate spouses do. Yeah, of course she sent him a message telling him selective things about the conversation in her office before I left Egirdir. Now I have an even more constant reminder of what I'm risking if I don't play nice.

"If that is all for this evening," I begin, but he interrupts me.

"The ISM folks called again—I've delivered over a dozen messages from them the past two weeks, Emily." Great, I know he's in a scolding mood when he uses my first name. "Tonight they called my apartment. How did they even get my private number?"

"Fine, fine, I'll call them first thing in the morning. Refuse to bring my mochaid until I do," I tell him.

"Don't have to. They said they'd be dropping by your house tonight or tomorrow night."

"What?" I whisper into the phone. "When did they say this?"

"Right before I called you; that was the real reason why I did."

"Then why didn't you say so right away?"

"Look, calm down, it's no big deal. They had some questions about Wynn this evening; I told them that he was a great pet...."

"They asked you about Wynn?"

"Yeah, yeah, I thought it was odd, too, but the doctor explained that they do routine check-ups in the home. They want satisfied customers. You weren't replying, so they're concerned there's a problem."

I step back but keep my eyes on Wynn. He's started his nightly conversation with the owl that moved into one of my trees this week. I don't think he fully grasps that it isn't really asking him anything. Soon he'll tire of repeating his name and explaining what he's doing here and just close the curtains before pouting about stupid animals.

"There isn't a problem," I say firmly to Lindsey.

"I know, Boss." Good, he's back to my title. "I told them that he was very friendly and seemed to be helping you relax more."

"Thank you," I say, then the lights go on outside, signaling movement. "Did they say what time tonight they were coming?"

"No, just tonight or tomorrow night. They did sound anxious, though." The doorbell rings, and Wynn sits up on the window seat. "Is that them?"

"I'll see you tomorrow, Lindsey. Good night," I say, then tell the telephone to turn off.

I look at Wynn, who has hopped down and run to me. I push him gently to the floor, and he nods before crawling next to me. I ask the visitors to identify themselves, and I hear, "It's Mr. Chase with Doctor Batsinow from ISM, Ms. Potter. We're just here for a client review. Have you not gotten our messages?"

Could Inandirmak have a deal with ISM? Is that why it was strongly recommended that I go there? Are they here to make sure I'm acting like part of the family? My thoughts are as loud as my heart pounding in my chest as I take a few steps toward the door. Yes, the screen shows the two men who went with me during the selection process at ISM.

Wynn whimpers a bit and brushes his face against my calf; he's huddled down on the floor. "Ms. Potter?" the same voice calls again, and I can see it is the businessman talking.

"Yes. Please open the door for our visitors," I instruct the computer.

In a few moments they are in my house. "Ms. Potter," the businessman says, holding out his hand, so I shake it, then just nod at the doctor, who is staring at Wynn with a look of distaste. "It's been six months, so I thought we'd do a checkup."

"I took Wynn for a checkup both before and after my winter vacation," I reply, watching the doctor as he steps toward Wynn, who shrinks back and holds my legs.

"That was a medical checkup; this is more about his performance and behavior."

"He seems very attached to you," the doctor says as he steps back.

"I should hope so; he is my pet," I reply in a harsh tone that makes both men look at me. "Look there's nothing wrong with Wynn; he's grown used to my house, to me, even my assistant, whom I'm told you've already spoken with."

"Yes, yes, we're sorry we had to do that, but you weren't replying to our messages. Biannual performance checkups are in your contract," Mr. Chase adds with a slimy tone to his voice. I'll be checking that tomorrow.

"We just need to check out his living environment and talk to him a bit, ask a few questions," the doctor says as he crouches down to look at Wynn. "Don't you remember me?"

Wynn looks up at me and then back at the two men before nodding and burying his head in my legs again. Either he's playing shy very well, or he's afraid. I've been trying to get him to open up more and tell me more of what goes on in his furry little head, so I decide to stay close to him. "Fine, I'll give you a tour, and you may ask your questions as we look around. It's late, and I do have work in the morning," I emphasize.

The businessman wants to look around on his own, because I keep needing to stop and slow down. I'm too worried to let them be alone for even a moment in the house. They look at Wynn's room and the bathroom; they seem to be fine, though they frown a bit when I say that many nights he just sleeps with me, until I add that his body heat and soft fur is quite comfortable.

Wynn is very good at speaking in the third person and with very short sentences, always looking up at me, when they ask him questions. He even lies to them a few times, saying that he spends most of his day sleeping or watching a few shows on the morph channel. When they ask about chores around the house, I jump in and explain that he's trying to be helpful, but there is only so much he seems able to grasp. OK, so we're both lying to them now.

The doctor gives him a once-over and frowns when I refuse to let him take blood because they already did that at his last visit, twice in two months, I remind them. Finally, when they are about to leave, I ask something that has been bothering me. "What is this really about? I mean, you can't have just asked for a photo tour and sent me a survey?"

The doctor looks at the businessman, who nods with a sigh. "To be blunt, Ms. Potter, there have been some reports of breakdowns in the training with some other morphs from this generation and the following. Since we know our training isn't at fault"—yes, I'm sure they are certain of that—"it might be on the physical or genetic level. ISM prides itself on providing only the best erotic pets available, so we are checking with every client."

I take a second to compose myself by looking down at Wynn, then back at them. "I haven't noticed anything odd about him. Well," I add—I have to give them something, like one of our clients might need to admit to a minor problem with a product while they go fix whatever is truly wrong before the consumer rights groups get too loud—"he was very shy after the incident with my half brother, but he's recovered from that quite well."

Wynn rubs against my leg as I pet his head.

"They are quite resilient," the businessman states.

"I should hope so, at the price," I deflect his praise with a threat of my own.

"Which is why we are doing these rounds; we have a responsibility to our clients," Mr. Chase replied. Touché.

"Thank you for doing so," I add with a smile as I motion toward the door. "I do have work in the morning, so I must ask you gentlemen to leave. I'll contact you if I notice anything odd."

They hesitate; they look at each other, then smile, bow, and leave.

I have the computer lock the door and reset all my security systems again. "Thank God they left," I tell Wynn as I kneel down and hug him.

"They lied to you, Master," he tells me.

"How do you know?"

"They smelled different, I can tell by smell," he says.

That's slightly creepy to think that he can know so much about us by smell. Wait, does that explain how he always seems to know how to calm me down or arouse me more? "Are you using your nose to manipulate me, little fox?" I tease him.

"Oh, no, Master, I would never do that," he says with a look down, but he's grinning.

I arch an eyebrow and pull him to his feet. "I think someone is in need of a spanking," I say as I lead him by the wrist.

"Oh, oh, Master, please," he says, struggling just a little, but laughing. He pays attention to the movies and shows I watch; I bet he tracks them by my scent now that I know he can do that. A little resistance play, as I used to call it back in college, is a great turn on for me.

I've gotten him lying across my lap, and I'm into the fifth stroke from my bare hand when the doorbell makes us both freeze in place. I help him up, and he scurries away so I can go to the door screen.

"Ms. Potter?" I blink as I see the doctor who checked out Wynn after Anthony attacked him and before we left for Egirdir at our door not more than a few minutes after those first two from the Institute left. I hadn't even noticed the lights turning back on until the doorbell rang.

"Your colleagues have already been here, Doctor Veveren. I've told them that nothing is wrong with Wynn, so good night."

"Please, I just want to tell you the truth, because they've lied to you," she says, turning her gaze downward.

Wynn has followed me to the door, and he looks at her, then at me before taking the hem of my shirt in one paw. "Please, Master?"

I flinch and open the door, saying, "Interesting how they can mimic so well, huh?"

She steps in and takes a small device out of her pocket that looks much like the device my father sent home with me to make sure the house wasn't bugged. "Yes, but if birds can do it, why not mammal morphs? Amazing what science creates, isn't it?"

I'm too stunned to do anything other than watch her for a few minutes as she enters my house, talking about how she saw we were back from our trip and wanted to do a checkup on Wynn, to make sure he was healthy, because she knows how tempting it is to overfeed them on vacation. As she's speaking she's walking around, looking at everything with her device.

Wynn follows her but does not seem afraid, so I follow his instincts and reply, "Oh, your colleagues didn't mention a follow-up because of the trip. They said it was a routine check-in that I'd need to bring him to your offices to conduct."

She looks at me and shakes her head slightly but simply comments on how the division of departments works and how she expects I can understand that. After a sweep of the public parts of my house she turns off her machine and faces me. "Good, you didn't give them enough time to plant any bugs."

"Bugs? Doctor Veveren, you'd better start making some sense, or I'll forget I'm a lady and force you to leave my home."

"Denise."

"What?"

"Please call me Denise, because I'm not here as a doctor so much as your friend."

"We aren't friends," I almost snarl, recalling all the things that have been said about Wynn over the past month and a half. I may have to pretend to be friends with everyone in my company, but I'll be damned if I tolerate it from the shop I got him from.

"You want me as your friend, Emily; you really do," she adds when I fist my hands in annoyance, "because I can help you make sure that ISM, Inandirmak, MTB, everything and everyone think that you and Wynn have a perfectly normal relationship."

The entire world drops out from underneath me. The next thing I know, Wynn is cradling my head on his lap while this bitch from ISM is holding my wrist and looking at me with a fake expression of concern. "How dare you make accusations in my house," I start to say when I'm interrupted.

"Master, please. Emalee," Wynn says, and the doctor just smiles at me. It looks like a genuine smile, not a trick, so I keep listening. "I trust Doctor Denise."

"Yes, he has the modification," she mutters.

I push myself up but let Wynn keep in touch with me. "You better start saying something that makes sense, Denise," I bite off her name, "or I'll call ISM and let them know you are here." There, two can play at this game.

She stands up, and Wynn helps me up as well. He kneels back down and snuggles against my legs, and my hand falls down to pet him automatically. "I will, but not here. Meet me here instead; I know this place is safe. Please, you have nothing to lose by trusting me."

Except everything I know, everything I've resigned myself to in order to protect our lives. I know this as surely as I know the sun will rise tomorrow as I let her leave without another word.

Part III

Private Revolutions

Chapter Twenty-One
In Our Image

For at least the twelfth time since we arrived at the Jungle I look down at him kneeling by my feet under the table. It's an upscale club-slash-café that I was shocked to learn I could get into simply because I had a customer ID from ISM. Is meeting in one of their own employee clubs Doctor Vevern's idea of safe? I'm sure we're being filmed as we sit here.

It is a nice café, however—less crowded, more light, roomier than the ones Inandirmak operates or co-sponsors. The list of companies on the place's board of directors outside looks like a Who's-Who of life sciences, though the one at the top of the list, Genius, I'm completely unfamiliar with. Metro Thunder Bay has a tight hold on the lake, so I suppose everyone wants a piece of the action here. The water attacks my father spoke about seem to have spread to a few other locations, if the news reports are correct. Who can tell? The corporate media spins one direction while city media spins another.

I reach down and scratch behind one of Wynn's ears when he lifts his head and lays it on my lap. I can feel him looking up at me, but I'm just trying to act like any other morph owner.

Because all other morph owners have to be convinced by their pets to meet with a mysterious scientist promising she's on your side.

"That is adorable." I look up to find Doctor Vevern standing next to the table, a smile on her face, her white lab coat a reminder that she didn't have far to travel from work. "May I?"

I frown. ISM basically threatens me, and she asks if she can join me. I'm tempted to say "no," but a whine from Wynn makes me pause. I simply nod my head.

She takes a seat and sets her order placard on the table. "You should order something other than, what, mochaid? The food here is good, nutritionally balanced but still tasty. Plus," she leans toward me and lowers her voice, "it looks less suspicious."

Bloody hell. "I'll have to leave Wynn here, Doctor Vevern, for you to do your test, so you'll excuse me if I'm not comfortable doing much here at all."

"Denise."

"Excuse me?"

"Please call me Denise, Emily. It will help separate the various faces we are going to have to wear to protect him and you, too."

"I can protect us."

"No—no, you can't. Why do you think ISM sent agents? Because your behavior was unusual enough that your own company contacted them."

"Them? Don't you mean us, Doctor?" Now I'm purposely trying to push her and get her to drop this act.

She sighs. "There's a surcharge for orders placed at the table, but if you insist," she replies, just in time for the server to bring her food and drink. "I'm sorry, but my friend here wasn't sure when I was arriving; could she place her order now?"

"It's a two-credit surcharge," the server replies but takes out his datapad and looks expectantly at me.

Great, now I have to order. "Just a breakfast shake then, the most decadent one you have, and do you have anything for pets?"

The server glances down, then nods. "Sure, of course, it's one of our specialties. Do you have an enhancement in mind?"

Enhancement? Doctor Vevern jumps in. "Immunity booster, this is a professional consultation."

The server's eyebrows rise a bit, but he only nods before leaving us again.

"I informed my colleagues that you called after they left last night. You were more comfortable with me since I'd made a house call previously."

I frown, but the doctor only nods her head. "I know you have no reason to trust me other than his word, his instincts, but we haven't engineered that out of them yet, so you really should listen to your pet." Wynn is clearly listening, because he nuzzles into my lap, adding to her plea with action of his own.

I let her lead the conversation into a simple recount of the holidays, focusing on how Wynn behaved and how much he ate and slept. I don't lie, but I do leave certain things out, like the conversations we've had and the signs he's been giving me for weeks that we were being watched, which I only later realized in hindsight. Yeah, I need to listen to my pet more, because obviously he's more aware than I have been.

After the server leaves again, the doctor pushes a button, and opaque screens rise up around us. "There we go; the consultation bubble is up now, so we can really talk."

"Or you're recording us even more clearly."

"I'm sure your father gave you something to determine that. Why not use it?"

"What makes you think that?"

"He is military, isn't he? Lake Geneva guard, I believe is what I read."

It's not surprising they'd know that. Going over my finances would have told them a good deal about me, even more than what I suspected, I realize now. I liked this world better when I actually thought I had some privacy. I set the device on the table, and it scans, then gives me the clear sign.

"When we took over the governance of this club, we set up these consultation bubbles, but you are correct to assume the entrance marked you, and a few recordings are going on at various points in the club. Can't get rid of everything without drawing attention."

"We?"

"Why did you go into advertising, marketing, Emily?"

"I don't see...."

"Please just indulge me."

I sigh and close my eyes until Wynn bumps my knees and looks up at me again. "I thought it was a good way to educate the public on a wide scale, plus I was good at figuring out how to get people to think a certain way."

"But you're in administration now. Is that correct?"

"An opportunity for advancement opened up soon after I joined—turned out I had decent leadership skills, too. What does this have to do with Wynn?"

"I joined ISM because my parents had a morph. A beautiful creature, but its inability to communicate resulted in her untimely death. A speaker came to lecture during one of my classes, and he said they had found a way to access the communication genes, to crank those up without losing the obedience of the morph pets. Ours had been a simple thing, a pet in the real sense of the word, but this would be a step up in evolution, a true servant for the world at a time when we were realizing that we needed help as a species. ISM offered me the biggest student loan buyout, so I came here."

Communication gene? That starts to trigger some old memory of my own, but the doctor just continues.

"There used to be a debate, a century ago or so, about what really sets us apart from other animals. Finally we figured it out—communication. Not just with other humans—animals communicate with each other all the time—but the ability to communicate with ourselves, to interact with the world up here," she explains as she touches her head with one finger, "and then turn that internal dialogue into sounds or gestures that change the way others think. That changes the way we think. Humans create reality long before they affect the environment."

I sigh and frown. "What does this have to do with Wynn?"

"ISM was one of the first companies to try to manipulate the communication genes specifically. Wynn is a fourth-generation result of that testing."

"And it worked, so why would ISM feel threatened? Wouldn't they be happy to have succeeded?"

The doctor smiled tightly and took a sip of her drink. "Some of us are quite happy. But some customers have complained that their morphs think too much, talk back, act up—you wouldn't want that, would you?"

"Wynn doesn't do those things, and even if he did—I'm bigger; I'm the owner; if I can't keep him in line, then maybe I don't deserve him." There, I've used that same reasoning several times with failed human relationships; however, right now it isn't reassuring me very much.

I can tell the doctor thinks that is ridiculous, but we both just let our mouths hang open when Wynn's voice rises up from the floor. "Master best master in whole world, Wynn stay forever please."

"He's been listening and understanding us," the doctor reacts first. "I'm very impressed, but then I haven't had the chance to really interact much with fourth-gens."

"But you create them," I challenge her, wary for anything that could prove her false, not that we'd have much of a shot getting out of the Jungle with her own people all around us.

"Yes, but I don't do the training, and only recently have I been involved in the final steps before sales are finalized. I do know that there have been a record number of returns, and recently they hired an entire new team for the genetics lab. I've been moved to medical, which I can do, but I want to know what's going on at the basic level."

"Why should I help you?"

"Emily, returns is a nice way to say that they've been killing pets. If the genetics are at fault, they aren't wasting their time recoding, only destroying. I assume you don't want Wynn destroyed. Or am I wrong about that?"

I should be surprised when she says it, but in my gut I've had this increasing feeling that the world isn't ready for Wynn. I've been taking him out less and less, which would drive me insane if I were him, but he seems content to do more for me around the house. Since I scan my house every night after I get back from work, I've been feeling safe—until the ISM men and the doctor here showed up within an hour of each other.

"No, not wrong; I—I—" I put both hands on him and can feel him trembling against me, "I have no intention of giving him up." I can hear my voice almost break, so I take a deep breath, and the doctor just watches silently.

I grasp onto the one hope I'm nursing. "I haven't complained, though, so why even visit me? How can he be in any danger?"

She smiles tightly. "You are the exception now; the majority of owners are complaining. Add to that the fact that your company thought you were behaving strangely, and it actually put you at the top of their list."

"All the owners are complaining?"

"Mostly fourth-gen owners, but also some third-gen." Doctor Vevern frowns and pokes her food with a fork for a few seconds. "This makes no sense, because since first-gen morphs, really, we've been responding to consumer demand for better communication—more service-oriented pets. I didn't sign on to see the company fail."

"Doctor, you are talking in circles; you need to be clear. What do you want from me, from us?"

"I want to offer you both a place in a study that I and some of my more independent colleagues are conducting, an alternative to the destruction program focusing on those pets who are not causing problems. We need to understand what is happening and assess the full potential of pets. If we can determine what you the consumer wants, then your pets need not be endangered, and we'll create a new market. The benefit for you is that you'll meet others of similar desires and requirements for pets, and have a place where you don't have to be afraid."

"You're saying 'we,' Doctor, but you aren't giving me a name," I point out with a determined frown.

"Oh, sorry; I thought you might have figured that out. We call ourselves Genius—a play on genetics, of course, but it also refers to the fact that all of us working on this new project are focused on understanding the genetic limits for intelligence. You'll be part of a new vision of corporation. One based on pure science with profit as a mere side effect," the doctor tells me, and the warning bells start ringing in my head.

"How are you funding this?" Following the money is always a good idea, and if a company or consortium of companies isn't involved, I'm even more suspicious.

"Ah, an intelligent question—usually owners just jump at the chance to save their pets and meet others in similar situations."

"I'm not usual," I tell her simply as I pet the top of Wynn's head again.

"No, I can see that," the doctor says and takes out a folder with a logo I haven't seen before on it. There's no name under it, and she doesn't clarify but simply opens it up. "This lays out the funding for Bio-Servants—our goals, the procedures we'll use, consent forms, all of that. It is a bit technical, but I'm sure you'll figure it out. We have grants from four cities and our own savings for this start-up. Cities love new companies, because we compete and help control the corporations. Please take this home and consider it. The telephone numbers are safe, not monitored in any way."

"How are you able to do this, doctor? My contract with Inandirmak won't be over for another decade. I'm sure your company has a tight rein on you, too."

"Life sciences are far more competitive, plus I've made back my loans now fivefold. I'm done in just two months, then I'll be working full-time for Bio-Servants."

Before I can speak again she pushes some buttons, and the screens go down. We take our time at lunch and discuss some of the latest news. It's all very civilized, and Wynn even crawls up on her bench at one point for a hug before she leaves us.

I call Lindsey on the way back home and ask him to meet us wherever he currently is. I need to know if I can trust him, because if I can't, I'm not sure how to fully understand this folder I've been handed. Wynn certainly won't be of much help, and so far trying to go it alone is only resulting in greater problems for me.

We pick him up at the corner of his apartment building complex, and he's dressed rather dully for a first executive assistant. He has his briefcase and is rubbing his eyes when we pull up. Without a complaint he gets in the back seat, and out of the corner of my eye I see Wynn turn around and watch him the entire drive.

"What's wrong with you?" I ask as casually as I can with my stomach in knots and my head buzzing with questions.

"Late night, bad night," Lindsey says. "I didn't know you

wanted to work; you surprised me, Boss, so I hope you can handle the fresh-out-of-bed me."

"Life's full of surprises," I say, and I see him cock one eyebrow in the rearview mirror.

"Hey, Wynn, you all been out shopping?" Lindsey asks as he reaches out, and my morph lets him pet him but doesn't reply beyond a yip.

"I should have gone shopping last night instead of the gang bang; that was a mistake," Lindsey says softly, and now it's my turn to frown a bit.

"I wish you wouldn't do things like that," I say as I grip the wheel more tightly.

"If someone would put a claim on me, I wouldn't," he replies with a pointed look at me.

Yes, that was one of the reasons I suspect that my predecessor left. Lindsey's actions suggest that he expects to move up in the company along a certain trajectory, and since getting back from Egirdir I haven't been much for sex with him. Of course, Madame Reizis did mention that Lindsey would make a good corporate spouse, and I'd be foolish to ignore what was basically an order when I have ten more years under their watch.

"That's part of what I want to discuss with you," I tell him. Now he sits up straighter, and even Wynn turns to look at me. "When we get home," I say, pulling into the corporate carpooling lane we pay good money to use.

"Wait," says Lindsey, sitting back from the island in the kitchen where we've been talking. Actually he's been listening to me, not interrupting, no shock on his face. Talking to him may be a mistake, I'm thinking, as I tell him about the vid clips Madame Reizis showed me. He runs both hands through his dirty blond hair, making it stick up. "Reynolds wasn't making those vids?"

I blink. "What vids?"

Lindsey leans forward toward me, placing his hands on the countertop. "There were some things he wanted me to do, but he wasn't willing to stake a claim. He showed me some vids of him and me, me out in the clubs, said he made them and he'd show Corporate. He forgot who controlled his scheduling and account claims, but he left me with no choice."

"You set up Reynolds?" This was a bad idea.

"He gave me no choice. I swear that's all it was, Boss," Lindsey tries to place a hand on top of mine, but I move, stand up, and start to pace. "Fuck! I would never, never do that to you, Boss. Emily? Please, this is insane, you're telling me our own company is spying on us, and now you're worried about me?"

Lindsey jumps off his chair, and I see Wynn go skidding across the floor. "What the hell? He was sniffing my... me."

I turn and see Wynn just blinking at him and then at me. "Why did you do that, pet?"

Wynn looks back at Lindsey then at me, and when I nod slightly he smiles at Lindsey and proclaims, "He good pet, no lie to Master."

Lindsey's mouth falls open, and he plops right back down onto the stool.

I hurry over and sit facing him again, tapping my thigh, which signals Wynn to kneel at my feet. I don't recall teaching him to do that, but he's been doing it since he arrived, and I've now been trained to use the signal without thinking much. "You knew he could talk, remember?" I insist to my assistant.

Lindsey nods his head slowly as his eyes start to focus. "Yeah, yeah, no, why did he say I was a pet?"

I snort and sigh. "Oh, I was trying to explain your job, and that was a simple way to make Wynn understand certain things about our relationship."

He narrows his eyes for a second, then cocks one side of his mouth before returning to the previous concern. "So as your pet you trust me then, right, Boss?"

He so is not just an assistant. I'd be lying to myself if I claimed I only wanted Lindsey because he was a good gatekeeper at my office and a nice way to relieve stress. That didn't change when I got Wynn, though I thought it might. "That depends on what you want to do about this," I reply, circling one hand to include all three of us, "and the vids I've shown you."

"Let me rephrase what you've told me so I'm sure we're on the same page." Lindsey stands, and I just watch as he moves away and runs his hands over his face, blowing enough air out of his mouth to make his bangs wave. "Inandirmak makes its executives buy anthropomorphic pets and uses them as a way to blackmail said executives into staying with the company and working harder for the company? What's to prevent you from going to MTB authority and reporting this, or to the global corporate authority?"

"I don't have the vids; only Egirdir has them. I'm sure they'd claim I was lying; then where would I find a job?"

"But Reynolds had them, some of them," Lindsey points out.

I think for a minute, trying to pull out what little information I know. "Wasn't he click-back? Wouldn't he know a lot more about computers than you or I?"

"Maybe, very possibly. Asshole sucked at administration, but he was a demon in the net. He had a jack port, I saw it many times."

A shiver goes up my spine when I hear this. There are very few people allowed now to interface directly with computers; they generally need the highest clearance from cities, and companies watch them closely, monitoring them for any misbehavior. The Zombie War made us all a little fearful when it came to putting anything mechanical or computerized into our bodies. "Is Reynolds still working for Inandirmak?"

Lindsey starts to shake his head, then comes back and picks up his briefcase. "You have a safe connection, Boss?"

"Yes, I've been careful about that," I tell him. "Wynn, go fetch my computer bag, that's a good pet."

"Don't ever call me that," Lindsey cautions as he takes out his computer and opens it.

"Have I ever?"

"No, but please don't start." He takes the bag from Wynn and uses it to set up a connection. He pauses as he looks at the extra equipment."

"We visited my father on the way back," I simply state, and that earns a nod while Lindsey logs on. Once back home I still felt unsafe, and my father was able to put me in contact with the MTB Guard director, who was happy to help me avoid Inandirmak, though I wouldn't be surprised if they wanted to monitor me. My father told me not to worry about it; the cities take care of their own. Am I their own or Egirdir's?

"Reynolds used to have me do all his personal accounting—I think just 'cause he liked to have me sit on his lap to do it." He looks and raises his eyebrows when I frown. "Sorry, too much intel, Boss. But if he hasn't changed his passcodes... There, I'm in his credit account." He is silent for a few minutes, and I fight the urge to lean in and look at the screen.

"No direct connection to Inandirmak, but he's getting a consulting fee from another company in Egirdir."

"I bet that isn't a coincidence," I say. There are rumors, always pooh-poohed by the companies, that some are old enough and large enough to have acquired political power in certain cities before the Water Wars, of which the Zombie War was merely one theater of combat. No one now would tolerate a direct connection between government and for-profit business, but conspiracy theories abound that the separation of city and company are not as great as we are led to believe.

Lindsey goes offline and disconnects. "No reason to be on longer than we need." He sighs as he packs things up then looks at me, sitting up straight on the stool. "What do you want from me, Emily?"

"I need to know your goals, Lindsey." He blinks, and his eyes widen a bit, but I just continue. "You have no interest in continuing your education, you run out and do gang bangs, is it, which you know can be dangerous, you've made comments in the past about my using or not using my executive privileges. So what are you hoping for at Inandirmak?"

"I think you know."

"I need to hear you say it."

He pauses and looks down, then moves slightly closer to me before letting his gaze travel up my body. Wynn presses close against my leg from his spot on the floor, which he had returned to after fetching the bag. "Corporate spouse. I want to be your corporate spouse."

I suck in my breath, then I take his hand. I've seen old movies and books where the man asked the woman to marry him after some long angst-filled journey where they had to fight against family and society to get to each other. What a bunch of romantic crap, hardly worthy of consideration. Yet we're about to embark on something possibly old-fashioned in that sense. "I'm not in the good graces of Egirdir, Lindsey."

"I know."

"ISM came looking for Wynn; they think something is wrong with him, and there's more I haven't told you," I continue, but he reaches out and puts a finger over my lips.

"I don't care. I'm not getting any prettier or younger, and you're the finest Watcher our office has had since I've been there, hell, maybe one of the best I've ever worked for, and I've worked a few jobs, and heard my mom talk about hers. I'm from a long line of executive assistants; I know the score."

"I'm not getting rid of Wynn, and I'm not letting them take him from me," I declare, and Lindsey smiles. "What is so funny?"

"Not funny, Boss; just this is why I want to be your corporate spouse. You bring loyalty and passion to everything you do."

"It could be tricky; Egirdir will still be watching me. Us." I swallow before asking the most dangerous question of all this afternoon, "Lindsey, Madame Reizis said that she thought you'd be a good corporate spouse for me. Who has your chief loyalty?"

He stands up and moves very close to me. I feel Wynn try to push between us, but he isn't strong enough. "You do. We can even do old-fashioned vows if you want, so you're assured of my loyalty. It isn't a big deal though, Boss."

"Why not?"

"If I'm on your side, you're going to shoot your way up the

ladder, and no one will ever take either of your pets," he emphasizes that word, "away from you."

"You're that good, huh?" I can feel a smile at the edge of my lips as he leans toward me, our noses almost brushing, Wynn pushing harder against my leg.

"Oh, I'm so much better than I've shown you, Emily. Boss? Whatever you want me to call you, dear."

I chuckle and tilt my face up and to one side. "Let's seal the deal then," I whisper before capturing his mouth with my own.

As we kiss I reach down and pet Wynn's soft fur as he leans against me, his arms around my leg, trembling for some reason.

Chapter Twenty-Two
Feelings Without Words

"Wynn, you have to pay attention, or the test isn't valid," the white coat tells me. i blink and look at her, it's the nice one, the one who helped me, Denise is what she keeps trying to get Master to call her, but i know i shouldn't call her that. i just bow, my head racing with a lot of things, very few of them the shapes on the cards.

Master isn't here with me; i don't know where She is; maybe She's with him. Lindsey. Her other pet, but he isn't a pet, not really, don't understand. i blink when the white coat touches the top of my head, scratching it gently.

"I know you miss your owner, but we do need to get through the prelims before we can decide what to do with you next. I need honest readings, so you must pay attention," she says with an edge to her voice that makes me swallow and nod my head.

"No, no, words, we use words here in the safe area, remember? I heard your master say that you were to use words with me, Wynn."

"Yes, Wynn remember," but i also remember the private conversation about how i shouldn't use the big words like "I," "me," "mine," and such things. Too dangerous until we know what these white coats really want. Since they haven't mentioned such words, Master assumes they don't know that i can use them. "Best to play along but be cautious," She said.

"Will you focus now and find the matches?"

"Wynn try better," i promise, but inside, my attempt to push back the other thoughts is weak, so i make myself stare at the next card she holds up then at the spread on the table before tapping one.

"That's better; that's what I suspect you can really do," the nice doctor says.

Matching shapes is easy; matching colors easy, but too hard when they ask me to say the shape name or the color name. i don't know many, and i worry that Master will be disappointed. i have no room to disappoint Her with another pet now getting Her time, even at home.

Later when She comes to pick me up, the white coats want to talk to Her, so we go into one of their offices. Master is listening to the white coat share the results while i sit at Her feet, head in Her lap, listening. Wynn is clever but lacks certain words, information, i can feel myself roll my eyes. Fox morphs are clever, make best pets ever, unless you are a human pet. i push that thought away and try to keep listening to what they are saying about me without reacting to it too much.

"Wouldn't trying to teach him the names of colors and shapes defeat the purpose of the testing?" Master asks, and i glance up. The games have a purpose? Oh, yes, to say how clever i am. i bet he knows all the shapes and colors, bet he could match everything. i'm not a stupid animal. i can know them, and i almost speak up before clenching my jaw tightly shut. Master is worried about us stepping over some line. Maybe this is like when we went out before and i pushed the cart or weared the clothes, but now She knows, so we have to be careful.

"Oh, no, part of the development of the brain that we want to study involves the ability to learn through communication. So our showing and telling him the words for the various colors and shapes will be directly testing this ability. It will allow us to gauge if the genetics work has made them more human or too human."

Human? Wynn not human, he's human, human pet, not supposed to be pets, but before i got further i catch something about my behaving and force myself to quiet down.

"Plus it is very simple, it honestly shouldn't affect how he behaves or interacts with others, if you are concerned about that, Emily."

i feel Master tense when the nice doctor uses Her name. She still does not fully trust her or the others here in this center—that is the word they used for the building and themselves. Not the Institute— somewhere else; i can tell by the smell and how it looks, plus the drive was different. Somewhere else, but still white coats everywhere.

i can tell that Master forces Herself to relax before She replies. "Well, it might actually help. I could say, 'Fetch the white shoes,' or 'the blue ones,' for instance."

i glance over and up to watch the nice doctor smile and laugh. "Yes, yes, it could have private benefits; just remember that some people aren't as open to these evolutionary changes as you or I may be."

"I'm fully aware of the social strictures," Master replies, and i can feel her anger rise, so i cuddle against Her lap, yipping a bit, trying to distract Her. When i can concentrate, i'm having fun here with the games. If i can learn more like Lindsey, help Her more like he can, all the better.

i pay very little attention when they discuss how often i can come to this center. That's a human concern; i'll just go where i'm taken and do my best for Master. i think they decide i'll come once a week, during the day while Master is at work, because as She looks down at me and accepts my nuzzling of Her face before we leave, She mutters, "You'll go to work once a week, too, then, Wynn. That should keep you less bored."

He's here again. Lindsey. i'm watching them from the window seat as they sit on the couch and look over these ebooks with lots of pictures in them. Catalogs, these are called; i learned that listening to Master whenever She gets one delivered to Her. i can see the pages, since they are viewing it on the big screen, but they aren't asking my opinion. They wouldn't like it. i don't want him here, i decided last night when he kissed Her at the door.

i don't know what wedding really means, but i fear it means he will be moving in here and then Master will never play with me again. What can a morph pet do against a human pet? i think and think until my head hurts. Nothing, i'm not smart enough to figure this out, even if i know what triangle is and what pink is and what line is and what texture is now.

"Oh, no that won't go with our coloring," i hear. i turn and listen carefully as he speaks up. They are looking at purple things—clothes, plates, and other things.

"Why not?" Master replies. "Why wouldn't violet go with your eyes?"

"My eyes are blue, yours are grayish green; that is not going to work at all." I cringe when he reaches over and places one hand casually on Her knee and She does not move away. "Boss, honey," She does raise one eyebrow when he says that, "Emily. I know what I'm talking about; these are the sort of things you shouldn't be worrying about. This is why I'm here, isn't it?"

"You're going to change my entire wardrobe, aren't you?"

"No, no, of course not," he says. He lifts a hand and waves it a bit as he pushes a button and the picture on the big screen changes. "Only the necessary things," he adds with a grin.

i smile as Master picks up a pillow and hits his head and shoulder with it. She is perfect as She is; i'm glad She'll punish him for talking like a bad pet. Those pillows can hurt a lot. i wait, but She doesn't continue hitting him, and his laughter makes me feel cold. That wasn't a punishment?

i don't want him here. i turn back and look up at the dark sky, hoping it will rain so he gets wet when he leaves. At least he always leaves. Then i get to sleep with Master in Her big bed and make Her giggle in much better ways. If i've been good while they do their work, i'll reach the sky, too, and then pleasure Master many times until She cuddles me to Her to sleep.

The nice doctor strokes my head after we get through all of the shapes and colors. She mixed them up, trying to trick me, but i'm not a stupid animal; i know the differences now. i eat the treats she leaves—chicken pieces, real chicken, not pet food—but as i eat i smell something else and look up. Master is outside the open door, and She has carryout with Her.

Who needs treats when She's here? i run out to Her and jump

up to hug Her about the waist, making Her take a step back before starting to laugh. "You're extra hyper today. What have you been giving him, Doctor?"

"Denise," the nice white coat says softly in a tone that i know means she is getting weary of reminding Master to use her first name. "Just a few fresh chicken pieces, nothing you didn't sign off on. He was a real trooper today. He has all the colors and shapes down now, almost has all the textures we've worked with as well. I suspect you've been doing some work at home?"

Master's petting of me pauses, and She swallows. "Not as much as I should, only some. It's all his own cleverness."

That's true. Master so busy with Lindsey and work now that we have little time for play. She promises this will change, but they are planning something and setting things up. i have no clue, but i don't like it one bit. i've been practicing on my own with the big screen like Master showed me. Took the big screen a while to understand my words, plus i had to speak slow, more clear, but now it knows all my words for shapes, colors, textures, test, page, next, score, on, off. The big screen is very smart like Her computer and pad. They all smell the same, too, so sometimes i think they may be same thing as the TV, some machine thing. Machines things are also created by humans just like morphs. i think we are much better, though, because i'm cuddly, but i'm not as smart.

i wonder if they will make machine pets, but that only makes me sad, so i turn my ears slightly to hear what the nice doctor is saying while i soak up as much petting as i can. Maybe she's saying how good i am again, and maybe Master will be so pleased that he won't come over. "How do you define his own cleverness in this case?"

"Oh, well, I set up a program on the house system like you suggested, then I showed him how to use it. He's been practicing, the logs tell me, sometimes for hours while I'm at work."

"He works your computer?"

"Well, he uses the home system—verbal commands; he doesn't use the keyboard."

"His digits would make typing difficult beyond pecking away, but then, we used to do that before it became a survival skill." The doctor's voice sounds a bit off, so i glance back at her, but she's just writing on her pad. "I think we should take a break, and I'll call you in a week or two. We have to compare and sift through all the data we've gathered from Wynn and the others. Plus this will allow us to test retention of information and skills."

"How many others?"

"You know we have confidentiality in place, Emily. I can't tell you that, just like you've agreed not to tell anyone you are bringing him here for testing, right?"

Master stops petting me as Her temperature drops and Her muscles stiffen. i turn before i can stop myself and growl, "Leave Emalee alone."

"Wynn!" Master's voice makes me cringe down onto the floor at Her feet. i can feel the air change around me, their scents change, the room itself seems to close in on me. "I'm so sorry, Denise. He's very protective of me. They tell morphs on that TV station of theirs to protect and help their owners. He's just taking it a bit too literally."

There is a pause, and i can smell fear coming off of Master, so i reach out and place one paw on Her shoe but nothing else. She can kick me if She likes; i deserve it for breaking rules so much. We both hold our breaths until the doctor speaks again.

"At least his behavior got you to use my name finally. I get yelled at, snarled at, even bitten a few times, at these tests," the white coat says, but i can tell that she's lying to us from her smell. i've never been afraid of her; she's always been the nice one, but now i put a paw over my muzzle to keep from telling Master that we need to leave. Speaking out right now would be very, very bad. The songs tell us that humans are quick to anger, quick to punish, and slow to forget. Stupid, stupid, wynn! Make things so hard now for all.

"I'll call you in a week or so, Emily. Just relax and enjoy your pet," the doctor says.

"Get up, Wynn. We're going home where we'll discuss your behavior this evening," Master tells me.

i rise on all four paws and follow like a pet should once we hit the outside. i don't even find the outdoors interesting on the ride like i always do. i just sit in the seat and stare at the metal and plastic in front of me, my ears trying to reach through the music She's playing to be aware of anything She says. She says nothing to me the entire drive, and it feels longer since it is only us in the car.

i follow Her inside and just stay on the floor after She locks the door. She prods me with a foot, and i look up at Her. "Stand up!"

i obey, and then She slaps me and i fall to the floor. "Stand up again!"

This repeats until i'm crying on the floor and She's stomping around the place and then stomps into the kitchen before stomping back. i look up as She kneels down and raises my head with Her hand under my muzzle. i haven't said anything; best to be quiet when my stupid words caused this problem. She applies something wet and cool to my face, and out of the corner of my eye i see She brought a bowl with a few ice cubes and water in it that She is dipping this cloth into.

She still smells so angry, but Her voice is different as She shakes Her head at me. "I shouldn't have hit you so hard. I probably shouldn't have hit you at all," She adds with a sigh.

i just stare at Her, then lower my eyes. When She says things like this that make no sense, i just try to stay small and still. i disobeyed very early rules She set up. She should do worse than this to me, but i don't mention that. i remember one show on the TV where a morph said such a thing to his master, and he was hurt so bad he never woke up again, and then he just disappeared. The big sleep, so easy for humans to send us there, where there is nothing but cold and dark and alone. The songs tell us so. Best to just accept what they do to us, never offer advice on punishment.

She holds me for a while, adding a rocking motion to it, and i can feel my eyes start to close. No, that's not good, so a light bite on my tongue wakes me up. Master is angry about something, so i need to be alert.

She stops at some point and hugs me very hard. My ears twitch when She whispers, "Thank you for defending me, but you don't need to do that, pet. I'm supposed to be protecting you. Please, don't make it so hard for me to do." With that She lets me go, gets to Her feet, and bids me follow Her into the kitchen for dinner.

Defending Her? i think on what She says as i use the controls to get my food and water then watch Her plate the food She brought home for Herself. i spoke up cause the nice doctor stopped being nice for a moment. i spoke up 'cause it felt good to do so. i spoke up 'cause there are feelings in my head, in my body, that i can't say to Master. i just don't know if the words i hear on the TV from humans would work, and the pets never say the things that feel right to me.

i eat my dinner quickly, then follow Her to the table and curl up around Her feet, looking up and rubbing my head against Her lap before just lying there as She eats. When She finishes, She taps the side of Her thigh, so i move and scurry to the living room with the screen and the window seat. i just kneel there waiting until She comes and sees me.

She approaches, so i sit up and put my arms around Her, resting my head on Her stomach. "wynn please Master," i say, and i take her hand in mine and stand up so I can look up at Her. "Please?" i beg, adding a little whimper that i know will work unless She is still angry. She doesn't smell angry anymore.

She smiles and reaches out to pet my head then leads us to Her bedroom, where Lindsey has never been. i'd know if he had been here; i check every day after She goes to work, and when he visits and leaves, i check again. She starts to take Her jacket off, so i put my paws over Her hands. "Please, let wynn help."

She blinks at me, then nods and allows me to help remove all the clothes She wears. i think She is better naked or in that nightie, but my stomach tightens when i think of Her out of the house like that. i concentrate on walking to put the clothes either in Her closet, where i sometimes sit to be surrounded by Her scent when i miss Her, or in the laundry basket, which gets full, disappears, then reappears empty. What happens to it?

i push aside the question and try to focus on Master's shoes and stockings next. These are hard to take off without tearing them, but i've been practicing. Go very, very slow, and use only the padded parts of my paws is the trick. She isn't in a rush but simply lies back on Her bed as i roll them down from knees to feet and then off.

She sighs and shifts Her body when i come back and lick along the bottom of Her foot. Her scent fills me, and i gently hold the foot i'm playing with in my hands. Long, slow licks are best; they do not make Her giggle or kick out, so i take my time, touching each part, slipping my tongue around and between Her toes. When Her scent and temperature start to change just slightly, i turn to the other foot and give it the same care.

i bet Lindsey never does this for Her. i see pets do this sort of thing all the time on the TV, and the white coats and handlers showed us vids many times about pleasing with our mouths and tongues. Every part of the pet belongs to the owner, so every part should be used to please owner. i never see humans do this to each other beyond kissing and chests and hands. i need to do things that he won't do, show Her how good a real pet is.

i'm doing it again—thinking about me more than Master. So i bite my own tongue lightly before starting the slow journey up Her legs one long slow lick at a time. i pause when Master moves back onto the bed so She's all on top of it, which makes me crawl up to join Her. Want so bad to jump up, but i force myself to go slow, one paw up, one body part up at a time as i lick my way between Her legs, and She spreads them apart with another sigh and a mumbled, "good boy."

As i lick along Her thighs Her scent changes again, becoming more earthy, more intense, more of the happy Master i want. i rub back as She reaches down and pets my head, leaving one hand on top of it. She'll signal me when it is time to speed up by Her grip in my fur.

i am very careful now, no air in certain human parts, only tongues, and no paws beyond merely holding and caressing. my nails are not sharp, but some morphs still have claws, from what i see on the TV and in the training vids. i gently separate the folds under Her pretty short fur that matches the red of Her head fur with one paw and then shift my body so i can hold my position for as long as She wants.

She makes a little gasp when i lick once, just a tiny touch that gets Her hand to flex and grab my head fur. It doesn't hurt; i like the feeling of Her holding me tight, moving my head, forcing me closer to Her scent and wetness. Some masters pull on ears—that can hurt—or pull on other body parts, using a leash or a crop to tell a pet what to do; i see it on TV and in training vids all the time. All that can hurt, but Master only hurts when She wants to for play or when She is angry.

She is not angry now, so i eagerly start licking at Her center in long and short strokes, changing as i have learned She likes. The nice doctor is surprised that i learn words for colors and shapes. i learn all the time with Master. Learn or Big Sleep, only two ways for any pet, the Songs say. Words are boring to learn, but Master wants it, so i practice every day, 'cause i may forget. i want to practice this every day, i decide as i slip my tongue into Her center and She tightens Her grip on my fur.

i tilt my nose up and over Her fur so i can breathe without the bad things maybe happening—air in certain human places can make pain, hurt, even kill, one vid said. i bet Lindsey can't do this, can't give pleasure and still breathe. As Her grip pulls me closer i speed up my licks, concentrating on the top of Her folds where that spot is that gets Her legs to clench and Her scent to concentrate even more. As She gets closer to the sky i wrap one arm around Her and try rubbing the fold i'm holding to the side with one digit.

Master sits up, gasps, and then screams, but Her grip is too tight for me to pull away. i keep licking, riding out the bucking of Her hips, sucking down the moisture that flows from Her freely. i'm afraid, because She's never made these noises before, and the movements of Her body are more hard, almost pushing me away.

At some point She lies down and tugs at my fur, so i stop

licking and crawl up to lay over one side of Her, my shaft lying between our legs. i look at Her as She blinks up at the ceiling and rests one hand over my back, stroking it a few times before releasing my head fur to rest that hand over Her eyes. Her temperature starts to shift downward, and Her scent relaxes, so i nuzzle against the breast right above my head but do nothing further.

"Are they teaching you more than shapes and colors at that place?"

Her question surprises me, so i just shake my head and whisper, "No, Master. wynn tell Master everything they do to him at center place."

"Well then you just keep on doing your own homeschooling, then, 'cause it was brilliant," She says with a chuckle.

She rolls us over so She is on top, and she lowers Her mouth to my muzzle, pressing Her lips there before rubbing Her nose against mine. "You are brilliant, and that's why we're doing all of this," She says, then lies down, curling around me, skin to fur.

my shaft is aching, begging for attention, but i just lie there silently. i think She just kissed me, like i see Her do to Lindsey and i see humans do on the TV. My muzzle is tingling and my nose is twitching as i feel Her lips and nose on mine. Doing all of this?

i blink into the dark as the house lowers the light at Master's muttered command. Kissing? She kissed me? i'm still going over every feeling of this until the sun is coming through the curtains and Master's mouth is swallowing down my shaft before She starts the day off with play that we haven't done for a while since he started coming around.

i smile as She grabs one of my legs and yanks me down to the edge of the bed. i offer my bottom to Her firm toy that She just adjusted around Her center. As She enters me, making me see sparks before my eyes, i'm sure Lindsey can't do this for Master either. Nope, we're doing all of this.

Chapter Twenty-Three
Bureaucratic Openings

I'm frowning at the form when Lindsey comes in with a big mochaid and a huge smile, his hips swaying just a bit, his face lit up like the sun. He's so excited for our big day, which may never come if I can't figure out a way to fill out these damned forms in a way that won't make the owners look at me or my private life more closely than they currently are.

"Boss, I bring you the fruit of several laboratories and maybe an actual farm or two," he announces before setting the cup on my desk, right next to the previous cup that I haven't touched. I hear him click his tongue, but I just glance back at him before staring at the screen in front of me.

I'm not sure how much time has passed, maybe only a few seconds, but I look up when Lindsey is suddenly there turning my chair away from my desk, leaning down over me, his hands on the arms of the chair. His eyes are looking very seriously down at me, but I don't like this position, so I sit up straighter and glare at him. He sighs and straightens but only moves back far enough to fold his arms over his chest. A glance at the door shows that he has shut it.

"I'm not aware of any campaign or personnel conflicts, so there aren't any," he declares. "That means your attitude is about personal matters. Me? The wedding? Wynn?"

"All of it," I say, then turn back to my computer.

I hear him clear his throat, but I don't look back at him. "You know part of my job here as your assistant is to help you with at least one of those. My future as your spouse means I should be able to help you with the other two."

I'm trying to ignore him, staring at this form and trying to figure out the best way to word the value of my acquiring a corporate spouse for Inandirmak. I'm just a VP, fairly new, so what exactly gives me the right to make this request?

"Hey!" I look up to find Lindsey leaning across the desk, his face inches from the screen. He turns and looks at it, then climbs further up so he can get a closer look.

"What the hell do you think you're doing?" I ask, sitting back and pulling the keyboard toward me.

"My job, even if you refuse to let me do it," he says with no title and no terms of endearment. He reads for a moment, and I can't process what to say because I'm so shocked by his behavior. First Wynn acts up, and now this. I'm losing control of the males in my life.

He looks at me, and I can see determination in his beautifully made up eyes, their edges tipped in something sparkly. I don't have time to be distracted by his good looks and tricks. "You need specifics, then, to fill this out. A model of a successful application or several would probably help, too," Lindsey declares as he pushes himself back off the desk and stands up. "I'll get you that, then, Boss. You look at other things for a while and let me do my job."

I just sit there and watch him leave, taking the first cup of mochaid with him. I reach for the second and take a sip, relaxing into the smooth bitterness and heat. I'm not getting anywhere on my own here; I might as well see what he can dig up. I turn to another report from our branch detective and smile when I see that Genius is talking with one of our rivals about an ad campaign. I can use my in with Doctor Vevern—Denise—to find a way in for us. That might increase my odds of getting this corporate spouse approved.

Apparently Lindsey is completely focused on his self-assigned task, because the next time I'm interrupted it is Connie standing just inside my door after a soft knock. "Boss," she says softly—she looks like her old self now, all recovered from the medical crisis just a few months back. "You have a call from President Andres Reizis, Human Resources Division. Line one."

Vetting my calls and visitors is a first assistant's job, but a quick glance outside shows Lindsey looking as intently at his screen as I was, but his fingers are flying over the keyboard.

"Excellent, Connie; put him through," I say with a smile that seems to help her relax, as she returns a smile, and her hunched up shoulders lower just a bit. She just nods and scurries outside, and in a moment my phone rings.

"President Reizis, what an unexpected pleasure. What can we do to help Human Resources here in MTB?" I'm using my most pleasant but professional voice. It is very possible that Corporate knows I've been looking at the spousal request forms, but I was not expecting them to really talk to me until I filled one out.

"Vice President Potter, I'm glad I could talk to you directly," the grandson of our CEO says lightly as he pops up on my screen. He is dressed rather elegantly for the office, but then who am I to tell the owners how to dress at work? His office may be his home, for all I know, but a glance at the map in the corner of the screen shows where the call is originating—in this case not in Egirdir but from the branch in Nyirripi on Lake Mackay. It must be important to have him up so early in his time zone.

"Of course, my time is your time, President Reizis. What can we do for Inandirmak?"

"Have you seen the news about Carson City?"

I blink, then nod. "It's been all over the news. Water pirates, violence, but the news I saw this morning reported that the city's army is handling the situation."

"Yes, well, that is what all cities say, isn't it?" President Reizis says with a slight grin. The tensions between cities and companies is always high, and while my livelihood may depend on Corporate, I know my living depends on the city, so I just listen and arch one eyebrow, trying to look non-committal.

"How does this relate to Inandirmak, if I may ask?" I venture after a few seconds of silence.

"There have been some attacks on the branch there, mostly threats, but Hendricks reports that his car was attacked at his apartment last night."

I sit up and put one hand on my chest. Of all of the other VPs here in North American I probably like Ashton Hendricks second best, though his environmental rants get a bit much. I didn't even know he had a car, since he is always bragging about how he refused the corporate house and stays just a few blocks from his branch in a company-subsidized apartment. "Is he all right?"

"Physically he seems fine, but he did sound shaky when I spoke to him just an hour ago." President Reizis pauses and looks down at his desk before looking directly back at me. "Potter, I have to ask if you have any room in your branch for any of the employees from the Carson City office?"

"Room?" I glance at the open door, then back at the screen. "Perhaps I should close my door so we can have a more private conversation."

"Yes, please do that."

Lindsey and Connie both look up at me when I go to close the door but say nothing when I just shake my head. Everyone in the branch may start gossiping, but my door is closed, so they can't know the specifics. I'll deal with any rumors that are sure to start flying when I'm certain of what I'm dealing with myself.

President Reizis nods at me when I sit back down. "Are you thinking of closing the Carson City branch over some water pirates? That seems a bit... extreme, doesn't it?"

He blinks at me, then chuckles. "I was told you were a go-getter, always pushing, questioning how things are done. It can be good, except when it isn't," he says, underscoring this last part with a dark edge to his voice, his eyes narrowing just a bit.

"Is this one of those times?" If I have a reputation for being pushy, and I know that reputation is what earned me this promotion, I'm damned well going to play into it.

"Not yet, but," he replies, pausing and closing his eyes for a moment. "What I'm about to tell you can go no further than you and me. Do I have your cooperation on that, Emily?"

Using my first name... that's either a threat or an attempt to pull me up to the big wigs and include me in something they believe can tie me further to the company. At least it isn't film of that damned holiday. "Of course, Sir. Rumors can only be harmful to all of us."

"There has been concern for some time now that the two lakes are not going to be able to support the population in that region much longer. Collaboration with other companies in the region confirms that the city has been hiding the lower water levels for at least two decades now, and the public reaction, negative as it should be, is escalating."

Carson City is supposed to be a diamond in the desert, an example of man's will over nature's revenge. To hold on to their water, though, it is also known as one of the most restrictive regions, with some of the most rigid immigration laws in the world and high corporate taxes along with far-reaching regulations of the residents' lives. Of course, this is what companies and other cities say; Hendricks always made it sound so reasonable, almost a paradise.

The President continues, so I focus on his words, determined to find a way to use this to my advantage in some fashion. "Water pirates are only the most visible sign of unrest in the region. We have reports that other companies have tried to employ their own security forces to guard their water lines, though of course, we at Inandirmak leave that to the regional directors. However, we have concerns, because mass protests from residents and rival companies increasing their own security causes our people to get nervous. Nervous people tend to do a poor job at work."

"Are you intending to pull out of Carson City, then? Simply move the employees around the existing branches?" We could certainly take on a team of theirs with their own contracts, but I don't fancy having to share power with Hendricks, no matter how nice he seems.

"For a while, at least. We thought you might have an idea of how to do this, given your knack for team building. Hendricks would need an office, but you would remain head of that branch until we can settle him elsewhere."

"Of course, of course," I say with a casual wave of my hand that is entirely too casual to be real. I'm sure the CEO's son knows it, because he half smiles. "I'm sure we can find room for him and some others, especially if they bring their clients with them." That makes his smile widen. *I've made the right move, putting things in the perspective of money, not my own authority.*

I lean back and place my hands under my chin in a tripod form for a few moments, like I'm thinking, then I lean toward the screen again. "If we could have one of their teams, a fully established team, to ease their transition, with their current client load, I'm sure we can offer them space to thrive in here at MTB."

"They have three teams, like you do, like all the branches are now trying," President Reizis reminds me, and I can see a gleam in his eyes that I can't quite decipher.

"Yes, since you asked my advice, I'd move the other two teams between the other Great Lakes branches. We aren't that far from each other, and I'm sure we can determine how best to divide up their support staff in just a few days of time. But," I say, looking around my room, "work space is limited, and unless Hendricks is bringing every client with him I don't see enough work at any one branch to support an entire extra branch worth of employees."

He nods seriously and then asks one more question. "Who do you recommend we approach?"

Oh nice, make me the one responsible for dumping these changes on my colleagues. I think, trying to remember if any of them reported any gaps or any problems at the big meeting or in our weekly planning convos. I smile as the answer easily comes to mind.

"The Chicago branch is always in need of detail-oriented support staff, and Vice President Main mentioned in a recent meeting that he wants to shake things up a bit there. Bringing in another team plus new clients would shake it up." That isn't exactly what he said, but that should make him happy, having more people to boss around.

"Welsand in Winnipeg can generally find the best person for the job. She mentioned at least two of her employees have applied for parental leave, so perhaps they could use the extra hands, too." Faye is a team player, and she did say that she was not looking forward to trying to juggle a few positions for a year or so. Parental leave is great for employee morale but a headache for administration. We've seen that already here, before I got my promotion. "Plus I believe they just acquired a new office space as well, so they can certainly accommodate another team."

The President listens, then his face breaks into a smile. "Excellent ideas; they mirror my own on the matter." Inside I sigh in relief. "I'll be in touch in a week or so should we decide to make this move. Keep your eyes on the news in the meantime. Good day, Emily."

"Good night, Sir," I say, mentally adjusting for the time difference.

I sit still for a few minutes, thinking about what has just happened. It could be a test, a check-in to see that I'm acting like I'm "part of the family," as I believe Madame Reizis worded it. I'm convinced that if I work my way up the corporate ladder fast, I can get more freedom for myself and protection for Wynn. I mean, until he pissed off Lindsey something fierce, my predecessor felt he had a lot of freedom to do things here in this office I hadn't even considered a year ago.

I can almost hear my mother ranting about the corruption of the company as she clings to her municipal loyalties. I can avoid that. I'm doing this to protect us, right?

I'm interrupted when I see the door open slowly and then Lindsey's head peek around the corner. "Everything fine, Boss?" he says in a very neutral tone he hasn't used since the first week I moved into this office. The day I let my hand wander up his leg and cup his ass was the first day he sincerely smiled at me, because he knew I was going to use all the assets the company was providing me with. Job security, after all, is a great aphrodisiac.

Isn't that what I'm really doing now, for all of us?

"Come in, Lindsey," I say firmly, and he opens the door wider and then leaves it open when I shake my head.

"I'm still working on the special project, but if Connie can't do something, I'm here," he begins until I shake my head again and push the call button for my second executive assistant.

He glances at her when she comes in carrying a pad and stylus.

They both take a seat when I nod to them, and Lindsey gets his own pad out with a bit of a put-upon look, but he says nothing.

I sit up straight and look at them both. "That was the President of Human Resources. What I'm about to tell you must stay only between the three of us." I wait for them both to go a bit pale, then Lindsey nods, quickly followed by Connie.

"There may be a need to find a few positions here on short notice. Connie, I want you to do an analysis of the building, find a way to make space for an entire new team, and look into housing options, including a PV-level apartment right here in the city, if not in this building."

She makes the notes and nods with a muttered, soft, "Yes, Boss," but stays in her seat.

"Lindsey," I say; his eyes turn to me, and he readies his stylus, all business, yet with a curious tilt of his head. "I need you to look at all our support personnel and see if there are any areas that could use an extra hand. I also need you to manage the rumor mill on this—make sure the staff and teams know their jobs are not in jeopardy here if we have to make an announcement next week. I know that as soon as my door is closed and I'm in here alone or with both of you, the rumors start. I used to be on that side of the door; I remember. We need to turn up the 'we're all one big happy family here at Inandirmak' message just a touch."

"To manage it, I'm going to need to know what's going on, Boss," he says simply, and I see Connie's posture straighten and her eyes flit between him and me. She would never think of making such a bold statement, but I expect nothing less from him.

"Of course," I say with a smile, more to calm Connie than him, and fill them in on the Carson City situation.

Connie gasps, quickly placing one hand over her mouth. That makes Lindsey's eyes widen, and he makes a very dramatic turn in his chair to look at her. She blushes, but then points out in a whisper, "I have something private to tell you," with a glance back at the door.

"Lindsey, double-check the door, please," I order, and he

simply moves to do it quickly. "We're one family here, Connie; you know that. Remember your close call at the end of last year? We take care of our own here at Inandirmak," I say as kindly as I can, but it feels a bit fake—something I'd best get used to if I want to rise up and get this corporate spouse approval.

She waits until Lindsey returns, and he's looking at her again. "I'm sorry I overreacted," she starts, but he hushes her, while I wave a hand for her to continue. "My parents, I was very little, you know, I don't remember well, but there was a drought where we lived. That's why we moved so far north. They, we, lost everything, including my brother."

And that's the thing we don't talk about but everyone keeps abreast of no matter what they might say on the publicity vids for cities and companies alike. We don't talk about the water, but we all read or watch the monthly fresh water reports. Conversations in restaurants and clubs die down to a whisper when the media cover any local, continental, or global water news. Growing up with an urban administrator and a city militia member for parents meant I was allowed to talk about it more than most, but even at home we used euphemisms to talk about the true dangers every living thing on the planet faces.

"We're all worried, so don't be ashamed of your reaction," I say, and I can see Lindsey smile approvingly out of the corner of my eye as I look at Connie, leaning forward with the best smile I can put on my face. "Even here in MTB we should be aware that every now and again some folks believe they have a right to steal from the rest of us. But we're good citizens just like Inandirmak is, right? We're just making sure we can help out the other branches if the need arises."

They both nod, but now Lindsey is smirking a bit, because he knows I'm using lines right out of the company manual. "Of course," Connie says firmly, and I'm almost shocked, because normally she is so hesitant in her speech. I knew the moment I saw her spouse that our dear assistant was not in charge of that relationship, not that I care one way or the other as long as she does a good job here.

"I'll get right on this, Boss," Connie says, standing up.

After a moment's glance at me, his eyes wide, Lindsey stands up as well. "Should this take priority over the other project, Boss?" he asks as Connie simply turns and leaves to do her tasks.

I sit back, bring my hands up to my chin, and make my fingers into a triangle I can rest just below it as I grin. "This is our highest priority, because I'm sure Corporate will make a decision to relocate them; the only questions are how soon and how many will come here."

He nods and starts to turn to go, but pauses when I say his name.

"Lindsey, I think this might actually be useful for the other project as well. Do you agree?"

He grins and taps the promise ring I gave him a few days after he agreed to my proposal. "I certainly believe it will, Emily." With that cheeky response he leaves me to find something else to occupy my mind until I can head home and see how Wynn's number homework is going.

He seems more eager to learn how to count than he was to learn the names of colors. I bet that's because Genius is linking it to his food and treats and even had the gall to suggest I use it in sexual play. I had him counting out strikes or strokes or pets or orgasms long before they got the idea.

That gets me back on track to working my connection with Doctor Vevern to my full benefit as well as hers. Within minutes I'm checking out our rival and working on strategies to bring the future campaigns for Genius into our Inandirmak family. After hours of searching I find an obscure article that mentions that a manager from a new company called Genius was talking at a global commission's annual meeting on farming last year. The summary for said speech says that Genius claimed that soon we may not need to endanger so many precious human lives on coastline plantations or on the shipping lanes.

I'm so absorbed in trying to find other information about this meeting and what it could mean that I jump when something touches my arm. "Calm down, Boss," Lindsey says, rubbing his arm where I must have automatically struck him. Father always made sure I could respond immediately to any sudden threat.

"Sorry, I didn't hear you knock on the door," I say, quickly closing down my computer but leaving the files so they'll pop up first thing in the morning.

"No problem, I can take it harder than that," he replies with a twist of his body as he slips in to sit on the edge of my desk. He smiles at me and runs one hand through his hair. "It's late, you know; everyone else is gone, company family mottos running through their heads," he assures me.

"What time is it?" I say as I look at the clock on the photo frame of Wynn and key in my lockdown code on my computer at the same time. "Bloody hell! Well, at least he's just at home, so maybe he won't be aware of just how late I am," I say, though I don't believe it. Even before he was learning to tell time he seemed to have an uncanny sense of how long I was gone and how long I should be gone at work.

"Why don't I come home with you then?" Lindsey says as he scoots closer to me and puts one foot right next to my knee. "I could work on dinner while you play with him for a while. Have to keep your pet happy after all."

"Both of them?" I tease as I reach for his foot, but he pulls away and stands up with exaggerated pout.

"Yes, both of us," he says, catching my hand and helping me rise. "I think it's time we three had a talk anyway, don't you? Especially with your clever plans today."

"Clever plans?" I say as I pack up my briefcase and prepare to leave with my future spouse in tow. "I'm just making sure this family will be protected."

Lindsey nods, and I see him pick up his own briefcase from the other side of the desk as we walk. "Indeed, as am I. Thus the conversation I think is overdue, oh master mine," he taunts me, jumping out of the way when I swing at him with one hand.

He smirks at me the entire ride down to my car and on the ride home. I think he's a bit too sure of himself, so I smirk as well but say nothing to betray how eager I am to see how this entire "conversation" works out.

Chapter Twenty-Four
Differences Between Pets

i'm waiting by the door when Master opens it and comes home. She's late, a good two hours late if i've learned to read the big clock in the living room right. i've learned cause She wants me to but seeing it only makes me worry more. Before i could just feel it inside or see it in the rays of the sun in the back yard or hear the sounds of others coming back or see the animals scurrying around as they hear the humans return. i felt it, but now i know it, and i wonder why it hurts more when She is late.

Been long time since it colder but i can tell that is coming soon too by the animals, the sun, and the plants outside. The clock is no good for that. The clock, i think, is mostly good for making worry. Why do humans want to worry? Don't they have everything?

i might ask Her that if She seems up to the question. Sometimes my questions make Her laugh, or nod Her head and then talk to me for a while. Rarely do they make Her angry as long as i've been good outside the house. i've been good since that last night She shook me then cried. i didn't ask Her why for that.

i'm smiling when She opens the door until the second scent hits my nose. He's back. Been long time since he's been back, not as long as big trip was, but i thought maybe She saw how bad pet he is and left him only for work. i catch a growl before it comes out and jump up to hug Master tight, looking around Her hip to stare at the other pet.

He smiles at me and just moves around us, heading toward the kitchen by himself as though he lives here. i whimper but Master just slips off Her shoes and smiles at me. "Lindsey's going to make dinner so that you and I can have some play time. Isn't that nice of him?"

i'm not sure what to say or do but Master just grabs my hand

and leads me back to Her room. Usually She likes what She calls build-up or foreplay. Not now i find as She pushes me gently toward Her bed with a "get ready" order before disappearing into the bathroom. i pause for one moment then open the drawer with the supplies i think She means. "Get ready" means i need to lube my butt because She's in a mood to play hard and fast, driving me to the sky over and over until i feel i can barely move.

i grab one of the towels She likes to use beneath me. i use the yucky cleaner every day for Her so there is nothing usually on the towel but humans are very weird about clean. As i spread it out i wonder why the white coats didn't just make us clean everywhere for the owners. Maybe if i count really good tomorrow Doctor Denise will tell me.

The thing that makes it less easy for me to ready myself are my arms and my claws. My arms don't like to bend around like this, so i always have to bend over far, easiest when i'm on my paws, my back toward the ceiling. My claws are short, and Master trims them, but they seem more sharp than Hers ever are. i think about stupid things or calming things to keep them at bay, hard when i'm slipping fingers inside myself to slick it all up good. i wonder why we have claws, too, when punishment is bad for using them on owners or owner's stuff. Thinking about that keeps my claws down, and soon i'm wet and waiting.

Turning my ears a bit i can hear Master doing things in the bathroom, and i can imagine what they are. Will She use the hip harness, the thigh one, or maybe the one that connects from inside of Her to go inside of me. i hope it isn't the last one, because She's more gentle with that one, and i can still smell Lindsey, and i need that scent pounded out of me and Her scent and mine flooding my nose and surrounding me.

She steps out of the bathroom and my shaft goes hard immediately when i see the thigh harness in place. She gets more levers, is that what She calls it, with this, plus i get to look up at Her, touch Her breasts, and my shaft will slip between our bodies. She takes me other positions too, but this is Her favorite with this harness. Those rare times when i'm sent to fetch one i almost always pick this one.

She stands there, hands on Her hips, Her breasts half hidden behind a bra, Her lower fur covered by cloth but not by much, looking at me with a grin. i scurry to the end of the bed and lay the towel down again before laying back, my feet up not far from my butt, legs spread so i can look down my body at Her. i whimper for effect and She laughs before walking toward me, the object of our play swinging as she moves.

On the TV one show had a group of morphs talking to the doctor again and saying that certain things about their owners were scary. One of these was the use of harnesses for play. Some said it looked like monsters or that it looked so big or so hard. Master just looks like Master, like Emalee plus good toys that i get to play with. Sometimes i think the morphs on the TV are not real, they can't really be owned cause who would talk like they do unless... i push the memories out of my head as She leans over me.

Her hair falls down around my face as She nuzzles me with Her nose. Then as She looks into my eyes, i feel Her push inside of me, making me buck up a bit and place my paws on Her arms. She slides in easily, and soon She's deep in me, Her leg pressing against my butt, Her stomach sliding over my shaft. i lick Her face and get a giggle before She slips Her hands under me and pulls me a bit closer but not off the bed.

Closing my eyes would make the sky sink lower faster, but i keep them open, watching Master's own eyes close then open, the dark parts bigger, Her lips parted as She moves Her leg and the toy in and out of me. Changes in Her breathing and scent can signal a lot of things for me when i'm pleasuring Her or She's playing with me. Her eyes, though, are the clearest signals. They change color, the parts change shape, they even narrow when She's about to change position to increase Her pace.

She does not like to hurt me on accident, She calls it. When i don't watch, sometimes i don't make the tiny move of my hips or arms or head, and then there is some pain. When i watch Her eyes and read all the other signs, though, i've figured out how to move just right so my whimper is one of pleasure, and She gets a firmer grip or a deeper angle or rubs me more.

She pauses and then lifts me up. Master is strong, though not as strong as some on the TV or in the Institute; they were men, too, so i wonder if that has something to do with strongness. i moan as i slip further down onto the toy, but She just lifts Her leg a few times, adding more but not going in or out. i can feel the stickiness between our bodies, and i've reached the sky at least twice so far when i bury my head between Her still clad breasts and start panting with another sky burst from my shaft.

i feel my shaft go soft, and Master chuckles as She turns around. "Not done with you yet," She says with a breathy chuckle.

She sits down on the bed, then lifts me up and off of the toy, separating us. i reach for Her, but She just sets me on the bed next to Her. i try to calm my breathing as She scoots back to lie against the pillows. i smile, though i'm a bit worried if i'll be able to do this position given how weak i feel right now. She unhooks Her bra and tosses it to the floor. "Hop up and ride, pet," She orders with a wiggle of a few fingers.

i nod and work my way to the toy, looking from it to Her before standing up and kneeling over Her, the toy at my ass hole. i take her offered hands and use them to help me slip down and over the toy. This is the smart toy, because i feel it turn with me as i lie down on top of Her more, my height bringing me to Her breasts if i tilt my head up. i use my paws to give support to my bucking up and down on the toy just a bit, just enough to make Master know i'm being a good pet, but also to hold up Her breasts so i can lick them, especially the nipples that are harder and darker than normal.

In this position my shaft pushes against Her lower fur, and while i can't come again so soon, between that pressure and my flicks against Her nipples, my paws gently caressing Her mounds, She reaches the sky, almost tossing me off if not for my readiness and Her fingers wound in my fur.

We both look toward the door that neither of us closed when

we hear a knocking sound. i growl a bit but bury my head between Master's breasts. He's here, right now, just when the cuddling would start.

"Sorry about that," he says.

Master grabs an edge of the bed cover and pulls it over us slightly with a "Lindsey, bloody hell," showing Her annoyance.

"I tried not to see much," he says but gives us no time to reply. "Dinner will be ready in 15 minutes or so. You may want to shower," he adds, and then i hear his footsteps move away.

Master lies there for a while, and I feel Her laughter before I hear it because I can feel the rumble in Her chest. After a few moments of laughing, She swats my butt and tells me to move it.

As we take a quick shower together, a wonderful rare thing, She says something about it would have happened sooner or later. i'm not sure what that means, but i feel growling building up inside my chest again, so i turn my face to the water and purposely swallow some to damp it down.

Master and Lindsey talk about a lot of things i don't understand. Mostly i tune it out, eating my food at Her feet, ears tuned up, just in case he should say something i should know about. Something that might imply that he's here to replace me. Master says that isn't true, but i know i shouldn't think about such things. She'll make the right decision. That's what humans do. They make the decisions, and we do as we're told. That's what any good morph would do. Then he makes Her laugh, and i feel the fur on the back of my neck go up. Focus on eating, i tell myself. Above me they are talking more about this wedding thing. They have a problem? i lift my head up at that. This is good. They have a problem means that maybe he doesn't move in? Maybe there would be no wedding thing? But then Master just says, "It isn't a problem. We'll fix it. I'm sure you'll be able to see everything that's going on."

"I did try. Hey, part of the job." i sniff and go back to my food. As i'm eating i think... problem... problem. But no. No that is too risky. Too dangerous. i keep my head down and finish eating. At one point he stands back up and goes into the kitchen proper. Master leans down and pets my head. i look up, place my head on Her lap, bat my eyes at Her, and try to keep Her attention.

"So, what do you think of him?" She asks me, and i just tilt my head to one side. Ah, She must mean Lindsey. i sniff again, and She shakes Her head. "Oh, you're not still worried about that, are you? I thought I explained it. He's work related. This is about work."

"Not only about work." His voice interrupting us draws my attention, but instead of putting my head back down near my food, i just burrow into Her lap further.

"Oh, what is that?" i hear Master say.

"Dessert."

"I didn't know you could cook."

"You didn't know I could cook?" He sets the plates down, and i arch one eyebrow, lift my head slightly and look at the table. i can smell it. It's that thing She calls chocolate. i don't know. Smells like the earth to me. Don't know how She could eat it. But then i'm not allowed to eat any human food. i'm not good enough. i don't know.

"Oh," Master says, "Where did you find this?"

"In your cabinets. Why? Was it for a special occasion?" His voice is worried. i can tell. i'm getting very good at figuring out human speech now, even if i can't quite mimic it yet.

"No. No. I just forgot that I still had some. My mother had sent me some a while back. What is this?"

"Just very simple cake. Flourless."

"That's basically candy." She says. "Wynn, Wynn." She's tapping my head gently, and i look up Her again. "Can you please get off my lap so I can continue eating?"

i sniff again but then lower my head back down. i really want to crawl into the other room. But no, i need to stay here where i can pay attention to what they are saying. To what he's saying.

They eat this chocolate-flourless-cake-thing for some time, and there is a lot of laughing. So the chocolate-flourless-cake-thing makes Master laugh. i scratch behind one ear. Could i learn to make chocolate-flourless-cake-thing? The idea whirls around in my head until Master pulls Her chair back, signaling they are done with their meal. i bounce up and dance around Her a little bit. Looking up hopefully, wagging my tail—even though it feels slightly unnatural to do that. I have seen on TV that morphs do that when they are happy. When they want attention. So i should try more to do it myself.

"Well, you're all energetic, and you're not even the one who had the chocolate."

"Boss." It's Lindsey again, and i glance at him. "Why don't you go look at what I've done? See if you understand my comments. I have more to do, but at least you could let me know if these are the sorts of things you need to know about the proposal."

"Oh, alright. I'll work." She says.

"Oh, there'll be play," he adds as he picks up the dishes. i turn to follow after Her, and he calls my name. I stop and look back at him. "Yeah, I was talking to you," he says. "Wynn, how would you like to help me do the dishes? Emily tells me that you are becoming very useful around the house." i just lower my tail and look at him. "It will give her more time to look at what I brought home, and the more time she looks at it—you know, time that you're not bothering her?" i sniff as he says this, fluffing up my tail a bit. How dare he assume i bother Master when She has work. i don't. Good morph... usually. "— the faster she'll get it done," he continues. "So if you'll help me, or at least keep me company, then I can take off earlier, and you can have her all to yourself. That's what you want, isn't it?"

There is a huge grin on his face, and he's folded his arms across his chest. Somehow he's moved closer to me. Now i'm forced to actually look up at him at a sharp angle. He crouches down so that he's closer to me. "I mean, if I were in your position, I'd want to have as much time with her as I could. While I can."

His eyes look a little colder, and there is a shock that goes though my body. i can't forget. He's human. All humans are better than all morphs. i've allowed him to see that i'm upset by him being here. Worried about him being here. Oh, stupid morph.

i nuzzle his leg with my nose and whimper a little bit. "wynn help," i say softly.

"There we go. Remember, I know you can talk. I can't hear your thoughts," he says as he stands up. Master says that too from time to time. Really not sure what it means. But i sigh and follow him further into the kitchen.

Doing dishes is not something that Master has me do. Something about wet fur not hi-geen-ic. Hi-gen-ic. I can't say the word. She doesn't want me touching clean dishes. Lindsey doesn't have me touch the dishes either, though he does have me point out where the different things go. "It's too bad you are covered with all that fur," he says at one point as though he is reading my mind. "Or maybe you could actually do the dishes. Free us both up. But this is a huge help. Now, where does this go?" he asks, holding up a pan. "I didn't use it to cook with, so I have no idea where it goes." i go to the cabinet and open it up. "Yeah, I noticed she doesn't have safety locks on it. I thought she might. You know, for kids, pets." i sniff again at him. "But I suppose you're much more clever that that. You know not to go digging around in things you're not supposed to."

"So why is it a problem that I put down that I'm British?" Both of us turn our heads as Master enters the room. Lindsey blinks a few seconds, and i blink as well.

"Oh, that," he says. "Well, when it asks about where you were born, and those sorts of questions—you put down that you were British. There's no Britain," he says to Her.

"I know there is no Britain anymore, but British is a cultural identity." Master says.

"Is it?" Lindsey adds. "I didn't put down that I'm—" He thinks for a few seconds. "American? Is that the right word?"

Master sighs. "I've always put down that I'm British."

"I think they want the city that you were born in. The principality."

"But cities don't matter anymore. Not to us. We're part of the corporate structure." Master says.

"Keep it British, then," he says. "It's just that no one else put down something like that in any of their forms. They all put down the cities they were born in."

"Fine." She says.

"Hey," Lindsey calls out, and She stops. "Doesn't mean you have to get rid of the accent. I mean, that's sexy. Just, you know, let's do it how everyone else is doing it."

They stare at each other for a few seconds, and i look from one to the other. "Yes," Master says, "Have to do it like everyone else. Have to be like everyone else," and She leaves.

"Why is this so difficult for her?" Lindsey asks, and i look up at him again. Is this real questions, or one of those fake questions that humans ask? Ones they don't want real answer to? Must be the second, because he goes back and finishes dealing with the dishes. He does them differently than Master does. She usually washes a few at a time, dries them, puts them away. But he's washed them all. Set them in the rack. Then he's drying them and putting them away. i guess there weren't that many dishes. After what seems like forever being in his presence, he pats his leg as though he is calling a dog. i am not a dog. Fox morph, not a dog. He crouches down again and says, "So, lets go in and see how she's doing. Remember, she has work to do. We need to let her do it." i roll my eyes slightly but turn away and head into the living room, where i hope Master is sitting. Yes, there She is, on the couch looking up at the computer screen again. Looking down at the smaller digi-pad that She has. i come over, lay my head on the couch next to Her, and look at Her.

"Hello, did you help Lindsey out? Did he help out?" She asks him before i even had a chance to answer.

"Oh he was a big help. He told me where everything went. Made it go a lot faster than rooting around all your cabinets."

"Thought you would have rooted around in all my cabinets when you were making dinner."

"Yeah but, you know, we needed some guy time too."

Guy time? She looks at him, then at me. "Wynn, why don't you go sit in the window and watch the backyard. I know you like

to do that. Lindsey and I have some work we have to do." So i
retreat to my favorite seat in the entire house. If Master isn't there.
Or if i'm not allowed to sit next to Master. i look outside into the
dark yard. i see little specks of light lighting up now and again.
Master said once these are called fireflies. i don't know. They don't
set the yard on fire. They don't seem to be made of fire. i just accept
it's another human word for things that i can't understand. And i
watch them, keeping one eye on them—on the couch. He's sitting
right next to Her again. Every now and then he touches Her arm,
She touches his leg. But there is no more laughing. And few times
i hear Master's voice harsh, hard—She's angry. And when i hear
that, i grin and turn back to the strange fireflies and watch them.

Chapter Twenty-Five
Playing The Game

Hendricks and some of his staff have firmly moved into our branch here. I'm looking at the documentation that Lindsey delivered to me, and I sigh. It's been three months since I made the decision to let them come here, not that it was actually my decision to make. Andres Reizis made it clear that, well, it was all for the Inandirmak family, right? I sigh again and put down the paper. We haven't mixed up the teams yet. His one team that he brought with him has been handling the cases that he brought with him—three cases. Relatively lucrative, though, to be honest, one is really geared more toward desert cities. And Carson City isn't the only one in trouble, it turns out. The news is reporting a fair amount of violence in several other desert cities around the world. I shake my head and pick up the papers again. I should talk to Hendricks again. I haven't really talked to him since the move. He has his office; his wife Lisa is with him. That's good to know. Maybe he'd know something about this whole corporate spouse process. We turned in the paperwork, but nothing yet. I flip though the pages again and don't see any problems. Of course, that first week you could have cut the tension in the office with a knife. We had several team meetings that week, reassuring everyone that their positions were safe, their roles were secure, and we were not going to be turning over their contracts. And when that didn't happen, people settled down again—eventually, though, we'll have to switch teams around. I mean, that idea is what got me this promotion. If I don't do it, it will look suspicious. Right now I can't afford for anything to look suspicious to the home office.

I buzz for Lindsey, and in a second or two the door opens, and he comes inside. "Hey," I say.

"Need something, Boss?" He's wearing a sky blue shirt today and has an earring dangling from one ear. He's been dressing up a bit more since we've filed the paperwork. But he has been flirting less with everyone else in the office, I've noticed. And I do notice. It's true; I spy on him. But I doubt I spy on him more than he spies on me. "What can I do for you?" he says again.

"Can you call Lisa and arrange a meeting between me and Hendricks?" I ask him.

He arches an eyebrow. Having Lisa here has been more of a problem for him than anyone else. He is supposed to be the executive secretary, and yet here she is in charge of another office right inside of ours. She isn't number one here, although technically Hendricks would have seniority, but that was the deal I made with Egirdir. "Sure" Lindsey says after a moment of hesitation. "I'll go talk to her face to face. She doesn't like me very much," he adds with a flip of his hair. He's also been letting that grow out a little bit.

We need to have a conversation about that. I don't like him looking too feminine, which is odd, because he is clearly a man. I push that thought away and shake my head. "Can you at least be civil to her?"

"Me?" He puts one hand on his chest and laughs, "I'm civil to everyone, even if they are too stupid to realize it. Anything else?" he asks.

"No, that should do it." I say. He nods and leaves the room, shutting the door behind him.

I look at the door for a second. I've been keeping the door shut a lot lately too. I don't know why. I stand up, cross to it, and open it back up. Lindsey glances back over his shoulder at me. "Why don't we just leave it open. We want people to know I'm here for them if they need me," I explain. Connie glances over from her desk as well and gives me a smile, then turns back to her typing. Connie has been taking all of this in stride. Of course, it's not as if Hendricks brought a second secretary with him or anything. Nope, we had to hire someone, and that was good, because it sent the message to the entire office that this was not going to be a lot of job cutting. Nope; in fact, having more people here could create more jobs. Of course, that's a bonus in Metro Thunder Bay, because we had to get permission from the council in order to bring in Hendricks and his team in the first place.

I go back to my desk and computer and check my messages. No one is having a crisis currently, so I go back to the clickback page and look at our latest campaigns online, making sure everything works. In a way being VP is not just about management; it is about beta testing everything, I think. I mean, I'm not the greatest computer expert in the world. I figure if I can use their pages and nothing seems broken, then the average person out there shouldn't have a problem with it either.

After I go though that, I sign off again, and pick up Wynn's picture from my desk. This—this is what I should be thinking about. I hold it in my hand and turn it on, and he starts laughing and chasing a ball around the floor. I changed the video weeks ago to something that made him seem more lively. More petlike. And that's important right now.

I took him back to the Jungle   the center. After they went through all of their data, they decided that they wanted to continue research. I wasn't too sure about it, but then I got another letter. The institute that created him wanted him to come in for a checkup. Yeah, right, a checkup. So I agreed and signed him up for more training at the Jungle.

The other night—what was it, three nights ago?—he came up to me as I carried in the groceries, helped me unpack it, picked up an apple, looked at me, and said, "If Master buys five apples and eats two, how many apples will Wynn have to play with?" I remember just being in shock. What was he saying? Then he laughed, "Three! Wynn will have three apples to play with." That's mathematics.

I put his photo down and turn it off again so that it's just a frozen image there, looking up at me with his big bright blue eyes. Mathematics. What are they doing? Are they crazy? If he goes around asking people these mathematical puzzles, they'll start asking questions. A lot of questions. I had a discussion with him about that and made it very clear that he is not to repeat that sort of little trick to anyone, not even Lindsey.

At least they are getting along better. Lindsey comes over about twice a week now, makes dinner, hangs out, and watches TV. He also looks at more wedding planning stuff—though last week I put an end to that. We aren't hearing back, so what's the point of planning? Lindsey just sighed and pouted in his rather exasperated way.

And now Wynn's doing that—I have to put a stop to that too. Going to the Jungle, learning mathematics, that's great, but mimicking Lindsey? I shudder. I don't need him mimicking Lindsey. I need a clear division in my mind, human potential corporate spouse vs. morph pet, because sometimes I think I might be confusing them.

Half an hour later, Lindsey knocks on the door and then walks in when I nod at him. "Have it arranged—he can meet with you later this afternoon or tomorrow morning."

"What fits best in my calendar?" I ask. He looks at his data pad and says, "Either will work. The next meeting you have is two afternoons from now. You have to meet with the entire team to go over that RH2O proposal." He rolls his eyes. "Yeah. RH2O, that's not going over so well."

I sigh, "Well ok, let's do it this afternoon, then, and get it out of the way. Um, here." I hand back all the papers he left in my office. "Did you actually look at these?" he asks, tilting his head to one side. "Of course... I glanced at them. Looks like everything is fine."

"Um." He puts the papers down and flips through them, then pulls one out and places it down in front of me. "This might be a problem," he says, pointing to a sentence on one of the evaluation forms.

"Someone's pregnant?" I ask. "I don't understand. She's going to be needing time off." I sigh. "OK, set up a meeting, then. She and I can talk and fill out the appropriate paperwork. See if there's anyone we can move around here, and if we're going to need to get someone else."

"Ok, I'll do that." He takes the papers back again and gives me a silent frown before he leaves.

Yeah, I need to be paying more attention to things at the office. I start by typing out an agenda for what I want to talk to Hendricks about, and half an hour later I discover that I actually have a lot of things to talk to him about.

First, I need his impression on how his people are doing. Yes, he gave it to me in the paperwork, but I want to look at him and see what his body language says. Second, I would like to know a little more about what happened in Carson City. Did he get all of his teams out? Are some of them still there? I mean, Inandirmak said they moved everyone out, but... I was remembering what happened in the city of my birth. It was a similar situation—company shut down, claimed the city regulations were too rigid. Turned out they had actually been stealing water—adding extra lines that they weren't supposed to. The company pulled out but didn't pull all of its workers out with them. So the city was left with—what was it—two dozen people who weren't citizens and had no right to water and no right to their housing anymore. I remember my mother almost pulled her hair out over the issue.

I sigh again. No, I need to know. I need to know if Inandirmak is going to keep its word, keep its honor. Ah, and then there is the annual meeting. Right now, both Hendricks and I are scheduled to go. I need to make sure he is OK with that. Maybe we can share a ride over. I guess there are a lot of personal things on the agenda, too, I reflect. I'm about ready to delete them, but I decide not to, because I do want to talk to him about the annual meeting, about having a corporate spouse, and about his pet ownership. If I can get his impressions, maybe I can suss out if he is an ally. *Be careful*, I tell myself—*he could just turn right around and report you to the home office. You don't need that, Lindsey doesn't need that, and Wynn doesn't need that.*

I've already bought my ticket anyway, so it would be a matter of seeing if he could get a ticket on the same flight, and if we could sit together. No, impossible—the Company has a lot of pull, because a lot of money gives you a lot of pull in this world, but... oh well. And then there's the question of how to talk to him about some of these more personal things. Hmmm. I put the agenda away, stand up, stretch out, and look out my windows onto the bay. So much water here—I did hear one of his people in the elevator the other day mention how crazy we are about water. We're just drinking water right and left. What is going on in Carson City? I grab my purse, put on my sunglasses, and decide I want to eat out this afternoon. Maybe I'll stop by the Jungle. Why not? There are some things I want to talk to the dear doctor about anyway.

I sit at the table in the Jungle and look at my food for a few seconds. I've already put down the privacy screen. I try to keep my eye out for Dr Vevern. Denise. I need to make sure I call her Denise, as much as it irks me to do so.

There she is, walking toward me. She seems a bit confused. Her face is making a slight frown, and she's glancing around her. Good, she doesn't have Wynn with her. I did ask for a private meeting with her. She steps up to the screen. I open it, she comes in, and I lower it back down again. "I'm really surprised that you came to see me," she says as she takes her seat.

"Oh, am I inconveniencing you, Doctor?" I say, tweaking up my accent just a little bit here. I have noticed that North Americans tend to react to it in a way that might be beneficial to me. "I hope I didn't bother you too much. I mean, you did say I could come back and talk to you anytime I wanted, didn't you?"

She takes a deep breath and then nods. "Of course—of course. It's just that you asked not to see Wynn at the same time."

"Well I thought he was in... testing? That's what they told me, anyway, when I asked about you. We haven't had time to really have lunch together yet, and, well, I did want to talk to you without him being here. He does have a tendency to be a bit nosey. I don't know if you've noticed that." I smiled.

She nods and then chuckles. "Yes, well, it is his type. Fox morphs tend to be a bit curious. They, and cats. Dogs can be, but they tend to give up as soon as they are told not to. Is there anything particular that you wanted to talk to me about?"

"Maybe you should order some food first," I say. I hand her the menu.

"Oh, alright."

I give her a few minutes while I look at my food and poke around a bit. It's not that the food doesn't taste good, and I need to eat. It's just that I have to be careful. Making inquires of this nature... I don't want her to think that I'm going to pull him out of testing. Although, depending on what she tells me, I may very well do that. That would put me right back... no, I don't want to think about that. I don't want to think about this right now.

Soon she calls in her order, and once it arrives we eat for a few minutes. As they take the plates away, I use the moment to bridge a question to her. "So, Denise." She glances at me when I use her first name. I see a slight tinge of pink on her cheeks. "I do hope it is alright that I call you that. Denise." I say again.

"Yes." She smiles widely. "Of course, Emily." She uses my name back.

I dig my fingernails into my leg with one hand. I really don't want her to use my first name, but if I'm going to use hers... "Yes, well, I'm glad that I feel comfortable being on a first-name basis with you. I'm a bit more formal, I'm afraid. It's taken me a while, but you've done wonders with Wynn." There, I'm just going to let that hang out there.

"Do you think so?" she said. "He's one of our more promising subjects. He's very clever. It's too bad we don't have any real way of testing them."

"What do you mean?"

"Well," she says, sitting back and folding her arms over her stomach for a second, "you see, with a human, we can give them standard tests. You know, intelligence tests, comprehensive tests, evaluations—things like that. But with a morph, we can't do that. Not only do they not know how to read and write to a degree necessary to do that, but they simply don't have the same cultural experiences. We don't have a true experience of their culture either."

"Their culture?" I pause and look at her for a second. "You made that sound like the morphs have a culture of their own."

"Oh yes." She sits up a little straighter. "We think that they do. Has he not talked to you about that at all?"

"No. No, he hasn't, really." But then I pause. He's said a few things. Every now and then he lets something slip. Something about singing. Songs reaching the sky. Every now and then I hear him talking to himself when he doesn't know I'm paying attention. It's like he's repeating expressions that he's heard. I just assumed he got that from the clinic. "I don't... he hasn't been... he doesn't share those kind of things with me, I'm afraid. But I'm so sorry for interrupting you. You were saying about testing and evaluating?"

"Oh, yes, yes. Well, we can't do it with standard testing, so we decided to evaluate their intelligence and potential simply by trying to teach them things."

"Ahh, like basic counting, reading the clock, colors, shapes... mathematics." I do sense my voice dropping a little bit there. I mean, that's what I really want to know about, after all.

She raises her chin slightly and gives a sharp nod. "Ahh, so that is what this is about. You aren't the first owner to come here with some concerns about our teaching what is really just basic arithmetic," she says.

"Whatever you think, I don't think it's standard for genetically engineered creatures to learn, is it?"

"No, no, of course not, but we're thinking ahead for what we might want to use these creatures for—you know, the Genesis project. Will they be capable of learning these things? Will they be capable of some higher understanding? Be able to follow more complex orders? Or are we going to have to completely re-engineer them mentally. Intellectually—you know," she says.

I just narrow my eyes slightly. "I was just so very shocked, you see, when he came up to me and started to talk to me about apples and... and playing with apples and eating apples."

"Yes, yes, we found that putting things in a more concrete context... often with food, or playtime, or nature and trees. Teaching arithmetic." Again she used that word, not the one I used, mathematics. "Put in that context, they seem to grasp it much more easily, as apposed to abstracts. Um, I'm sure that's true for human children as well. When you first start teaching them arithmetic, you might say if—if Billy has five candies and Julie takes one away, how may candies does Billy have? You know. You use things like that. It isn't until you get into mathematics that you start dealing with things that are not quite so concrete."

"Is your goal to teach them that, then? I'm not sure that that's necessary."

"No, no. Not at this point. It's just that...." She sighs and leans over the table, very close to me, and lowers her voice—unnecessarily, because the privacy screen is still down. "Miss Potter." Ahh, she is referring back to my preferred name. "I do hope you don't withdraw Wynn from the program. We are making... incredible observations. It's increasing our knowledge tremendously."

"Are people already pulling out?" I asked directly.

"As I said, you aren't the first with these concerns. But, um, I can bring you another brochure, more forms. You know."

"You want to lay out what you are going to do for me in a new contract?" There, that sounds like something a consumer rights activist would say. If they are displeased with the product or service, don't just accept their answer; demand a new contract. Protect your rights. Remember, as a citizen you can do this.

I never thought I would be one of those people relying on that. Not since—I pushed the thought away. "I want to trust you, Denise," I say, purposefully using her first name, "I really do, but as we were discussing, ISM—they may want to harm Wynn, and I just can't allow that. But you said that your program would try to understand him better and offer him some protection at the same time. So I would prefer not to pull him out, but I do have to think about what's best for him. "

"Of course, of course," she says. "I understand. Let me step out, and I can get you new information, if you don't mind."

"That's fine. I have a little while longer that I can wait here. Perhaps I'll order dessert."

"Yes, you should do that." She stands up, I lower the privacy screen, and she steps away. I don't bother to raise the privacy screen again, simply sitting there. I call in an order for dessert. Something simple, easy, relatively light. I don't feel like spending money for chocolate or having to think about working out a lot if I order anything too fattening. They seem to grow a lot of food right here at this restaurant. There are definitely things on this menu that should be priced higher than they currently are.

After I wait for my order, I take out my phone and check it for messages. Nope. None. So I text Lindsey and let him know that he should make sure that my meeting with Hendricks is still scheduled. I will make it back in time. Just, what I am currently doing may take a little longer. He writes back immediately.

"You OK Boss?"

"I'm fine," I tell him. "Set up the casual corner."

"OK Boss."

I put my phone away, and within moments my dessert is delivered, along with another serving for Dr. Vevern, who returns mere moments later. She comes in, and I put the privacy screen down again.

She pushes a folder across to me. "All right. Here you go. It's updated information. If you agree to all of it, there is a place for you to sign. Um, twelve others have already signed it, but—"

"But what?"

"But we've lost seven. We have a few more that haven't come in. They don't seem to be too worried about it, or not worried enough to come in for it yet. I do hope that you understand what we are doing and agree to let Wynn continue. He does seem to enjoy it a great deal."

I look at her and then look down at the folder. "Give me a few minutes," I say. It's pretty standard. Actually not a lot is different from the first one I looked at and agreed to. There is, however, advanced training. Oh. Basic arithmetic. Huh. Household work. I pause here—they'll be surprised when they find he knows how to do some of that, I think. Basic motor skills. "Motor skills?" I say out loud.

"Um, like exercise. See how much his body can move. I'm sure you may have noticed that his body, while it may look humanoid, is definitely not human. His legs, his arms—there are unique angles. The connection between the muscle groups and the bones...."

"Yes, yes, I understand. Down here." I tap my finger on the section I just looked at. "Reading and writing? I know it says basic, but—"

"That is only if he continues to the next phase. You see?" she taps the folder again, and I see the text.

"Ahh yes. It will be only a select few that are chosen for this, and they will have to get our permission. This sounds acceptable. I do hope, though..." I say, holding my finger over the digiform I would have to sign. "I do hope that you are emphasizing to Wynn and the others that these are not everyday skills that they are being taught. I would hate for them to endanger the program or themselves," I say, leaving "Or me" unsaid, but I think it clearly to myself, "by doing things that are unusual."

"Oh, we are! We are," she said. "We are. And if he should speak out or act out in any way, I want to you call me personally and let me know about it."

I stare at her for a few seconds and nod at her curtly. "This seems acceptable." I tap my finger on the screen, sign my name, leave a genetic print, close the folder, and hand it back to her.

"Excellent. We'll then send a copy of it to your home computer. Which is still where you want us to send documents to?"

"Yes," I say simply. I don't want the company knowing more than it needs to, so I'm using my home computer for all of this. Technically, the company owns the house, but with my father's help I've set up secure firewalls and traps.

"Excellent. Oh, I'm so glad you came to talk to me about this. Several of the others that have withdrawn—they just simply pulled their morphs out of the program. Didn't talk to us at all about it. I know we are doing cutting-edge things, very risky, but I promise you, Emily, it will all be worth it. Not just for you, not just for Wynn, not just for me, but for all of us. What we are working on with Genesis, it's going to improve things for all of us."

I smile and take a bite of my dessert. The berries and fresh cream taste real enough, fresh enough, and yet they are turning sour in my stomach. When was the last time I heard the expression, "It will benefit all of us?" I smile again and force myself to finish my meal.

I have about 40 minutes or so once I'm back at the office before there is a knock at the door and Lindsey opens it. "Boss, Vice President Hendricks is here."

I sit up straighter. "Oh yes, yes, excellent." I stand up, push my desk chair in, and actually walk to the door as Lindsey opens it. He takes a few steps in, and Hendricks follows him—and behind him, I guess that must be Lisa, his wife/executive assistant. "Ashton!" I say, holding out both my hands to shake his. His eyes widen a moment, but he takes them. "I just wanted to connect here—talk a little about how you're settling in. Well, we really don't think we need it recorded," I say with a slight chuckle. "Lindsey." I look directly at him, and he blinks a moment. "Why don't you and Lisa go get some tea and do your own discussion on how things are settling down?"

He tilts his head to one side a moment and then smiles. "Of course. That sounds excellent. Lisa?" He turns around and gives her one of his most charming smiles. "Have you been upstairs to the executive lounge? You know we can go there, right?" Before she can even lodge a protest he has his hand at the small of her back and is steering her away from my office.

Hendricks glances at them and then back at me. "Oh, he's smooth," he says after a moment.

"He is," I say. "Won't you come in?" I motion to the corner, where Lindsey has already set up some beverages on the table next to the two comfortable chairs and nice couch. Yes, we'll sit on the chairs. I glance at the couch and remember some activities that were enjoyed there just a few days before, hoping that Lindsey has had the foresight to clean it well. I'm sure he has. As Ashton steps in I close the door behind him and follow him. I take a seat as he waits, kind of looking at me, wondering what seat he should take. I take the one closest to the table and the treats that have been laid out, leaving him with the one closest to the window. Now, technically I'm offering him the superior seat in this alcove. He doesn't say anything, but he does have a little grin plastered on his face when he takes a seat. There, this may be my office in my city and my branch, but he is senior to me overall in the company. This is a subtle way of letting him know that I know this, even if dynamics have changed here a bit. "You like tea, mochaid, caffeinaid, just plain water... oh, look." I pull off a napkin that is over a tub of ice. "He has chilled fruit juice as well. Not sure of the type."

"You know," Ashton says, sitting back, "water would be fine. Just plain water... You have so much of it here," he adds after a moment. I smile at him and transfer the juice bottle out so that I can use the ice—waste not, want not, remember—in our glasses. Just plain, ordinary, Metro Thunder Bay water. Best kind there is. It says so right on the bottle. It says so on all of our tax statements, too. I pour us each a full glass with ice, then I actually put the water bottle in the tub of ice and cover it back up with the insulating napkin. There, that will keep the ice and water chilled. As for the juice bottle, it should stay chilled for some time, should we want it later. We both take a sip and sigh.

"Yes, I heard there was a water issue in Carson City," I say. He did bring it up, giving me permission to discuss it. We haven't discussed this issue at all. We've actually discussed very little; that's why I wanted to meet with him.

"Yes, Carson City is—I don't know how close you have been paying attention to the news," he says as he runs his hands through his hair. Hmmm, I wonder, is it thinner? It might be thinner. Might be stress; I'd be feeling stress if I'd been effectively demoted, as he's been.

We're both VPs—we're both go-getters, putting our best foot forward, leading in a direct fashion, aren't we? Yet I notice that he's feeling unusually uncomfortable, as a bead of sweat falls down the side of his face. I'm feeling even more comfortable than normal with him in my office, more in charge, in control, like a VP. Looking at my colleague, I consider the facts of his needing to come into my territory and what that suggests in our very insular world.

To be blatantly honest, the role that I now play here in the company is a much more comfortable role for me than being one of the many underlings. A lot of people look at Leslie, Lisa, Connie—the support staff—and think they're weak. They're not, of course. Lindsey is anything but weak. In fact, he can be quite the little bitch when he wants to be. I couldn't do what he does, just following orders with a smile, and using my charisma and manipulation to get my way in a subtle fashion. I'd be highly uncomfortable if I lost my position and had to resort to less direct ways of exercising my power. That's it. That's why he's uncomfortable, and I need to find a way to embrace my authority without ignoring his experience.

"Are you too warm?" I ask. "I could turn the temperature down a little bit."

"No—no, that's fine," he says. "I'm just a little nervous. I'm not sure what you wanted to talk about. Is there a problem?"

I sit back, hold my glass for a moment, and take another sip. Then I lean forward and put my glass on the little table, making sure to use a coaster. "No, I don't think so. I was looking through the personnel reports. Your team seems to be doing an admirable job under the circumstances."

"Circumstances," he repeats the word. "Yeah, under the circumstances. You know, the two of us here, this probably won't work for very long." Well, that was amazingly forward, I think. Here I was, wanting to have a friendly conversation, and he's pushing us into much more confrontational territory. I have no intention of competing with this man for my position here at the branch. That was a ridiculous notion, especially since I've done much more for the Company that he has, and I've been here for a much shorter amount of time.

But I push all those thoughts aside and smile. "Hey, it's okay," I say in a soothing voice. "I don't foresee there being a problem. Right now I'm helping out a colleague. I'm helping out the

Inandirmak family. We have to think about the greater good here.
We can't just think about our own jobs."

He chuckles a moment and glances down. "Yeah. Greater good.
I'm sorry. I'm just very—I'm just very nervous. Lisa's been
worried, and Aaron isn't adjusting well."

"Aaron?" I repeat the name.

"My son." he says.

"Oh." Damn it, I curse myself internally. I should know he has
a son, shouldn't I? Shouldn't that have been in his file or in a report
or something? But I swear the name is just a complete and utter
blank for me. "Your son is how old?" I ask, trying to hide the fact
that I'm completely clueless as to the direction our conversation
has suddenly taken.

"Um, he's not that old—I mean, he's eight. You know, he's only
in third grade, but still, children don't like to move around. They
find it a challenge."

"Hmm, is that so?" I say.

"Well, didn't you, growing up?" he asks.

"I didn't move around." I said. "Not until I was much older
and my mother took a different metropolitan position."

"Metro," Hendricks said. "Oh, so you have citizenship status."

I shrug slightly. "I did. I suppose technically I still do. But I am
one of Inandirmak's now. One big happy family." I repeat.

He nods slightly. "Yeah, it's—it's a choice, isn't it? I mean, Lisa
and I are fine, but Aaron..." He shrugs a bit. "So..." He leans
forward. "Speaking of kids, are you planning on having some,
then?" My eyes widen a bit. "I heard through the corporate
grapevine that you've applied for a spouse? Lindsey, I assume?" he
asks, looking towards the door. Ah, yes. I shouldn't be surprised
that the rumor mill works both ways. I should be more on top of
it, though. I should've known he had a child, for example.

"Oh yes, I didn't know that would be common knowledge.
We just filled out an application."

"Oh, they're contacting colleagues, other people in the
Americas. You know. Getting feedback. Do you think you are
mature enough? Do you think Lindsey is a good match?"

"Really?"

"Don't worry; I said that, from what I've observed, it looked like it was about time you settled down."

I frown just slightly. "Oh well." Then I blush. At least I hope he thinks it's a blush. Actually, I'm angry. How dare they ask Hendricks what I'm doing here? He hasn't been here that long, and we've interacted maybe four or five times at most. Clearly in a horribly superficial manner, too, given the fact that I didn't know that he had a child or the child's name. "Well, thank you. I mean, I hope that you were able to tell them the truth. You haven't been here for long, and we certainly haven't had very many meetings."

"Hey that's fine. In my opinion, if you want to get married, that should be your right. You know, in the Metros, all you have to do is have been born there, or at least one of the spouses must have been born there, and one of them has to have a job there. I hear in some areas group marriages are recognized."

I nod my head. Yes, that was true. There were a lot more types of legalized marriage in the cities, which was interesting, because they held very tightly to their citizenship status. But companies? Well, I've never applied to be married other than here, and that fairly recently. What did I really know about it? "Oh I don't know. I've never been married before, or even applied to be married before. Apparently this wasn't such a big deal a long time ago."

"Hmm, and people used to water their lawns whenever they wanted to, too," Hendricks says casually, but I can tell he's very nervous about it.

"Now, you mentioned Carson City," I say, trying to ease us back to the conversation. "Do you want to talk about what happened there?" Of course, the question is, do I want to talk about it? Not really. I mean, I have been watching the news, and it hasn't been good. Last I heard, martial law hours had been extended. But I keep all that inside and wait for Hendricks to say something. I can see he is clenching one fist, and he takes a big breath.

"Ah. Yeah, well. You know, our home was vandalized there. That's when I contacted the company. We didn't run," he tries to explain. "The average person found out where I lived. I had to think about everyone at the branch."

"Of course," I say gently. "Of course."

"Kind of foolish there. The branch president—you know he's gone most of the time. So I kind of had to make the call."

I suck my breath in through my teeth. "Yes, I had thought about that recently myself. What if a crisis happened here and the President wasn't available?"

"Well, you know, that is sort of our role, to step in when he or she can't or doesn't have the information. It's just that they spend so much time at the Home Office." Hendricks says.

"Yes. But it isn't like they don't communicate with us."

"No, no, they communicate. They just—it's just hard to understand what was going on there if you weren't there."

"What was going on there?" I ask, a little more firmly this time.

He looks at me and nods his head. "Um. Well, the city declared martial law. At first they were charging some of the companies with water theft. We weren't doing it. I swear we weren't. But..."

"Were other companies?" I pushed a little further.

"Maybe. I've just sort of been watching the news casually." His eye twitches, and I think that probably means he's lying, but I don't push it.

"Of course, I mean if you wanted to settle here. It's a good idea to be firmly aware of what goes on in MTB."

"MTB?"

"Metro Thunder Bay. Kind of short for it. You have to get all hip with the local lingo." I say with a grin.

"Oh. Yeah. Yeah. That would be good. That would be great."

We sit silently for at least a few minutes, then I look towards the table again. "Oh, it looks like Lindsey has little—uh, cookies for us." I make sure I use the more appropriate and common word from here, even though I'm dying to say "biscuit." Biscuits are—well, biscuits are something different, Lindsey would tell me. I put a few onto the plate and hold them out to him. I am not going to let him refuse this.

"Oh, thank you," he says. Then I smile, because I just learned something very important about Ashton Hendricks. He is comfortable with letting me taking the lead. I take a few cookies of my own and nibble on some.

"You know, I was thinking that perhaps we could go out some time and talk about how you are settling in. And Lisa—and Aaron. If you need any help navigating the Metro?" Now he looks at me a little more closely, so I smile wider. "Well, to be kind of blunt, I also wanted to ask you about the whole corporate marriage thing. How that is working out for you? How long you had to wait? Did I make any stupid mistakes on the application?"

He chuckles a little bit, saying, "Well, not if they've started asking around, you haven't. As far as I know, they don't start asking for other people's opinions unless they think it's an acceptable business decision."

"Ah, I suppose that's good to hear."

"As for how long, actually, Lisa would know more about that."

"Yes, but it seems like you know... something we shouldn't take so much time here at work discussing. So, I thought that we could meet out at a restaurant, or you could come over. Bring the whole family. Including your pet?" He looks up at me. See, I might not have realized that he had a son, I may not have done all the personal digging I should have, but ever since he didn't go to the annual meeting with his morph, I did some digging. There's a rotation that has to go to that meeting—and Hendricks, every single time he can, has requested to take it off. Which means he's missed three meetings in the past eight years. It's crazy. See, if your name comes up in the rotation and you don't want to take it off, they don't go to the next name in the rotation; instead, they ask for volunteers. Which is interesting, because it'll throw off the entire dynamic of the meeting. But the mere thought that Hendricks has been able to do this has suggested to me that it isn't so much about corporate brainstorming and business as it is about the pets. And the fact that Hendricks doesn't want to go suggests that he's not any more comfortable with the Showing and Sharing than I am. But I have to be very careful about how I word that. "I mean, I have a fox breed, and I understand you have a morph as well. Although I didn't get to meet her. It is a her, right?"

"Yes," he says, "Yes, it's a her."

He doesn't say anything else, and I kind of tilt my head to one side. "You know, Wynn doesn't get to meet very many people. Especially other morphs—except, you know, once a year. And let's be honest, that's kind of stressful for them, all that performing they have to do." Ashton has put his glass down now and folded his hands in his lap. "But I'm not sure if there was a ferret morph there." He glances up at me. "Her name is Renee, right?" I say, and Hendricks's face goes a little pale. "You know, I think Wynn would love to meet Renee. I would love to meet Renee—and Aaron and Lisa, of course. You know, you've been married for many years now, and I think your family can be an excellent model for what I hope my family can become."

He glances down to his lap and then finally back to me. "I see," he says slowly. "You are very good," he says, and I blink at him. "Very good." And he leans forward and takes another cookie off the tray. "Much better then I was at your age."

"I'll take that as a compliment," I say.

"You should—and yes, we should get together. How about at your house?" Now he narrows his eyes at me slightly. Ah, so if he puts it in my territory, then somehow I won't be able to hide things from him.

I smile. "That sounds fine. I know that Lindsey loves to cook. He's probably a better cook than me," I add with a laugh, and Hendricks chuckles a bit, looking slightly confused.

"Alright. Is he living with you already?" he asks after a moment.

"Lindsey? No, not yet. We don't want everyone to think we are rushing into this marriage. Although it gets kind of hard sometimes. He's quite a man," I say. The fact is, Lindsey has never spent the night at my house. I've never spent the night at his apartment. It never occurred to us to do that before. It makes me wonder whether perhaps we should be spending more time together, spreading the image around that we really do want to be together. "Is there a time in your schedule? I mean with Aaron's school and everything I don't want to make it difficult."

"Uh, I'll have to have Lisa—"

"Have Lisa look into it," I finish his sentence. "I understand. So, let's talk about the teams, then, why don't we?" I say, making my voice a little more formal. "I mean, while we are here waiting for those two to get back from tea, we might as well get some actual work done. Or at least the facsimile of actual work, right?"

"Yes, yes," he says. We begin talking about his team, my three teams, and how we might start mixing them up. Some time later, there is a knock on the door, and Lisa and Lindsey come back. Lindsey looks like the cat who ate the canary. And Lisa?

Oddly, Lisa looks a little flustered; she ignores me and looks directly at Ashton, who stands up immediately and goes to her. "Thank you so much for dropping by," I say.

"Yes," Ashton responds briefly. When he turns around, I can see that he is holding one of her hands in his. "Yes, and, uh, Lisa," he says, turning to her. "We have been invited—the entire family— over to Emily's house."

"Oh," she says. "Um—I see. Uh... I'll have to check with Aaron's schedule," she says, looking at him. They look at each other kind of oddly.

"Oh, take your time. We don't need to do it tomorrow night. Just in the next week or two, I think. Get to know each other a little better. I think we can learn a lot from you." They glance at each other again, and I see Lindsey arch one eyebrow off to the side. He's busying himself now, moving towards the table to pick up the treats.

"Yes, yes. I'll get back in touch with you in the next day or two," Hendricks says, holding out his hand to me.

"Yes," I say, and I take his one hand in both of mine again, and he seems slightly flustered. "Yes, we'll do that. Thanks for stopping by. It was nice to meet you, Lisa."

"Ma'am," she says and allows Hendricks to escort her away.

Lindsey steps up to the side, and I can feel the tray bumping into me. "Inviting them over—to your place?" he says.

"Yes. And I said you are going to cook."

"Oh. Wonderful," he adds. "So, I'll put these back in private storage here. Next time I won't even bother with all these drinks; I'll just bring water."

"Yes, I think that's all he really wanted."

Lindsey looks at me a second. "Sure." Then he leaves, and I close the door behind him. No, in fact I'm completely sure that water wasn't all Hendricks wanted. But sharing a bit of food and drink wasn't what I wanted either. Maybe I got a little bit of what I wanted from him. I just hope I didn't reveal more than I should have.

Chapter Twenty-Six
Business & Pleasure

Lindsey is looking at me over his shoulder as I pace back and forth across the entryway going between the living room and the kitchen, both of which are basically open to the front door. Wynn is sitting by the front door looking at me, too, though unlike my assistant he can be fully focused on me.

Lindsey clears his throat, and I find him directly in front of me. "You should be working on dinner," I say, the words tight, making me sound harsher than I feel.

"It's all done, in the oven or frig, just waiting," he replies.

I feel a cool, wet nudge on my hand and look down to find Wynn looking directly up at me.

"See, he's worried about you, too," Lindsey adds, drawing my attention back to him.

"Worried about me?" I ask. "I've done my part. I set the water to chill." I gesture toward Wynn, who grins at me. "We set the table for five, plus an extra dish if Renee will be eating, too. I've picked the music." As I continue Lindsey just nods, and soon I find myself sitting on the couch with my pet curled up on one side of me and my assistant on the other, holding one of my hands. "How did I...?"

"That's how nervous you are. You didn't even notice that we steered you in here to relax," Lindsey says. He winks, but I can tell it is directed beyond me to Wynn, who nuzzles my hand and makes one of his huffing sounds that I think means that he's either annoyed or self-satisfied. "You need to just relax a bit, or you're going to go to the door too soon and send out all sorts of negative energy when they arrive. If anyone should be nervous, it should be Hendricks or his spouse, not you or I. This is your house, your realm; no invading queen should feel completely at ease here."

I frown slightly at his reference to our earlier conversations about the Hendricks family. From all outside views they seemed to be the standard Indandirmak family: a proper dominant executive with a supportive corporate spouse and one child who was excelling at their educational programs as well as having a head for something creative or good people skills. Just the type for the future of the company in the decades to come.

But both of us picked up something from that afternoon meeting that suggested it's just a show for Egirdir. On my end I'd felt the classic submissive tendencies from Hendricks, while Lindsey chuckled that Lisa had tried to steer their outing, and when he allowed it slightly, she just glowed with more than business triumph. She has an air about her, was the way he put it, and since he's flexible and used to my needs, he let her push a few things, though he made it clear he's not just anyone's boy.

Lindsey has always known what to say and do to get me turned on, but it's never the classic submissive role with him. No, he's far too manipulative for that, but then again, if he's merely guiding us where I most want to go, I've never seen the harm in it. Far less stressful than having to be the one with all the ideas all the time. Better to be aligned in all our goals than just physically compatible, my younger days had taught me.

"You make it sound like we're at war," I sigh and let my hand start petting Wynn, one true way to get me to relax, I've discovered.

"Think of it more like a potential alliance," Lindsey offers as he sits back but continues to hold my hand.

Between them I'm effectively trapped into trying to relax. I see them glance at each other, and I'm shocked at the thought that Wynn might be learning a bit too much from my assistant in terms of getting me to do what I need to do without pushing me directly. "When did the two of you starting getting along so well?"

"Wynn first pet, Lindsey smart, he know," Wynn says softly, with an edge to his voice.

"That's right, that's exactly correct," my human pet confirms with a light chuckle.

Perhaps my encouraging them to get along is backfiring on

me. Or *maybe not*, I consider, as I realize that my pulse has finally returned to normal. I really am nervous, a dangerous feeling to show tonight, or any day in the office.

As though in answer to my assessment the doorbell rings, and the computer announces that the Hendricks family has arrived.

I turn to Wynn. "Remember what I told you about tonight? No talking ever." He nods seriously at me and gets down off the couch to scamper off to his window ledge, where he can observe and appear to be shy rather than risk too much interaction.

"Remember what I said, Boss," Lindsey says as he helps me stand up. "Let me do most of the small talk. We'll see who answers and how, and that will tell us how to play this."

I smile and nod then head to the front door as he returns to the kitchen to do his duty, as a good spouse would.

"The trick is to make them believe that you have other options, then the price will come down," Lindsey is saying to Lisa over dessert. I've been listening and watching, my eyes wandering over to Wynn and Renee by the window, where they have been quietly eating and watching us during dinner.

"Back in Carson we had limited connections, almost none at the end," Lisa replies with a glance toward her husband. I've been carefully watching these little glances. She's angry with him for coming here—not specifically to the house, but to MTB in general. He seems to be accepting the blame a bit too readily.

"Oh we have a lot of connections here; we have a city contract for all their citizen announcements," Lindsey says with a soft smile, and I return his wink in my direction. "You weren't given a list of our reciprocal stores? You should have received one with the welcome package."

"Headquarters sent us very little, but then the move was sudden," Lisa says again with another glance at Hendricks, who flinches just enough that I notice with my careful eyes.

Lindsey puts his fork down and takes her hand, causing her to tense up for a second until he releases it. "Sorry, sorry, I can just see how stressed you are. Emily doesn't like her guests to be stressed, isn't that right, Boss?"

Now it's my turn to talk, so I nod my head. "Perhaps we should move this to the living room while Lindsey clears everything away?"

I'm expecting Lisa to offer to help as any spouse or assistant would; instead, Hendricks stands up and takes his plates, and then hers. "Ash," she says softly, and he looks at her hand on his arm, "I'll take care of that, dear; why don't you go relax, pour us a drink, if that is allowed?" Her final question is directed toward me.

"Yes, we'll make drinks and have them waiting for you both," I agree as I stand up. As I pass by Lindsey I lean over and kiss his cheek, earning a rolling of his eyes. I don't think I've ever kissed him on the cheek, but after I do so, Lisa also kisses Hendricks this way and sends me a serious look.

Ah, yes, all of my bells are ringing now. He may have the corporate title, but she's the one who rules their family. She even picks up their son, Aaron, and hands him to my fellow VP, who takes him with a grin and follows me out to the living room, where the pets turn toward us.

Renee sits up and looks at Hendricks, then nods and comes over to him, sitting so that her head is in his lap after he sits at my urging. Aaron moves to sit on the floor by their pet and proceeds to stroke her, though she ignores him and just gazes up at her master. There's something in her body language that is making me uncomfortable, so I look at Wynn, who is sitting up on his window seat looking at me under his longer head fur, his head slightly bowed.

I walk to him and pet him gently, bending down so I can whisper in his ear, "Everything go well so far?"

"Yes, Master, but," he says, licking his lips and nuzzling into my neck, "she is strange," he says, softly adding a lick to my face.

I look at my guests and see that Renee has used one leg to push the smaller Hendricks a bit further from her. The little boy isn't reacting as I'd expect him to; he isn't demanding her attention or pouting, just sitting there with a dejected frown. "Wynn, could you keep little Aaron company? Just let him pet you, no biting or play like we do?"

My pet looks up at me, then at the child, and nods before

crawling down and across to the boy. "Hendricks, if Aaron wants, he can play with Wynn a bit."

My colleague looks at me, his son, and then at the pet in his lap that he has been touching with a calm but distant look on his face. "Oh, I'm sorry, I'm so selfish with Renee, and she really isn't a pet for children, you know." He glances at Wynn, who is lying flat on the floor, looking at the boy, who is staring back at him. "Is he safe with children?"

I pause to consider that question. Wynn primarily watches more adult shows on the morph channel, but he also watches more general programs, and I've seen that several of these deal with human families and even children. I nod. "Of course, Wynn has been learning a lot about families, you know, so that when corporate approves," I say, letting the implication hang in the air. We did write down that we wanted two children ideally, so it would make sense given all the other preparations we are doing that we might also train my morph differently. Maybe we should talk about this some more?

Hendricks blinks, then smiles. "You're taking this corporate spouse application very seriously."

"I take all business matters seriously," I reply as I step to the bar set in one corner of the room. "I also take my personal matters seriously," I add as I look across at the sofa, where the two morphs and two humans are lounging. Young Aaron has finally reached out and is petting Wynn, not always in the correct direction, but my pet is accepting it, huffing and smoothing his fur down only to have it fluffed up again by the child.

"Just don't forget to have fun, too," Hendricks comments as he leans down and kisses his pet on the mouth.

I feel the glass I'm holding slip from my fingers, but luckily the countertop isn't far below, so it just makes a loud enough sound to jerk my mind back to the drinks I said I'd prepare. He kissed her, on the mouth, right in front of me. Even in private I've only done that to Wynn once; his mouth isn't—it just isn't, but I push those thoughts aside and get out the water and flavor mixes along with a clear bottle of basic alco. My mother has a small collection of alco inherited along family lines, but I'm not wealthy, nor have I inherited it yet, so I'm stuck with the basics I can mix together to make decent if not professional-grade drinks for all of us but the child. "What would Aaron like?" I call out.

Hendricks looks up at me, then at his son, who is now lying on the floor just petting Wynn, who is also just lying and watching me, his blue eyes twinkling as they often do when he's feeling relaxed and paid attention to. "He's recently decided that mixed punches are his favorite. There was a time when if it wasn't orange he wouldn't even look at it."

"Daddy!" Aaron says as he starts to sit up but finds his lap full of Wynn's head as my pet playfully pounces and distracts him. Good boy, sensing the potential for the evening to turn a touch negative. Wynn has a great ability to read emotions in humans, I've been learning, something the doctor says is a skill not all morphs have.

"I'll mix a bit of several flavors in for him, then. What do you and Lisa want?"

"Lisa prefers a simple lemon kick, and I'll have a straight kick, if you don't mind."

"It's why I asked," I tell him with a chuckle as I turn to the bottles and five glasses. In them I pour water, a good 4/5 into the one and 3/5 into the others. Then the first four get a shot of alco, and finally the flavors, adding in each one to the child's and then two extra fruits as well.

I set them on the tray and start to call to Wynn when Lindsey and Lisa return. Lindsey arches an eye at me and takes the tray. "Who gets what?" he asks out loud, then leans closer to whisper, "You were not about to ask Wynn to carry, were you?" Even this minor service had Lindsey a bit unnerved the first few times he saw Wynn carrying food or drinks to us. I've gotten so used to it in the past two years that I honestly hadn't thought about it.

We exchange worried looks, then I take my own drink and direct him with the others before sitting down in one of the other sofas we bought recently for this dinner. Soon Lindsey is back at my side, and Wynn has crawled to sit at my feet, little Aaron following him.

"You've trained him to deal with children?" Lisa asks as she sips her drink; her eyes, though, are looking at her husband.

"Given that we hope to soon have permission to marry, and I'm not getting any younger," I say with a smile and a shrug.

"Wynn is actually a fairly smart pet," Lindsey adds and just smiles at my look. "Emily made a good choice, thinking well into the future with this one, just like she does at the office."

"That must be why MTB is doing so very well," Hendricks comments.

"I think Egirdir values this area more," Lisa states softly.

"Why is that?" I really should be more focused on our goal of assessing their opinions about morphs, but I can't pass up the opportunity to learn more about what happened in Carson City; I can use it later if I need to.

"Lisa," Hendricks says softly, but she only glares at him.

"Oh, please, I can tell right way that these are our sort of people, Ash," she tells him and then looks at me. "You value Wynn, right, a bit more than a mere morph. And Lindsey a bit more than a corporate spouse, right?"

I set my drink down and cross my right leg over my left knee, letting my hands rest in my lap. "Why wouldn't I?" Next to me Lindsey has stiffened and is about to open his mouth when I put one hand on his knee.

Lisa smiles and puts her arm around Hendrick's. "That's what I thought. We have a great deal in common, and that could be to our mutual advantage, Ms Emily Potter."

Silence reigns for a while, then I get a very hennish idea. "Lisa, have I shown you the rest of the house?" I try to make it a question, but it comes out as more of an order. She arches one eyebrow but stands and follows me.

I give her a short tour as we hear the men trying to have a conversation that wasn't about business or city concerns, then I take her to my bathroom and shut the door. She looks at me, tosses her head back, and smiles. "I don't swing this way," she laughs, "but I am flattered. I have no doubt you are the more dominant of us two."

Her words made me pause for a second. Anyone could use the terms; it made it quite difficult to have a sincere conversation these days unless there were lawyers present to determine what each was willing to give and take, direct and follow. Even Lindsey and I were struggling a bit with the corporate paperwork and the dynamic I was most comfortable with. I decided to take her comment at face value.

"Then you won't mind being up front with me and tell me exactly what you mean by 'we have a good deal in common.'"

Lisa leans back and rests against the countertop. "You are a strong woman, and so am I, but unlike you I didn't have the city or corporate connections to get the education I would have needed to advance to your level. Ash, on the other hand, was expected to advance well beyond his own comfort level, so he went out to find some relief from the pressures of work. I caught on quick; I may only be an assistant, but I'm not dumb."

"I can see that. Neither is Lindsey," I add.

"Oh, yes, he's interesting, huh? He could have gone a lot further but really dislikes the pressures of authority. Much easier to move down the ladder than up it unless there is something you want."

"What do you want?"

Lisa blinks a few times. "You're very stressed about this whole thing. First time making a poly-share?"

Now I blink and take a step back. Poly-share? She thinks—oh, no, we've completely misunderstood them—but before I can say anything Lisa blushes.

"Oh, I see, I thought, we thought, you were forceful with Ash in your office, and the offer to meet us here with the pets, we just, well, I'm very sorry."

Wait, I can use this. "No, you aren't entirely mistaken," I say as I step toward her and put a hand on her arm. This only makes her blush deepen. "We aren't even poly, you know? We're really only interested in certain things, plus friends; who couldn't use more friends?"

Now she's smiling, and the blush is fading. I think we've come to an understanding, but I won't know until we meet again, just the adults this time. We set that meeting for a week from Friday, back here again.

As we leave the restroom and return to the men, I can tell that their conversation has also changed, and Lindsey gives me a full smile when I take my seat next to him.

"I'm not sure that went as well as it could have," I say as I'm slipping into my pajamas.

"Really? I thought it went very well," Lindsey says from the bedroom. "I'm fairly sure that Lisa is running things in that family, and I'm also sure they're not thrilled by Indandirmak—it may or may not have something to do with the ferret," he adds.

I look down at Wynn, who has followed me back to the bathroom to get ready for bed. He rubs his head against my leg but says nothing. He hasn't said anything for hours, so I lean down and capture his muzzle in my hand. "Did you learn anything, pet?"

He blinks at me with his big blue eyes and then huffs a bit, so I let go of him so he can talk. "Renee different," he says.

"Different how?" I look up to find Lindsey standing in the doorway in nothing but pajama bottoms. He started staying over a week or so ago, but beyond the three of us sharing a bed, sex has been nonexistent since we began this experiment. If we are to present the image of a couple who wants to get married, we need to show we're moving in that direction with or without the company backing. My mother suggested that this would send a message that we might turn to the city for backing if our request was denied.

"Stare at Wynn all the time," my furry pet replies. I smile a bit as I realize how comfortable the two of them have become. The first night Wynn refused to share my bed, he even went back to his room, and I was about to go after him when Lindsey suggested

I let him get used to the idea in his own time. The next night Wynn slept on the floor nearest to me. By the third night he was on my side of the bed, and since then I've been in a lovely sandwich between two males who know how to please me, though neither of them have.

"Stare at you? Is that something morphs don't normally do?" Lindsey is now kneeling down on the floor so he and Wynn and can talk more easily. The first time Lindsey knelt down I asked him why, but he only smiled and replied that it wasn't that unusual a position for him to be around me anyway. That comment had earned me a glare from Wynn. I've learned that every animal and human personality trait you might think exists certainly does exist in Wynn, though he is never direct about his displeasure, and it is still a challenge to get him to refer to himself in the first person.

"No, no staring challenge, who best, but Master," Wynn says, looking up at me, "said be nice to Renee, so head hurt about what to do." Ah, a battle for dominance, is it? Sort of what Lisa and I went through, though she caved quickly, perhaps a bit too quickly. "Dominant" is not a description I'd use for either of my pets; just thinking that makes me chuckle, and both of them glance up at me.

"Just thinking how cute you both look down on the floor," I tell them.

"Yeah," Lindsey says as he stands up. For a moment I wonder if I've pushed him too far. He must have his limits—lord knows he isn't slow to demand his duties and rights as my assistant at work—but he just steps to the side, inclines his head, and motions toward the bedroom. "Your bed awaits, Boss," he almost purrs out the sentence, making Wynn huff again and put one hand on my hip as he looks up at me.

I arch my eyebrows just slightly and then make a decision. Sooner or later this would have to be tried, so I step quickly past them and study the bed for a moment. With a wave of my hand, I command, "Pull the cover back up. We aren't quite ready to sleep yet."

Lindsey frowns but goes to do as I say while I feel Wynn clinging to me, his face looking up from where it rests against my belly. "Play?" he asks eagerly, his tongue darting out to lick his lips.

"You want to play tonight?" I tease him back, stroking his head fur but glancing up at Lindsey.

"Yes, long, long time no play with Master."

"I'll go wait in the living room then," Lindsey says as he turns.

"No don't go. I want us all to play tonight."

Lindsey freezes in place as Wynn bounces onto the bed with a squeal of pleasure and immediately starts to turn his back to me so I see his tail rise invitingly. Lindsey turns toward me but says nothing; his eyes are darker, his face wary.

I can't back down now. I have to stay in charge here, just as in the office and the research center; if I'm not in charge, then we don't stand a chance, I'm sure of that. I tilt my head to one side with a smile. "I'm sure you've wondered what it's like to be with a morph, particularly Wynn," I tell my human lover and assistant, the man I hope can help me create a safer future for everyone in this room.

I feel my eyes go wide as Lindsey's tanned cheeks turn a bit red. I don't think I've ever seen him blush before, ever, not even when he tells me these outrageous stories about his sex life in an attempt to make me jealous. "Wynn is well trained. I had excellent reports from the Sharing session at the annual meeting; I recall how you noticed his attributes, shall we say, the first time you met him."

Out of the corner of my eye I see Wynn has turned around, lying on one hip, his jaw a bit open, his eyes wide.

"Well, I'm a man; we notice that sort of thing," Lindsey suggests, but his blush is getting deeper. He isn't saying no, he isn't walking out, he clearly has thought about it. I need to remember how difficult it was for me at first.

"Nothing too big tonight, just a little playtime; I'll supervise," I add, and amid all the talk I've worked my way to him so I can put my hand on his arm.

He looks down at my hand, then up at me, his normal sexy smile on his face. "Oh, I see, Boss," he says, using that title, and I raise my chin a bit. "Well, then you tell us what to do, and we'll do it."

I feel a flutter in my groin as my test is met with a countermove that offers me more authority while also letting Lindsey set the boundaries. This is something I bet a morph trained as Wynn is will never be able to do. I nod and motion to the bed again, where Wynn is now sitting up, looking at us both.

"Wynn, can you play with Lindsey as I tell you?"

"Yes, Master," he replies, but his tone is a bit dead, reminding me of Egirdir.

I reach out to pet his head, and he moans softly, twisting to move closer to me. "I'm going to be right here, Lindsey, and you aren't going to do anything that I don't tell you to do, right?" I add that part with a glance at my assistant.

"Every move is at your whim, Boss," he replies, and I note the blush is almost gone from his cheeks. Perhaps giving me this role is relieving him of responsibility? That's a turnon I've never understood myself, but it seems to have worked for many partners in the past.

I smile one of my slight, hopefully seductive smiles and go to sit by Wynn, who moves to lie in my lap, face up, his erection still there, though he has been watching us with increasing wariness. I look at Lindsey, and Wynn directs his gaze that way as well. "In that case, boy," I say, and the word makes my assistant blush a bit, "you will remove your clothes."

I learned a while back that giving orders in a positive and direct fashion works well for Lindsey and for Wynn, too. Wording things different ways elicits different reactions and attitudes. If Lindsey wants to be free of any guilt or fear, I think I know how to do that.

Lindsey doesn't have much to remove, and soon he's there in all his tanned glory. Except for one thing—unlike Wynn, his erection isn't ready, but I bet we can figure out how to fix that.

"Pet," I begin, smiling a bit when this also gets Lindsey's attention as well as my morph's. I place one hand gently under Wynn's chin and direct his gaze back to me. "Go over and caress Lindsey—just touch him everywhere, but do not rush. Do you understand?"

"Yes, Master, Wynn do nice touching," he agrees with a glance at the subject of our conversation.

I make a little shooing motion with my hands, and soon Wynn

is off the bed and kneeling in front of Lindsey, his head at groin level. At first Lindsey is tense; he even takes a half step back, until I catch his eyes with my own. "You may tell me what you are thinking, Lindsey, but you will let him touch you everywhere. Do you understand?"

He blinks at me, then whispers, "Sure, Boss, just touching," he adds in a lower whisper.

Wynn glances back at me, and when he turns his head I can see that my human pet has lost more enthusiasm. "Just start, Wynn; I was a bit unnerved myself at first."

That confession makes both males look at me for a second, then Wynn just leans in and rubs his furry face against Lindsey's thigh.

I hear the sharp intake of breath, then the relaxing sigh as my morph continues to simply use his lighter face fur back and forth, up and down on Lindsey's legs, working from hips to feet. As is common with men these days, Lindsey is completely smooth except for his head, where he might grow a mustache, or at least attempt to do so. In theory men should be hairier than women, but I've never personally dated such a man, whom we jokingly call thralls after an ancient species of homids. Who would want to be so hairy with summer temps normally in the upper 80s here in MTB?

When Wynn reaches down to Lindsey's feet for the second time I issue a new command. "Tease his feet with your tongue, pet."

Both males glance at me, but Wynn soon has his tongue out and is licking the tops of my would-be spouse's feet. Lindsey loves to be at my feet, possibly more than he likes to be between my legs, but other than a few massages I've done in the weeks since we've been working the marriage angle, I've stayed away from his.

"Boss, I'm, you know," Lindsey begins to say, and then gasps as Wynn does something.

"Ticklish? I know, but he's on the top of your foot, and you are standing; you will submit to this," I add, hardening my voice slightly and enjoying the shiver that goes up his body.

"Yes, yes, I will," he repeats back and gasps again. I can't see clearly, but I bet Wynn is finding a way to work his tongue between the toes, and that might be right on the edge of tickling him.

Just as I'm about to tell Wynn to pull back because Lindsey's gasps are taking on a giggling edge, my morph rubs his face back up along the left leg and stops at the hip to glance back at me. I can see that his black dick is hard and even glistening. He looks directly at me, his blue orbs deep and dark, and runs his tongue along his upper lip. "Master like watching," he says.

I see Lindsey's left hand come up and pause just inches from Wynn's head. His mocha eyes, now looking at me, next glance down at my morph before returning to my gaze. "Yes, she does, it seems," he says with a surprised tone to his voice.

I frown slightly and issue another command to regain control. "Lindsey, you will come over to the bed, but you will not lie down on it yet."

This earns an arched eyebrow, but he lowers his hand without touching Wynn and steps around him to come and stand in front of me by the bed. My morph stays where he is until I gesture toward the bed. "You lie on the bed, face up, Wynn."

"Yes, Master," he says as he quickly scrambles over and up onto the bed, laying his head in my lap without an explicit order. "Now?" he asks, looking between me and Lindsey.

"He isn't very patient," my assistant comments as he shifts and rests his hands behind his back, which forces his hips and his own growing erection forward more.

"Part of their genetics, I'm told—once horny, they can get demanding," I tease, stroking Wynn's face with my fingertips.

"Lucky I'm not a morph, then," Lindsey replies, shifting on his feet slightly. "I will," he goes on, using the word I've been employing, "wait patiently for your next instructions, Boss."

"Patience is as much attitude as action. At least Wynn's are in alignment," I tease as I stare back into Lindsey's darkening gaze. When he's turned on, my human pet's eyes change color just slightly, though I've been told by numerous lovers over the years that my own change quite a bit depending on my mood.

Keeping my eyes on Lindsey I count silently to twenty, gauging his reactions as Wynn wiggles beneath my hands, which are dipping down to stroke his neck and chest before returning to caress his face. "You will touch Wynn now using only your hands. Starting at his feet and working up to his face."

"Yes, Boss," he says, mimicking Wynn's own confirmations of my orders.

Lindsey kneels and takes Wynn's left foot in his hands. "I am allowed to talk, correct?" he asks and then smiles when I nod. He kneads Wynn's sole and then the rest of his foot, and my pet tosses his head and looks up at me. "The soles are harder, kind of rubbery, but the fur is very soft. Oh, you don't like that, huh?" he says as Wynn kicks out a bit.

"Why?" I ask, capturing Wynn's chin in my hand as I stop caressing his fur.

"Wrong way," he says, and I nod.

"Yes, he doesn't like having his fur moved in the opposite direction it grows in, just so you know. I won't stop him from kicking you if you annoy him too much," I warn.

"Ah, sorry, little pet," Lindsey says, and I see his hands smoothing the fur back down.

"Little pet?" Wynn and I both repeat, and this gets a grin from Lindsey. "If I'm your pet too, then I'm the big pet and he's the little pet, in multiple ways," my assistant adds with a chuckle.

"I'll restrict your speaking privileges if you don't focus on your task," I threaten, and this makes Lindsey pause. I learned a long time back that the worst thing I can ever do to Lindsey is control his means of communication. Half of everything he does every day is a matter of his talking with or to others, sending emails, reaching out by phone, even typing out reports. If I let him, he'd be a never-ending chatterbox even during sex.

He looks up at me and swallows. "Sorry, Boss," he apologizes, and I'm surprised at the sincerity in his voice. "I will focus on describing what I'm doing from now on."

"And feeling," I prompt, earning a nod and slight smile from him.

After a few seconds of massaging Wynn's feet, he looks up at me with a puzzled expression. "No claws or nails? Wait, now I feel something, but very short."

"Part of the standard preparation, I was told, though I've wondered about that since. They told me several things were standard that I now believe were not."

"They? The ISM folks? Not The Jungle or Genesis?"

"Ruining the mood with too much chatter, boy," I say firmly. I really don't want to be thinking about all the ways I'm sure I'm being lied to right now when I'd love to feel my own center hot and moist, feeding off the energy I was hoping to generate tonight.

"Don't make Master turn off." I chuckle when Wynn issues his own commands and gets a startled look from Lindsey in reply.

"Yes, sir, little pet," Lindsey chuckles as well, then runs both hands up Wynn's leg in the wrong direction, causing him to squirm and attempt to kick out. He looks at me from where this places him, poised above the bed and the morph, our eyes just a foot or so apart now. I can see the slight tremor in his body from the stress of holding the position for more than a few seconds.

"You will get on the bed now, boy, so you can reach my morph more easily and amuse me," I add with a tilt of my head.

"Yes, Boss," he says, then he places a knee up by Wynn's side as he smooths the fur back down his legs.

Wynn moans softly as his body is touched in a more pleasant way. "I'm going to stop touching you, pet," I tell him as I take his chin in my hand again. "You are to pay attention to how Lindsey touches you, but you ask me for permission for any other play. You understand?"

"Yes, Master, Wynn toy tonight?" he half asks as he lets his arms fall down to his sides and spreads his legs a bit more. Trust a morph to find a way around my rules in this fashion.

I catch Lindsey grinning at me as he pets Wynn's fur up over his hips, ignoring his groin for now, and into the lighter fur around his dark nipples. Wynn arches up as the nubs are brushed over, and I nod at Lindsey to continue.

My human pet's hands continue to take a slow journey over

Wynn's entire body, going from his chest to his shoulders then downward along his arms. He picks up each hand and arches one eyebrow when he finds it far more humanlike than Wynn's feet were like human feet. The fingers are not quite as dexterous as ours, and the nails are definitely harder, but still very, very short. With a muttered comment on the similarities, Lindsey jumps up to caress Wynn's neck and face.

His muzzle is still muzzle shaped, but not nearly as much as the animal he is derived from. Still, it is clearly not a human face, and I can empathize as Lindsey's erection fades a bit when he strokes the fur and finds Wynn's shockingly blue eyes looking directly back at him. "Please," my morph begs softly, his eyes darting between us.

"Have to obey the Boss," Lindsey tells him, and now they are both looking at me.

I wait for a count of five before I give another command; it helps build a bit of expectation that rarely harms the mood. "You will be more forceful in your touching, Lindsey. Wynn," I say, touching his chin again to get his attention, "you may beg and wiggle all you wish, but I decide the actions now."

"Yes, Master," Wynn says, then he arches up again with a groan as Lindsey's hand moves back to his nipples and starts massaging them in earnest. I watch closely for every action and reaction, and soon I can hear both males' breathing quicken.

Wynn reaches out and touches Lindsey's leg, and my assistant freezes for a second as he looks to me for direction.

"That is fine, give and take a bit, gentlemen," I say, and my words result in both of them turning toward me. "I use the term loosely," I say. Fact is that I'm getting a bit bored, and I want this show to pick up some speed.

"Just touching still?" Lindsey asks.

"You will be doing a lot of touching, of all types now, for my amusement," I order as I move a bit and position Wynn so his head is resting between my legs but still on top of my thighs.

He makes a sniffing sound then grins and glances up at me then at Lindsey. "Master turned on, too," he states.

"Good, that's the plan, yes?" Lindsey grins at me as he reaches down with one hand to finally touch Wynn's cock. It easily fits into his fist, but the texture is a bit different—I know first hand—so my assistant makes a bit of a face, then just chuckles as he strokes it once, twice, three times before returning that hand to a dark nipple.

"Mean," Wynn moans as he thrusts up with his hips and looks at me with trembling muzzle.

"Not mean, just building up," I tell him as I stroke his face and neck.

"Only touching, little pet," Lindsey says, locking eyes with me. "Boss is in control here, remember, I'm just a puppet."

A puppet whose strings are very loose right now, so I decide to tighten them up when I realize that Lindsey is teasing both of us when he repeats the combination of dick stroking with nipple rubs two more times.

"You like the taste of cock, right Lindsey?" My question makes him pause again and that blush return to his face.

"You were always telling me about your great nights and days off in so much detail. Bet you never went down on a morph, though." He looks up at me; his eyes have a heat in them that I've seen numerous times when he's on his knees between my legs.

"You will go down on Wynn and see how he compares to your old single days." Lindsey swallows, then nods his head without a word before scooting down and then lying on one side. With a glance at me again, he moves over and sticks out his tongue to just test the black tip.

Wynn immediately starts to buck, so I place my hands on his shoulders and whisper an order for him to remain as still as possible. This means he will wiggle a bit, but Lindsey shouldn't have many logistical problems now.

Since he is smaller, though a bit differently shaped, with a sharper tip, it is easy to deep throat my morph pet—I've done it dozens of times now myself—so I'm not surprised that within moments Lindsey has swallowed him to the root. After a few seconds, Wynn starts to tense up, and Lindsey releases him with a pop.

"Boss," I look at my human pet, and he's dark red in the face but hard below as he speaks. "Is it safe to, you know, to, um...."

"Swallow?" I finish the sentence, and his blushing goes toward purple. "It is; I've done it myself." That earns a shocked look, because, to be blunt, I've never gone down on Lindsey; I simply haven't needed to, and before Wynn I always found it a bit difficult to give a great blowjob. If I can't do it great, I see no point. "It will taste different, but it is safe."

Lindsey nods slowly until Wynn's moans turn into a needy keening sound. "Sorry, little pet," he mumbles as he returns to the black cock once more.

It doesn't take long, and soon Wynn is begging for permission to come, and I give it with a chuckle. When he is finished Lindsey sits back and wipes his mouth with one hand. "Weird; it's not as salty, more sweet?"

I nod, then I motion back down toward Wynn's groin again with one hand as I continue to cradle his head on my thighs and stroke his neck. "But you aren't finished yet, boy."

Lindsey looks and then frowns. "Are you kidding me? So soon?"

"Soon? This little pet," I say, using his own words now, "has a good three more to go before he'll be able to focus on you. Since I haven't seen him with a human male, I'm anxious for you to get to the task so I can learn something new tonight while we still have time."

Lindsey takes a deep breath and sighs. "Sadist," he mutters as he bends back down.

"Yes, yes," I chuckle as I reach down and pinch one of Wynn's nipples to add to the sensations. "But we all knew this when we decided to start living together."

As I sit there, watching, directing, then participating, I'm feeling more confident than ever in this plan.

Chapter Twenty-Seven
Humans Are Strange

From where i'm sitting i can see the entire ceremony happen. Master's father has my leash in his hand but he's just grinning widely as he sits on the hard seats that hold about four humans each. Lying just on the edge of the aisle, as they call this wide carpeted section between the seats, i can see Lindsey blush as Master raises this cloth over his face to give him a kiss. They had made jokes back and forth about how he had to wear white and this veil thing even though it was old fashioned. i think that means it is something you do cause the human songs say to do it but i don't know. They tell me many things when i asked. Asking lots of questions in hopes of getting Master to think more about this marriage thing but after a while it became clear that this was something they had to do and i couldn't stop it. i stopped asking then cause it only hurt my heart and head to hear answers.

One of the company leaders is beaming from the front of the room but i don't remember his name at all only that i had to spend time with him at the last Sharing. He wasn't cruel and he didn't want much more than to fuck me and see me scamper about the room for a while before then. He was just someone i had to tolerate before i was sent back to Master.

Lindsey met us at Master's father house, that tall building with the many floors after the big Show and Share thing. Then we went to see her mother in another place with accents more like Master's when She's excited or trying to sound more important. Her mother is very active and very wordy, talking a lot, and making Master angry cause the bad brother was there for one day. i hid in my room or stayed with Master or Lindsey at all times. Bad brother only glared at me and i wanted to bare my teeth but stayed good pet and looked away.

No bad brother here today though the mother is here sitting

on the other side of Master's father. i glance up when my ears catch her crying again but her scent says this is a good cry not bad one so i turn back to the event. Now Master is putting something on Lindsey's hand and then he's giving Her something too, contract rings i think they called them, special rings not like the ones they wear for dress up. Then they kiss again and turn around to smile at the group.

There are a lot of people here, i could count them i think but it was boring to do so after a while. Master says She won't share me with anyone other than at the big meeting or the other human group they've been seeing for months now with the family with the little human and the weird female morph who just looks at me. i can feel that ferret girl's eyes on me again and i pointedly ignore it as Master takes my leash from Her father and has me walk with them down this aisle. i put my head up proud cause i bet most pets not real part of day like this. On the television they never show pets with humans at big events like this.

i get to sit on the floor between Master and Lindsey at the next part of the event. They have a dinner where everyone who came to the ceremony comes to eat and make speeches. They tell how good Master is at Her job and how much help Lindsey is to Her. They say how Master and Lindsey will increase profits and connections for the next generation. It is all so much old news i already know or words i'm not sure of and soon i'm trying to distract them both by rubbing against their legs.

That only gets me a little petting, a few bits of food that taste terrible, and a few taps of warning to my head. i try to settle down but i'm afraid to fall asleep cause there are so many people around and only a good dozen morphs with them at this part of it. i don't want to miss an order and be shown up by any of them.

Lindsey been staying at Master's most nights for long time now but when the boxes come i'm surprised. They say something about finally settling down as they move his things into various spots around the house. That's when i realize that Her human pet is staying for good. i try to find shows with the whitecoats or others that help me understand this and they all talk about family. i'm a bit confused so when Doctor Denise asks me if i have any questions one afternoon i take a risk.

"What is family for humans?" i ask in my most soft voice, looking at her from beneath my head fur, one hand resting on the table where i've been selecting shapes to fit in other shapes. Fun play but also hard at times.

"Human family?" she changes what i said but i nod anyway. Whitecoats here always repeat or resay what i say back to me. As though they can't understand me, silly cause i say good words, very careful when speaking. "Ah this is about the wedding and them moving in together," she says with a slight smile.

i nod again and put my other hand on the table, bringing them closer together as i make my eyes wider to watch her closely. Is more than what i feel but humans like more than what we feel at these times, not so much other times, i've learned in my two years outside the Institution. Sometimes i make wrong choice but not much now.

"As you know, your Master cannot mate with you, so if she wants to have children of her own, she needs a human mate. Their business offered them this opportunity, so they took it. May not be the best choice," the good whitecoat explained, pausing for a second, "but if it works for them, that's all that matters. I shouldn't judge; we want Genesis certified ourselves, after all, and all of you are a big part of that."

i just nod even though i don't understand it all. At Institution, whitecoats would mate us and we'd never see that mate again or maybe even they take things from us while in little sleep the songs say. i don't know but humans need lots of others to see them set up these things. Even here i know they have asked Master to mate me but She says no so far. i don't really have idea if this is good or bad just not the ferret girl cause she is very bossy when she does talk, trying to be like a human, staring the rest of the time.

"Status is very important for us humans," Doctor Denise continues so i focus on her talking. "Given the need to control the population, we start with potential children's status and try to keep the rest at bay. Doesn't always work, but then, we need folks to be on the coasts, don't we?"

Coasts is a bad place from what i can piece together. People without ceremonies or status go there to do something dangerous. Lots of talk on the news about coasts and storms, deaths of humans, important work but many die. I flinch a bit when Doctor Denise continues.

"Of course, if this all works out, your kind can take over those jobs, and we can just eliminate the unclaimed from the get-go," she says with a smile.

i nod my head again and watch as she dumps out the shapes and colors, has the table make a new set, and then tells me to do it again. i frown a bit cause this time colors not match with shapes but soon i have it cause i'm smart morph, more than many humans the good whitecoat says with a wink at me. i feel cold in my stomach and sink down further in the seat.

Master is sitting down, i'm by Her feet as Lindsey brings the last of their food to the table. My food is on the floor by me but i'm waiting for them to start. Never say i have to wait but i see it make Master happy so i force myself to stay still. Her hand in my head fur helps much but it is removed when he sits down.

He gave me the extra good food and for a moment i look up at him but he doesn't look back. Maybe he being here is not so bad.

There is quiet for a bit, only talk about food, then Lindsey says something that makes Master's temperature and scent change. i perk up my ears to listen harder. "I thought you were going to suggest we make a kid; I was not expecting that," Master says.

"No, no, that would be too fast," Lindsey says, then he continues, "The records in company show that a kid at 30 months post marriage correlates to faster promotions, but anything less than 12 months results in stagnation and anything longer than 46 results in slower promotion rates."

There is a pause and then Master sighs before replying, "Of course you've done the research about that. So where did this civic marriage idea come from then? I doubt they'd be happy about that in Egirdir."

"Your parents, and mine," he says back to Her. Now they have my full attention and i sit back, my food forgotten. Didn't they already have this marriage thing?

"Really?" Master doesn't sound happy, and Her body is tense, Her scent changing to reflect that.

"I'm a citizen here, and you have status back in Antrim; we come from municipal stock." That word make Master tense more. "We have a legal right to a civic marriage. Just think, please, Emily, this gives us extra protection. I went to the last annual meeting with you and Wynn; I know what that is about now."

"You were with spouses and soon-to-be spouses."

"We still did things, saw things." Now Lindsey pauses and his scent and temperature are changing. "They had us watch you all, the big event, the in room exchanges, we had our own things as well."

"Why didn't you mention before now?"

i move closer to Master, rub against Her leg and She reaches down to stroke my head fur and face.

"I saw how you and him were after that; I didn't want any of that to distract us from the wedding. It was a big deal, Lisa told me, that we had it there in Egirdir; it showed a great deal of hope that the Reizis family has for you. I couldn't risk you not being the happy bride."

Master removes Her hand and leaves the table so i follow close behind Her. She exits the house and goes into the backyard so i pause at the open door. "Aren't you coming out?"

i look around but do not see Lindsey, so i guess she means me. i haven't been out here yet, only watching from the window. i take a tentative step then run to Her, kneeling at Her feet, looking up at Her, my hands just touching Her legs for support. "Master?"

"You heard everything we said at dinner, right? I know you listen and understand most of it, Wynn."

She doesn't seem angry so i nod.

"There are two types of marriage status—legal status, that is; there's another bunch that aren't legal, I'm sure. You can have both, but it's a tricky game to play with the company. I won't do anything to endanger you; you know that, right?"

"Master love wynn, protect wynn," i say, repeating back a few words She's said to me multiple times, then add, "wynn love Master, protect Master."

Master moves so i move back a bit and soon She's at the same level as me, kneeling in front of me. i feel funny, like i did at the place they took me to where the ferret girl hit her master while his spouse was watching and told her what to do, and Lindsey knelt by Master's feet like i did and She hit him though She was not angry. After a while i figured out when the changes in Her body meant She was going to hurt Lindsey but he never acted like it hurt in a bad way. Her body isn't like that now so my stomach gets tight again.

"There are good things and bad things about what Lindsey is suggesting. It will take me some time to think about it, for him to do research, I don't want you to worry, pet, just trust us to make the best decision. Can you do that?"

She looks at me as though i have a choice. Maybe this is like the sex games where She needs me to ask, to act a bit human. "i can do that, Master," i say very slowly and very softly.

"Everything good out here?" Lindsey's voice makes us both tense for a second then Master stands up but keeps a hand on my head.

"Yes; now if you haven't done the research on civic marriages and Inandirmak, I need you to do that. We're going to make an informed decision, one that is the best for all of us."

"Yes, Boss, as you say," Lindsey replies. He steps to the side to let us back into the house.

When the door closes i linger for a moment looking outside. i really didn't get to explore it at all.

i'm looking out the window again into the backyard where i've been allowed to explore now big hands of times. Lindsey takes a chair out and sits and watches me since Master is busy with the work stuff. Still hate work but Lindsey is nice to me and we always share Master's bed together. When they come back from work i can smell him on Her but he sits outside and watches me so i can tease and play with the stupid animals and see the big world. One time i played too hard with a stupid animal and Lindsey said that was a secret he would hide from Master and not to do it again. He cleaned me up, took the unmoving stupid animal away, and never told Master. Never asked me for anything for that and he still sits outside with me.

i like Lindsey but i will never tell him that.

i can see the clock, i can see outside change, the human clothes change, but i do not know how much big time is over but i know the showing and sharing is coming again. i act like i do not care so Master is not unhappy.

Let me think, three showing and sharing, three candles on the cake she let me have some time before, is that three years? Wynn getting old. i look at my reflection in the little mirror in my room and the big one in Master's. No, still pretty pet, still white and big blue eyes. Be pretty, be happy, be good pet, yes, i do all of that cause i'm smart Doctor Denise tells me.

So much time away from me on this civic thing and work now. Master is late again, i can see on the clock and Lindsey is making clicking noises as he checks their food in the warmer again. "You want your food, Wynn?"

i look up at Lindsey and shake my head. Before i had to think of what to do with my body, my words, to tell humans right answer, now it just is there and i do it. Pet type may be smarter or something like that, Doctor Denise says when she isn't talking to me but i can still hear her.

"Of course, be more patient than me, why don't you?" Lindsey states with a sigh in that way i know is half teasing and half sad. Maybe Lindsey not really know that i am best pet for Master so he feel sad when i can be good and he can't? No, his scent is off for just sad, he is worried, about Master?

i pause then kneel up and put my arms around his legs, resting my hand on him, whispering, "Master fine, Wynn and Lindsey eat with Her cause good pets." He just chuckles weakly and pets my head fur.

The house tells us that Master is here soon so we separate and set table up with full meal, extra small glass for Master of something with a sharp scent that Lindsey tells me not to drink. Controlling rolling eyes i go to wait by door.

Master almost runs into me when She comes in, swinging her case, a lot of sweat and eagerness floating off of Her that surprises me. "Oh, damn, pet, almost tripped over you," She says with a smile as She lets me hug Her upright, something i have only been doing newly since the cake with three candles. It is only for a short moment then i kneel again and follow Her into the house where Lindsey also hugs Her and takes Her case.

"Should I have stayed today?" he asks. See, he goes to work, too, and most times comes home with Master but sometimes he comes home first. i do not know why and i never ask 'cause not my place.

"And done what? Waited for me outside? This was a VP & P meeting; closed, though a Reizis was there too."

Lindsey frowns as he brings out their plates. i wait for Master to sit then kneel up to lay my head in her lap while they do their prayer thing. That is thing i do not understand. Humans make whole world yet have things they treat like morphs should treat them, except not because mostly they just do the prayer thing and toss out terms. i never see them with their masters so i think they cannot be. Master only start this prayer after Lindsey brings up civic marriage, something about a show of faith in local customs. i'm not expected to join them so i don't pay attention to it.

"Well?" Lindsey pushes after a few moments of eating.

"They said they will evaluate things after the next annual asked and if I'd be willing to start operations in Antrim for them," Master says softly.

"What?" Lindsey's voice is harsh and i clutch at Master's leg until She shoos me off with a wave of Her hand.

"I know you wanted to stay here, closer to your friends and family, but it's a counteroffer they made. They didn't have to; they still hold most of the cards, you know. Your debt is free, but mine is not."

i only hear this word, debt, a few times, something work has over Master.

"Only four more years," Lindsey states.

"You want to wait four more years? Maurice only knows how many horrible things they'd have me and Wynn do by then."

i catch the whine in my throat and simply nuzzle Master's leg.

"We've put so much time into figuring out what they want here."

"I know, and I'm willing to stay with the original plan, but debt free, Lins," Master emphasizes. "Antrim is fairly open-minded; we could keep Gaia and just add in the Trinity, I'm sure. We'd claim it was your heritage, and as much as my mother clings to tradition, the civic laws are not religious based or biased."

There is a pause then Lindsey's voice is a bit squeaky when he replies. "It gets cold there, can they even grow their own food?"

"I grew up there; it's fine. They know how to deal with the big storm; the lake is pristine, heavily guarded; the university has become top notch; morphs are rare, but we don't take him out much now."

"Wynn like backyard," i say. That was risky, but at least i didn't slip up and use other words in front of Lindsey. We keep some secrets from him still.

"See? He's not thrilled by the idea either."

Master looks down at me and frowns slightly. "We'd have a yard there, I'd make sure of it, for both of you," She turns Her gaze across the table then.

Lindsey bites his lip; the faint scent of his blood reaches me, but i just huddle closer to Master's legs. Pets aren't allowed to harm self, bad punishments happen when they do but She doesn't seem to notice. i go completely still though with the next words from his mouth.

"Your brother? Isn't he living with your mother there?"

Master's scent changes as She reaches down and grabs my fur in a very intense way, not hurting, She doesn't dig in or pull, just holds me tightly in Her fist that was just petting me casually from time to time. "I'll deal with him personally if I have to, tell mother if she can't control him, we won't do this deal. Perhaps Inandirmak would be helpful...."

"No!" Lindsey says slamming his hand down on the table. I whine and wrap my arms around Master's leg and the chair at the same time. Unlike me, he feels comfortable raising his voice and disagreeing with Master but never like this before. "We're doing all of this to be free of them, Emily! They don't give out favors without taking something in return. I know first hand. The things I had to do...."

Master's scent changes again and her voice softens and then i note that Lindsey is afraid, worried, only a little angry when his new smell hits me. "I don't want the details, Lins. I promise if I can't make my mother send him away we'll stay here, stay on course. We're tough enough, right?" and Her grip in my fur loosens so i can look up at Her question.

i swallow down a whine and nod my head. i would survive Showing and Sharing as i have three times now. i would survive Her brother but just not alone with him please.

Lindsey huffs and they go back to eating for a bit until he brings up another thing. "Haven? Do they have clubs like that there?"

Haven is the place we have gone to with the human family and their ferret girl who stares at me and acts like a human too much. It is place where Master hits Lindsey and ferret hits her master, it is a confusing place but no one touches me so mostly I just feel strange there watching them, listening to them, do their strange human things.

"I'm not sure they are exactly like that, but I did learn to do some things at a club in Antrim growing up. Also visited one a few times in father's city, just so you know."

"I'd want to be certain, and I want to know we are a united front against your brother, Inandirmak, all of it, so..." Lindsey pauses and i can feel the air change around us again as he gets very serious, "I'd want you to accept my code."

This sets Master off, and She stands up suddenly and walks out of the dining room into another, i hear a door open and close as i scurry after Lindsey. "Stay here," he tells me firmly when we see Her outside in the backyard walking back and forth, Her arms folded over Her chest, Her face hard.

i go to the window and watch them. There is a lot of pointing, arm moving, shaking of heads, and Lindsey finally kneeling down holding one hand up at Her as She shakes Her head a few times, takes a few steps away then back and finally touches His hand with a sharp nod of Her head. He moves fast and soon he's placed Her hand on top of his head.

This code must be the thing they've argued about before. It came up at Haven first then at dinner again with the family plus ferret. Now and then it comes up again along with other words i do not really understand: war, zombie, kink, global security sanction. But also with words i do know: trust, control, safety, power, freedom, though i don't get them working with the other words. This may have to do with me more than i want i think as i see as Master motions toward me and Lindsey nods but keeps the hand he has taken firmly on his head.

It is strange that humans make us with better eyes for darkness than them. This isn't the first time i've thought that, it isn't something i'd ever say outloud not even when Doctor Denise says i can ask anything because we have privacy. As Master holds only my leash and onto Lindsey's hand as we walk through the dark parts of the club, it just comes up in my mind again. Humans made me this way, must be reason, and Master asking me to lead them through is reason. wynn more than pet, wynn helpful like at home.

The club has different areas that somehow humans control so that when we step into a little more light there is also more sound, too much sound, making me tug at my ears in discomfort, but we keep moving forward. Master wants to be in the brighter, quieter space not far ahead.

i stop when Master tugs my leash gently and then look. Them.

The ferret girl is leaning into her master while his wife is waving at us yet keeping one hand on the morph. i shake my head then stop myself hoping no one has seen me. Is bad of me to not like Master's friends and their pet? Still don't like them.

i move forward again when Lindsey leans down to me and places one hand on my shoulder, whispering that we need to get moving. The club is very crowded tonight and i have to stop a few times to let humans pass me. I counted the morphs once, tried to think of how to count it better. Not every human has a morph but more morphs than i see in any place at one time, even at the stores just for our stuff that Lindsey or Master take me to once a month. Master figured out She did not like taking me to human stores and says expense worth the hassle of other stores. That means She loves me.

i count time in the human way but also the morph way from event to event, encounter to encounter. We've had sex thirty-seven times just master and i and nine times all three since the big dinner argument. Before we go to this Antrim they had to come here, had to talk to the Haven people to meet Lindsey's demands.

Could wynn make demands and get more food, more sex, more time alone with Master? No, just morph, human pets very different.

The other human who works with master, his wife, and that ferret girl are there just ahead waiting in a circular room with one, two, three, four, five, six, seven... lots of humans but only two other morphs. The woman in charge of Haven steps forward and kisses Master's face twice then does the same to Lindsey but only strokes my head.

Master kneels down and looks at me as the wife steps up beside Her. "wynn, go with Miss Lisa for a while, stay quiet and just watch. Don't worry about anything you see or hear. I'm only doing what Lindsey wants." She hands my leash to Lisa who smiles at me and led me over to where her man and the ferret girl are standing with others in a circle.

Master and Lindsey go to the center with the woman who kissed them and they all touch a computer on a stand at the very

center. i can't see very well and the people in the circle repeat back
some words so i'm not sure what is happening.

They say a lot of words i don't hear often from humans except
on TV shows. Lindsey is Master's property, slave, tool, but they
don't say pet, guess 'cause that already true. Master is Lindsey's
guide, owner, user, all seem like already there but maybe now he
disagree less or not at all with Her. Zombie war... i still don't know
what that means but it was all over the TV lately, i think always
more this time of year, called, what, summer, right.

The woman in charge says that this place, no, their people, have
special legal rights, all civics, must uphold honor. Master and
Lindsey agree and do something on the computer that i can't see
even when i stretch up as high as i can. Miss Lisa lets me cause i'm
quiet but when ferret girl stretches she taps her head hard making
me smile just a bit. i can see Master put something against the back
of Lindsey's ear, maybe the one he puts computer line into.

Then he starts screaming and screaming louder than any
human i've ever heard. So much pain, his body but Master in pain,
too, their scents tell me. i strain to reach them but Miss Lisa and
her man pull me back while the ferret girl stares at me.

Then the sounds and scents change, becoming the ones i
sometimes catch bits of when they get home from work or when
they are in the bedroom at Master's home alone for a while. i can
see them come together, fall to the floor, the humans in the circle
close in except for Miss Lisa and her man who stay with me and
the ferret girl. Soon i can't see anything and hear little than the
sounds of humans all touching the sky over and over again.

"So wynn, how have you been this past month?" Doctor Denise
asks me when i see her next. Master took me out of meetings for a
while after the big Haven circle as i'm calling the event in my mind.

Master and i have had sex forty-two times since then and three
of us twenty-three times with Master and Lindsey only seven times

alone. They want me to understand they have very tight bond now but i still at center of family they tell me over and over. i sigh not at Doctor Denise but at the memories her question brings to my mind.

wynn not at center, Master center of all things. They tell me cause they want me feel safe with changes. i not see many changes. Lindsey still speak up, still act up, Master still Her.

"wynn?" Doctor Denise's voice makes me blink. She looks at her pad and does a few things saying "Have you forgotten me in just a month?" but her question seems worried not playful on the surface like most of her questions are.

"wynn remember Doctor Denise," i say softly. "wynn practice numbers, time, colors, objects," i start listing off the various things we've been working on for so long now. True that i do practice even in front of Master and Lindsey but i don't tell Doctor Denise everything from there because it would be bad, both Master and Lindsey tell me to keep some things private, meaning just with them.

Don't tell humans all things i think and feel, our songs say and i still follow that.

Doctor Denise smiles and her worry scent fades a bit. "Then let's just do basic skills tests today."

Chapter Twenty-Eight
Click-Back Flexibility

I look up at my reflection in the mirror and splash cool water on my face. Taking a deep breath I step back and look at the two remotes. I've only used Wynn's maybe a half dozen times in all these years, always on the lowest setting. I've never used Lindsey's. I didn't want to bring them with me, but it's illegal to take Wynn anywhere without it, and part of Lindsey's requirements for us to even check Antrim out.

The things I do for my family.

Putting a smile on my face, I walk back into the main room of the hotel suite to find them both waiting for me. Wynn bounces to me and hugs my legs while Lindsey just smiles and pick up the day bag we'll be bringing. "My pets ready to meet my mum again?" I ask as lightly as I can.

"Yup, let's do this," Lindsey says with resignation in his voice. Wynn just nods against my legs then holds the handle loop on his leash.

Off we go once more into the city to check out what could be our new home, our new salvation.

As we ride in the taxi I look around and marvel at how little things have changed. Not that I should be surprised really. MTB may have added on a few new areas and upgraded some buildings, but here my mother and her fellow councilors work hard to maintain what they have without wasting anything. Let's just pray that a storm doesn't come off the ocean so we can move on to the holiday torments before making our final decision.

Lindsey is repeating much of the local history and company spiel that we've heard over the past few days. Who he's talking to I'm not sure, but the other passengers are just ignoring him while they stare openly at Wynn.

I'm just ignoring them all as I keep one hand firmly on Wynn lying across our laps and nod at Lindsey as he points out everything I already know. If it makes him more comfortable with the idea of moving, he can chatter all he wants.

We come to the neighborhood entrance and exit the taxi. The last mile we'll need to walk, since vehicles other than bicycles or skates are forbidden in this area so close to the main waterway. Lindsey grumbles a bit, since he's a spoiled inner city kid, but Wynn just bounces merrily along, mindless of the looks we get from the folks who live here.

"Emily Potter?" An older man calls out to me as we walk by his fence. I pause and look at him. "Why it is Agatha's daughter! You back for a visit?"

It takes my brain a moment to recall, but then I smile. "Mr. Worthson, how are you doing?" I say, walking toward his outstretched hand and clasping it in mine. He was my mother's campaign manager for many years until she won lifetime status on the Council. I used to imagine they were having an affair but never had confirmation.

"I'm fine, fine. Neighborhood watch commander, you know," he says as his eyes move over to examine Lindsey and Wynn.

"This is my spouse, Lindsey, and my pet, Wynn," I say as my human better half steps forward and shakes Mr. Worthson's hand and my morph better half curls closer to my legs. "Don't be shy, Wynn," I try to encourage him with a glance at my mother's compatriot.

"Is that the morph then that Agatha said you were getting? Part of your job or something? Quite strange the things you all do over there," he states as though that is a fact. Transport between continents has become much more difficult so we've fallen back on media and rumors to learn about each other.

"Well, the company I work for is headquartered in Egirdir, but I work in the Lake Superior branch," I tell him.

He frowns and steps back. "You know you have citizenship here, Emily, you could probably get it for your spouse here, even if you do bring your... pet... with you," Mr. Worthson tells us seriously.

"That's part of why we're here actually. We have an appointment with my mother, so we'd best be going on," I say, turning slightly away.

"You hurry it up, then, Agatha don't like being kept waiting," he says with a wave of his hand as he walks over to one of his trees and looks at it, though I can feel he's still watching us as we walk just two houses further on.

My mother is there waiting for us and makes some comment in passing about how we just made it on time and how she must apologize for keeping the city screen up during our visit. Lindsey chuckles but gives a look to say that he can't believe how rude she is before he intercedes and goes off to get the tray she's left in the kitchen to bring out to us.

"Does it eat human food?" mother asks as I sit down in the parlor with Wynn kneeling by my feet.

"Wynn already ate," I say, getting a pouting whine from him in return, "but we brought appropriate food for him as well. Don't trouble yourself about it."

"Good, good; we don't have many of those things around here, so I wouldn't know what to give it."

Lindsey arches an eyebrow at me as he returns with the tray, which has biscuits, small sandwiches, and tea on it. "Shall I pour?" he asks, taking a seat next to me and across from my mother.

"Do you know how?" my mother retorts, but not meanly; it is just her way.

"Been practicing," Lindsey replies as he deftly takes the pot and pours out three cups, making the appropriate inquiries about sugar or cream. The display is all very decadent and I'm sure meant to impress upon my spouse how my mother expects her daughter to be treated. I know we rarely had such fancy fare every afternoon when I lived here.

"That's fine then, just fine," mother says with a smile as she accepts her cup and hands him back a plate with a few of the treats.

Wynn whines again and looks up at me, but I just shake my head.

"It seems well behaved. I remember Roggy would always try

to climb up on your lap to steal a biscuit from you," mother says, referring to her late dog.

"Morphs aren't animals," I begin, then stop when my mother's smile quickly snaps down into a frown. Not the place or time for this discussion.

The rest of the afternoon is spent with her telling Lindsey all about my childhood and her position on the Council, the advantages of Antrim and how a nice young man like him could probably make friends quickly with the right introductions. She puts up tons of pictures on the main screen, with her work display, confined to the bottom left quadrant during our entire visit, remaining quiet.

She even splurges to impress by having dinner ordered in from a fancy caterer who is also a dear friend of hers. It all goes so well until we are almost finished with the meal.

"Mum? Sorry I'm late. Had a probable at the studio—singer thinks she needs to be on her feed with the fans all the fucking time." Wynn has planted himself under my chair by now as Anthony, my half-brother, walks in and stops to stare at us.

"Anthony, darling," my mother begins as she stands up, Lindsey following suit and eyeing the newcomer, "mother told you that she had guests today and you needed to eat elsewhere until I called you."

"Forgot, sorry," Anthony begins as he steps forward and snags a bit of chicken with his fingers. "Plus this is my home," he adds with a glance at us. I hope he hasn't noticed Wynn, because my pet is shaking so hard it's making my chair move beneath me.

"What do you mean this is your home?" My words are a bit shaky, and that isn't from Wynn.

"Of course; been living here since you kicked me out over that animal of yours," he replies with his annoying voice.

"Anthony, darling, mother needs you to leave."

"You still have that thing, or has it died? What do they live, like a year?" he continues and bends down to try to look under my chair. "There it is, just as ugly as ever."

"You need to step back." I look up to find that Lindsey has moved closer and is now on the same side of my chair as my half-brother. Lindsey isn't huge—he and I stand pretty much toe to toe—and my brother is a skinny little artist who pretends his obnoxious eating habits are a sign of his sensitive nature rather than merely a sign of a spoiled brat.

"You the spouse, then?" Anthony asks with a huff as he stands up and crosses his arms over his chest. "Yeah, you look pretty much like what I'd expect Queen Em to want around."

"Mother, you told me that he didn't live here anymore," I say, finding myself turning toward her as Wynn crawls out from under my chair and tries to hide along my side.

It is rare to catch my mother the politician without a comeback, but now she just swallows for a second and puts a hand on my half-brother's arm. "Anthony, darling, you need to leave Mother alone for a while with your sister, please."

He ignores her to keep focusing on Lindsey. "She let you fuck it yet? It's nice and soft, huh, cries a lot given the fact it's just a whore... Fuck!"

We all freeze when Lindsey's fist connects with Anthony's face and blood spurts from his nose, sending him to the floor with his hands over it.

"What a self-centered bastard you are," Lindsey states as my mother goes to comfort her son and leaves me sitting in shock.

My mother lied to me. I'm not naïve, but I thought she understood the problem with him and Wynn being anywhere around each other. The law may only apply in MTB, but isn't she always preaching about how if the urban centers don't respect each other's rules there will be chaos again, or worse, corporate control, like it was before the Zombie War?

"How dare you hit my baby!" mother screeches, and that puts me into action.

"Indeed. Just like an infant," I state as I put a hand on Wynn's head and stand up. "We won't be moving to Antrim, so you don't need to keep lying to me, Mother."

"No, no, you," she stammers, looking to me then at my half-brother, "go put a cold pack on it, darling," then back to me, "I miss you so much, Emily. He'll move, he has a girlfriend now, I'm sure she'll..."

I cut her off with a huff. "Too late. Good bye, Mother."

With that Lindsey releashes Wynn and escorts us out of the house.

Within a few steps he calls a taxi, and we head toward the entrance to wait for it. My mother doesn't even try to come after us, and I realize I don't really expect her to.

He could so easily turn this into an "I told you so" moment, but Lindsey just takes my hand in his on the silent ride back. Back in the hotel room he whispers to Wynn, who slinks off, then returns free of his leash and carrying my pajamas in his paws as he walks out on his legs, barely tottering at all in his steps.

"You were right," I begin, but Lindsey puts a gentle finger over his mouth.

"Master wants to believe the best about her family," he says, and Wynn nuzzles my hand in agreement.

I shake my head and caress Wynn as I kiss the tip of my spouse's finger. "You two are my family, not her, not anymore," I tell them.

They continue to just nuzzle against my exposed body parts for a while until I can feel myself relax. I recall a recent meeting at the club where a speaker bemoaned the fact that submissives were so aggressive these days. I can't help but chuckle at how even more ridiculous that sounds now.

"Think she's happy?" I hear Lindsey's voice ask, and I hear Wynn's confirmation as he swallows one of my fingers and causes me to suck in a breath.

That's what I want, I decide as I sit up, pulling myself from them. "Wynn, undress Lindsey," I say simply.

Both my pets stand up, and my spouse gives me a grin as he takes a relaxed position, allowing my morph to manipulate his body as he needs to remove his clothes.

Wynn used to look at me all the time while he did this, searching my face for hints that he was doing it correctly, but over the years he's gotten far more confidence than I bet anyone would

like to know his kind is capable of. He starts with the shoes and
socks because, as he huffed once, they get in the way, and I
thoroughly agree with that sentiment. Then he unbuttons and
unzips everything but leaves the clothing on while Lindsey tosses
me a look and I just shrug with my own smile.

Then Wynn stands up and looks up into Lindsey's eyes, letting
his gaze trail down. I've often wondered if he does this because
this is the one time in his life where he gets to take his time and
look at a human man up close, feeling if not his equal then at least
that he has a right to gaze back just as Lindsey still finds his similar
yet different body fascinating when the roles are reversed.

Now Wynn does look at me, and I nod my head. I can feel my
body start to heat up and get wet as I watch, but I keep my hands
under the bedcovers, not wanting to add to the excitement this
performance alone can give me. Lisa once asked me if I ever jilled
off watching my two pets together, and I said I preferred to make
them work for it later. She seemed a bit confused by it, then just
giggled and said two sisters didn't need to have the same approach.

I look down for a second trying to push the recent events from
my mind. These two are my family, but the Hendrickses are
probably a second family to me now, something I never would
have expected when I agreed to share my branch. Lindsey makes
a little noise that draws my attention back where it belongs.

Even though I didn't tell him, Wynn is using his tongue to push
aside the clothing until he is forced to use his paws to fully let the
shoulder of Lindsey's shirt fall down his arm and onto the floor.
"You're a tease," Lindsey softly growls and earns what I am utterly
certain is a smirk from Wynn before he turns his head to lick along
Lindsey's back until he reaches the other shoulder.

My smile deepens as Lindsey just automatically reaches back
and helps Wynn balance himself, since reaching this high requires
he rise up on his toes. He walks so much better now, but still,
morph toes are apparently not as stable as ours, and he still topples
over if not careful.

Once the shirt is on the floor Wynn bounces over to me with
a "Hey now" from Lindsey following him. "Master have fun?

Wynn go further?" he asks me with sharp blue eyes looking directly up into mine from his position crouching down by the foot of the bed.

"You just like to tease Lindsey," I counter and shoo him back with a hand gesture that makes him bounce a bit in his rush to obey.

"You've created a monster," Lindsey tells me as Wynn circles him a few times until he kneels up at his feet and reaches for the trousers.

I don't say anything as I tell them both to turn a bit so I have a better view, which results in some shuffling and grunts until I can see it all more clearly. Already Lindsey's cock is straining the fabric, but soon it is freed, and they both look to me. I crook two fingers, and they come back to bed with Lindsey's head in my lap and Wynn lying beside me, his head lying on Lindsey's groin, waiting for the word.

"Not yet," I instruct as I run my fingers down my spouse's face and chest until I'm pinching his nipples and Wynn is moving his head just slightly—enough, I know from experience, to make the fur move soft and seductively over bare skin.

I lean down and whisper, though I know that both can hear me, "Perhaps Wynn should go down on you while you go down on me, then we switch it before the rush kicks out."

Both of them moan, since that has become one of our favorite games. Lindsey has no problems with touching Wynn or vice versa, but I can tell he really dislikes touching me after Wynn has; Wynn doesn't seem to care, so it is simpler to just go with his preferences, since I get a ton of pleasure either way.

I've just removed my undergarments when the telephone rings and draws our attention. "You've got to be kidding me," I gripe as I swing off the bed to murmured protests. We are supposed to be here for business, so I have to take this, and we all know it, even if we aren't pleased.

My grip tightens on the phone, and soon Wynn is at my feet, Lindsey pulling up his trousers. Whatever my spouse might miss in terms of my body language, my pet never does, and they are both looking at me anxiously. "No; I'll be down in a moment though. If you'd be so kind as to call the police, I'd be grateful," I tell the night manager of the hotel before hanging up.

"Who?" Lindsey begins as he sees me pulling my hair back in the mirror and slipping back into my shoes barefooted.

"One guess," I toss back as I pause at the door.

"Should we come?" he says, grabbing his shirt.

"Only if you can keep up, but this time he's mine," I state as I walk out the door. I barely register that Wynn is keeping pace with me as I stomp down the hallway and the stairs to the main lobby where my damned half-brother is waiting.

I stop when Wynn stops a few steps behind me. "Stay here. Do not interfere, pet, do you understand?"

"Wynn understand," he says in a shaky voice.

I catch his muzzle in one hand and force him to look at me. "Do you understand?"

He takes a short breath then states very softly so that only I can hear, "I understand, Master."

I nod and turn to take the final four steps out into the lobby. Behind me I hear a "fuck" in Lindsey's voice, but I don't bother turning, hoping he realizes what I have to do, since I failed to react appropriately before.

Anthony is there, glaring at the manager, who has pulled back from the counter and has a privacy base held up to his mouth, hopefully calling the police as I asked. He sneers at me as I step toward him and place my hands on my hips to look as calmly at him as I can while my heart is pounding and the blood is rushing into my limbs in anger.

"You took off without saying goodbye to your only brother," he chuckles in that sickeningly sweet voice that seems to get others to treat him like a baby.

"Did I? That's funny, I didn't think I had a brother to say goodbye to."

"Oh, her temper's on the rise—I better watch out," he tosses at the hotel manager as he swoops closer to me. His face has gone blank as he tries to stare me down, as though his few inches on me are intimidating at all. "You hurt mom; I don't like that."

"You hurt mum, over and over again," I say, holding my ground as he raises a hand, "touch me and it may be the very last thing that you do," I tell him. "Are you getting this?" I add more loudly, and I see Lindsey out of the corner of my eye with his handcam up.

"I surely am, sweetheart," he says as he moves closer, drawing Anthony's gaze to him.

"You want to document something, asshole, how about my nose where you hit me earlier?" His attention is turned toward my spouse now, and I'm able to step aside, placing him more directly in the camera's view.

"You were threatening me and my pet as well as interrupting a private dinner where you had been told to not be; he was defending me," I say, and this makes Anthony's eyes swing toward me again, then swing back. I glance where he is and see that Wynn is frozen in the hallway looking back at him.

"Over this... thing? That was years ago; can't believe the thing is still alive even. I thought they just lived a year or so, then you upgraded or something. Shit, why would you want to keep that fuck around with your new spouse?" Anthony tries to push me, then realizes it isn't working and turns toward Lindsey and the camera. "You can't get it up or something? Not enough man for my sister?"

I chuckle at his response, "I'm not sure anyone is, but at least I don't have to rape and assault someone else's property to feel my dick get hard."

That gets my half-brother to growl, and I find my hands wrapped around his arm as he's about to let a punch head toward my lovely man's body. The moment of shock is all I need to jerk my knee up into his torso and my arms upward to slam his own fist into his head.

"Stop threatening my family!" I yell as I kick him and send him stumbling back.

"Stop this instant!" another voice calls from the lobby doors as two officers come inside, their baton stunners out.

"Now you're for it," Anthony sneers as he stands up and wipes his mouth off.

"What's going on here?" the officer asks, and I nod at the hotel manager, who tells them who I am and how I came back earlier this evening complaining about a man he believes to be the one here as he points to Anthony, who does us all a favor and interrupts repeatedly until the other officer has to point his baton at him to keep him quiet.

Then I'm asked the same question, and each of us in turn, including Wynn, who only comes forward if I hold him, is asked for our explanation. Lindsey hands over a copy of his recording, and finally the officer in charge looks at my half brother and holds out a warrant for me to consider. MTB and Antrim have a civic trade agreement that includes security sharing, and I'm pleased to be let off with a warning, while Anthony is led away in cuffs.

I thank the hotel manager and slip him a hefty tip after the authorities pull away. I make it back to my room before I start to cry. Leave it up to my stupid American half-brother to ruin a decent visit.

Soon we'll be in Lausanne, and things can calm down with my father. At least everything runs smoothly around Lac Léman.

Lindsey's smile fades after Master's father takes us up to the same room we've stayed in every year when we visit. But this is the first time we've come here before the big yucky meeting where everyone but Master touches me and watches me. i'm already on the bed testing it out, kneeling up to look out the window at the humans and buildings below. It looks different than before, less gray, less white.

"The three of us in here?" i turn when his annoyed voice hits my ears. He's... his scent is a bit hard to determine, not angry really, not afraid, no wait, a little bit. i turn from the window to watch Master's reply.

"I know it's a bit small, Linds," She begins, and he shakes his head.

"No, no, not that, but the three of us," he says, pausing and running a hand through his hair, wincing when he reaches the end a bit sooner than he's used to. Must have been hard to have it cut so short to impress Master's mother only to have the scary man show up and ruin it all. "We don't spend every night in the same bed."

Master tilts Her head to one side, and Her scent goes from confused to comforting as she steps toward him. "Oh, I see. No, no, we three, all three of us," and She looks at me then, so i hop off the bed and go to them as She finishes, "will sleep in the bed. No one is getting the floor. Do we agree?"

i blink up at Her, realizing what this is all about. Yes, back home Master shares bed with Self more than me, me more than Lindsey, three of us last of all. i should point out that i am a good pet and the floor is fine. i should do that, but i don't. Instead i hug Her legs and caress Lindsey's with my face for a few seconds to show i agree.

"Oh, good, good, it will be a very cuddly sleep then," Lindsey says with a chuckle, but he smells calm again.

"Great! Now that that is settled, we have someplace we'd like to take you, since we got here so early in the morning," Master says as She releases him but keeps a hand on my head.

"Right now? I haven't even unpacked," he says, but She just grabs his hand and pulls us both down the stairs to the living room, where Her father is watching the screen.

"We're going out for a picnic," She says, and Her father stands up and nods his head silently. Something is off—i can smell it on him, but it isn't my place to say, is it? "We'll be back in a few hours, well, in time for dinner," She tosses off as Lindsey gets their coats.

"Be careful, Em, the snowfall was a bit low this past year," Her father begins, and it is like he is both lying and not as he steps closer to give Her a hug and his scent surrounds me for a second as he pets me. "Take your phone with you; keep it on," he states, and Master just nods with a smile.

i should tell Her? i shouldn't tell Her?

By the time i think i know what i should do i'm in the pet cart behind Her bicycle, and we are headed up into the mountains again to the place where humans and morphs live happy. i love visiting this place every year with Master, who is welcomed, though She won't make a commitment there no matter how often they ask since i spoke up.

Mr. Monroe and Catria greet us, and Master is soon showing Lindsey around. i can't take my eyes off of Her human pet because he is not comfortable here, though he does a good job for a human in pretending. This year the village has a new playground where human children and young morphs are playing while the older ones watch until a bell rings and they all run off.

"They all go to school together?" Master asks as we follow them toward a building that has lots of bright colors on it, more than i can name easily.

"No, not the morphs, not really," Catria says with a smile while Mr. Monroe pauses to talk with someone who has run up to us. "They are there to watch the children and play with them; if they learn anything it's by accident. Their intelligence is quite limited, after all."

i huff, and Master tosses me a glare as Lindsey puts an arm around me, giving me a harder squeeze. "wynn cold," i toss out, trying to cover. Doctor Denise says i'm as smart as any of the smallest humans we saw on the playground. My visits to her and my skills are one of the things we do not mention here or to anyone beyond Lindsey. Keeping it from him so long was the most angry he has ever been when She told him.

They give us lunch; we didn't bring a picnic at all this time, and we talk with more of the humans here, though the morphs are still very quiet. When we get ready to leave so we can take a slow bike back down, Lindsey gets very close to Master. i tilt up my ears and listen, because he's so scared it has been making my tummy hurt for hours now.

"We need to go now. Something is wrong here," he almost growls, and Master steps back before Lindsey grabs Her arm. She looks down at me, but i just nod, though the only thing i'm picking up is his fear. "I found the bugs in the office, didn't I?" he partly states, and that makes me scrunch up my eyes a bit as i imagine little things running around the office that i hear much about but have never seen. Master is always looking for bugs at home, and if i find one when She is gone i toss it in the trash.

Master nods, and we head off, slightly more quickly than we normally would. Both She and he are quiet as they bike, and i grip the cart sides like always as we bump along. i bet i could bike, but that would probably be bad in human eyes.

We return the bikes to the store we got them from, but the man behind the counter just points out the door. We look and find Master's father and another man dressed just like him waiting outside.

"Is there a problem, Dad?" Master asks as we go right up to them.

"This is my chief assistant Jaggi," Her father says. "We need to ask you three to come back to the house with us and answer a few questions."

"What? What's going on?" Master begins, but Her father motions toward the street we need to walk along to get back to his place.

Lindsey puts his arm around my shoulders and steers me as we follow them, Master's voice demanding answers until Her father snaps with a "By Saint Maurice's Badge, Em! For once stop acting like your mother and just do what I ask."

This Jaggi man is walking next to Lindsey and i and just gives us a smile that seems to not match his scent one bit. Now my tummy hurts all on its own.

"Are you sure you've never signed anything with them?" Master's father asks Her again, and She crosses Her arms over Her chest. "When this goes down, if we find something I can't protect you, Em."

"Nothing—we've, I've, signed nothing with them. I haven't looked at their online information since that first visit here three years ago. We just go up to look around every year because they don't treat me like a freak because I have Wynn with me," Master explains.

Lindsey is in the other room after he answered a lot of questions. He's trying hard to be calm for Master, but he's worried, as am i.

i press closer to Master's leg, and that Jaggi man smiles down at me again.

"All right, I believe you," Her father says then holds up a hand, "Not as your dad, but as head of the Guard here. Is that everything?" he asks, turning toward the other man.

"Are you leaving in two nights then?" the man asks Master as his eyes stay on me.

"Yes, I have a business meeting that I must get to," She states for the last of many times. Should i be keeping count?

"Then that's it, as long as you make your flight," the man tells Her, his eyes finally leaving me.

Master just sits there, petting me rather hard, as Her father leads the other man out. She looks up when Lindsey comes in and sits on the edge of Her father's desk and looks between Her and the two men still talking by the door.

When Her father returns, She just stands and heads upstairs to the room we're staying in. "I'm sorry, I'm trying to protect her," i hear him say as i pause at the bottom of the stairs, wondering if i should follow, if Lindsey will.

"It's what I want to do too, Sir. How long has this..."

"Since before they found her. It broke my heart when I saw her on the surveillance, but any long-term investigation requires patience. I didn't think she'd go for them, but then she kept going back."

"She hasn't been happy with Inandirmak for a while now," Lindsey states, glancing at me and shaking his head when i start to take a step up. Without an order from Master i'm supposed to obey him, so i just glance upward, then crawl to his feet and look up at him and Her father as they talk.

"She does love this little guy, doesn't she?" Her father asks with a pet to my head.

"We both do." Lindsey's hand joins his and i wiggle around trying to get them to let go as competing man smells hit my nose. Master calls this "put it back in your trousers" time, but they don't seem to be making any moves toward their clothes. They release my head, and i scoot a bit toward Lindsey.

"Look, when this goes down, and it will be soon, I'll let you know, son."

Lindsey's scent changes to a friendly one, a prouder one, and i can see him smile a bit. "How soon are we talking?"

Her father puts a hand on his chin and scratches it for a second. "Within two weeks, probably sooner."

"If you give me a heads up first, a day or so," Lindsey suggests, lowering his voice slightly, "I can run interference with her."

i snap my head back, because he's lying about something.

They touch telephones, and then Lindsey takes me upstairs to find Master staring out the windows. "What kept you?"

"Just talking to your father, he's going to let us know when this is about to go down."

Master makes a noise that sounds a lot like when i huff, and Her scent matches the feelings i have when i do it.

"It will be when we're in Egirdir," he continues as he sits down on the bed close to Her and pulls me onto his lap.

Master looks at us, then lifts Her chin slightly. "And?"

"Do you think it's easier to use my backdoors in central or from MTB?"

Master sits down next to us and begins to absently stroke my leg. "Are you thinking we can use this somehow?"

"Well, we both know that it isn't quite as open as they'd like the metros to think, so maybe."

"Maybe. Let me think on it," Master says as She leans in to kiss him, then me.

Chapter Twenty-Nine
Into The Black

The leopard tom is being a bastard to me this time around. i feel his claws dig into my thighs as he pushes into me over and over again. He's small compared to many of Master's toys but about the same as Lindsey, though they take care to prepare me. True, we are supposed to prepare ourselves before we are called out, but that doesn't stop the hitting, the claws, or the meanness of the other morphs.

Every Showing seems more violent, but i never hurt the others more than i must. It would make Master sad. i'm a good pet, i make Her happy.

"Look at me," Lockin growls, soft enough that the viewers are not likely to hear. We perform for them, but we are not stupid animals; we know how much they can see and hear, because the Showing is on in the waiting area.

i don't even glance back at him but tilt my head back farther so i can keep my eyes on Master, sitting just where she always sits. As in the past Showings but the first, the man who comes to the house with the ferret girl and often is at the club is sitting next to Her. Unlike the others i can see and hear, they just sit and watch. Master keeps Her eyes on mine every time i am in here now. She told me it was to lend me strength. i only know it makes what is done to me and what i do seem farther away.

"Bitch," Lockin growls again and digs his claws in, making me tighten my grip on the bench i'm lying down on. He hates that i lie this way, face up so i could watch Master more easily. The order had not said to lay face down, but i can tell from his smell that he's annoyed and afraid of my position.

"Tod," i correct him as i let a smile show for a second before he cuts it off with a particularly deep thrust and stays there.

Suddenly his breath is on my face, and he is leaning over me, one hand on my head, forcing me to look at him. "Why like this if you don't look at me, tod?" he demands. The humans are whistling and clapping, but I gave up trying to figure out why a long time back. "What are you looking at?"

"Master." i try to move my head, but he is much stronger than me, probably as strong as Lindsey, so i frown at him. "Master order this one look at Her."

He releases my head immediately and eases back to continue thrusting. Even he, big morph that he thinks he is, won't go against a human's orders. i look up at Master, who has leaned forward, the friend man's hand on one of Her shoulders, until I manage to nod and vocalize some fake joy, and She eases back in Her seat.

i only take my eyes off of Her when finally i am the alpha of the scene, and then only long enough to make sure i'll be licking and touching the bitch i'm paired with right so her joy is real. Humans watching do not know, but i do, and i let the little white fluffy thing cuddle close to me as we walk out, letting her lead us so i can keep my eyes on Master until the gate comes down on another Showing.

Watching Master is a way to feel safer, to feel more distant, but i can only grip the walls where the man with a strange voice and bad breath has me pushed as he continues to spank me. Sharing means Master is not here, and only a stranger is touching me, ordering me, hurting me.

This morning for breakfast Lindsey came, and we had a private meal, the first ever at this place. They both petted me lots and told me they were proud of me; Master gave me extra food, and Lindsey sucked on my cock until i squealed and begged Master to let me touch the sky.

i heard them very softly talking while i used the shower. They were afraid but also excited in a good way. i didn't understand, so i started to sing softly to block them out. Afterwards we went for a little walk before Lindsey had to leave to go to something called spouse events that he sounded bored by.

Lunch and dinner were the normal group thing before i am

got for the Sharing. Tonight will be my last one this time, so i focus my mind on the breakfast as the man i'm serving turns me around with one push and picks up one of my legs to raise it painfully high before thrusting into me again.

i do something forbidden: i hate being here.

"We'll see you in a few weeks. If the weather cooperates, we plan to do a stopover at the Great Lakes casinos in Detroit, just for a change," Ashton tells us as he and Renee wait with us in the main lobby.

"Oh are Lisa and Aaron joining you?" I ask merely for politeness's sake, since I'm trying not to be worried. Where is this big police action my father promised? We've been waiting all bloody week for it. Lindsey told me two mornings ago that he had been able to find a way into the computers and has a ton of data he's safely stored away.

It doesn't mean anything, though, unless a world of trouble can descend damned soon. Lindsey bends down and looks through our carry-on bags again and then pets Wynn, who is doing a bad job of not being nervous. Thank goodness that is easily explained by the fact that he has to ride in the pet section of the plane.

"No, no, Lisa has just arranged for us to have a few days alone," I can hear Ashton saying, but it is the ferret girl jerking on his arm that gets my attention. "And a bit of, you know, training, too," he says, turning a bright red.

If only I found such a reaction as sexy as I used to, but I've shared too much with their family to really find my colleague more than a useful ally.

"What are they interrupting for?" I hear a man's voice near us say. Both Ashton and I look up at the screen, where they were announcing our shuttle arrivals until the Egirdir news broke in. Their logo is flashing for a few more seconds, and I see everyone waiting, including the Reizis family members acting as hosts, who have also stopped their chatter with various employees to look up.

"Breaking news out of Lausanne just moments ago," the male anchor announces as his female colleague nods her head.

The camera changes angle, pulling back so we can see the male anchor reading the sheet as well as a graphic of the Lausanne municipality. "It has been confirmed today that after years of investigation the Lausanne guard has arrested and charged a James Monroe with attempts to coopt civil land and water under a private name."

There is a collective gasp before the room goes quiet. Lindsey steps up and puts an arm around my waist. Out of the corner of my eye I see that Ashton has an arm around Renee's shoulders as she stands up and wraps one around his hips. I meet Wynn's eyes as he looks up at me. "It's all right, pet," I tell him.

"It will be," Lindsey adds, earning a small shove from my elbow into his ribs. We exchange glances, and he puts a hand on Wynn's shoulder as well when my morph whines.

I don't need his sense of smell to know that everyone in this room is worried now. For a private entity to try to control water is a major sin and has been for over a century.

The screen changes, and I have to tighten my self-control as a video of my father and the mayor of Lausanne appears. "We take our duty to our citizens quite seriously here in Lausanne," the mayor is saying. "Our elite guards have been diligent in their investigation, working slowly to make sure there are no gaps in the evidence before charges were formally filed this morning. We are certain that James Monroe has been using his nature community as a front to steal water from the good people of Lausanne. Their so-called community is really a branch of his company, which has branches in several municipalities around the globe. We urge all civil governments to take a hard look at the companies who have negotiated contracts with them because we have also uncovered evidence of a multi-private conspiracy to wrest control of water and land resources from their rightful owners, the citizens of that area. Captain Grant of our guard and I will now take a few questions."

I can feel the mood of the waiting area change as people start talking softly. I feel Ashton's eyes on me before he speaks. "Isn't that your father, Emily?"

I nod with a shrug. "This must be why he insisted we stop in before coming here this year. Normally we spend a few days with him after this annual meeting." I think that sounds like enough truth to hide the lie, and Ashton's nod confirms it as I feel Lindsey's hand caress my back a few times.

"Humans angry, worried, why?" Wynn asks softly, and I look down to find him pressed against Lindsey's body as he looks up at me with what I recognize as fear on his face and in his body language.

"The news is something important," I tell him without details. He might be able to understand, but we made a decision to tell him as little as possible in case this fails. If something happens to Linds and I, at least Wynn can have a chance to find a new owner or go to the Genesis Project, where Doctor Vevern assured me he'd be taken care of for life. "Don't worry about it," I start to say until the mid-caress pause of Lindsey's touch and my own senses tell me someone has joined us.

I turn to find one of the Reizis daughters stopping by our group. "We're asking everyone to please come back into the arena for a bit so we can all watch this important news together, as a family," she tells us before inclining her head and moving on to the next group.

"Oh-oh," Ashton whispers, "this can't be good."

Like the good employees we are supposed to be, we three follow everyone back into the arena. Not everyone has a spouse with them at the annual meeting; indeed, I got permission for Lindsey because we said we were trying to have a baby and we are basically newlyweds. Everyone does have their morph, so in all the space is much fuller than normal, but still not crowded.

The big screens are all turned on to various metro newscasts around the globe with subtitles and no sound. The investigation and arrest in Lausanne is slowly making headlines as we sit, watching and waiting. For a few minutes everyone is in shock and very quiet, then the muttering starts again, but this time it is asking a more immediate question: why can't we leave?

"What are they doing?" Ashton asks with a glare around us. He turns to me, and I notice that Renee is unusually close to him, under his arm, practically wrapped around his torso, even shaking. Not quite the cold little dominatrix that Lisa chuckles about when we go to the club or get around to talking about sex. "Emily, I think something is off. Do you feel it?"

"I'm sure they'll tell us something soon. There are dozens of us here; we will demand answers if they don't," I point out.

Lindsey has taken out his computer and glances up at us. "You have some emails from back at the branch, both of you," he adds with a smile.

I pause, then understand what he's doing. My father, bless Saint Maurice, has continued his gifts of privacy, as he calls them, and we've integrated each into our house and computers. Will that protect Hendricks? Only one way to find out. "We might as well use this time productively. I'll check with my teams; you check with yours."

Ashton whispers something to Renee, and she pulls away to lie on the seat next to him, looking only at him. Speaking of things being off, this seems quite unusual behavior for them. I pet Wynn and tell him to be good and just be still, which earns me a pout but a nod all the same as he settles down but looks at the screens then me and Lindsey as though guarding us. What a silly idea.

Once we three are online we start looking at emails, and I set up a private chat with Lindsey on invisible. "Hendricks. This is Emily. We have set up a safe space here to chat."

He jerks a bit, sitting up straighter, and glances at me, but I just shake my head slightly and keep typing.

"Unless you draw attention to us."

Another pause, then he replies, "I only have one email about this, an automatic news alert."

"Me, too. But we can discuss what is happening and say we are monitoring things back home."

"What's going on?"

"Do you like working here?"

He frowns and types very slowly. "Why?"

I pause now to think. Once I type this, either we win or we lose; there will be no going back, no matter how much privacy Linds and Dad have managed to buy us right here and now.

A message pops up from Lindsey. "Make it simple, Boss."

"I feel we could run the branch much better without these annual events. I find them distracting."

Ashton looks at me, then back at his screen. "I hate them; you know I take off any one that I can."

I let go of a breath and continue. "My father is in the Lausanne guard, captain of the unit. He says they will push for global investigations into all companies."

"All? Here?"

"Yes." I pause again, trying to determine how to word this next question. "Do you feel like you are part of this family?"

The reply is immediate. "No. This isn't a family; we aren't family to them."

"I agree. We should probably get off now; I see Madame Reizis at the podium."

We both close out, then turn to our "mother" in this fake family and watch as she looks over the crowd, willing it to quiet down and succeeding in a few moments. "I am so sorry for the delay in your departures. We believe it may be in the best interest for us all to stay here and see what is happening. The Egirdir Guard has asked us to keep everyone safe."

There isn't even enough time for her to take a breath before someone speaks out. "You can't hold us here!"

"You will be taken care of, I assure you, as head of our little family. You know we have the room and resources; you can check in with your branches online."

My back stiffens at the next shout. "We aren't a family!"

Ashton looks sharply at me, and I turn to Lindsey, who just looks down with a grin. I turn back to my colleague, who has tilted his head and is giving me a glare.

Madame Reizis is silent for a few seconds as others call out the same thing. One of her sons steps forward and demands silence, though it takes him a good minute to get it. Lindsey's done something, but I'm not sure what, so all I can do is watch and hope he and my father are more clever than I think.

"Of course we are a family, a business family," Madame Reizis states, but that just causes more muttering around the arena.

Her son steps forward again and orders us to go back to our rooms, spouses and morphs included. We can watch the news there and contact our branches. They will arrange transportation when it is safe.

By the time we are back in the hallway to my room I've noticed several presidents and vice presidents talking in small groups. Margaret and Zandy nod at me as they talk and walk; Bailey seems rather annoyed by something that Jim is saying. I'm glad that Faye took this time off; perhaps we can get more information from her. When they try to talk to either Ashton or me, we just wave them off and continue down the hall to our neighboring rooms.

Ashton glances at me, then at Lindsey. "An hour, then, we meet to see if anyone has concerns back at the branch?" He states it as a question, but for the first time I see a glimpse of what got him a promotion. He might hate being in charge, but he can take the lead if required, and I'm content to accept his directive right now, so I nod in agreement.

Once in the room, Lindsey takes out the device and scans for bugs again, but apparently they have not had time to plant new ones, even though maid service clearly came through. We have only one to worry about then: the one pointed toward the bed area that is only supposed to record during the Sharing.

"Master?" Wynn's voice makes me look down and find him kneeling by my feet, looking up at me. "Go home?"

"Not yet, pet, not quite yet. There are some issues going on right now that everyone needs to deal with."

"Human issues?" he asks, and Lindsey gives me that look he always does when my morph shows himself to be a bit more clever than a normal pet. I haven't told my spouse everything, though he is fully aware that the training that Wynn goes to once a week is helping him be more useful around the house. I probably should, but for some reason I still worry about what might happen should he truly understand what this foxmorph is capable of.

"Well, sort of human issues. More how some humans are going to react to the current situation," I add, trying to give him something but still remain vague.

Wynn nods and jumps up on the bed to curl in the center of it, where he can watch us and the screen that Lindsey has now turned on.

"I'm glad one of us is really calm about this," Lindsey says as he pulls out our computers and sets them up again.

"It will just be an extended holiday, then. This is basically a five-star resort, you know," I tell him as I walk to him and put my arms around his neck to give him a kiss. I ignore the small huff from Wynn and nuzzle my spouse's ear while whispering, "Can you find out if they are recording now?"

Even though this is far from a romantic situation, Lindsey's nuzzling along my neck sends a thrill down my body until he whispers, "I'll get right on that, Boss."

A few more seconds of kissing and nuzzling, then we part so he can get down to work.

I sit on the edge of the bed and lift up one leg, looking at Wynn, who scrambles onto the floor and removes my shoes. Sitting back up, I pat the bed, and he jumps up next to me with a flip of his tail in Lindsey's direction, earning a huff from my human pet in return. How much of their reactions to each other is jealousy and how much play, I don't know, but so far there haven't been big conflicts between them.

Master, Lindsey, and i watch the screen forever, it feels like. At Master's house the screen is often on, but no one looks or listens much. After a long time I go to the window ledge in the room and look out for a while. That is when the other man and the ferret girl come over.

The world here is different than back home, bigger space, but still i can see the huge fence around it all. Some humans are outside doing things with the plants and objects. i try to ignore Renee when she comes over and sits on the other side. In a few moments i realize i don't have that creepy feeling i get when she watches me. i look to find her looking outside.

"Your life so good," she whispers, and i jerk back from her. Glancing over my shoulder i move closer to her, but the humans are on their smaller screens and talking in soft tones. i could listen, i have very good ears Doctor Denise tells me, but now i want to hear more from this jill, who is acting very odd. "Wynn is happy with Master?"

i nod and scoot closer still. "Wynn very happy with Master and Linsdey. Renee happy?"

She shakes her head, and i'm stunned. We never say that, we never shake our heads to that question, you don't even think, you just say yes if you are ever asked if you are happy by anyone, morph or human, whitecoat or suit. Then she nods and shakes her head before turning to me. This time her eyes are not staring at me in the creepy way, and i can see tears in them.

"Being that way for Master, for Master Lisa, is hard," she confesses.

"That way?" i find myself asking before glancing back and making sure we haven't been noticed.

"Like a human, like a master, this one doesn't like it," she continues, then turns away from me, pulling to the side of the window ledge and curling in on herself.

i blink several times. That is what has been bothering me from the moment i met her and the other human family. She's been acting like one of them, no, like Master acts if she is pretending to be mean or is angry. It isn't right. It isn't natural for us to be like that. If it isn't right or natural, it has to be order from her Master making her like that.

i turn back to the window and look out again. There is a problem with the humans. Morphs don't matter for that, but here, with another morph, maybe i can help Renee be more right and natural. How? This will take a long time.

We have a long time. We are here for many more breakfasts,

lunches, and dinners, with playtime outside and Master going to meetings sometimes. Lindsey takes care of Renee and I, and there i see her start to act more right as she does what Lindsey says.

Lindsey is a good human, just like Master he cares about me, and now about Renee, so while she is running off to get something he left by the water on a walk back one day, i gently bump into his leg. "What is it, Wynn? You tired?"

"No, Wynn play lots more," i assure him, then stop and pull on his trouser leg once. He stops, so i speak more. "Renee not happy acting like human Master."

Lindsey's eyes go wide, and he crosses his arms over his chest. Back where i was before Master, this would scare me, but Lindsey only does it when he wants more words from me. Sometimes Master folds arms when She is angry, but never Lindsey. "Renee told to be like Master for Master, you know?"

He nods his head slowly but doesn't say anything, so I talk more. "It not right, not morph, not natural for that," i emphasize.

"Natural is not a word I would use for you all," he starts to reply when i interrupt.

"Renee sad. Wynn happy. Want Renee happy."

A smile comes over Lindsey's face, and he lets his arms relax to pet me. "Aren't you just a great friend, then? When this situation is worked out, and it will be," he says, though he sounds and smells unsure of that, "then I'll see what I can do to help Renee be happy. That work for you?"

i yip and agree. i trust Lindsey now. We will fix this for Renee, then she won't stare at me anymore.

"Good. Right now we need to focus on what Emily and Ashton need, though. We might just be on the edge of a revolution here."

i have no idea what that means, but focus on Master is something i'm best at. i repeat that statement to Renee later, who sighs and then nods.

It took days and two visits from Egirdir guards at the headquarters to get a meeting with Madame Reizis. During these days Ashton, Lindsey, and I have had ample opportunity to talk with the other VPs and presidents, including everyone in our North American region. I had planned to walk in with nothing but Lindsey's recordings and a few veiled threats, but now I have almost everyone I've spoken with behind me. Unless this fails.

When I am escorted into Madame Reizis's office I can see that the stress of the past few days has been great. Never before would I have seen more than a few regal gray hairs or the tiniest of wrinkles around her eyes. She looks like she hasn't slept since this entire hurricane started.

Interesting how it mimics the current storm blocking all North Atlantic travel, but unlike those storms, her reaction isn't expected. She looks almost like she can feel, like she's almost human.

"Vice President Potter, I'm sorry to have kept you waiting. As you know, we are dealing with a challenge to this family," she tells me with a tightening of the edges of her mouth that might be an attempt at a smile.

I smooth out my skirt as I sit, then tilt my head slightly to the left. "Are we? I thought the company was being questioned, not my family."

The edges of her mouth tighten further as she leans back in her chair and glares at me. "I thought you and I understood each other."

"We do. You want to protect your family, your real family. That's what I want, too."

"We are all one family," she begins, the edges of her mouth and her eyes taking on what might be a smile. I'm not as naïve as I was three years ago, the last time I was in her office; I see right through it.

"You protect your family's lives, their wealth, their power. You make us aid you through blackmail. That's not how I was raised to treat my family."

She snorts, a sound that surprises me enough that I start to chuckle until she leans forward on the desk. "Blackmail? Isn't that what you're about to try? Do you forget how much I have on you? Your spouse?"

"Probably no more than we have on you."

She frowns at me, so I continue. "Did you know that one of your sons, Deniz, the middle one, has been recording the happenings here in your house for over a decade now? Seems like he feels he simply won't have enough power once you pass on and the eldest takes over controlling interest. Sibling rivalry, huh?"

I practiced giving these speeches for hours in the bathroom, where there was no recording device, over the past several days. I still feel a flutter of fear in my chest, though I'm forcing myself to remain relaxed in pose. By Saint Maurice's Badge, if her morph were here I'd be pegged for sure, but it's just us, and hopefully Lindsey and Ashton watching and recording.

Madame Reizis says something in her native tongue that I can't understand before taking a slow, deep breath. "What do you want? A Presidency? Another branch? More money?"

"Desire for more money, more everything, is what is causing this mess, wouldn't you say?" There, that's the first thing I've said off the top of my head, and I don't think it sounds half bad. Best to move on to "the suggestion," as we've been calling it in talks with others.

"Then what do you want?" Madame Reizis demands with a low tone.

"Franchises."

She sits back a bit, relaxing her posture. "Franchises?"

"Yes, I realize that it is an older concept, with everything either global or local these days, but it still does happen. We ask that you turn over real control of each branch office to either the VP or president working there. In turn, your family would be paid a franchise fee, let's say twenty percent of profit"—collectively we thought it best to offer a very high margin, since it meant freedom for us all—"and we'll offer our employees buy-in rights to the branch, so we become citizen-owned businesses. Aside from the metro actually owning them, this is what most of them really want in their cities."

"We? You've been talking with others about this, not just business as usual? While here?" When I nod she suddenly smiles and sits back in her chair. "This is funny, and very timely, though I doubt all of this is a surprise to you, huh, daughter of a guardsmen?"

I just keep control and smile back at her. "It is a very generous offer. If metros start digging they will find out that your family controls over 80% of the voting rights here. You'll be kicked out of most of them, if not all of them. You aren't the only ad agency around, after all."

"You'd all be out of work. Do you all want to move to the coasts that badly?"

I can't help but grin at this idea, because it is one we discussed. "You choose creative and brilliant people for your company. Do you actually think most of us don't have citizenship status somewhere? Given our experience, we're sure we'd all find positions elsewhere."

"You might have to move."

"Small price to pay."

She is silent for a few moments, then nods her head. "The Titan Project?"

"You can keep that; after all, it's just an idea right now."

"How can we be certain you'll not go off and start a new agency or join a rival firm?"

"Same as now. You keep all your recordings; we keep ours. Collective guilt, I believe is the term you used."

Madame Reizis thinks for a bit longer, then nods as she moves closer to her desk, sitting up straight to get to work on this agreement. "It will take some time to work out the details...."

"No, we have the proposal right here," I say as I set the tablet on the desk. "It's locked; you can't change one word, but we've had legal in every branch go over it."

She picks it up and begins reading. I can tell by her body language that she isn't thrilled by some sections, but she keeps reading. Finally she looks up at me. "Do you have the power to sign this for your branch? What about Hendricks?"

I lean over and tap the screen until the document saying he and I agree on this offer comes up, and then a copy of the MTB franchise agreement appears with his signature already there, minus the date. "I can sign for us, then the others are waiting to come in as well."

I could point out how every passing minute is one minute closer to their records being ripped apart by investigators or the fact that the Morison Colony branch has an appointment in just two days with the guard there. I really don't want to have to go down that road, but I will if I must.

As I'm about to say it Madame Reizis takes her ID out and scans it on the tablet, then takes out her data pen and begins signing. I really want to cry right now as I feel the world grow a bit lighter and shinier around me, but I maintain my façade of calm.

We just won. All of us just won, and there was no blood spilled, as some feared might happen.

I take out my ID, then sign. Within minutes the Egirdir and MTB branches confirm receipt and validate our IDs.

We both stand up and shake hands when Madame Reizis's grip tightens and I allow her to pull me closer. "We had decided we'd franchise for 15%, so thank you for making me a better offer, Chief Potter."

My smile falters for a second, then I chuckle. "Well, done, Madame Reizis, well done."

When I get back to the main lobby of the compound, the representatives from each branch who agreed to wait for me are there. I stand silent, then break into a grin. "You'd best get in there and get your franchises in order!"

After a few well-placed slaps on the back and words of congratulation, I see Ashton, Lindsey and the pets waiting a few yards away.

As I walk toward them Wynn breaks away and runs toward me, knocking me to my knees with his hug.

"Master happy now," he says before starting to kiss and lick my face, making me laugh.

"Congrats, Ashton," Lindsey says when they stop and smile down at us. "Now you all just need to divide up the realms, and we'll be set."

"Let's hope it's this easy," Ashton says, but he offers me a hand up when Wynn finally releases me.

"Oh, no, you aren't spoiling this, American," I taunt him back before leaning in to kiss my spouse. "Lindsey, arrange our flight out of here as soon as possible, and get us into a hotel for the rest of this stay. The sooner we can start off independently, the better."

Chapter Thirty
Family Business

Lake Superior is so much closer now than it was to my previous office. I'm sitting at my corner desk looking out on the water and the metro guards patrolling around it. You'd think after all this time my office wouldn't thrill me as much, but given that it's mine, as much as civil property can ever be mine, I doubt that feeling will ever go away.

Inandirmak's building was confiscated by MTB, and in its place, once we'd signed some exclusive agreements with the Council, we got this new all-purpose delight a mile closer to the water. Given that we now need to spend a quarter of all our time promoting and managing city business, it seems like a fair deal, plus it gave us an excuse to expand to a four-team model. Nothing comes for free, right? Not even freedom, and who is really free these days?

I look down at my desk and see the vid of my family. First there is Wynn and me, soon after I got him, then the one where he's looking up at me before running around the old house, then stopping and looking up at me again. This fades into the image of Lindsey at our first ceremony, then the second at City Hall for the civil one. Now I'm holding Joshua and looking up, my hair plastered to my face with sweat; I hated Lindsey's recording everything, but what can you expect from a first-time dad? Then there's Carol and Lindsey moving stuff around in this office, setting it up just right as her wife and I look on, giving annoying advice. Finally there's Wynn looking up at the camera, a red Santa hat on his head as Joshua hugs him and giggles right into his ear.

I put a hand on top of my just-expanding tummy and flip the video to live feed for a few seconds before I'm interrupted by a knock on my door. Lindsey walks in with a smile, Lisa close behind him. She came back to work with Ashton on the other side of the floor and seems so much happier than when she stayed at home with Aaron and Sara. "You ready, Boss?" Lindsey asks, cocking one eyebrow.

I turn off my desk and stand up with a nod of my head. "Everything's ready to go?" I ask as I join them and we walk through the floor.

"I just double-checked, and Ash will meet us at the daycare, so we can all go together," Lisa tells me with a smile and a gentle touch to my stomach that earns her a frown.

We've kept the same team spaces in this new building, and the semi-open floor plan for meetings, but the individual department spaces are on the floor below, so they have all the equipment they need. Below that are our studios, where we shoot three to four ads and about a dozen civic announcements a week. I couldn't have imagined all of this in our hands when the Monroe arrest triggered global investigations and break-ups of over a dozen private multi-urban companies. That Inandirmak eventually collapsed wasn't our fault; every former branch's chief officers kept our word, saying nothing, but that didn't keep the Reizis children silent as they fought for the final scraps of control. I'm sure Madame Reizis was furious, but I had warned her, hadn't I?

"Good morning," I call out as we walk by the people currently meeting in the team areas. For the three of us to be together—heck, for the four of us plus our kids and pets to be together—isn't unusual, except at this time of day. We wanted to celebrate the entire day, not just part of it.

The daycare is on this same floor, halfway between my side and Ashton's. We are the only dual team of original executives left, though a few other regions had to consolidate after the investigations and sentences were finished. Most didn't get along particularly well, and early retirements were frequent. I still speak with most of our old executive team, though Faye left and joined the Winnipeg Council, and Bailey has settled down in Chicago as a professor at the university there, where his rants make him an interesting lecturer, I'm told.

Ashton turns to us as we near the daycare. He puts a finger up to his mouth and points to the one-way mirror that parents can look through when they don't want to disturb but do want to check up on their children and pets. We step up and see what he's looking at.

Master Joshua is giggling again, but not in my ears. No, that had fallen to this new child human who has finally gotten around to noticing me. i wince as the child pets me with a flat smack of a tiny hand that really doesn't hurt too much but which still jars my shoulders. i'm not as young as i used to be.

"Not so hard," Master Joshua commands, sounding a bit like Master Herself and thus getting the other child to stop. "Wynn's getting old, he needs gentle touches," he says, demonstrating the action. It's true; i just turned ten last week.

"Puppy?" the new child says, looking between me and Master Joshua.

"Tod," i say automatically, making the child jerk away and blink at me.

"Wynn fox called tod," Master Joshua says, then he points to himself, "Joshua human called boy." He points to the new child, "Nancy human called girl."

Ah it's a girl human child; they look basically the same to me, and they smell basically the same too until they get a lot older, like two of the workers here who help the adult teachers. Not quite adult humans, not child humans, sometime in between; that is the focus on the television about human problems.

Master Joshua throws his arms around my neck and says "Wynn is my bestest friend!" making the girl giggle again. Too bad he hasn't learned to gentle hug me like he now gentle pets me.

i sniff the air and then turn my head toward one of the walls. "Master Joshua please let wynn go?" i say, putting my paws over his arms and whining a little in my throat.

"Let's go talk to Aaron and Renee; she's a girl morph, a ferret, called a jill," Master Joshua tells the girl as he releases me, letting me take a deeper breath.

i crawl to the wall, then stand up sniffing at it, listening, touching the glass, until i find the spot and rub my head against it.

"How does he do that?" Lindsey says as he stands next to me, one arm around my waist, resting just on the top of my tummy.

"I don't know. The first time I met him he did that, too," I say as I move my hand and his face follows it.

"Renee's got their attention now, poor thing," Ashton chuckles.

"No, I think that Sara is going to try and help her," Lisa points out as their toddler runs over and tries to push between their morph and my son's poor decision.

I couldn't believe that Renee wasn't happy being a little dominatrix until I watched her more closely with Ashton a few times, with Lisa, and finally with Aaron, who is at the nearby public school we all send our children to. Bringing it up with Lisa had been problematic, and I thought we'd lost their friendship for certain when we only saw Ashton at the office for a few months. Whatever they had to do seems to have worked, since once we started seeing them again Lisa was more firmly in charge, and Wynn told me that Renee was happy like him.

Watching him react, however—he manages to sense my presence on the other side, where he should not be able to see me, hear me, or anything—I hope he is happy. I feel a tear start to fall and wipe it away.

"Let's go then, so this party can get started!" I state and grab Lindsey's hand to pull him after me.

"We need you all to come with us on an outing!" Ashton announces as he walks into the daycare. The nannies just look at us; their assistants stop what they are doing and turn to them. "Everyone is coming with us. Don't worry, it's a good thing, I promise," he tells them. Whatever they did has made them all happy, I'd say, because the old Ashton would have made all sorts of soft excuses before speaking out to a group larger than three.

Now he takes the lead in most internal meetings, and I deal with the clients and Metro Council.

Wynn waits until Joshua runs up to Lindsey, then my pet scampers to me as fast as he can and kneels to hug me, resting his face against my tummy. "Children treating you well?" I ask him, and he always just nods and says he is happiest pet ever.

Of the other morphs, only Renee comes forward, the rest hovering and looking at us and the nannies. "You, too, pets," Ashton tells them, "your masters will be joining us; you won't get into trouble."

While I can't condone what Inandirmak did to our pets and to us, it turns out that morphs are a great way to get loyalty from your fellows at work. The head of each department now makes enough to buy a high-quality morph, and a few of their assistants have purchased other morphs, bringing the zoo, as Lindsey calls it, to a grand total of thirty-two morphs and fifty-nine children. As with all technology, they have become available to the middle class and are now an everyday part of our lives.

I put a hand on Wynn's head and caress his furry face. Mine is still special, though, undoubtedly the most brilliant ever made. There are still some things we must hide, so I just take the leash from my pocket and clip it to his collar, so I can lead him to the escalator down to where the party has been set up in the auditorium on the ground floor.

As we walk back through the team area Ashton calls out, "Call your departments, call your families, tell them to report to the Auditorium—you, too, come join us; that's an order, not a request," he adds.

Soon we are joined by others, and then we see even more as we transfer to the next set of escalators on the fourth, third, and even second floors. We all work and live together in this building, a requirement for MTB, but we do not have stores or restaurants, so we must be part of the greater urban community at the same time. The only ones missing will be the children in school, but we've planned an all-day celebration, so they'll join us late this afternoon.

How many are there of us now? I wonder as I look out at the faces all sitting in the seats as Ashton gives a brief introduction to today's schedule of events. Lindsey and Lisa are sitting in the front row right with the kids and pets, but I can see Lisa mouthing the words coming out of her spouse's mouth. Well, at least he's more outgoing, if not more spontaneous, and she is a big part of what keeps this place running. He finishes by introducing the Council representative we've asked to speak today.

Councilman Freemont talks about the history of Metro Thunder Bay and its focus on empowering the citizen to create whatever life she wants as long as we respect each other. He talks about the role our company, Enlightenment—the name we gave it with a 71% employee/owner vote five years ago to the day—is playing in promoting and maintaining MTB as one of the most sustainable cities in North America. It's a good speech, and he delivers it well. He should, considering fourth team helped him with it.

Then it's my turn, and I step up to the podium, without a prewritten speech, so Lindsey can only nod and watch Joshua to make sure he remains calm. I look at Wynn and see him smile, and that gives me energy to tell the story of how we all got to be part of Enlightenment.

Everyone listens, nodding, tossing out little affirmations, or clapping on and off, as I recount our history. While I may not have prewritten my exact words, I did practice how to go through the details, second team helping me with that last week, though they did an admirable job of keeping things quiet.

Then I come to the part I didn't practice with anyone but myself. I turn my gaze solely to Wynn. "Pet, come up here."

He pauses, looks at Lindsey and Joshua, then goes to the floor to crawl to the steps and up to the podium. I wish he could walk now—that seems to cause him less stress, but that would not be wise right here and now. I step out from behind the podium and move with him until we are in front of the audience. Then I take a second and just caress his head before looking at my audience.

"Some of you have asked me why I fought so hard for

Enlightenment. Where did I get the idea we could be a franchise, a citizen business, focused on the betterment of not just our bottom line but our city and each and every person and pet in this room? This," I explain, looking back at Wynn and ruffling his head fur, "is why I started. These are our pets, not our children, not our spouses, not our co-workers, but our pets. For hundreds of years humans and their pets have lived in harmony, countless studies revealing that both groups benefit from a positive relationship. They are not weapons used to coerce our loyalty but connections between us."

I can see that only the highest and oldest members of our company understand, so I quickly step in front of Wynn and finish. "We are connected, all of us, each of us dependent on the other. This five-year anniversary is only a tiny step in our bright future. Please do enjoy today's celebration. We have a lovely buffet set up in the next room, and we'll switch that out twice more as the party continues. Save me a seat!"

I look down at Lindsey for a moment before the Councilman and Ashton come to shake my hand and pet Wynn. He looks guarded for a second, then gives me a grin and two thumbs up before scooping up Joshua and heading toward the breakfast buffet.

The next day I send Lindsey and Joshua off to go shopping and visit family in the city, since it is our day off and I need to do something I couldn't do yesterday, either because there were too many people around or simply because I'm a coward. I'm watching Wynn patrolling the shared garden space outside our back door, not interacting much with the younger morphs but pausing where he and Renee used to lie and do whatever it is that pets do when they aren't paying attention to us or roughhousing with each other.

He misses her so much, I can tell, though I've never let him know that I'm aware. I know he'd deny it, something about being a good pet. Doctor Vevern told me that it affected his testing with them for weeks, and that was a very helpful thing for them to learn about morphs. That woman creeps me out sometimes, but Wynn seems to like working with her once a week, so I've continued to let him go. Renee was two years older than he, and one day she was here, the next Ashton was very quiet, and then the following day Lisa brought a new pet, a bitch hybrid, into the daycare.

I let him stay outside for a few minutes more, then I open the door and call for him. He turns to me and comes over as quickly as he can, but I can see one of his shoulders is a bit stooped. "Was Joshua being too hard on you again?" I ask him as he slipped by me.

"Just a little boy," Wynn tells me, rising to his feet once the door is shut and the curtains drawn over it. "How I make you happy, Master?"

My throat tightens up for a second on his words. We let Lindsey in on our secret right after the last Inandirmak meeting, but when Joshua is around we must continue with the traditional morph behavior, because he's too young to understand why it has to be a secret. "Simply by being here," I whisper to him as I bend down and hug him gently.

He pets my back in return, then licks my face until I'm chuckling and backing off. "Then I want to play with Master," he tells me, squinting up at me now that he can't see as clearly as he used to.

"We'll do that, I promise," I say as I lead him off, one arm around him, helping him walk. "I sent the boys away so that you and I could have a talk."

Wynn goes stiff for a moment, then nods as I have him sit up on the couch in the position he is most comfortable with. "I'm going to go get us some treats, you stay here, watch some telly if you want, pet," I tell him with a kiss to his nose before heading to the kitchen.

After eleven years I know how he thinks, so I know right now that he's full of doubt and fear, trying to figure out what I want and how he can make me happy. Two years ago I had a discussion with Doctor Vevern when Lindsey and I decided to apply to have another baby, and we were concerned about how that might affect

Wynn. She assured me that as long as I gave him time, just me and him, and I included him in family things, he'd be happy. She also said he was unusually bright and that the testing had been beyond their wildest dreams. I never pressed about that, though she was not as opposed to my latest decision as I thought she might be.

Wynn will be a different matter altogether.

Funny. That sounds like Doctor Vevern's voice from the living room. I get the tray and hurry back, catching the last of her words. "Project will be a perfect match for us. The advances in morphology are going to help us reach out to the rest of the solar system much more quickly and with less risk than we could have imagined even a decade ago."

She's standing at a podium in the center of The Jungle, with other scientists I've seen there behind her, and reporters gathered around. I glance down to find Wynn staring at the screen, so I turn back as well when a question is asked. "Risk to humans, you mean?"

"Of course, to humans—sorry, perhaps I should have specified," Doctor Vevern says with a smile. "Genesis has been focused solely on improving morphs so that they can be of maximum benefit for humanity."

"Has your work had anything to do with the recent decrease in morph prices?" another reporter asks. "They used to be the toys of the elites, but now the average citizen in most regions can afford one if they save up for a just a few months."

Doctor Vevern's face goes a bit red, and her voice is a bit rough. "They aren't toys; they have never been toys," she says, but she is interrupted by a cough behind her. "It is difficult to say what our research has done to the market. Most technologies decrease in price once they become tried and improved upon over the years."

Another man, one I don't recognize, moves into Doctor Vevern's place and ends the press conference. That's when I see the news headline, Titan Project to Use Morph Builders, as the screen shifts to an anchor recapping the event before turning to her group of experts.

"Master?" Wynn's voice draws my attention, and I find he's straightened up and has his hands under the tray.

"That was timely," I saw as I let him help me set it on the table and then sit beside him.

"We talk about Jungle?" he asks as he takes a pet biscuit from his side of the tray. We've been getting him the luxury morph foods more and more, and he grins as he tastes it.

"Yes, yes, you are a clever pet," I agree, taking one of the human treats for myself.

We nibble for a while, and then I just plow ahead. "You won't be going to test with Doctor Vevern anymore."

He stops nibbling and lets his hand fall to his lap, where his almost constant erection is wilting. "Wynn do something bad?" he asks softly, falling into old habits that are triggered around me only when he's afraid.

"No, no, not bad," I say, reaching out and stroking his arm, which gets him to look up at me silently for a moment. He's using his senses to determine if I'm lying. Like I said, I've learned how he thinks so well over the years. "But it's been years, and frankly I want you around more. As you could see, they are doing just great there. You know," I add with a light squeeze of his arm, "she tells me that you are the best help they've had."

He nods but licks his lips, though he doesn't speak.

"I'm thinking that Joshua is a big boy now." That gets a look from Wynn, but he doesn't say anything or even huff in annoyance, "and with Ellie on the way I'll be very busy again, so I'd like your help more."

"More?" he repeats, eyeing me now with confusion. Good, that means he isn't thinking the worst, because we decided after Renee that we were not doing that unless he was in so much pain there wasn't a choice.

"Yes, I'll need you more at the office and at home. Lindsey will be taking time off to raise Ellie, so Carol will take on more of his responsibility, but she can't do more personal service like you and he can."

Now he shakes his head, and I'm shocked—but then, no, not really—by his next words. "I'm not too old, Master? You can't, you aren't as rough as you were; I remember last time I ask you say it not a good idea."

I close my eyes. Yes, I've been neglecting him. It took Lindsey to see that as well as to point out that he doesn't like things quite as rough as I have been making them between us. I could offer words, I could make promises; I could then turn around and break them.

I reach up and take his muzzle firmly in my hand, harden my voice, and just act. "Don't question me, pet. I won't tolerate it. Do you understand me?"

A quick glance down shows his erection is back and he leans toward me trying to nod his head.

"You want to shake your head, nod it? Well I don't care what you want to say, I'm in charge, and I'll do with you as I will, because I love you, damn it."

We both freeze at the words. I release his muzzle and run my hands down his arms slowly, our eyes looking directly into each other. "I do love you. I think you were the first... one I loved," I tell him, and I feel my eyes filling with tears.

"I love you, Master, I love you so much," he tells me, coming into my arms.

All my other plans for the day fall away as we just let our hearts direct the next few hours.

"Lock the door," Master tells me after Carol leaves. i stand up from my pillow by Her desk, moving slowly, swaying my hips as best i can to give Her a view as i obey. i pause with my back to the door and look at her, letting my head fall for a second before meeting Her eyes. "Master is stressed," i simply say as i walk back toward Her.

i move purposely, sexily as Lindsey calls it. He was all full of words once he started his leave to watch little Ellie. He forgets that i was here first, that i was the one making Master less stressed first. He can believe what he likes, but i know the truth.

i come around to Her side of the desk and find She's kicked

off Her shoes already. i appreciate the gesture as i get to my knees and crawl under the desk, knowing that i want to spend as much time pleasing Her as i can.

i start by running my face along Her legs, urging Her thighs to part and release Her scent. There was a time i would have needed to be touched first, or i would have begged to be touched first. i am always hard around Master, but i can wait until the end to touch the sky, knowing it will be all that higher for the wait.

i lick and tease Her folds and thighs, going fast then slow and fast, letting Her scent and Her fingers in my head fur direct me. She moans and shudders, then flies high and higher until Her body is clenching against me.

i see Her push the button that locks the wheels of Her chair, and i crawl up Her body to see if She wants me inside of Her. "Do it, pet, be with me now," She whispers.

Entering Her is easy. i can tell that i am no match for Lindsey's cock, but She simply pulls me closer by wrapping Her legs around me as i thrust quickly into Her. This is a gift i do not think any morph gets with a human. Not even when Lindsey and i obey Master together, putting on a show as they call it, do i get to do anything like this to him. i can't hold back, but Master doesn't mind.

She helps me slide off and walks me to the couch, where we cuddle. i don't even try any more to go get a washcloth or to offer myself to Her again. She's in charge, and i'm happy to let Her move me where She wishes. "You fine? Not in pain?"

"i love you, Master," i say back to Her instead of a direct answer.

Finally after Her continued inquiries i have to reply, "Best pet ever," earning a hug as i let my eyes shut. i hear the songs of my people as Master continues to rock me and whisper Her own love for me over and over.

wynn is luckiest morph ever.

About the Author

Several small presses have published TammyJo Eckhart's fiction and non-fiction since 1996 — Circlet Press, Greenery Press, Blue Moon, Ravenous Romance, Masquerade Books, Alyson Books, Python University Productions, and The Nazca Plains Corporation.

A skilled storyteller, TammyJo enjoys reading her fiction to live audience so she is happy to travel in her region to perform readings, sell/sign books, and lead workshops and discussions on various aspects of BDSM, gender & sexuality, or the literature, culture, and study of science fiction, fantasy, horror and other types of speculative fiction. She has been a panelist, Game Master, and speaker at multiple kinky conventions, professional science fiction and fandom events, and at private organizations.

A huge but picky science fiction, fantasy, horror, and slash fan, TammyJo is also a prolific book reviewer writing 2-6 reviews a month for various scholarly and mainstream publications since 1999. Her review shelf generally stores around a dozen books at any given time so she has been known to turn down offers to review books when one just doesn't seem to fit into her fields of interest or experience.

TammyJo earned her PhD in ancient history with minors in women's history and folklore in November 2007 from Indiana University in Bloomington, and uses both her scholarly knowledge and twelve years teaching experience in her reviewing, writing, and storytelling. She has consulted with authors and publishers on history matters for non-fiction and fiction works.

TammyJo's ongoing RPG, set in the "Ghoul: Fatal Addiction" variation of World of Darkness 3.0, runs at several science fiction conventions where she is always looking for good actors/players to embody her complex characters. She has been a consultant and reviewer of RPGS and board games for the past few years.

TammyJo is the founder and main author for The Chocolate Cult (http://thechocolatecult.blogspot.com/) where she takes readers through sensible and sensual explorations of all matters chocolate.

TammyJo lives in Indiana as head of her poly, kinky household. She has a husband of 22 years and a slave of 14 years who she loves dearly and happily manages daily.

Feel free to learn more about TammyJo at tammyjoeckhart.com. Or follow her latest adventures at thetammyjo.livejournal.com and various online communities you can find at her main website.